D1630219

9112000265134

KARAN GHELO

GUJARAT'S
LAST RAJPUT
KING

KARAN GHELO

NANDSHANKAR MEHTA

Translated by
TULSI VATSAL and ABAN MUKHERJI

PENGUIN
VIKING

VIKING

Published by the Penguin Group

Penguin Books India Pvt. Ltd, 7th Floor, Infinity Tower C, DLF Cyber City,
Gurgaon 122 002, Haryana, India

Penguin Group (USA) Inc., 375 Hudson Street, New York, New York 10014, USA

Penguin Group (Canada), 90 Eglinton Avenue East, Suite 700, Toronto,
Ontario, M4P 2Y3, Canada

Penguin Books Ltd, 80 Strand, London WC2R 0RL, England

Penguin Ireland, 25 St Stephen's Green, Dublin 2, Ireland
(a division of Penguin Books Ltd)

Penguin Group (Australia), 707 Collins Street, Melbourne, Victoria 3008, Australia

Penguin Group (NZ), 67 Apollo Drive, Rosedale, Auckland 0632, New Zealand

Penguin Books (South Africa) (Pty) Ltd, Block D, Rosebank Office Park,
181 Jan Smuts Avenue, Parktown North, Johannesburg 2193, South Africa

Penguin Books Ltd, Registered Offices: 80 Strand, London WC2R 0RL, England

First published in Gujarati as *Karan Ghelo* 1866
First published in Viking by Penguin Books India 2015

English translation copyright © Tulsi Vatsal and Aban Mukherji 2015

10 9 8 7 6 5 4 3 2 1

ISBN 9780670087693

Typeset in Adobe Jenson Pro by Manipal Digital Systems, Manipal
Printed at Thomson Press India Ltd, New Delhi

A PENGUIN RANDOM HOUSE COMPANY

KARAN GHELO

1

From the writings of a bard we know that in the Samvat year 802, that is AD 746, a certain town was established in Gujarat. Vanaraj's decree was proclaimed in the waning hours of the night, at three o'clock, on the Saturday of maha vad satam. Learned astrologers of the Jain sect were summoned and, after studying the charts, prophesied the destruction of the town in AD 1297. This new town was named Anhilpur-Patan, now known as Patan or Kadi-Patan. Today, there are hardly any signs to suggest that Patan was once a large and thriving city. Huge blocks of marble lie abandoned in the vicinity of the fort. The passage of time, attacks by Muslim fanatics, constant wars, and the ignorance and greed of the Marathas have reduced the stepwells, ponds and temples constructed by the Rajput kings to ruin. Even so, it is clear that 700 years ago Patan was the capital of a powerful kingdom. The greatness and splendour of the town have been described by a number of poets and chroniclers. The author of *Kumarapalacharitra* says:

'Anhilpur covered an area of eleven kos; and within this were several temples and schools. It had eighty-four squares, eighty-four bazaars, and a mint to manufacture gold and silver coins. Different castes lived in their respective localities and there were specific areas where ivory, silk cloths, diamonds, pearls, rubies, aromatic bath oils and other merchandise were sold. There was a separate bazaar for bankers. Doctors, artisans, goldsmiths, sailors, bards, genealogists, each had a market of their own. All eighteen castes were represented in the town and all were content. Adjoining the king's palace were a multitude of buildings for storing weapons of war, housing elephants, horses and chariots. Accountants and other officials had their own quarters. Every variety of commodity had its own customs house. Here sales taxes and excise duties were levied on goods such as spices, fruit, herbs, camphor, metals and luxury items from Patan and other cities. The town was a centre for goods from all over the world. Excise worth one lakh tankhas was collected daily. A person only had to ask for water to be offered milk. There were many Jain temples in the town and by the side of a lake stood a shrine to Sahasralinga Shiva. People strolled carefree amidst the shady groves of frangipani, coconut, jamun, sandalwood and mango trees entwined by every variety of creeper, and alongside tanks of nectar-sweet water. Learned discourses on the Vedas were offered for the edification of the people. There was no dearth of Jain theologians or of reliable and skilled merchants. There were also many schools that taught grammar. Anhilpur was a sea of humanity. To count the people who lived there was as hopeless as measuring the waters of the ocean. The army was also large and did not lack for belled elephants.'

This description is certainly exaggerated, but it is undeniable that Anhilpur-Patan was once a prosperous, sprawling and attractive town. On Ashwin sud 9 of Samvat 1352 (AD 1296), that is on the day our story begins, the *brahmanwada* wore a festive look. Garlands hung from every door. Delicate rangoli patterns were traced in courtyards. People sauntered cheerfully along the streets. Brahmins clad in dhotis, *angavastras* and *paghadis*—some even sporting a topi—could be seen walking with a brisk, purposeful air, as if intent upon some important business. Their faces suggested a long-standing enmity with the barber. Their heads, chins and cheeks resembled fields before the commencement of the monsoon, scattered with the stubble of grain as yet unharvested. Quite a few of these demigods were proceeding towards a large mansion in the brahmanvada. The haveli was spacious and attractive. It had four floors and an opulent exterior. It was surrounded by an immense wall at one end of which was a large entrance gate, surmounted by a balcony. The *nobat* and shehnai were being played from the balcony that day. Entering the doorway, one stepped into an open courtyard decorated with exquisite rangoli patterns. On all four sides were enclosures, one of which housed elephants, horses, chariots and other vehicles; in another, Patels, banias and other townsfolk who had come to demand justice of the king, waited their turn; the third had offices for clerks and other officials; and the fourth served as a chamber for the policemen and watchmen. Also seated here were Kathis of the lineage of Raja Karan—terrifying figures, over six-feet tall, strong-limbed, cat-eyed and brown-haired; Kolis, short-statured but well-built, bow and arrows at their waists; dark and vigorous Bhils, professional looters and fearless warriors; and Rajput soldiers of more refined visage and superior status but valorous nonetheless. The haveli in the centre of the compound was built of stone of different types and its walls were decorated with floral designs and animal and human figures. Low windows projected outwards, their balconies supported by exquisitely carved brackets. From the entrance hallway, a staircase led to the first floor; several household servants sat gossiping here. The room opened out into a courtyard with a columned veranda on all four sides. Banana trees stood like pillars and thousands of red and yellow marigolds bloomed in the spaces between. Garlands of mango leaves were strung across the columns of the veranda and with its profusion of adornments,

3

the haveli resembled Vaikuntha, the heavenly abode of the gods. Bare-headed brahmins sat before a large altar that had been set up in the centre of the square. Gathered on one side were the womenfolk and, on the other, the men. The third was occupied by the king's entourage, while from the fourth, guests kept an eye on the activity as they whiled away the time chatting about this and that. It was the last day of Navaratri and a sacrifice for the Goddess was being performed. Brahmins chanted the *Chandipath*, sesame seeds spluttered in the sacrificial flames, serpentine plumes of billowing smoke rose and mingled in the clear blue sky. Freshly chopped firewood and other hard-to-burn substances, together with the intermittent pouring of ghee from enormous ladles into the sacrificial vessel, produced huge bursts of flames. All this, not to mention the bevy of delicate Nagar brahmin beauties, finely dressed and bejewelled, the fair-skinned and good-looking Nagar gentlemen in their handsome turbans chewing *paansupari* in the company of other men, and the din of incessant chatter, can only be imagined—only a skilled poet or painter would be able to render a faithful description of the scene.

Bhana Patel sat with the other Patels. He was the most imposing and intelligent-looking of them all. A Kanbi by caste, he had been gifted many *bigha*s of land by the king for his policing, and he also had the lease of a fair number of *pargana*s from the revenue of which he paid the king a share. He was around sixty years old but certainly proved the falsity of the adage, 'There is no fool like an old fool.' Though he had grown fat on rich food, his mind was as sharp as it had been during his youth. Moreover, his intelligence seemed to increase with each passing year. The minutest details connected with the land—how the kings of yore treated the peasants, the rate of land taxes in their time and the manner of collection—were all stored in the treasure-chest of his memory. On the opposite platform, on a raised seat meant for higher ranks, sat the Jain merchant Jethasha. His business houses graced every town. People had such confidence in him that he could command credit from even the most unlikely sources. His ships traded in foreign lands and his wealth was numbered in lakhs and crores. Fortune-tellers who could gauge a man's qualities, intellect and nature by looking at his face would be thrown into confusion at the sight of Jethasha's visage. From his face it was difficult to divine that he had a knack for business and the acumen to accumulate and preserve wealth. He was so obese that his kinsmen constantly worried about how they would carry his corpse should he die suddenly. His pendulous stomach, the result of accumulated fat, had so many large folds that small objects could remain hidden in them for years without him being any the wiser of their existence. His barber must have had a hard time holding up the great roll of flesh around his neck before the work of shaving could commence. His face was equally fleshy. His eyes were tiny and set deep in folds of flesh, their continual twitching a reminder of his obsession with the glitter of gold and silver. Thus sat Jethasha, bedecked in diamonds and pearls. Being a devotee of Adinatha, he had no great faith in the sacrificial ceremonies for the Goddess; nor did he believe that he would gain bliss in the afterlife by listening to the mantras—he had come there merely to please his host.

In the Nagar brahmin camp there was one man more brilliant and handsome than the rest. He was seated on a large *patlo* fringed with silver. He was clad only in a dhoti and a rich Kashmiri shawl. He wore a diamond wristlet and an armband, and on his fingers sparkled rings of diamonds, rubies and other precious stones. Around his neck were strings of pea-sized pearls and diamonds; his ears were adorned with even bigger and more lustrous pearls. From his appearance it was clear that he was a personage of importance, and his air of dignity commanded respect. He was of medium height and though one could not describe him as fat, he clearly leaned towards plumpness. His skin

5

was fair, his face oval and his nose and ears shapely. His sharp eyes radiated intelligence. This gentleman's name was Madhav, and he was Karan Raja's prime minister. His intelligence had given him such influence over the king that the latter never took a step without consulting him. Madhav managed all the business of government. The king was a mere puppet and Madhav the de facto ruler. Many who had gathered that morning in the palace had done so only to please the powerful minister.

The *havan* was almost over. The sacrificial fire was rekindled for the offering of the last coconut. The brahmins prayed with renewed vigour. The crowd became restless, impatiently waiting for the ceremony to end. The last flames burst from the *kund* as the final sacrificial offering was made to the Goddess. Loud shouts of '*Jai Ambe*', 'Victory to Mother Amba', rent the air, making children jump up from their seats. After a while, when things quietened down, Madhav's family priest, Gormaharaj Vijayadatta Pandya, arose with the container of *kunku*, the *ashaka* of the havan and *prasad*. With such a wealthy patron, the priest did not lack for money. He was grossly fat and his stomach so substantial that seven laddoos could easily be packed in it with room to spare. Vijayadatta applied tikkas on the foreheads of the women and men, pressed grains of rice over them, offered the ashaka, recited the mantra of blessing and distributed small portions of prasad to the elders. Gathering the children around him, he made them jump and dance like frisky puppies awaiting the promise of food, then suddenly threw the prasad up in the air, setting them scrambling on hands and knees in search of it. The shouts of the children, the pushing, shoving and fighting as they tried to retrieve the prasad without stepping on the sacred offerings, the delight of the bigger children as they grabbed more of the prasad, and the disappointment of those who got only a little, created an amusing spectacle.

After the prasad had been distributed the children dispersed, and with the havan coming to a close most of the guests returned to their homes. The womenfolk went back to their chores. The brahmins collected their dakshina, and knotting the grain and whatever else they had received in the corner of their dhotis, departed to perform havans elsewhere. Apart from the prime minister, Madhav, only the moneylender Jethasha, the prosperous landlord Bhano Patel and Gormaharaj Vijayadatta Pandya remained. As friends of Madhav and the most prominent citizens of the town, they did not think it proper to leave immediately like the rest of the crowd, so they reclined against bolsters near the prime minister's patlo. After a brief interval of silence Madhav spoke, 'Gormaharaj, has the havan been performed properly? There was no botching up, I trust! Today havans are being performed at several places, and the brahmins are naturally in a hurry on a day that is propitious for fees. And you, I suspect, would like your brethren to earn as much as possible, which could perhaps lead to slips. Of course, you are not the kind of person to make mistakes. I merely ask as a formality. Forgive me if this offends you.'

Of course these words made the priest angry. He was saddened too, to think that his patron suspected him of such little faith in the Goddess as to rush his brethren through the ceremony for monetary gain while neglecting the correct performance of the ritual. But Madhav's family priest, a frequent visitor to court, had heard often enough how an inferior in the employment of the powerful should behave. He was in the habit of controlling his thoughts, so suppressing his anger and with his characteristic calm expression he replied, 'Honoured host! You have never spoken to me like this, and I am really surprised to hear such words from you. I fear your opinion of me has changed somewhat, and when the attitude of a person like you changes, it makes me fear greatly for the future. For the first time in my life it has been suggested that I could have deliberately made a mistake in the performance of the havan of Ambabhavani, the primal power, the originator of all creation, and mother of the world. You know that all the gods slumber during this Kaliyuga. Ambamata is the only divinity fully awake and watchful; and all are aware of her power. At different times she appears in different forms and performs miracles. While in general it is wrong to use abusive language without good reason, worshippers do not consider it sacrilegious to utter outrageous words when performing a *bhavai* in front of the Mother. Our religion forbids us to drink liquor, but the devotees of the Goddess partake freely of it. Our *Dharmashastras* consider violence in any form the worst sin, yet, in the sacred precincts of the Goddess, goats, fowl, oxen and such are sacrificed; and what is even more amazing is that the slain animals are portioned out as prasad and many a worthy, who at any other time would never dream of eating meat, breaks the customs of his forefathers and, to please the Goddess, ignores the injunctions of the *Dharmashastras*. When people go on a pilgrimage connected with Ambabhavani, how vigilant they have to be! Not a drop of oil must be used in the ritual. If one misbehaves at any of her shrines, the consequences of that action are felt immediately. The slightest change in the prescribed ritual incurs her wrath, and punishment in one form or another is certain. For the nine days of Navaratri, the Divine Mother, together with her companions, flies across the sky in her chariot at sunset. If a person happens to sit with his head uncovered in a balcony, at a crossroads or in any other open space, and the chariot passes over him, he is bound to succumb to a disease that year. Besides this, one has to maintain the greatest caution around the lamp of the Goddess and items connected with it. So, as you can see, I am fully aware of the Goddess's greatness and power; and, in spite of this, do you really think I would bungle the ceremony? O Lord! My heart overflows with distress when I hear talk of the greed of brahmins. The heyday of the brahmins is past and their earnings have dried up. What sort of talk is this?

The poor brahmins are powerless these days. How times have changed! No one, neither the king nor the people respect them. God forbid, but it is this sin, this lack of belief that will be the king's undoing. From Lahore all the way to Delhi, Hindu rajas are being crushed by the foreign barbarians. It is due to this very sin that Lord Somnath's temple was destroyed, and the ruler of the kingdom ruined. Still, the good deeds of the kings of yore act as a barrier protecting the land. It is only due to prime ministers like you—the guardian of cow and brahmin—that the brahmins can survive. As for the great benevolence of previous kings, what more can I say? Listen, sir. Let me give you just one example.

'When Raja Mulraj, the Solanki ruler of Gujarat, grew old, he went to Shristhala (Siddhapur) to expiate his sins. Shristhala is considered the holiest of all pilgrimage sites. It is the bestower of wealth and whosoever visits it attains liberation. From Gaya, heaven is three *yojana*s away; from Prayag, one-and-a-half; but heaven is only a hand's breadth away from Shristhala, where the river Saraswati flows to the east. To that *tirtha*, Mulraj invited brahmins from far and near. A hundred and five brahmins came from the place where the Ganga and Yamuna rivers unite; 100 from the Chyavanashrama of the Samavedis; 200 from Kanyakubja; another 100, resplendent as the sun, from Kashi; 272 from Kurukshetra; 100 from Gangadwara; from the Naimisha forest 100; and 132 more from Kurukshetra. The king prostrated himself in obeisance before the brahmins and they gave him their blessings. "Thanks to you, my birth as a human at last stands validated," he said. "Now my desires can be fulfilled. Therefore, O brahmins! Please take my kingdom, my wealth, my elephants, my horses and whatever else you desire. As your humble servant I surrender myself to you." The brahmins replied, "O King of Kings! We are not meant to rule a kingdom, so why should we accept it only to destroy it? Parshurama, the son of Jamadagni, took the world by force from the kshatriyas and twenty-one times attempted to give it to the brahmins, but they refused." The king said, "I will protect you. Continue to perform your daily worship as usual free from care." The brahmins replied, "Learned men say that troubles accrue to those who live close to the king. Kings are egoistical, crafty and selfish, therefore, King of Kings, if you desire to give us a gift then gift us beautiful Shristhala, where we can live in contentment. Use whatever gold, silver and diamonds you wanted to gift us to beautify the town." Overjoyed, the king bowed down to the brahmins and handed over Shristhala, together with cattle, gold, chariots decorated with garlands of diamonds, and other gifts. In addition, Mulraj bestowed the prosperous and charming town of Simhapur (Sihor) to ten brahmins. He granted several other villages in the vicinity of Siddhapur and Sihor to others; and gave Stambhatirtha (Khambat), together with sixty horses, to six devout brahmins from Somavalli. Mulraj's successor, Siddharaj, endorsed this gift and gave an additional hundred villages in the land of Balak (Bhal) to the brahmins. And when the brahmins from Sihor complained about the wild animals in the vicinity and requested the king to let them live in Gujarat instead, Siddharaj bestowed Ashabali village on the Sabarmati river to them and waived the taxes on the grain they took from Sihor. Blessed are such kings and their progenitors! They have proved the worth of their existence. They have freed themselves of 84,00,000 cycles of rebirth. Now they are shining stars in the firmament.' Having made his speech, Gormaharaj Vijayadatta sighed deeply and lapsed into silence.

Listening to the woes of the brahmins, Bhana Patel could not refrain from enumerating his own and those of the farmers in general. 'Brother,' he said, 'it is not the brahmin alone who is in this unfortunate situation. The condition of the farmer, too, is not good at present. The rainfall this year is less than what it should be and the harvest is not as plentiful as it usually is, in spite of which the revenue collector threatens to extract the royal share by hook or by crook. Are we less oppressed? We are allowed to harvest the grain on the condition that it is stored in the village grain-yard. Then the zamindar, the government official, the bania who measures the grain, the farmer and the watchman, all gather on the threshing floor. First, 40 per cent of the grain is set aside for the king. A slightly smaller amount goes to the *karbhari*, the government agent, the village watchman, the bania who measures the grain, the headman, for the crown prince's personal expenses, for the temple of Vishnu or Devi, for the lake, or the welfare of the dogs. Finally the farmer strikes his basket in protest, crying enough is enough. The remaining grain is then divided equally between the peasant and the zamindar. Yet, if the king wants to get his daughter married, or spend on equally important matters, it is the peasant who has to pay. Not just that. During the Holi festival, either the tax due from family genealogists and mendicants is reduced or they are given the right to a certain number of measures of grain. This practice may continue for either just one year or indefinitely. This is the manner in which the income of the village is extracted. When such is the usual plight of peasants, what can one say about their condition when the monsoon fails and the crops don't ripen? The prime minister says that no concessions will be made, that there is no point going to the king, begging and pleading and requesting arbitration. It is his opinion that no pity should be shown to the peasants and, to strengthen such a belief, he constantly reminds them that even Lord Rama's pampered subjects did not hesitate to criticize him.[1] But Bapji, it is not like that. Peasants constitute the pillars of the system; the country depends on the farmer and the farmer appreciates the benevolence of the ruler. Bapji, you must be aware that in the days of King Bhimdev, when the rains did not come for a year, and the peasants of Dandahi and Vishopak could not give the feudatory Kanbi ruler his share of the produce, the king

11

sent a minister to look into the matter. He caught hold of the wealthy farmers, dragged them to the capital and produced them before the king. One morning, when the king's son, the honest and trustworthy crown prince Mulraj, was out with a servant he noticed these people whispering fearfully amongst themselves. He immediately made enquiries through his attendant and on hearing the facts was so moved that his eyes filled with tears. Some time before this incident, impressed by Mulraj's equestrian skills, the king had promised to grant him whatever he desired. Mulraj now asked his father for the annulment of the tax. The king very willingly agreed to do so and set the farmers free. Filled with gratitude, many of them stayed behind, and those that went back to their own lands spread Mulraj's fame far and wide. But the unfortunate Mulraj died soon after. The next year, when the crop was plentiful, the Kanbis brought the king both the present as well as the previous year's share. Bhimdev declined to accept the latter but the farmers entreated him to appoint a local panchayat committee to settle the matter. The panch decided that the share of grain for both years should be accepted and the revenue used to build a temple to Tripurushaprasad in honour of Mulraj.

'Such behaviour is typical of peasants. Therefore, Bapji, do not blindly do what the prime minister says, but ponder upon the example I have narrated.' Bhana Patel fell silent, immensely satisfied that he had put forward his case under the pretext of being engaged in pleasantries.

Prime Minister Madhav, having listened intently to both Gormaharaj Vijayadatta and Bhana Patel, turned to Jethasha and enquired, 'Well, Shah! Would you, too, like to pour out your woes?' Jethasha had made a tidy profit in his business that year, and had no doubt that the merchants were the happiest people in the world. But, because he felt he ought to say something, he boasted, 'I have recently dispatched a considerable amount of *manjeeshtha* dye to Stambhatirtha and Bhrigupur (Bharuch) ports. Moreover, my agents from Bet Dwarika, Devpatan, Mahuva, Gopanath and elsewhere inform me that they have received large consignments of goods on my behalf. With this we should be able to put a roti or two on our plates. We would have done better, but this year pirates looted the merchandise from my ships near the ports of Suryapur (Surat) and Ganadeba (Ganadevi). Luckily, the gold *mohur*s had been concealed and were not stolen; otherwise it would have been time to declare bankruptcy. Bapji, there is nothing more to tell you, but it would be good if something could be done about the pirates, otherwise the merchants will get wiped out. Also, the excise duty on imports and exports is rather high and it would help if this could be reduced. You are shrewd, so there is no need for me to say more, but how can one remain silent where one's self-interest is involved? There is a proverb that states that unless you ask, even your own mother will not offer you food.'

Madhav listened attentively to all that was said. He aimed to secure the goodwill of the populace by doing what they desired. The prime ministership had not been handed down to him through his forefathers. He was born to a poor man in Vadnagar town. When he was sixteen, Madhav had come to Patan in search of a job. At first he worked as a clerk, doling out salaries to the soldiers of the army. His quick-wittedness, intelligence and honesty obtained him the position of treasurer. Gradually he had become the favourite of King Sarangdev. When, after Sarangdev's death, his sons fought over the succession, it was Madhav's ingenuity and scheming that brought Karan to the throne. From that day, the sun of Madhav's good fortune began to rise, and as soon as Karan Raja felt that his throne was secure, he offered Madhav the prime minister's post. But a prime minister's job is burdensome and full of risks. To keep the king and his subjects happy at the same time is always difficult. Madhav understood this. He longed to gain popularity among the people and make his name immortal by doing good and beneficial things for them; but he knew only too well that his authority stemmed from the ruler's favour, and he had firmly resolved to keep the king pleased at any cost as well. Most former prime ministers of Gujarat had been banias by caste, and now the banias felt that by giving Madhav the prime ministership, the king had disregarded their rights. They did not miss a single opportunity to criticize Madhav in front of the king, and the prime minister had to manoeuvre his way carefully around them. In addition to this, he also had one eye focused on acquiring wealth for himself; because not even for a moment did he believe that he would remain prime minister forever. Madhav's predicament was a difficult one. The kingdom of Gujarat was bound by Achalgadh and Chandravati in the north; in the west it extended up to Modhera and Jhinjuwada; in the east to Champaner and Dabhoyi; and in the south it stretched right up to Konkan. But after the death of the good-natured Bhimdev, discord had spread across the land. The Parmar kings of Achalgadh did not pay their tribute regularly. The other feudatory rajas were feudatories merely in name. Only if Karan Raja renounced the pleasures of the capital and took up the sword would the kingdom's former glory be restored. Only if Karan waged successful wars, and only if the various feudatories continued paying tribute and the state's income increased, could the brahmins be appeased; the peasants, as Bhana Patel suggested, be given more leeway; and a reduction in excise duty, as requested by Jethasha, be effected. But this seemed highly unlikely. Therefore, the only road open to Madhav was to keep the king happy and stock the treasury however he could. It was a dangerous option. To be prime minister was to lie on a bed of thorns. When all are dissatisfied, and the king is easily swayed, even the highest rank affords little security. Yet the thought of pandering to the king for his own selfish ends was distasteful.

There was yet another reason for the prime minister's unease. He had no children and there was a real fear that he would remain childless. What was the point of accumulating wealth through questionable means? There would be no one to enjoy it in the future. His cousins would fight over his property and instead of being grateful would gang up to slander him—such wounding thoughts caused him great unhappiness. Besides, according to the Hindu *shastras*, the life of a person without sons is contemptible. Thoughts about the fate of his soul after death oppressed Madhav—he had no son to lead the lament when he died, to light the pyre and perform the funerary rites. The desire to immortalize one's name is natural and this can be achieved either through one's descendants or through altruistic deeds. Madhav had no hopes of a lineage nor had he yet had the opportunities for philanthropic deeds, and so, though he held the most important post in the kingdom, though the king did not so much as drink a glass of water without his permission, though a mere gesture of his was enough to raise or ruin the fortunes of men, though he was blessed by Lakshmi still, when he dwelt on the future, he was reduced to a condition so pitiable, even a villager would not envy him.

2

On the tenth day of Ashvin sud, that is on Dussera morning, there was great excitement outside the durbar hall. Syces groomed and bedecked their horses, mahouts were busy with their elephants, and the king's servants readied the chariots for the Dussera procession. Attendants, harem servants, royal jesters and wrestlers stood around anxiously for their conveyance. There was much coming and going at the tailor shops—everyone wanted new clothes for the occasion. None of the town's tailors, washermen or shoemakers had slept the previous night, and many impatient customers had spent a wakeful night with them. Even so, there was such a throng outside their shops that it was a wonder that no one was crushed underfoot. Drains usually kept open to carry away the monsoon rains had been covered that morning, and the surface of the street resembled a mirror. Along it, the young girls of Patan had traced designs with coloured powders, either freehand or with the help of perforated moulds, and now they stood debating among themselves whose pattern was the best. A festive atmosphere pervaded the entire town. Women dressed in fine clothes and jewellery milled about, their high spirits bursting into song. Schools were closed for the day, and groups of children could be seen everywhere. In the courtyard from where the procession would begin, shopowners looked forward to the fees people would pay for a place in their balconies. Sweetsellers, florists, toymakers and food vendors had a spring in their step in anticipation of good business. Those who had fasted for the past ten days or had lived only on fruit bore the appearance of emaciated and hungry wolves that morning as they daydreamt about the feast that awaited them.

The king's palace stood inside the fort, along with a number of other palaces. It rose fifty yards above the ground. It was a square structure, built of black stone embedded with crystal. Facing the main entrance, which was named Ghatika, was a triple-arched gateway. A terrace ran along the considerable width of the building at a height of about fifteen yards, affording a view over the entire city. Below the terrace was an arched corridor, and two victory towers stood on either side. The façade was carved with fine decorative reliefs and painted with battle scenes from the Ramayana and the Mahabharata, as well as episodes from Krishna's life. Inside, the rooms were brightly painted; mirrors hung from the walls.

The moment the sun made its appearance that morning, and nobats and conchshells began to sound the hour, the king came out of his bedchamber. Ordering his favourite horse to be brought to him, he went for a short ride. He bathed and offered puja to his family deity, Shiva, attended by several brahmins. The brahmins chanted Vedic prayers and the king gave them their customary fees. He ordered grain to be distributed to the thousands of beggars who had gathered outside. That done, Karan Raja donned his ceremonial clothing and jewellery and prepared to make his way to the durbar.

The ornate crystal-columned durbar hall was wide and spacious. The floor was spread with a large mattress, covered with a white sheet. Bolsters were placed on the sides, and facing the king's throne, seats had been provided for the leading officials,

17

high and low, depending on their rank. The throne was covered in brocade over which was spread cloth of the finest and softest Bengal muslin. Alongside was the throne for the heir-apparent, but as Karan had no son yet, this stood empty. The next seat was occupied by Prime Minister Madhav, splendid in an embroidered paghadi and brocade coat, and covered with jewellery of gold, pearls and diamonds. Beside him sat crowned princelings, feudatories and other vassal rulers. On the opposite side were ambassadors from Udaipur, Jodhpur and other kingdoms, whose job it was to declare war or negotiate peace, and to pass on information about the goings-on in whichever durbar they were posted. There were also spies in the guise of royal officials, ready to gather inside information about the country. Military officers too were present, their status depending on the number of troops under their command. Most important were the notables, who were entitled to a ceremonial *chhatri* over their heads, or a nobat drumbeat preceding them. Soldiers with swords, daggers, spears and shields stood at attention; there were Vedic scholars, pundits, astrologers and learned brahmins; and right in front sat the bards and painters, riding instructors, dance teachers, jesters and magicians. In one corner were bejewelled courtesans dressed in expensive finery, their posture, fluttering eyes and suggestive manner attracting the attention of everyone.

Bearing golden sceptres and calling out 'Rajadhiraj, king of kings, Khamakhamaji, bestower of plenty,' the standard-bearers announced the arrival of the king. Everyone rose to greet him. The *chopdars'* voices grew louder and the hall reverberated with their cries. Karan Raja ascended his throne. The chopdars stationed themselves at the entrances to prevent any more people from entering the hall, and the guests settled down.

Karan Raja was at the prime of his manhood. He was thirty years old, and by God's grace and a habit of disciplined exercise since childhood, his body was lean and strong. He was a tall man.

His complexion was wheaten, his nose aquiline. His pursed lips suggested a determined character, one who would pursue his chosen task come what may. However, because he often acted thoughtlessly and with haste, the word *'ghelo'* (foolish) had been added as an epithet to Karan's name. His almond eyes were perennially bloodshot, giving him a rather fierce expression, striking fear in the eyes of wrongdoers. Pure kshatriya blood flowed in Karan's veins, and his valour was praised everywhere. He had two shortcomings—one was his excitable and impatient nature, the other his sensuality. This last trait could be discerned in his eyes, and his personal behaviour made it apparent to all. Karan's forehead was broad, his eyebrows thick and set close together, and the strength of his character was evident to any observer.

On this occasion, the king was clothed in expensive garments. A brocade paghadi, crested with diamonds and pearls, covered his head. He wore a brocade angarkha coat, and in the Banarasi sash tied around his waist were tucked a diamond-encrusted sword in a gold scabbard, and a dagger ornamented with diamonds and pearls. Pearl necklaces and diamond pendants hung around his neck. He wore brocade trousers, a gold anklet and sequinned velvet shoes. Two *khidmatgars* fanned him gently.

The durbar commenced. Brahmins chanted blessings. A courtesan entertained the audience with a song. Her suggestive manner and flirtatious gestures soon put Karan Raja in a good mood. As it was the festival of Dussera, a poet recited some verses celebrating Rama's victory over Lanka. A second bard recited a poem in which he described the visit of the Pandava princes to the kingdom of Virat. A learned discussion on the finer points of grammar followed. Finally, an artist displayed his painting of a beautiful woman, and extolled her loveliness. The official proceedings now ended, and the guests began talking among themselves.

It was now ten o'clock. The fire in the king's belly had grown fierce, and he rose from his throne. The chopdars announced his departure, and the audience dispersed. Karan Raja strode to the dining hall, and seating himself on a low silver patlo, had a hearty meal served on a gold plate. He finished with some betel nut and made his way to his bedchamber. His personal advisors, the Gormaharaj and a bard, were waiting for him. Every day, after lunch, it was the king's practice to listen to the brahmin discourse on subjects such as kingly duty, law, statecraft and other issues as propounded in the shastras. 'What shall we discuss today, guruji?' he asked. The brahmin thought for a moment and replied, 'Rajadhiraj, for several days now, I have been wanting to discuss the question of the king's duty and conduct, but the right opportunity never presented itself. Perhaps we could discuss this today. I hope that once Your Majesty has heard what I have to say, you will try and follow the precepts.' The bard had his own views on the subject, not indeed from the shastras, but from his interactions with people, and he prepared to join in the discussion. The Gormaharaj began with a story from the Mahabharata.

'Grandsire Bhishma said, "A country without a king can never prosper. The physical well-being of its people, all their virtues are worthless in the absence of a ruler. It takes just two men for property disputes to arise and when many come together, they begin to oppress one another, and the law of the jungle prevails." In this manner, the first humans made each other's life a torment. Finally, they appealed to Lord Brahma to appoint a ruler. Brahma asked Manu to become their king but Manu said, "Lord, I am afraid to take on such a sinful job. A king's job is a hazardous one; it is burdened by responsibility, often requiring one to act against one's principles." The petitioners reassured him, "Do not fear, Manu. We will offer you a good bargain. Half of all our gold, and half of all our beasts shall be yours; you will receive one-tenth of the grain and your wealth will increase continually. You will receive the taxes levied on prostitutes. Duties on lawsuits and taxes on gambling will also be yours. Moreover, just as the gods obey Lord Indra's command, so will you have authority over all rich and learned men. Become our king, and you will become powerful. No one will be able to strike fear in you, and you will rule over men as peaceably as Kuber rules over the *yakshas*. A quarter of the spiritual merit that your subjects acquire will accrue to you. Just as pupils consider their own teacher to be the best, and the gods honour Indra as their greatest leader, those who want to rise on life's ladder will have to regard their king as the best and worship him, for he is their protector."

'When Yudhishthir heard these words, he burst out, "Birth, death, one's lifespan, the limbs of one's body, where these are concerned there is no difference between a king and ordinary people. Why then should strong, brave men honour the king? And why should the king be worshipped? Why should the happiness and sorrow of his subjects depend on the happiness or sorrow of the king?" Grandsire Bhishma then described the origin of kingship and explained how the welfare of the world depended on the ruler.'

The bard was very pleased to hear the extent of the king's powers extolled in this manner. 'Truly, Maharaj,' he said to Karan Raja, 'the king is indeed divine, the representative of God on earth. And just as God can do anything he pleases, so can the king.'

But the brahmin said, 'Stop. Don't be in such a hurry to jump to conclusions. For greater than all men, greater than the king himself, is the brahmin. The *Manusmriti* tells us that the first thing a king should do when he gets up in the morning is to honour the Trivedi brahmins and follow their advice.'

The bard countered, 'But it is also said in the *Manusmriti* that no one dares to look at the king, for like the sun, his gaze blinds the eye and burns the soul. He is fire, he is water. He is the judge of sinners, the lord of wealth; he is greater than the seas, the master of the sky, a powerful god in human form. His wrath is death, and destruction is certain for one who, even in a foolish moment, shows enmity to the king.'

The brahmin said, 'That may well be, but even so, a king must honour brahmins and cannot act without their counsel. The shastras tell us that no matter what his difficulties, a king should not anger the brahmins, for once their wrath is aroused, they have the power to destroy him, his elephants, his horses, his chariots and his entire army, instantly. When aroused to anger, brahmins can create new worlds and new rulers, bring to life new gods and humans. How can a king prosper if he displeases them? Besides, as Manu says, the power of the brahmin depends on himself alone, but the authority of the king rests on others. If a person harms a brahmin who is skilled in the shastras, there is no need to refer the complaint to the king, because the brahmin's knowledge entitles him to punish the wrongdoer himself. No matter what wrong a brahmin does, his punishment cannot be as severe as for other people. The *Manusmriti* says that whatever the nature of a brahmin's crime, the king has no right to impose the death penalty on him. He can expel the guilty brahmin from his kingdom, but he cannot confiscate his wealth or harm his person. And in another text it is said that even if a king is desperate for funds, he cannot impose a tax on those learned in the Vedas.'

The bard was astonished to hear this. He had no idea that brahmins were so powerful. God has truly conferred great power on these pampered priests, he thought enviously. However, as he did not know of any *shastric* injunctions against them, he said, 'Enough of this. Now let me tell you how much is expected of a king. This is how the historian Mrityunjaya describes the advice Raja Bhoja, the king of Dhara gave to his grandsons, Bhartrihari and Vikramaditya.

'Calling his two boys to him, the king explained to them what they should study. "You must work hard and study grammar, the Vedas, Vedanta and Vedangas, the science of archery, the moral law, music and other arts. You must become skilled horsemen and charioteers. You must become proficient in all kinds of sports, learn how to lay siege to a fort, how to assemble an army and disperse it. You must nurture all manner of kingly virtue. You must learn how to gauge the enemy's strength. How to fight a war, prepare for a journey, conduct yourself in the company of important men, analyse contentious issues into their component parts, build relationships with other rulers, distinguish between the guilty and the innocent, mete just punishment to wrongdoers, and rule over the kingdom with justice and benevolence." The two boys were then sent to study under the finest teachers, and soon excelled themselves.'

Halfway through this recital, yawn after yawn escaped from Karan Raja, and thanks to the burning heat of the October sun assisted by the king's own habit of taking a nap, the raja never learnt how both Bhartrihari and Vikramaditya went on to become famous. When the bard had finished his tale he found that far from listening intently to him, the king was fast asleep. Leaving the room, the bard and brahmin let him enjoy his rest in peace.

While the king surrendered to the goddess of sleep, forgetting both this world and the next, and slept the sleep of the dead, both the fort and the town were buzzing with activity. Dressed in fine clothes and new shoes, a stalk of corn stuck in colourful new paghadis, men strolled down the main street, some singly, others with small children by their side. Some sat on balconies or in their shops. Rajputs and other military men strode importantly, weapons tied to their waists. Bhils, Kathis, Kolis and other tribals hastened to give them right of way. Calling out 'Make room, good sirs', Dheds and other untouchables made their way

23

slowly through the street, and those obliged to move away did so with a curse. Often, a horse or an elephant would start in panic, causing confusion and sending children shrieking. The wives of rich businessmen were borne in covered palanquins to visit the homes of their husbands' colleagues, relatives and acquaintances. The wives of the poor and the middle class walked about openly, confident that they would not be pestered on the way. Terraces and balconies were filled with spectators. Some had climbed on to roofs or treetops while others lined both sides of the street. Shopkeepers had whitewashed their shops, strung garlands, and displayed all their wares.

Outside the fort, Kathiawadi, Sindhi, Kutchi and Kabuli horses, bedecked with the finest saddles, pranced, pawed and stamped their hooves restlessly. As if unable to stand still, powerful elephants swayed from side to side, swinging upraised trunks and sending people scattering. Palanquin-bearers parked their empty palanquins by the roadside and wandered about, enjoying the scene. Foot soldiers and cavalrymen, their weapons in readiness, waited for the procession to begin.

Raja Karan was dressed in the same clothes and jewellery he had worn that morning, only adding amulets with mantras on his wrists as protection against the evil eye. The king's elephant was stronger and taller than the others; it was draped with a cloth of gold and had gold anklets on its legs; pearl necklaces hung on its forehead. The royal umbrella was wrought in silver and gold and embedded with precious stones. Behind the king sat Prime Minister Madhav bearing a fly whisk; he too, wore the same clothes and ornaments he had worn that morning.

Leading the procession were drummers seated on elephants and camels, bent over their drums. Cavalrymen and foot soldiers were followed by dignitaries and important court officials on horseback or in carriages. Filling the spaces in between were wrestlers, jesters and common folk. Finally, the king arrived on his elephant. The sounds of many musical instruments could now be heard, among which the *rangshingda, bhungal* and shehnai were most prominent. Karan Raja bowed his head in acknowledgement to the waiting crowds, and the people bent low and greeted him joyously as the procession passed. Garlands, flower bouquets and single blossoms rained down from windows. The crowd scattered flowers on the street, and the rich showered gold and silver flowers on the king. At that moment, Karan Raja's subjects were so overcome with love, they would have gladly sacrificed a few years of their lives and presented them to the king. He looked so handsome that the women cracked their knuckles on their foreheads to keep him safe from harm.

The procession wended its way outside the town for a short distance and stopped in front of a shami tree. Many brahmins had already gathered there, waiting to perform the shami puja and collect the fees that would be distributed. The moment the king dismounted from his elephant, a brahmin came forward and said, 'Rajadhiraja, give something so that the puja can begin.' The brahmin was immediately presented a bag of money. The other priests also approached their own patrons, saying, 'Maharaj, on this day Lord Rama vanquished the evil Ravan, and the sons of Pandu entered the city of Virat. It was on this day that Arjun and his brothers worshipped the shami tree and hung their weapons on its branches. Which is why you will earn merit by worshipping the shami tree, the Invincible Goddess, today.' They then bathed the tree with *panchamrut*, sprinkled water on it, adorned it with flowers, sandalpaste and *gulal abeel*, set offerings of food and asked the king to circumabulate it. Each of the ten *digpalas* was propitiated in turn, starting with Indra, Guardian of the East.

Then the king and the others removed the rakhis which had been tied around their wrists on the day of Raksha Bandhan and offered them to the tree. The brahmins took a bit of soil from the roots of the tree, a few leaves, some betel nut and grain and gave them to the worshippers, asking them to carry these in an amulet whenever they went on a journey. Once the puja was over, the dakshina due from the king was handed over to the brahmins, and individual worshippers also paid their fees, each according to his ability or the customs of his forebears. Even though the customary amounts were paid, the brahmins, as was customary, grumbled about the bad times, wondered fearfully what the future held in store for their children and, as the final amounts were distributed, the grumbling turned to swearing, and the swearing to fighting, and had it not been for the presence of some older priests who put a stop to the farce, some blood would have undoubtedly been added to the offerings to the Invincible Goddess.

Let us now leave the squabbling and protesting priests and follow the king as his procession returns homewards. A little way ahead, the king stopped to offer puja to the Goddess Gadhechi Mata, Protector of the Fort, and gave dakshina to the attendant priests. Then the convoy made its way back without further delays. There was a large square outside the fort, where thousands had gathered. Here the cavalrymen, foot soldiers, horses, elephants and the king's elephant came to a halt. Wrestlers, fattened on milk, yoghurt and ghee throughout the year, were wrestling, watched by a large crowd. In one corner, two soldiers were engaged in mock combat. Both had blunted spears and carried leather shields, and each time the loser was thrown from his horse by a blow of the spear, the crowd would clap and cheer wildly. One Rajput fought against a mounted spear-holder with only a sword, managing to unseat his opponent without touching him. Several Koli soldiers had created a circular target of mud, and aimed feathered darts at it. Cavalrymen walked their horses around the square, or made them prance in a circle. The festivities ended after about an hour. The horsemen and soldiers made their salutations to the king and left for their appointed tasks. Recounting and criticizing the events of the day, the crowd slowly made its way home.

The king dismounted from his elephant and entered the palace. He changed out of his formal clothing and jewellery, offered puja to the deity and performed *arti*, and then went to the *chandrashala* for his dinner. Raja Karan made it a practice to have his evening meal alone with his queen, with no one else present in the room. Silver seats had been placed and the queen served the meal in gold plates. After the meal ended, cups and glasses were brought in and the king drank liquor made from grapes and mahua fruit. He had his body massaged with sandalwood oil and relaxed on a swing that hung from silver chains. The room was aglow with the flickering light of silver lamps. The watchmen standing guard outside the windows surmised that the raja would soon fall asleep. But shortly afterwards Raja Karan got up from the swing and put on some ordinary clothes and worn-out shoes. He concealed his face with a scarf. Summoning a servant, he informed the man that he wanted to visit the town incognito in order to gauge the mood of the people, and asked him to take a flask of water and accompany him. The servant did as he was ordered, and the two men slipped out of the back door of the palace.[2]

Darkness was falling. The shops were closed and most of the townsfolk were at home asleep, exhausted by the events of the day. A few sat at their windows, exchanging gossip with their neighbours. In front of certain houses, men could be seen standing open-mouthed, watching and listening to the women who had gathered to sing songs to the Goddess, criticizing the lyrics, the manner of singing and the raucous voices of the singers. In the prostitutes' quarter, women decked in expensive clothes and jewellery, with flowers in their hair, did their best to lure passers-by into their web of lust. Some unlucky souls fell into their trap, and for a moment of pleasure, sacrificed a lifetime of

27

true happiness. Others surrendered to the charms of music in the homes of professional dancers. Like insects to a flame, foolish men were drawn to the sounds of the instruments, and blinded by a veil of lust, they imagined they were in Vishnu's heaven. In narrow alleyways and on broad streets, a few men moved about silently, their faces covered by scarves, waiting for an opportunity to make other people's property their own. Here and there, shameless couples walked the night. Raja Karan observed all these things and made a mental note to discuss them with his prime minister. But so far he had learnt nothing about the real concerns of the people. Whatever political talk there was, concerned the day's festivities. Everyone was full of praise for the king's appearance, his character, his clothes and jewellery. This was not what the king had in mind, and he decided to venture out of town.

The guard was bribed to open the gates and Karan Raja walked into the open maidan beyond. It was a full-moon night and the sky was brilliantly clear. The maidan was lit by a silvery glow, and the strips of grass looked like emerald rings on a maiden's fair hand. Not a single living creature was in sight, but frogs croaked in puddles, the sound of crickets was unceasing, and from somewhere the hissing of a snake could be heard. The king walked on until he reached the cremation ground. Although it was a moonlit night, the shadows of trees cast an eerie darkness, adding to the fearful atmosphere of the place. Looking into the distance, he noticed a group of women circling a fire that had been lit under a tree. Karan Raja was curious to see what was going on. He was armed with a sword and dagger, and felt no fear. But his servant had begun to tremble and with folded hands he begged, 'These women are *dakini*s, witches, spirits or something. There is nothing to be gained by going close to them.' But once Karan had got an idea in his head, he was not one to let it go; besides, retreat would be a blot on his Rajput valour. He had made up his mind, and go he would.

When the witches saw Karan Raja approach they glared at him, their eyes round with anger. 'Hey you! King or slave, whoever you are, what business is it of yours to come here?' they demanded. 'How dare you interrupt our rituals? Have you left your home in a fit of temper? Are you already so weary of life that you are willing to be trapped in the jaws of death? Leave this instant, or we will tear you to bits and picnic on your blood!' The raja was not one to be cowed by women. Drawing his sword from its sheath he said defiantly, 'I am a kshatriya, a Rajput, Raja Karan Vaghela, ruler of the Gujjar kingdom, and as you are here in my territory you are my subjects, and I demand that you tell me who you really are.' When the apparitions realized who the man was, they came forward with hands folded in supplication, and one of them said, 'Rajadhiraj, we were once the wives of brahmins and merchants, but all of us died in childbirth. Our husbands married again and did not bother to perform the death rituals for us, which is why we are in this unfortunate state. O Raja, we beseech you to make them perform the necessary Narayanbali sacrifice, and free us from this limbo.'

The king noted the names of the husbands of the spirit women and promised that he would take steps to free them from their condition. Delighted, the witches said, 'Ask for a boon, O Raja, and it shall be yours!' The king asked to know about his future, and one of the spirits replied, 'Maharaj, we do not possess much knowledge of the future. But since you have been so obliging, we will give you a piece of advice: As you know, women have been the cause of great upheavals in this world. Because Ravan abducted Sita, Lanka was destroyed and Ravan himself killed. The battle of Kurukshetra occurred because Duryodhan had Draupadi's garments stripped from her in full view of the assembly, and in the course of the battle not only the Kauravas, but the Pandavas and crores of their supporters also lost their lives. So beware, O King! Be wary of your

29

dealings with women and have as little to do with them as possible.'

The weight of these words raised so many questions in Raja Karan's mind that he was scarcely aware of the journey home. He would have continued walking in this dazed fashion had his progress not been interrupted by a crowd that had gathered in front of a small Shiva shrine waiting to see a performance of a play based on the *Viratparva*. The king felt like taking a look, so he and his servant fought their way into the hall where the play was in progress and the Pandavas, each in a different disguise, had come seeking work.

Absorbed in the action of the play, the king forgot about the warning of the witches. But, by now, his servant was overcome by the effect of opium, and his nodding and yawning set the king yawning too. Realizing that it was nearly morning, he decided to return to the palace. Before leaving he thought he would spend a moment for darshan at the shrine, but as he reached the door of the temple he heard the tinkling of a woman's anklets and in spite of himself he stopped to catch a glimpse of her. The king's senses deserted him. The woman was another Padmini! Her face was like the full moon, and the blush of pink that suffused her fair cheeks made even the pink of rose blossoms pale in comparison. Her mouth was small, her lips the colour of light coral. She laughed softly, her teeth like beads of pearls. On her nose was a ring of fine lustrous pearls. Where they touched her coral lips, they glistened like dew on the red leaves of a lotus. A small black spot adorned her cheek: and if, as the Persian poet Hafiz felt, both Bokhara and Samarkand were fair exchange for the black mole on the face of the beauteous maiden of Shiraz, then surely all of Gujarat was an inadequate price for that spot. The woman's eyes were slightly elongated and naturally black, their blackness heightened by a fine line of kajal. She was delicate, yet sensual. She moved with such grace, she could not help wound the heart of every man whose gaze fell on her. Her eyebrows were fine and curved like Indra's bow. The arrows shot from those brows by the god of love must destroy the peace of mind of many. The red tilak on her forehead was like a spot of blood on a snow-covered field. Her braid was as thick as a serpent's hood and just as black. If let loose, the hair would fall to her waist, but now it lay coiled at the nape of her neck. As for the rest of her body, surely it had been fashioned by the incomparable skill and workmanship of the Creator. Who could resist such beauty? A man is, after all, only human. Swayed by desire he is unable to think rationally, so it is no surprise that Karan Raja stood transfixed, driven out of his mind with longing.

The woman left the shrine and the king came out of his trance. 'Am I asleep or awake?' he exclaimed. 'Am I dreaming? Come, servant, pinch me so I can be sure that I am awake. What have I seen? A celestial maiden from Indra's heaven? Was it a nymph intent on enticing a brave warrior? Did the great Goddess herself assume human form and favour me with a vision? If so, what a foolish, sinful man am I, not to have fallen at her feet and worshipped her!'

The servant wondered if his master had lost his mind or was babbling in his sleep. To shake him out of his stupor, he said loudly, 'That was no celestial maiden, nymph or goddess, Maharaj. She is the wife of Prime Minister Madhav, and the servant with her had a gold thali with sandalwood paste, flowers, incense—so she must have come here to do puja.'

It was as if lightning had struck the king. 'Madhav's wife?' he said in a shocked voice. 'Our Madhav's wife? A swan married to that crow? Is that a fact? You're not lying to me? A woman fit to live in Indra's heaven, a woman made to be worshipped in the royal shrine, a woman who should light up the palace, such a woman is the wife of a miserable brahmin? A brahmin who is presently prime minister, it is true, but who knows, tomorrow or maybe a few years hence, he could be begging for alms, cloth bundle in

31

hand! O God! This is truly unfair on your part! Is a woman like this meant for a lowly brahmin or, for that matter, for anyone except a kshatriya? Is this jewel intended for someone who cannot protect her? Surely this cannot be. Surely there has been some mistake! She was created for me alone, and it is only because of some slip of fate that she is not mine. But now the time has come to rectify the error, and to give back the poor soul the rightful dues that have been denied to her for so long. She must be taken from Madhav. Should I then ask him for her? But that would not reflect well on me. Besides, he is a Nagar, and there is no likelihood of his parting with her. When it is a matter of pride, Nagars are not far behind kshatriyas. So what is the way out? I must send armed men to Madhav's house and forcibly abduct her. Madhav can be brought around later with arguments, bribery or deceit. Women are slaves to fine clothes and jewels and Madhav can be of no use to her in this regard. Ultimately he will realize where his self-interest lies and will agree. There seems to be no other way out. So tomorrow, at the opportune moment, the plan must be set in motion.'

Karan Raja returned to the palace and lay down on the swing but sleep evaded him. At that moment, his queen seemed like a shrew, and he tossed and turned, unable to think of anything except Madhav's wife. O Karan Raja! Alas for your thoughtless nature! It will prove to be your undoing. Have you forgotten the advice of the witches already? Do you not have a care for the consequences of your actions? You think that what you have in mind will be easy to accomplish. But, you fool, you are sowing a poisonous seed and the fruit it will bear will be the destruction of you. But it is too late for Karan to change his ways. He has been wilful since childhood, and has made no real effort to control his self-indulgence. Now he is being swept along in the river of desire, and there is no telling on which shore he will be washed up. The epithet 'ghelo' that historians have bestowed on you is truly apt, Karan. You are a fool, a veritable fool.

3

As Karan Raja thrashed about in an agony of lust thinking how best to have his way, the night gradually weakened its hold, giving way to that contentious interval between darkness and dawn. The sky was crystal clear. With a golden key, Arun, the charioteer of the sun god, unlocked the great doorway of the east and proclaimed to the slumbering world that it was time to rise and get to work. Like truant children who play on the street and run away when their teacher approaches, the stars hid their faces one by one, aware that if Arun had arrived Suryanarayana could not be far behind.

The moon had already set. The morning star, who the villagers say guards the spot vacated by the dying moon, stood undaunted for a while; then it too disappeared. Indra traced showy patterns in the eastern clouds to give a warm welcome to the sun god. Lotus flowers turned their faces eastwards in greeting. White water-lilies drooped low, their petals closed. Bees, like lovers, buzzed around them. Wafted on the cool breeze, the delicate fragrance of the champa, chameli, sevanti and malti delighted the senses. From every corner roosters—mace-bearers of the sun—announced his arrival. Sparrows emerged chirping from their nests. Crows cawed. Caged parakeets and mynahs woke their masters with sweet calls, and melodious birdsong filled orchards and groves. Nobats and conches sounded in the temples to awaken the gods. The homes of the poor were filled with the rumble of the grinding-mill, the chatter of the women, and the singing of *prabhatia*s and bhajans. The hammering of block-printers, goldsmiths, ironsmiths and coppersmiths resounded from the distance. In some homes, the insincere lament of dry-eyed women could be heard as they wailed over the souls of those long dead. The sound of *choghadia*s and other instruments came from the king's palace. Students sat on verandas, revising the previous day's lessons. The sons of banias practised writing in their copybooks. Let loose from their stalls, cattle happily followed the cowherds to graze. Conscientious housewives busied themselves cleaning their homes and making things comfortable for their families; their ill-tempered counterparts flapped about muttering and grumbling, cursing their children and scolding their husbands.

Good-for-nothing idlers and opium addicts lay in bed yawning and complaining, but the hardworking and enterprising were up and about. After a light breakfast, shopkeepers made their way to their shops, giant keys in hand. Some were still opening their establishments, while others had already swept their shops, done puja, arranged their wares and were now sweeping the road in front. Townswomen, skilfully balancing pot upon pot of water on their heads, gossiping about their husbands, mothers and sisters-in-law, and flirting with any unsuspecting male that crossed their path, wended their graceful way home. At Sahasralinga tank, brahmins, themselves unbathed, lectured others on the merits of bathing and offered to keep an eye on their clothes for a fee. Bathed and freshly clothed, *chandla*s smeared on foreheads, people proceeded for darshan of the gods. Owls and bats—kings of the night—sought refuge from crows and other birds in the safety of trees. The chakor bird concealed itself in a secret place at the departure of its lord, the moon. Thieves, having successfully accomplished their goals or sighing for lost opportunities, returned home. Amorous couples, pale and listless after a night of indulgence, crept home like stealthy thieves. Travellers, on foot, on horseback or in carts, carefree or anxious, were on the move. With loaded bullocks and songs on their lips, washermen trundled towards the ghats. Students of archery practised their skills and Rajputs exercised their horses outside the town or in maidans.

That morning in Madhav's home, a woman with her head bent in worry, sat on a small stool in deep thought. Her rumpled dress, her unkempt hair, and the paucity of her ornaments enhanced rather than diminished her graceful beauty. Her limbs were so delicate that the mere act of holding a silver tumbler of water seemed enough to sprain her wrist. She was eighteen, in the first flush of youth and her name, Roopsundari, matched her beauty. But why was she, Madhav's wife, so anxious that morning? On waking, she had discovered that her husband, ready to leave town on work, had already gone downstairs and instead of seeing his beloved face, she had caught sight of a broom lying in the corner; a cat crossed her path as she left the room; and glancing out of the window she saw a whore walking down the street. Worried about her husband's trip and fearful about what might befall him during the day, she begged him not to go. But the work was urgent, he was commanded by the king and being a Nagar he was not particularly superstitious, so he disregarded his wife's forebodings and went on his way. After he left, she told herself that omens have no power over events. She knew that even a twig could not be broken unless the Creator so wished but, in spite of that, she could not help thinking that an evil person will not rest till he has played his evil role, and she prayed to the Goddess that whatever danger might lie in store for Madhav should be rendered as harmless as a pin prick.

Reflecting thus, Roopsundari washed and dressed and went downstairs. The astrologer dropped by later that morning and the minute she saw him she recalled the inauspicious portents she had seen. The astrologer calculated the positions of the constellations, and having thought for a while said, 'The signs do not appear to be unfavourable, but according to the scriptures whatever clothes and ornaments you were wearing at the time should be gifted to the brahmins. I know your horoscope by heart, and it, too, shows no adverse influences. Only the comet Rahu appears to be a problem, so it is better that you give alms today. You do not have to donate much. A single mohur will suffice.' Roopsundari immediately brought down the clothes and ornaments she had worn in the morning, and offered them to the astrologer along with a gold mohur, bowing low as she did so.

She had just finished her puja when she heard a commotion in the outer courtyard of the mansion. She sent a servant to find out what was going on and was informed that scores of the king's soldiers had surrounded the mansion and her guards were being slaughtered. Roopsundari fell to the floor in a dead faint. The cowardly servants hid in corners but others more loyal and courageous grabbed shields, swords and whatever weapons they could lay their hands on, and got ready to fight. Keshav, Roopsundari's brother-in-law, pushed her behind him, and waited, shield in hand. He was a young man of about twenty-five years, and thanks to his brother Madhav, had never had to worry about earning a living. He had spent his youth exercising his body, wrestling, fencing and honing his skills in the martial arts; this had enhanced the natural strength of his youth. Strong and well-built, with fiery eyes, the impetuous Keshav was ever ready to plunge into the fray. Madhav was aware of this failing, and although he had appointed Keshav to a high post, he rarely allowed him to get embroiled in inflammable situations. Keshav was not as handsome and fair as his brother, but now the angry blood coursing through his veins gave his complexion a rare glow. While to others he appeared a veritable tiger, he was as meek as a lamb at home, and his adamantine chest housed a soft and gentle heart. He had ordered his attendant to fetch his favourite sword; holding it in one hand and grasping his shield with the other, he stood like a rock in the midst of a stormy sea, determined to protect Roopsundari against the surge of attackers, ready to slay as many as he could before surrendering to death. The noise in the courtyard grew louder, and he heard the metallic clash of swinging swords. If Keshav had had his way he would have plunged into the thick of the fracas; but his first duty was to protect Roopsundari, and he would not budge from the spot. Just then, a hundred men entered the house; with bloodcurdling cries they cut down the guards at the door and rushed forward. Keshav was ready to welcome them. With one blow he severed the first soldier in two, and with another decapitated the second.

The other soldiers hesitated a moment, and looked at their captain for the next move. The captain addressed Keshav saying, 'Listen, brother! We have not come here to fight. The king desires Roopsundari and if you hand her over peaceably we will leave without further bloodshed. Otherwise, we will be needlessly obliged to commit *brahmahatya*. So consider well what you do.'

Keshav went red with rage. 'If your ungrateful, despicable, lustful king wants Roopsundari, and if you have been sent to abduct her, you can take her—but over my dead body. A Nagar will never disgrace his dharma, lineage or caste just to save his own life.'

The captain gave his men the signal to proceed. They fell upon Keshav, but he stood his ground and managed to slice through five or seven of them before he gave up the fight. The odds were stacked against him. With blood pouring from his many wounds he finally succumbed to death, and with a terrifying scream his soul fled this cruel and scheming world to stand in front of the Great Judge.

Keshav's dying scream jolted Roopsundari out of her swoon and seeing what was happening around her, she cried out, 'O God! O Shiva! What sort of divine anger is this?' As she collapsed back in shock, the king's soldiers grabbed her, whisked her out of the house and delivered her to the palace.

Roopsundari lay on a bed in the chandrashala. Karan Raja was seated beside her. Her hair hung loose and dishevelled. Her eyes were wild with fear and though conscious, she was confused by the sudden and strange turn of events. The king tried to comfort her, to get her to compose her thoughts, to reconcile herself to the situation and accept it. 'O Roopsundari, my beloved, the light of my life, the jewel of my heart, why don't you speak? Gladden my heart with your sweet words. Like a plant wilting in the scorching heat of the desert yearns for a few drops of rain, I thirst for your words. Abuse me, revile me, curse me; your words will be like balm to my heart. Yes, I forcibly abducted you. I separated you from your wedded husband. Your brother-in-law died a needless death trying to protect you. For all these I am truly sorry. I know that you have suffered a great deal, but bear in mind that everything I did was for your sake. It is my intention to marry you and make you my chief queen. You will not want for clothes and ornaments. Lakshmi, goddess of wealth, will be like a slave to you. I will give you happiness such as you have never dreamed of. Today your husband is the prime minister and all your needs are met but what of tomorrow? If calamities come and poverty knocks at your door, will you have the strength to bear them? God has not created you to suffer. You were born to grace a palace, and the veil that hid your true destiny has now been removed and the purpose of your existence fulfilled. So give up your futile grieving. Had it not been God's will, these events would not have come to pass, so your resistance will be construed as a sign of rebellion against the will of God. In any case, there is nothing you can do about it. On the contrary, if you try to fight the inevitable, you will invite great sin upon yourself.'

The king's insistent pleading had not the slightest effect on Roopsundari. Wave upon wave of thoughts swept through her mind: O husband mine, you fulfilled my every desire. Even before you became prime minister and were poor, you deprived yourself to indulge me. When I asked for water you gave me milk; when I was at fault, never once did you utter a harsh word. Alas! Those happy times have passed. When will I see your beloved face again? When will I be able to take care of you? Who will wipe away your sorrow with a smile when you, careworn, enter your home? O! Wretched, ill-fated woman that I am, how will I ever be able to repay you? No one can take your place. Though I have been unable to conceive children, you never once said anything to add to my pain. Ah! Woe is me! Those days are gone but as long as I live I shall never forget you. O God, O Father of the world, do whatever you will with me, a sinner, but keep my beloved husband in good health, wealth and happiness forever. Heed this heartfelt prayer of mine! O my brother-in-law, even if my tears fill an ocean, they will not be enough to express my sorrow. I, whom you always treated with courtesy and respect, whom you looked on as a mother, watched you writhing in blood trying to protect me. You sacrificed your strength and youth, your hopes, your wife, and your life for me in this terrible manner. You died in the full bloom of youth for my sake. How shall I ever avenge this? O Keshav's wife, Gunsundari, my heart breaks in two when I imagine what you must be going through at this moment. Alas! What will happen to you now? You are just sixteen and wretched fate has already made you a widow. How will you live out your days? Curse me with a thousand curses to assuage my guilt for bringing you this boundless sorrow. Who will look after you now?

There will be no happiness for you even in your parents' home. Your sister-in-law will taunt you and feed you dry rotis. Your life will be a living death, and for that I am responsible. O God! Why did you curse me with such beauty? It is this cursed beauty that is the cause of these calamities. When will I be released from my sins? The fire of repentance will burn in me to my dying day, and whatever the king says and however many comforts I obtain, I will be consumed by it. O Lord! I pray that that day comes soon. What good was it to have been born a brahmin, and that, too, in the highest Nagar caste? To be forced to marry twice in one lifetime, and not be faithful to my husband! Heaven knows what sins I must have committed in a previous life! I am now as good as dead to my caste, my community, my relatives, parents, brother and sister. I know I will meet my loved ones again some day but can it ever be the same? Will we be able to gather together for a meal? The whole town will despise me. In the king's palace I will be hated by all. The other queens will be jealous of me. And what guarantee is there of the king? At present he is infatuated with my beauty. But beauty is fleeting. When it vanishes with illness or old age he will turn to other women, and I will be left to rot alone. True love is more than skin deep. False is the love born of attraction. But I am helpless. What can I do? What has happened has happened. Who can fathom the workings of fate? What has been ordained cannot be prevented. What is written cannot be erased. I have no option but to silently accept whatever befalls me.'

While Roopsundari was lost in such thoughts in the king's palace, a sombre mood pervaded the town as well as Madhav's home. The news of Roopsundari's abduction and the death of Keshav caused an uproar in the entire town. In homes and shops, at crossroads and neighbourhoods, the story was endlessly repeated.

Everyone pitied Madhav for the calamity that had befallen him. People wondered whom the king would now appoint as his prime minister, and speculation was rife. The king's evil deed had shocked the populace. 'Today it was Madhav's turn, tomorrow it might be ours,' was the thought in everyone's mind. Moreover, a brahmin had been slaughtered in the capital and no one knew what retribution would be visited upon its citizens by God. Gloom spread over the town. Women sat discussing the plight of Roopsundari. Some felt that she should have killed herself when captured, as it was far better to die than to dishonour the Nagar caste by marrying a Rajput. Others sympathized with her helplessness. 'How could one be expected to take one's life? Was it Roopsundari's fault that God had made her so beautiful? If she had to become a Rajput so be it, but how could she be expected to kill herself?' Some women wondered if it was even possible to live in a country where the king, who should be like a father to his subjects, lusts after one of his own daughters and forcibly kidnaps her. 'Today it is her; tomorrow it will be someone else. God will not tolerate the king's crime. Wait and watch, in a few days' time something terrible is bound to happen. His queen will be abducted and the sins of the king will be visited upon all of us. Whatever God has willed will come to pass.' Some of the more wanton women were thrilled. 'Today she has been singled out, tomorrow our turn might come,' they thought, and planned ways and means of attracting the attention of the king. 'What's so special about Roopsundari that the king has come under her spell when there are so many more beautiful women in the town? We are in no way inferior to her. Anyway, what will the king do with a barren woman like her? Will she be able to produce an heir for the throne? Well, there is still a lot of time. One must be patient and wait for the opportune moment.'

In Madhav's mansion the atmosphere was dark and depressing. Neighbourhood dogs howled. Men and women sat huddled in groups near the entrance. Nagar gentlemen, clad in white, some weeping openly, waited to bear Keshav's corpse to the funeral ground. But not one of Madhav's old friends, men who had considered themselves part of his family, who had basked in his glory, visited him frequently and greeted him obsequiously, could be spotted in the group. Like fish deserting a shrinking pond, like magpies abandoning a field after the corn has been reaped, like buzzing flies rejecting food no longer sweet, those parrots who had feasted in the lush green forests of Madhav's favour, those worshippers of the rising sun, the flatterers of the powerful and revilers of the fallen, were nowhere to be seen in the vicinity of Madhav's home.

Madhav had not been prime minister for long, but during that period he had done a lot for the country, which is why so many people grieved for him. His own relatives as well as Keshav's in-laws had gathered in the house. The haveli resounded with their cries and they beat their breasts red. Blood streamed down some chests, and had the pounding continued one of the mourners would doubtless have swelled the numbers of the dead. Around fifty headless corpses of the slain guards lay in the outer courtyard, and members of their caste were laying out the bodies and preparing them for cremation. Their wails, and the lamentations of grieving women, added to the turmoil. Servants who had narrowly escaped death bewailed their lot crying, 'Why were we spared? Why did we not give up our lives for our master?' Gunsundari's mother, sister, aunt and other relatives sat in one corner of the veranda, while at the other end, on the floor purified by cow dung and covered with darbha grass, lay Keshav's corpse. His wife sat facing the body, her head bowed.

Gunsundari was wheat-complexioned and tall for her age. Though she was not generally considered good-looking, her body now glowed with the rush of emotion. Her eyes were vermilion-red and terrifying. She looked like some angry mother-goddess waiting to be supplicated. Even her mother did not have the courage to approach her. She was gazing at her husband with such intensity that she was oblivious of the commotion and lamentation around her. It was clear that the overpowering desire to become a sati would soon consume her, but so far she exhibited no signs of this. Her mother, herself crazed by sorrow, feared that the intensity of her daughter's anguish would drive her to immolate herself. Till now she had firmly believed that for a girl, death was preferable to widowhood. As a widow, her daughter's presence would scorch the family like a red-hot brazier. Having her around would rekindle their grief again and again; and the sight of her tormented soul would prevent the flame of sorrow in their hearts from being extinguished. On the other hand, if Gunsundari were to become a sati, their grief would be intense but it would not fester endlessly. Yet, surely it was preferable for her daughter to live as a widow than end her life? Of course, the family would have to endure the shame of her widowhood, but her daughter, dearer to her than life, would be there with her and bring comfort to her heart. She would be there to advise her, keep her company and help her in the housework. And a widowed daughter would prove invaluable in her old age, to nurse and take care of her when she was feeble and bedridden. Time is a great healer and a young girl's grief will lessen; and a daughter, even though widowed, is a daughter after all, whose presence brings joy to her parents. Thus Gunsundari's mother (the mother of one whose name mirrored her rectitude, and who was indeed superior in virtue to her more beautiful sister-in-law, Roopsundari), reasoned to herself. On the other hand, how wonderful to have a daughter become a sati! Gunsundari's fame would spread not only in the town but throughout the whole of Gujarat. She would bring renown to her community, increase the prestige of her family, and her parents would be considered fortunate by all. Moreover, as the shastras said, her deed would bring salvation for herself and her husband, and the gods would rejoice.

Filled with religious fervour, Gunsundari's mother came to the conclusion that it would be far better for her daughter to die than to live. But to fathom her daughter's mind she asked, 'Child, it is being said that for your husband's sake you are going to sacrifice your life. If this is true, do what you think is right, keeping in mind our caste obligations, my age and condition. I will not be able to live without you and if I follow in your footsteps, think what will happen to your father and your little brothers and sisters. How can I, your mother, watch you die? How can I, an old woman, bid you farewell and continue to live? This can never be. So banish such insane thoughts that are the result of intense grief, and prepare to live out your life bearing stoically whatever difficulties God sees fit to bring your way. Perhaps your days may be numbered and you will not have to live long. But how can you knowingly take your own life?'

Blood rushed to Gunsundari's face, her eyes grew angry, and she began to tremble violently. Yet the words she uttered were clear and forceful: not by a single tremor did they indicate the great sorrow that had befallen her. 'Live? How can I, a wretch, remain alive when my beloved husband who had made me his own; with whom I had hoped to spend my days both in happiness and in sorrow; who indulged me in every way, never uttering a harsh word; who was as fierce as a tiger in his dealings with others but as gentle as a calf at home has, as if in anger, deserted me by his untimely death? No. Never! I will follow him wherever he goes and share whatever fate has ordained for him. Live? Should I obstruct the progress of his soul and deny it everlasting bliss, in order to prolong this miserable existence of mine for a few more days on earth, when it is in my power to wash away the sins of his past life, which have led to his unnatural death? Live? Having exchanged my ornaments for a string of rudraksha beads and my beautiful saris for garments of white? Live? And be banished from life's activities—to be considered so inauspicious that even my shadow must be barred from defiling happy events. Live? What happiness will life bring? What will be the point of it all? It is a thousand times better to die than to endure a living death. Of this I have not the slightest doubt. So prepare the funeral pyre to receive me and my husband. *Jai Ambe!* Gunsundari's impassioned speech had an immediate effect. All the women gathered around her and touched her feet in reverence, chiding those who wept.

The priest now asked for two *pindas*; one was placed on the darbha grass under the corpse, and the second one in the courtyard for his departing soul. While preparations for the funeral procession were underway, the women led Gunsundari to another room and bathed her. She donned expensive clothes and adorned herself with as many costly ornaments as she could wear. The rest, which she distributed to her sister, sister-in-law and other relatives, were gladly accepted by them as the prasad of the sati. Then smearing sandalwood paste on her forehead, and untying her wet plait, she approached her husband's corpse. The crowd that had gathered from the entire neighbourhood and town, swelled and surged forward as if for a darshan in a temple. They touched Gunsundari's feet and she blessed them all. After a short silence she began to speak. 'O people of Patan, listen well to what I have to say. When Lord Shiva's father-in-law did not invite Shiva to his grand yagna, his daughter Sati, wild with anger at the insult to her husband, plunged into the fire-altar and was burnt to ashes. In her next life, she took birth as the daughter of the Himalaya mountain and married Shiva once again. In the same way, I too, shall sacrifice myself on the funeral pyre of my husband, and will be born again to wed him once more and resume the flow of my interrupted happiness.' As cries of *'Jai Ambe!'* filled the air, Gunsundari applied vermilion paste on her palms, put chandlas on the foreheads of the married women, consoled her friends with a comforting touch, and stretched out her hands in benediction. Women who had brought their sick children held them up to be healed, and were rewarded for their faith when their listless children revived at the sati's touch.

The time for the funeral procession was now at hand, but the crowds showed no signs of dispersing. Finally, with great difficulty the priests managed to clear the haveli and bring out the dead body. Instead of the usual loud wailing that accompanies a funeral procession there was a profound silence to honour the woman who would soon become a sati. Scattering *hinglok* powder in front of her, Gunsundari entered her palanquin. And now the crowds chanted '*Jai Ambe!*' as they surged around the funeral procession and Gunsundari added her cries to theirs. The cacophonous din of rangshingdas, shehnais, *turais*, dhols, nobats, bells, gongs, conches, *thalis* and *jhanj* rent the air. The procession made its way to the town gateway, where childless women eagerly awaited the sati's touch to make their barren wombs fruitful. Gunsundari not only comforted these women but also blessed those who were unhappy at home; or had oppressive husbands; those fearful of early widowhood; and those whose children had died at childbirth. Men desirous of success in their endeavours gathered around her clamouring for her blessing. Finally, all those who had inadvertently harmed, reviled or insulted her came forward repentant, and were forgiven by Gunsundari.

The corpse was now carried outside the town and lowered onto a platform, and the customary pinda offering was made. At that moment, a ragged-looking Rajput disengaged himself from the crowd and with hands folded in supplication said, 'O Mother! From time immemorial it is the custom for a sati to leave behind the vermilion-smeared imprint of her hands on the town wall; and to bless the king and his subjects. You too, should follow this custom.' In a flash, Gunsundari picked up a handful of burning cinders, rubbed her hands black with them and flung them at the horrified townsfolk. 'The king,' she cried, 'who abducted a blameless woman, the wife of his own prime minister, a brahmin girl of the Nagar caste? The king, who banished the man who was

46

ever his well-wisher and strove for the prosperity of his kingdom? Who caused the slaying of the minister's brother as he tried to prevent the capture of his sister-in-law? The king who is now also responsible for the death of a woman, who though soon to gain immortality as a sati, leaves behind sorrowing parents, brothers, sisters and relatives due to her untimely death—that king, the cause of all this devastation, will soon lose his kingdom and wander the jungles homeless, his queen will be captured and his daughter will suffer endless torment before being forced into the arms of a stranger; he will long for his own death, but when the time comes, not a soul will know when or where he breathed his last, not a trace of his existence will remain, his enemies will occupy his palace, and the kingdom of Anhilpur will be utterly destroyed. Its wealth will be looted, the rich and powerful will be uprooted from their land, and not a trace of this town will remain. O Goddess Jagadamba! May my curses bear fruit! If my words prove to be in vain, consider me to be a sinful, wicked, false and hypocritical sati. O ye thirty-three crore gods, come to my aid! Let these words come true.'

Gunsundari's impassioned curses and wild demeanour so alarmed the Rajput that he started trembling uncontrollably and a host of conflicting emotions raced through his mind. He would have fallen to the ground if the bystanders had not supported him. This extraordinary reaction aroused intense curiosity, but before he could be questioned, the Rajput seemed to vanish into thin air, and everyone wondered if he was some divine apparition. As it was, the crowd was agitated by the curses flung by the sati. The rich resolved to conceal their wealth; courtiers started speculating about possible calamities; others, with solemn expressions on their long-drawn faces, began to recall the former misdeeds of the king. Secretly pleased at the prospect of turmoil and confusion, the unscrupulous and the cunning prayed for the early downfall of the kingdom. The poor and the weak resolved to abandon the town knowing that when troubles come, it is they who always bear the brunt.

When the procession finally reached the cremation grounds, the pall-bearers floated the corpse on the river and began to prepare the funeral pyre. The crowds watched transfixed as the brahmins made ready to merge the corporeal body back into the elements from which it had emanated. A square pyre made from the woods of babool, agar and sandal trees was prepared, and a wooden enclosure, covered with grass, thorns and other inflammable materials was erected on it. Heavy logs were arranged on top. An opening on one side provided just enough room for a person to enter. The sati descended from her palanquin. Not a trace of doubt clouded her face; and the firmness of her step belied the imminence of her doom. Her unsmiling face reflected an inner calm and a determination to carry out her resolve. She came and stood before the pyre, waiting for the funerary rites to end before bowing low to the four quarters. Then turning her face towards the sun she cried, 'O sun god! You stand revealed in front of us and your radiance is everywhere. You are the root cause of all life; not only do you illumine the world, you also uncover the deepest thoughts of living creatures. Therefore, I pray, burn away my sins to ashes and make me pure.

'O Lord of life! If I have been a true and faithful wife, fit to become a sati, take me in your arms, otherwise let me not be touched by your flames.' With head held high, Gunsundari began to sing the praises of the Lord.

> Thou art the refuge of the poor,
> All-merciful and compassionate,
> Bestower of plenty.
> The earth and all its creatures bow low
> in gratitude.
> Thy light illumines the sun and the moon,
> O creator of oceans, trees and mountains.

Flowers of field and garden,
Fragrant and lovely.
Flawless the mantles of green spread over the earth.
Myriads of insects dance in the breeze.
Birds fly gracefully under the skies.

In woods and forests wild beasts abide in peace.
Thy divine leela who can understand!
Yet the sinful stay enmeshed
Caught in endless pursuit of desire.

God's wondrous maya is unfathomable;
And the cause of suffering is sin.
O Lord! I humbly beseech you
Burn to cinders my evil deeds.

Gunsundari thrice circumambulated the pyre, removing her ornaments and distributing them amongst the brahmins, and by the time she completed the last round she was so oblivious to the world around her that she lost her footing. Her family priest caught her by the hand to steady her, but afraid that people might think she was faltering in her resolve, Gunsundari snatched her hand away from him and faced the dumbstruck crowd as they watched in mesmerized silence, sweat pouring down their faces in the unbearable heat of the afternoon sun and the stifling crush of bodies. Not a breath of air disturbed the awful silence, not a leaf stirred, and the waters of the Sabarmati were as clear and still as a lake. Self-preservation is a law of nature. Wealth, property, wife, children—all that one holds dear—are willingly sacrificed to it. Yet here was a woman, her faculties intact, so drugged with religious fervour, with such unquestioning faith in the holy scriptures, that she was willing to commit an act whose horror she had never seen and could never have imagined! It was a spectacle so strange that it seemed as though the universe had stopped in its tracks, wonderstruck.

Now the sati was eager to join her husband. She entered the wooden structure, cradled her husband's head in her lap, and gestured to the brahmins to proceed. Pouring liberal quantities of ghee on the pyre they lit the dry grass and twigs with flaming torches. The logs caught fire and the roof of the makeshift enclosure caved in. Rangshingdas, turais, bhungals, dhols, nobats, and shehnais blared, cymbals clashed, thalis were beaten and people covered their ears against the thundering noise. Screams of 'Jai Ambe! Jai Ambe!' pierced the din. The frenzy reached horrifying proportions, impossible to describe. Not a single cry escaped Gunsundari as her youthful body was crushed under the collapsing roof and she and her husband were enveloped by flames. Their mortal remains dissolved into the elements, leaving their souls to be judged before the King of Kings.

The crowds dispersed, sorrowful, momentarily indifferent to the things of this world. Only one Rajput remained. His heightened sensibilities convinced him that he had heard the agonized cries of the dying sati. What did such inauspicious omens augur for the future? What should he do? He sat down and wept like a child in distress.

The sinner can never rest happy. He fears retribution at every twist and turn. The fall of a pebble sounds like the roar of an onrushing avalanche. Peace of mind evades him by day, and sleep at night. He is tormented by doubt, real and imagined, and the unquenchable fire of remorse consumes his body. His wealth, his family, his servants, and all the outward comforts of life are no protection against the sin that gnaws at his heart, until he faces a death devoid of all hope and with the certainty of hell awaiting him. Such was the pitiable state of mind of that Rajput, none other than Karan Raja himself.

4

What evil times have befallen me, Lord Rama! O cruel fate! Wherefore your anger? What have I done to deserve the sorrows piled on me? Now I understand why the king ordered me to go out of town that day. That despicable villain was bent on destroying my family. A more ungrateful king was surely never seen on this earth, nor will be seen again. Has he forgotten to what lengths we went to place him on the throne after Sarangdev died? The stratagems we had to employ? The plotting and scheming? And the many promises he made to me when he ultimately became king? They were nothing but lies. Before long, he forgot what he owed me. More fool I, to have nurtured that young viper only to have him strike at me as soon as he reached adulthood. Surely God will not tolerate such ingratitude. But what's the point of thinking about the future when, at this very moment, he's enjoying the fruits of his foul deed? If only I had listened to my wife that day and not left town, perhaps these misfortunes could have been avoided. Yet who can resist fate? What providence has decreed must come to pass. But surely no man deserves to endure so much all at once. That the king should have seized my wife is enough to lacerate my soul, but in addition to have my brother, whom I loved and raised like my own son, die such an untimely death, is beyond bearing. O Keshav, you gave your life, but at least you did not allow your wife to be taken from you while you were alive. Your sacrifice has not been in vain. That the strong should protect the weak is only right, and the knowledge that you gave your life to do so, and that you are now dwelling in Kailashlok, is my only solace at this moment. But it seems that your death did not satisfy fate. Motisha has just come secretly from Jethasha's home to tell me that Gunsundari has committed sati. I don't know whether to rejoice or mourn. Our family has been wiped out. It is pointless to hope that our lineage will continue. Yet the family name will live on. Gunsundari's sacrifice has ensured the glory of our family, indeed of our entire caste, for the next seven generations.

How strange is the condition of man! How uncertain his greatness. Here today, gone tomorrow! It is nothing but the dry grass in the meadow, liable to burn in an instant; it is like a shadow at sunset, which seems so imposing, yet dwindles away in a moment; it is a dream that cannot be grasped when one is awake. What was I on Dussera day, and what am I now! I have come here on foot, walked ten kos without pause, and am alone. Where are all my soldiers, my servants? And yet, by the grace of the Goddess, I am alive. Had I died, that wretch would have lived happily ever after. But now I will become his nemesis. I will stalk him. I will not allow him a moment's peace. I will not rest until I have avenged his deeds. O revenge, child born of anger, awaken in my breast! I have need of you. As long as there is breath in my body, dwell in my heart! The tentacles of revenge are spread throughout the world. One may condemn it, but this does not have the slightest effect on its intensity. Even inanimate objects take revenge. If I hit the wall with my hand, it will hurt me in equal measure. Is that not revenge? If you throw a stone at a dog, will it not bark and attack you? If you trample a snake underfoot, will it not bite? If tormented, even the meanest creature will take revenge if it has the ability to do so. The shastras continually urge us to forgive, to be merciful, but this has never prevented anyone from taking revenge. Don't the Puranas give us examples of even the gods avenging themselves? Revenge is the safeguard of the world. Without it, the world would stop functioning. If you slap a man, he will slap you twice. Only if he is too weak to do so will he go and lodge a complaint with the king and seek justice from him. But this is the recourse of the powerless. A man whose property has been stolen, or who has been harmed in some way, will take revenge, or get someone to do so on his behalf. Learned men tell us that if everyone who has suffered injustice takes revenge according to his own inclinations, there would be no order left in the world; it would be the short road to destruction, and therefore, the king must be consulted in the case of each wrongdoing. And if one does not get justice, then one should rest assured that God himself will mete it. But a king is not always impartial, nor is he always just, and there are occasions when one cannot take this route. What if the king himself is the criminal, who will judge him? To rely on divine justice is for the helpless. It is taking the easy way out. If one is magnanimous and forgives every guilty person, the number of criminals would increase, and the responsibility for that would be on oneself. Only a few really fear the punishment of God. Who can vouch for it? If the ruler abdicates the role of judge and instead tells people that they will have to fear the punishment of God, I wonder how many would be deterred from crime. So revenge is the only option, and since in this case the evildoer is the king himself, one must take revenge personally, and only if this is impossible should one entrust the task to God.

These thoughts swept like waves through the mind of the young man who was wandering by the Sabarmati river, at the foot of the steps that led to the Rudramala shrine in Siddhapur. He was overcome with rage, and all nature seemed to endorse his mood. The current in the Sabarmati was so strong that animal carcasses and even whole trees were being swept along in it. The roaring of the wind made the man's heart beat wildly. The cloud-filled sky was dark; it was impossible to be aware of a person until one had collided with him. The rain fell steadily. Branches crashed to the ground and some trees were in danger of being uprooted altogether. Lightning cleaved the sky, and in the intermittent flashes of light he could see the pillars of the Rudramala temple, its decorated gateway, and the spires of the smaller shrines. Then thunder came, so ferocious, it seemed as if the whole temple complex would collapse. At that moment, when the wrath of God was evident everywhere, is it any wonder that a mere man should be overwhelmed by the force of his rage? Is it any surprise that Madhav's mind, instead of gradually becoming calmer, was being raised to even higher peaks of wrath? That in those dark surroundings he was ready to do dark deeds?

Madhav was shivering, the state of his body a reflection of the state of his mind. He listened once more to Motisha's report, but this only added fuel to the fire of his anger. He even forgot to thank Motisha for what he had done. At a time when all of Madhav's friends had deserted him, Motisha had abandoned his home, his wife, his children, his livelihood—everything— to help his friend. Jethasha, the powerful Jain financier had expressly forbidden anyone from making the slightest contact with a man who had aroused the king's displeasure, but Motisha had somehow managed to escape from the town. This is what true friendship means, and such bonds develop only in youth, when emotions are strong. As one grows older, increasing self-centredness drives away love, and strong friendships are rarely seen among older folk.

As the night advanced, Motisha and Madhav went to the rest house attached to the temple. But Madhav could not sleep.

Thoughts of revenge had possessed his body and he thrashed about thinking of what form his revenge should take. Just as he was falling into a wakeful sleep, his eyes were forced open by a sudden brilliant light. It emanated from a beautiful woman who stood before him. 'O lady of vengeance!' Madhav addressed her, 'whether you are human or fiend, tell me, how should I avenge myself on this evil king?' The woman replied, 'Madhav, I am Bhavani Ambamata, mother of the universe. You are a Nagar and thus a devotee of mine. I dwell on the top of Arasur mountain. If you come there and have darshan of me, I shall tell you what action to take.' So saying, the woman disappeared, and when Madhav looked around there was no one to be seen.

Convinced that the Goddess Bhavani would help him, Madhav decided to leave the very next morning for her shrine and follow whatever advice she gave him. Once this decision was made, Madhav's mind quietened. Exhausted by the day's events and the turmoil of his thoughts, he finally fell asleep and did not awake until sunlight streamed into the room, sparrows and other birds called noisily to one another, and sadhus sang in loud voices as they went about their activities. As soon as he awoke, he went into the village and bought two horses. Then, having completed the preparations for the journey, he and Motisha started in the direction of the Goddess's shrine.

To avoid encountering the king's soldiers on the highway, the two friends travelled along the banks of the river. For a few days, they passed through settled villages, but as they neared the source of the Sabarmati, the landscape became more hilly and wild. They made their way through a valley filled with fruit-laden trees, surrounded by thickly forested hills. Evening fell as they rode along the desolate bank of the river, and the dark hills were terrifying. They heard the cries of tigers, wolves and foxes, and the harsh sounds of nobats being played by naked tribals. The Bhils were making a sacrifice to their goddess, and the flames from the fire snaked between one mountain and the next. Finally, the travellers arrived at a small temple of Koteshwar Mahadev that stood at the source of the Sabarmati, at the foot of the pilgrimage site of Ambabhavani, and here they rested for the night.

The next morning, Madhav and Motisha decided to take the winding route up the mountain to Danta village, to avoid the dangers from both tigers and bandits. Danta lay in the domain of the Parmar kings, devout worshippers of Ambabhavani, and although this was not the time for the annual pilgrimage to her shrine, they came across many people who were on their way to the temple to fulfil a vow they had made to the Goddess. It was a long but easy climb, although the road was uneven and twisted in some places. The pilgrims were dressed in garments of red, white and yellow. Some carried gleaming swords. Some wore gold jewellery that glittered in the sunlight, creating a long golden necklace as the row of devotees wound up the path. From time to time, the colourful travellers would disappear behind the mountains, then suddenly emerge again from the shadows. A stepwell had been provided at one flat stretch, and everyone rested here for a while. Refreshed, they continued on their way, and soon the gloomy and depressing path gave way to a sweet-smelling meadow. Those ahead cried out that the temple was in sight, and those on horses dismounted and fell on the ground crying, *Jai Ambe! Ambemataki Jai!*

Situated on the peak of Mount Arasur, where the Aravalli mountain range ends in the south-west, was Ambamata's shrine. Small, and not as beautiful as many of the better-known temples in the area, it was surrounded by a high wall, and within were quarters for priests and servants, and rest houses for pilgrims. A small armed force was also stationed here, but since Ambamata did not need the protection of men and weapons, the Goddess had prohibited the building of an entrance gateway that could be locked to keep people out.

The Goddess was Durga, consort of Shiva, daughter of Himalaya and his consort Mena. Unlike in nearby Pavagadh, where she was worshipped in the form of the fearsome, all-devouring Kalika, here she was Bhavani, dynamic source of creation, and Amba, the great Earth Mother. Her temple at Arasur was an ancient one. It was said that the *mundan* ceremony of the child Krishna was performed at this very place; and it was here that Rukmini later came to offer thanks after she was saved by Srikrishna from marrying Shishupal. The feet of countless pilgrims who visited the site had worn smooth the paving stones of the courtyard.

Having cooked and eaten a meal at the temple rest house, and rested a while, Madhav and Motisha went to have darshan of the Goddess. Now, it is true that the Mother appears in different ways to different people, but to Madhav she manifested herself in a truly extraordinary form. She appeared as a *mleccha*, one hand wielding a sword, while with the other she grasped a man by a tuft of his hair. Madhav stood in front of her in amazement. And as he watched, the man somehow extricated himself from the Goddess-barbarian's clutch, leaving behind only a fistful of hair. As Madhav pondered over the meaning of this vision he suddenly remembered the dream he had had at the Rudramala dharamshala in Siddhapur. He realized that the barbarian was the Turkish sultan of Delhi, and the man in his clutches was none other than Karan Raja. The meaning of the vision was clear—the Turkish king would besiege Karan, and the raja would abandon his kingdom and flee. The Goddess had shown Madhav the path of revenge just as she had promised! Now he must make his way to Delhi and persuade the sultan to attack Gujarat.

Madhav bowed down to the Goddess in gratitude. He offered her flowers and coconuts, money and jewels. He presented clothes, a pennant, gold and silver utensils, a bell and other items required for her puja. That night, he sent up a tray laden with the flesh of goats and fowl along with an offering of wine. Throughout his stay at Arasur, he used only ghee instead of oil. In return for his generosity, Madhav was allowed the honour of fanning the Goddess. In turn he gave gifts to the three Audichya brahmins who had the exclusive right to officiate at the temple—a position they had secured by paying the raja of Danta a certain sum of money. The next morning Madhav spread further goodwill by distributing sweets to them and to the other brahmins, and giving them an appropriate fee. Next, he finally requested them to place a *kunku* handprint on his shoulder as a mark that his pilgrimage had been successfully completed.

Since nothing further remained to be done, Madhav and Motisha visited the nearby shrine of the Goddess Aparajita on the banks of the Mansarovar. They then decided to go to Gabargadh, a hillside fort that stood to the west of Ambamata's temple. Seen from a distance, the low hills in front of the fort looked like an arched entranceway to the cave where, it was said, Ambamata once lived. 'A long, long time ago,' the priest of the place told them, 'Ambamata's cows would join the cattle of a certain cowherd and graze with them all day long. When night fell, they would return to the mountain. Finally, one evening, the cowherd, determined to discover who the owner of the cows was and demand a grazing fee come what may, so he followed the cows when they returned to the mountain. When he passed through the cave, he found himself in a beautiful palace with many rooms. In the main hall, seated on a swing and surrounded by her companions, sat Mataji. Gathering his courage in his hands, the cowherd asked Mataji, "Do these cows belong to you?" "Yes," she replied. Encouraged, the cowherd went on, "I have taken these cows to graze for the past twelve years, and now you should pay me." Mataji gestured to one of her maids and ordered her to give the cowherd a handful of corn kernels from a heap lying on the floor. The woman filled a winnowing basket with the grain and handed it to the cowherd. Disappointed and angry, the cowherd left the palace, flinging the corn in the courtyard. When he returned home, he discovered that the pieces of grain clinging to his clothes were bits of gold! The next day, the cowherd tried to return to the mountain, but he could not find his way and Mataji's cows never came back to graze.'

Motisha now wanted to visit some Jain temples in the vicinity, and since he, a Jain, had accompanied Madhav to Ambaji's temple, Madhav could not refuse him. According to legend, when the Jain merchant Vimalshah was minister in Gujarat, Ambamata had bestowed much wealth on him. The minister, however, used the money to build 360 shrines dedicated to the Jain tirthankar, Parshvanath. 'Who helped you build these shrines?' Ambamata questioned Vimalshah. The king replied that he had built them with the aid of his guru. Mataji repeated the question three times, and three times Vimalshah gave the same answer. Then Mataji spoke. 'Run for your life!' she warned. Vimalshah fled to a crypt in one of the shrines, through which an underground passage led to Mount Abu. To make her displeasure known to all, Ambamata burnt all but five of the Jain shrines. The burnt remains of the 355 others were still scattered about on the site.

Later, when Vimalshah built a Jain temple among the Jain shrines at Mount Abu, he had an inscription inscribed on it to appease Ambamata's wrath.

O Goddess Ambika, you whose leaf-like hands are red like the tender leaves of the Ashoka tree, you of wondrous beauty, whose chariot is drawn by a tawny lion, on whose lap two boys sit, may you destroy the sins of the repentant.

The inscription continued: *Vimalshah was commanded one night by the wise Ambamata to build the temple of Yoginath (Adinatha) on the hallowed mountain.*

This command was honoured in the year 1032, and on the pinnacle of Mount Abu rose the temple of Adinatha to whom Vimalshah pays homage.

Madhav and Motisha now prepared to visit the many holy sites of Mount Abu. They walked up a pleasant path that bordered a small stream. The sky was cloudless. Koels called out from mango groves and from bamboo thickets birdsong could be heard. Partridges sat in friendly discussion with doves. The knock-knock of woodpeckers' beaks echoed through forests fragrant with flowers and fruit-laden trees. Bees searched for nectar in the white and yellow flowering vines. From time to time, a Rajput on horseback, sword in hand, would pass by on his way to Ambamata's shrine. Once the travellers came across a gypsy encampment where the bullocks had been set free to wander. They passed through a flat, sandy valley dotted with patches of arable land. Ahead lay fields cultivated with grain, a few small villages and streams that flowed from distant hills. Now Mount Abu could be seen through the mist. A thread-like road wound up the side of the mountain, sheltered by a canopy of trees. As Madhav and Motisha climbed higher, they came to a steep, sheer rockface in front of which was a maidan. Here, surrounded by trees, stood Vasishthamuni's temple. The travellers stopped to rest awhile in the temple grove. It was filled with fragrant flowers and the scent of kevda was everywhere. A small stream flowed into a tank from the mouth of a cow-faced rock, the sound pleasing to the ear. A black stone statue of the sage who had brought forth the four great Rajput clans from the fire-pit at Achaleshwar stood within the precincts of the small shrine. Every morning, afternoon and evening the place reverberated with the beating of drums.

Beyond Vasishthamuni's shrine, shallow stone steps cut into the mountainside led the long way up to the flat plateau of Mount Abu. It was a totally new world, an island floating in the sky. Rocky outcrops and hills, small and large, with villages nestled on their sides encircled it. In the centre of the plateau stood a lake fed by several streams. On the highest peak, Muni-Shikhar, the travellers could see a small shrine commemorating a sage, while on another stood the famous Achalgadh fort.

A cold, shivery wind from the south was blowing when Madhav and Motisha reached the top of Muni-Shikhar, and wrapping black woollen blankets around them, they lay down in the shelter of a rock. The view was breathtaking. Rays of sunlight pierced the clouds that swirled beneath their feet. On a dizzyingly sharp peak, protected by a wall, they could see a small fortress. Below, on one side of the mountain was a natural cave, some ten square yards wide. Here on a panel of rock were carved the footprints of Sage Dattabrighu, an avatar of Vishnu. It was to glimpse these footprints that Motisha had wanted to make the difficult journey up the mountain. In one corner of the cave were placed the wooden sandals of Saint Ramanand, guru of the Sitabhaktas. A priest from this sect lived in that desolate spot; he began ringing his bell the moment he spotted the travellers, and did not stop until Madhav gave him alms. A pile of walking sticks besides the saint's sandals commemorated the faith of the pilgrims who had made the perilous journey to the shrine. Small cave-like hollows in the mountainside indicated that this place had been inhabited from ancient times and there were several round holes which seemed to have been dug more recently to hold cannonballs.

The monsoons had just ended, and in the clear air the flat sandy plain which stretched to Balova and all the way to the Jodhpur fort could be seen. From time to time the fertile valley of Bhitril was visible all the way to Sirohi and, in the east, the Aravalli hills reached up to the clouds. Here in the centre stood the famous temple of Ambamata.

If you looked straight down you could see a steep hanging rock, but if you looked up and turned your gaze a half-circle to the right, you would spot the fort of the Parmar Rajput kings. Lower down were the Devalwada peaks. A blue sky, sandy earth, marble shrines, small dwellings, vast jungles and hills high and low offered a wonderfully varied view.

Descending from Muni-Shikhar, Madhav and Motisha walked to the firepit of Achaleshwar. About 450 yards long and 120 yards wide, it was carved out of the mountainside and lined with brick. Perched on a rock in the centre of the kund stood a temple dedicated to Mataji. Five shrines honouring the five Pandavas stood to the north; while to the west was the temple of Achaleshwar—unmoving Shiva—the Ishtadev of Mount Abu. A modest, undecorated building made from black slate, it was placed in a large courtyard and was surrounded by smaller shrines. To the east of the firepit, a stone structure housed a two-and-a-half-foot-tall marble statue of Adipala, the founder of the Parmar Rajput dynasty. He had been sent to earth to overcome the buffalo-headed demon who drank the holy water of the tank at night, and the statue depicted the king killing the monster with an arrow.

Madhav and Motisha made their way next to Achalgadh fort. After a stiff climb, they entered the lower fort through the Hanuman Gate. A second gate led to the inner fort; but there was nothing worth seeing there apart from a large lake named Shravan-Bhadarvo after the names of two monsoon months. An apt name, as the lake remained full even in the height of summer.

Now all that remained to be seen were the Dilwara shrines, and to get there Madhav and Motisha had to go past Vasishtha's shrine once again. The area between the shrine and the Dilwara peak was rich and fertile, with cultivated fields, villages, streams and trees; in some places it appeared as if a lush green carpet had been spread across the land. ****The temple precinct of Dilwara was located on the plateau of the mountain, by the side of the beautiful Nakhi lake. Little tree-covered islands dotted the lake and waterfowl swam contentedly in its waters. The main shrines had been built by Vimalshah and Tejpal. An inscription stated that Vimalshah's shrine had been constructed in 1032—the first Jain temple on this holy mountain. The shrines at Dilwara were not large, and had plain exteriors, but the interiors were so profusely carved that it is almost impossible to do justice to them in this account. The main octagonal dome of the shrines was surrounded by several smaller ones. Built entirely from white marble, the carving was so intricate it was difficult to imagine how such exquisite work was possible, except in enamelled jewellery. Carved here were not merely geometrical patterns; also depicted were men and women going about their daily lives, seafarers, market scenes and scenes of battle. Today, in the 1860s, every Englishman who visits the shrines is full of praise for their exquisite beauty, and is convinced of the considerable architectural abilities and great artistic skill of Indian craftsmen.

The sheer beauty of God's handiwork, and of art inspired by faith, the bliss of walking through sanctified ground, the experience of so many wondrous sights, the great good fortune of being in the glorious presence of living gods—all this filled Madhav with such joy that the turmoil in his soul subsided, the fierce revengeful thoughts that had invaded his heart curled up in a corner, and he began to forget some of his great suffering.

It is not surprising that in a place where one experiences the open-handed grace of the divine; where the greatness and power of God are revealed, and the insignificance and pettiness of man exposed; where the eternal nature of God's work and the transient creations of mankind are apparent; where God's love is heaped unstintingly on man, beast and all living things, the soul should be humbled and quietened.

Madhav's ugly and vengeful thoughts, though somewhat weakened, had not been completely destroyed. So long as he remained in that sacred space, Madhav's mind was tranquil, but as soon as he stepped out into the Mewar plains and there was no longer anything to distract him, they returned in full force. Besides, he and Motisha were now entirely on their own, and as they went over the same subject over and over again, the fire of revenge flared up once more. The road seemed endless, the food without flavour, and had Madhav not been overtaken by other events, he would have undoubtedly fallen ill on the way and died before he could carry out his evil plan. But thanks to the ill-fated destiny of Gujarat and the rising star of the foreign invaders, this was not to be.

As Madhav and Motisha continued their journey, they met a group of pilgrims on their way to Gokul and Mathura. Eager for some company, the two joined the group, saying that they, too, were going on a pilgrimage to Badrinath-Kedarnath. The pilgrims belonged to a number of different castes, and in the afternoon all of them would settle down under the shade of trees to cook their own meals and while away the hot hours, waiting until the early evening to start walking again. Some were travelling on horseback, others in carts, and their company lessened the tedium of the journey.

Among the pilgrims was an old bania woman, so suspicious and so anxious for the safety of her little bag of money that, even though embarking on a pilgrimage, she had found it impossible to part with her wealth and, unlike her fellow pilgrims, had not left it behind in the care of some relative or trusted friend. She kept her purse, with the hundred-or-so mohurs that she had earned after a lifetime of drudgery, with her at all times, pushing it deep into her armpit when she went to sleep at night. Like a sleeping dog she would be startled by the slightest touch, screech loudly and wake everyone up. Her fellow travellers would tease her mercilessly, poke fun at her during the day, and purposely startle her at night. For the old woman the prospect of spending the slightest bit of her money was a fate worse than death. Her one desire was to give a small sum in charity during the pilgrimage, leaving behind enough to pay for a sumptuous funeral feast for the entire community after she died. She had never earned the respect of her kin while alive, but she hoped that her grand funeral would be the talk of the village, for it was her opinion that such a talked-about death would find favour with God and earn her a good place in heaven.

The old woman had a nephew who had accompanied her on the pilgrimage. He was desperately poor, and though she had no children of her own and no one else to leave her money to, the old crone would not part with a paisa even if he were to starve to death in front of her eyes. She intended to hand over her money to the village headman before she died, instructing him to give her nephew whatever remained after deducting the cost of the funeral expenses. The old woman was fond of her nephew in her own way, and she had looked after him like her own son whenever he had fallen ill, if for no other reason than that, should he die, there would be no one to light her funeral pyre. But if he brought up the topic of his dire poverty, she would immediately change the subject, or say she had no money to spare. It was not surprising, therefore, that the nephew cared nothing for the old woman. If after he had gone hungry for four days she could not be persuaded to give him a stale roti, it was unlikely that she would part with her money while she lived. So the nephew waited eagerly for her to die, but the more impatient he got, the longer her lifespan stretched. She suffered from a number of diseases, but she was like a seasoned old pot, and these had not the slightest effect on her. As time went on, the nephew grew more and more desperate, and the woman more stingy.

When the woman decided to go on a pilgrimage, the nephew hoped that she would hand over her money to him for safekeeping, but when his expectations did not materialize, he sold his few meagre possessions and decided to accompany her on the journey. The crone did not like this one bit, but what could she do? She certainly could not prevent him.

It was the nephew's intention to kill the woman during the trip. But the old hag was so alert and they were in the midst of so many other people that he had been unable to carry out his evil plan. The lack of opportunity made him irascible and his murderous thoughts grew stronger with every passing day.

Finally one night, when everyone was fast asleep, the young man went up to the woman, grabbed her by the neck, and as she opened her mouth to scream, stuffed a rag in it. He squeezed her neck until she collapsed and died. Extracting the pouch from under her armpit, he buried it by a tree, and taking care to mark the spot, went back to sleep. Early next morning when the pilgrims tried to wake the woman up, she did not respond. As they attempted to raise her by her arms, it was discovered that her pouch was missing. Their suspicions aroused, they examined her more closely by the light of a lamp and realized that she was dead, but no one could say with certainty how she had died. The nephew now came running, gave a loud shriek, beat his breast and wept loudly. As everyone began speculating that the woman must have been murdered, the nephew dried his tears and casting a quick glance around the crowd, pointed out that there were two strangers in their midst. Although one of them was a Jain and therefore, unlikely to have killed the old woman, he had strong suspicions about the second man, who was a brahmin, and suggested that he be searched thoroughly. Madhav was seized, and when some money was found among his belongings, the nephew insisted that Madhav was the culprit. In spite of Madhav's repeated denials, it was decided to take him to the neighbouring town and lodge a complaint before the ruler.

The next day, when everyone was busy cooking in the rest house, the nephew approached one of the king's officials and related the whole tale. His palm adequately greased, the official decided that the nephew would not be implicated in the crime. Later that evening, when the young man arrived at the court loudly shouting 'Justice! Justice!' the official led him directly to the king. The plaint was heard, with the official adding his own bells and whistles to the story, whereupon the king ordered the accused to undergo an ordeal by fire, and directed the official to make the necessary preparations.

The next day, thousands of people gathered at an open area outside the town. The nephew was the first to arrive. Madhav was escorted there by the other pilgrims and the official took his place on a mat under a neem tree. A fire was lit a short distance away, the outer metal casing of a cartwheel was placed on it and the red-hot wheel brought before the official. First, the nephew was asked to lift it off the ground. 'O Suryadev,' he importuned, facing the sun, 'if what I say is true, do not allow my hands to get burnt.' He made as if to touch the wheel with his finger, whereupon the official cried out, 'That's enough! You have passed the test! Now it's the brahmin's turn.'

Madhav began to tremble and the blood rushed from his face. This convinced the onlookers of his guilt, and their whispering only increased his despair. In order to gain time, he asked leave to bathe by a nearby well. He stood for a while wondering what his next move should be. The saying 'Truth always prevails' is all very well, he thought to himself, but to believe that the hand of the guilty would burn while that of the innocent would be unscathed by the ordeal is nothing but superstition. The sacred texts are of no help—at times they say that divine intervention is more evident during Kaliyug; at others, that the gods are asleep in these dark times. Honest people starve in this world, while the dishonest ride around in carriages; there is no sign of God. It is in the nature of fire to burn whatever touches it—the question of guilt or innocence is simply not relevant. It is pointless to put my faith in my innocence and try and lift the wheel—my hand will definitely get burnt, and I will be judged guilty and hung. It is preferable to jump into this well and die.

But just as Madhav was about to leap, he heard a voice saying, 'Satyameva jayate.' No one was around, and Madhav felt sure that it was a sign from God asking him to have courage.

He drew water from the well, poured it on himself and went back and stood before the heated iron ring. Hands folded, facing the sun, he said, 'Lord Surya, you who stand manifest in all your radiance, from whom no deed can be hidden, you who know the innermost secrets of men, if indeed I have murdered the old woman, then let my hands burn, but if I have been falsely accused, let me lift up the wheel as lightly as I would a flower.' He bent down to pick up the wheel, but the sight of its angry, red-hot glow made his courage fail him once more and he backed away. Just then, however, the image of a string of ants walking across the wheel's rim flashed through his mind. Madhav's courage returned; he picked up the wheel and hung it around his neck. Amazed by this spectacle, the onlookers were convinced that the gods had not abandoned the righteous even in this Kaliyug but were offering a helping hand to the just. The official removed the iron wheel from Madhav's neck, and praising him profusely, led him back to the king, who realizing that Madhav was a brahmin, showered him with gold mohurs. Madhav had never accepted any such gifts before, but now, well aware that he must make his way to Delhi in pursuit of his mission, and that he had very little money left, he reluctantly accepted the mohurs. Then calling for Motisha, he took leave of the pilgrims, and the two friends left the town.

⁓

But without a guide they lost their way, and soon found themselves in a forest. The farther they went the more dense the forest got, and by the evening it became so dark, it was impossible to walk another step. Fearing wild animals, Madhav and Motisha dismounted, and tying up their horses, decided to spend the night in the branches of a tree. Just then two brahmins, wielding naked swords in their hands, emerged from the darkness. Four pairs of eyes locked gaze. Finally, one of the brahmins spoke.

'Greetings to you, O generous patron, may all be well with you. We are here to beg for alms.'

'Sir!' said Madhav, a surprised tone in his voice, 'the sight of brahmins begging for alms with naked swords in their hands is one I have never witnessed in my entire life. So kindly tell us who you are and what your business is, for it seems you have an unusual tale to tell.'

'Honourable patron,' the brahmin replied, 'we are brothers, followers of the path of Vedanta. Some years ago, when we had no work and were reduced to extreme poverty and subject to the daily taunts of our wives, we decided to take up a profession. At that time, a famous Vedanta scholar happened to come to town to give a discourse and we went to hear it. This is what the speaker said: "This material world is an illusion, brothers; it is the conjuring of a trickster. Just as a magician makes his audience see water where there is nothing but dust, so men are deceived by appearances. There is nothing real save the individual soul and the Universal One. Everything that we see around us is the creation of our senses; it is not really there, it is a mere illusion. Just as all the things we see, the words we hear, and the sensual pleasures we enjoy in our dreams vanish the moment we awake, so too, our lives are merely a dream. So friends, striving for wealth in this world is in vain. All distinctions between 'mine' and 'thine' are pointless. In truth, nothing is 'mine' and nothing is 'yours' either."

'The speaker's words made such a powerful impression on us that we decided to become Vedantists immediately, and not differentiate between "mine" and "yours" any more. One day, when we were at our patron's home, we noticed a purse full of money lying around, and we thought to ourselves, "People generally refer to this as money, but in reality it is nothing of the sort; it is actually a mirage. Besides, this world is a harsh place, one's life lasts for a moment, and either our patron will die leaving this money behind, or the money will no longer be in his possession—this much is certain. The first possibility does not seem likely, and in any case will not do us any good. So the money must be separated from the patron today. In any case, 'his' money and 'our' money are one and the same." My brother and I took the purse, but just as we were leaving the house, our patron's wretched servants caught us and we were dragged before the king. The king, too, had a veil of ignorance over his eyes, and he insisted on distinguishing between "mine" and "yours" and, acting quite contrary to the teachings of Vedanta, sentenced us to five years in prison. We lived there for free, we were provided with board and lodging without having to make the slightest effort. But then we were released. Now what were we to do? We live in a deluded world, one in which people, instead of seeking the means to eternal oneness with the divine, are busy wrangling over what's mine and yours, and like buffaloes yoked to a wheel, remain trapped in the 84,00,000 cycles of birth, death and rebirth. However, we knew that we would land ourselves in difficulties if we tried to persuade people to follow the sublime teachings of Vedanta, so we decided to renounce the worldly life, and we have been living in this jungle for the past three months. But for those who have tasted the good things of life, how is it possible to exist on roots and fruit? Which is why we come out at night in search of a patron. You are the first people we have met, so if you believe in the principles of Vedanta, hand over the clothes and possessions which you assume are yours to us, else we will ensure your instant union with the divine with the help of our swords.'

Greatly amused by what he had heard, and certain that the state of their stomachs had affected the state of their minds, Madhav handed the brahmins a gold mohur, which pleased them no end. Bidding them farewell, he cautioned them that the teachings of their guru had not yet been adopted by the world, and that if they continued to insist that there was no distinction between 'thine' and 'mine', they would be despatched to greet their Maker by their own swords. The Vedantists blessed him and departed.

5

In days of yore, present-day Delhi—situated on the banks of the Jamuna, and adjoining Hastinapur of legendary fame—was ruled over by Rajput kings. When the last king of the Tomar dynasty died without an heir, Prithviraj Chauhan ascended the throne of Delhi and Ajmer. During his reign Delhi was attacked twice by the Musalman king, Shahabuddin Ghori. His first attempt ended in defeat, the second in a decisive victory. And with the capture of Prithviraj, Delhi fell to the Musalmans.

Padshah Qutbuddin was the first Muslim king of Delhi and he and his successors did their utmost to beautify the city, extend its frontiers and enrich it with wealth looted from the coffers of defeated Hindu rajas.

It was now the year 1296, and as Diwali approached the city wore a festive look. At night, bazaars and homes were brightly lit, and during the day people strolled about, decked in fine clothes. But in the midst of this gaiety, a cloud of foreboding loomed on the horizon. Just a few months previously, the mild-mannered, kindly and peace-loving Delhi Sultan Jalaluddin Firoz had been treacherously murdered. During Jalaluddin's reign his subjects had been happy and content, justice was meted out evenly, and people were not arbitrarily oppressed or persecuted for their religion. But it was well known that the new ruler, Allauddin, was the complete opposite of his predecessor. He was renowned for valour and a love of warfare, and it was feared that his belligerent nature would result in a kingdom perpetually at war. The populace also feared for their lives and property, for the king was known to have a cruel, cunning and implacable nature and a reputation for iconoclastic zeal.

Allauddin's treachery towards his uncle Jalaluddin Firoz was still fresh in the minds of the people of Delhi. They recalled how the old emperor had met his nephew by the river outside Kara; how Allauddin, with a show of loyalty, had stepped forward, alone, to reverently touch his uncle's feet; how trustingly Jalaluddin had held his hand and bade him rise, and patting him affectionately on his cheek had said, 'From your infancy have I raised you like my own flesh and blood. I showered more affection on you than on my own son, that you would never have the slightest doubt of my love.' At that very moment the treacherous Allauddin signalled to his guard, and Muhammad bin Salam slashed the emperor's shoulder with his sword. Shocked, Jalaluddin tried to escape in his boat, but the wounded old king was held fast by Akhatiyaruddin, hurled to the ground and decapitated. The heartless Allauddin ordered the impaled head to be paraded through the town and displayed in front of the army.

After Jalaluddin's death, his queen Malekajahan, without bothering to consult the nobles, had hastily enthroned her younger son, Kadarkhan, alias Ruknuddin Ibrahim, and had sent urgent messages to Multan where her older son Arakalikhan, the rightful heir to the throne was encamped, urging him to send his army to support his brother. Not only had Arakalikhan refused to come to her aid, he had sent word that a river can be dammed at its source but its flow cannot be stemmed once it gains momentum. Allauddin's army now arrived at the outskirts of Delhi. But when Kadarkhan collected his forces and prepared for battle, he found that many of his supporters and nobles had deserted him and gone over to the enemy. Accompanied by his mother and a few trusted retainers, Kadarkhan fled to Multan. Meanwhile Allauddin entered Delhi and immediately struck coins in his own name. He sent a considerable army under his brother Alafkhan and Zafarkhan to capture Multan and bring back the two princes. The siege of Multan lasted for two months. Finally, the civilians as well as the soldiers agreed to hand over the fort to Alafkhan on the condition that the lives of the two princes be spared. Agreeing to this and promising to uphold his pledge, Alafkhan took charge of the princes. Word was sent to Allauddin that the mission was a success.

The emperor was delighted at this long-desired outcome. There was now not a single claimant left to dispute his right to rule. He organized a lavish celebration in the city. Not only were his Muslim subjects kept happy with liberal gifts of money, even his Hindu subjects were commanded to pray to their gods for the emperor's continued success and prosperity. Leading brahmins were summoned and paid handsomely for the rituals. Angered by Allauddin's patronage of an heathen religion, and fearing that prayers to false gods would enrage the one true God, many devout Muslims begged the king to desist. But Allauddin paid no attention to them—he was eager to win the goodwill of all his subjects and gain their affection. This act of the headstrong emperor was deeply resented by many Muslims. They bore their grudge sullenly, but waited for an opportunity to retaliate.

Allauddin ordered that Alafkhan's proclamation of victory should be read out in all the city mosques on the holy day of Juma—which happened to coincide with the Diwali festival. At noon, as soon as the call of the muezzin was heard across the mosques of the city, the Muslim population of Delhi, decked in their finery, went to offer prayers. Meanwhile, in the Hindu temples, festivities were in full swing. Brahmins bellowed mantras, their voices rising in proportion to the size of the offering. Thousands flocked to the gaily decorated shrines. Around one of the more famous temples, where a large number of brahmins had gathered, the noise rose to a deafening pitch. At that moment, a procession of devout Muslims on the way to their mosque, enraged by the ostentatious celebrations and the great favour shown by the emperor to the infidels, began to curse their gods, going so far as to beat up some brahmins with sticks. But the Hindus had not yet been reduced to abject helplessness. They refused to take the insults to their gods, or to submit to the beatings like dumb cattle. Some of them struck back at their attackers, a skirmish ensued, and as the Hindus far outnumbered the Muslims, the latter were severely beaten up—a couple to the point of death—and forced to retreat. The news spread like wildfire, and from lanes and by-lanes, from every crossroad and mosque, armed Muslims spilled on to the streets to confront an equally violent sea of Hindus. Terrified people bolted their doors tight and anxiously wondered what this savage battle which was being fought with swords and daggers, sticks, stones, roof tiles and whatever other objects that came to hand, would lead to. In this free-for-all, Hindus viciously attacked men with beards, while Muslims showed no mercy to the clean-shaven in their midst. Both sides lost many men. Many were mortally wounded; some fell to the ground exhausted and were crushed underfoot by stampeding crowds. The screams of the dying and wounded and the din and uproar of the fighting deafened the ear. It is difficult to predict how the riot would have ended had the king not come to hear of it and sent his army to quell the carnage.

Many rioters beat a hasty retreat when they saw the sultan's men advancing towards them. Some took refuge in neighbouring homes while others hastily seated themselves on verandas to prove that they had no part in the rioting. Most of the Muslim rioters managed to flee from the site, hoping that the Hindus would be blamed for starting the disturbance. The commander immediately ordered an end to the rioting and the surrender of all weapons. Realizing the futility of continuing the fight, the rioters obeyed. The ringleaders were rounded up and taken to the palace. There were more Hindu than Muslim prisoners; and the Hindus were more fearful of the outcome. They had abandoned all hope of coming out of the situation alive and they prepared to face and bear whatever was in store for them. Presently, the prisoners were brought into the presence of the emperor.

Allauddin sat in splendour on his golden, diamond-studded throne in the midst of a full durbar. Dressed in costly raiment and ornaments, his appearance dazzled the eye. There was no dearth of gold, diamonds, pearls and rubies. Nothing had been left undone to enhance the sultan's pomp and splendour, for the extravaganza was designed to exhibit his unlimited wealth, and not with a concern for good taste. Such an excessive display of riches by a newly crowned king has never been chronicled. The wealth had come from the kingdoms of southern India, wealth that had been accumulated over centuries. From the works of Muslim historians we learn that when Jalaluddin Firoz ruled Delhi, Allauddin, then governor of Kara, had attacked Devgadh, and the vanquished raja had been compelled to make peace by offering him 600 *maunds* of pearls, two maunds of diamonds, rubies, emeralds and topaz, 1000 maunds of silver, and 4000 *than*s of silk apart from countless other costly items. Though this account bears the usual stamp of exaggeration it is clear that Allauddin had returned from the south laden with fabulous wealth. To this he had added the wealth extracted from his own province so that there was no other king to equal him in riches. It was said that 17,000 servants were at his beck and call. He used his fortune lavishly to enhance the splendour of his surroundings.

Thus sat Allauddin Khilji, in all his splendour, on his throne that day. His forbidding appearance struck fear in the hearts of his subjects. It appeared as if God had sent him for the sole purpose of subjugating the rebellious people of Hindustan and ruling them with an iron hand. His round eyes glinted dangerously like those of a tiger, without a vestige of pity or forgiveness. The raw strength of his rugged physique made even the most powerful nobles cower before him. His rule would prove to be so oppressive that even today he is remembered throughout Gujarat as Allauddin the Murderer.

The sultan sat surrounded by his senior ministers. On one side were his vazir, Khwaja Khatir, considered to be a very upright man, and Khwaja Sadruddin Erif, better known as Sadrejehan, the chief justice of the civil court, the Diwani Adaalat. Umadtulmulk Malek Hamiuddin and Malek Ayzuddin, two learned and wise clerks, were also present. On the other side were Nusratkhan, Delhi's chief of police, Malek Fakkruddin Kuchi, chief justice of the criminal court, and the head clerk, Malek Zafarkhan. Apart from these important players, many courtiers, governors, kazis, maulavis, generals, fakirs and dervishes were also assembled.

It was in this durbar that the rioters were made to stand. The emperor ordered justice to take its course and the guilty punished. The accused were brought before Malek Fakkruddin Kuchi, the chief justice of the criminal court, who released them on bail, ordering them to appear before him the next day. The accused presented themselves at the appointed hour and were interrogated by Fakkruddin who apprised himself of the facts and the reasons behind the disturbances. Had the judge been unbiased, he would have laid the blame for starting the riots on the Musalmans, who had not only insulted the gods of the Hindus but also killed a number of people. But the Hindus had retaliated by attacking and slaying Muslims, and this, in the eyes of Malek Fakkruddin, was a major offence. The very reason for the establishment of a state is to protect the weak from the strong; this has been, in fact, the main duty of a king from ancient times. If people were to take the law into their own hands and mete out summary justice for perceived wrongs, then the whole edifice of society would crumble, men would become like packs of wild animals, life and property would not be safe, and not only would happiness be destroyed but society itself would disintegrate. Therefore, in a well-regulated kingdom, people have no right to any private vendetta. The aggrieved individual does not have the right to take the law into his own hands but must approach the king for justice, because the king, being an impartial observer, is generally free from bias towards either party, and his judgement is not clouded by the enmity and strong passions that prevent the adversaries from thinking clearly.

Though it is generally agreed that this is the wisest course, people do not always follow it. And even when they do, often it is not out of the conviction that it is beneficial to all, but because it is not in their power to take revenge themselves. The reason for this isn't difficult to understand. Like the lower animals, man too, has been endowed with certain instincts by God, and before these the intellect often has to admit defeat. Swayed by his instincts, man often acts without thinking; and there are occasions when he just does not have the time to think. To counter violence with violence is instinctual to man. Forbearance and forgiveness are products of reason. Only when instinct is nurtured and tempered by the power of reason do forbearance, pity and forgiveness come into play. Most people are incapable of conquering their instincts with the help of the intellect, and when any form of disturbance arises they retaliate without thought. At such moments, they are oblivious of the king or the rule of law. This tendency is so commonplace and natural that lawgivers have taken it into account when framing laws. And if the accused has been provoked or if the victim has given the perpetrator a strong reason for his criminal act, then these factors are taken into account, and the strength and validity of the reasons put forward to justify the crime determine the severity of the punishment.

77

In this instance, the Hindus were definitely at fault. They had disturbed the peace and killed and wounded many Muslims, and for that they deserved to be punished. On the other hand, the Muslims had needlessly hurt and provoked the Hindus and beaten them up without cause. In the ensuing riot, though only a few Hindus had been killed, it was not because of restraint on the part of the Muslims but because they were outnumbered. Therefore, in the eyes of the law, the Muslims should have been held equally guilty and should have been punished accordingly.

But Chief Justice Fakkruddin held different views. He was swayed not by the fear of God, but by the opinions of the Muslims. Justice was far from blind in his court. She had one eye turned towards the Muslims, her scales of justice were tilted favourably towards them, while her sword hovered menacingly above the Hindus. The dispenser of justice, too, wore blinkers with regard to the Muslims. Trapped in the web of prejudice, he was convinced that every true Muslim must have been aflame with anger at the munificence showered by the emperor upon the idol-worshipping infidels so that they could hold lavish celebrations in their satanic temples. The Muslims had done nothing wrong; they had been provoked to frenzy by the emperor's ungodly acts, and it was he who was solely responsible for the deaths. What did it matter if several infidel Hindus had lost their lives— sooner or later they were headed for hell anyway, and the world would be better off without such sinners. By killing Muslims, the Hindus had committed the greatest of sins and their punishment should be great. Having reasoned thus, Chief Justice Fakkruddin said, 'It is true that the riot was started by the Musalmans but there is no proof that those who have been brought here are the culprits, therefore they are innocent. The Hindus standing before me have taken part in the disturbances and have caused the death of many Muslims, therefore twenty-five of them should be punished by being buried up to their waists in the ground in front of the temple where the altercation took place, and pelted to death with bricks, stones and eggs.' People's reactions to this varied depending on who they were. Muslims were delighted; they felt that the punishment meted out to infidels who had dared raise their hands against the faithful was appropriate and just, and praised the judge for his impartiality and superior powers of reasoning. On the other hand, the Hindus in the audience were dismayed and feared that their own turn could come at any moment. When they heard the unfair, cruel and one-sided judgement the prisoners stood for some time in stupefied silence. They then addressed the chief justice saying, 'Your honour, if these are not the same Muslims who instigated the rioting, then we, too, are not the ones who first started it. Therefore, we cannot understand the reason for holding us more guilty than them.' The judge had no answer to this, as there was no reason for such a judgement other than his bigotry. Greatly affronted by the gall of the prisoners he said angrily, 'I do not need to investigate whether or not you started the riot. The fact that you took part in it and that many Muslims perished is offence enough—the punishment is less severe than you deserve.' He commanded his men to take the prisoners away and to inform him as soon as his orders had been carried out. The ill-fated Hindus got no further chance to speak. They were dragged out of the court to the temple where the rioting had begun and kept waiting while twenty-five trenches were dug.

It is impossible to adequately describe the horrendous scenes that followed. A bloodthirsty rabble of Muslim spectators gathered there, impatient for the stoning to begin. They came prepared with stones, bricks, rotten eggs and other missiles. Religious bigotry had wiped out all traces of justice or pity, and like wild beasts and vultures they waited in gleeful anticipation of the dreadful end that awaited the innocent Hindus. No Hindus were present at the site except the wives, children and relatives of the unfortunate twenty-five who they had come to meet for the last time. But even this solace was denied the condemned men, as their wives and children were prevented from approaching them. Their cries and laments only added to the wild excitement of the onlookers who showered curses on Hindus in general and the prisoners in particular. Forced to listen to both the curses of the crowd and the lamentations of their loved ones, the condemned men prayed fervently to God to hasten their end by ensuring that the weapons aimed by those beasts masquerading as humans did their job effectively.

At a signal from the chief of police, stones, bricks and anything else that could be thrown rained down upon the innocent Hindus. No one could be expected to survive for long under such an assault. Heads were split, bodies crushed and mangled and the ground was soaked with blood. Some died instantly or of internal injuries; some fainted and those who were still conscious screamed in agony. The tussle between life and death did not last long. One by one, the condemned succumbed to death and in an hour's time the stones were falling on inert corpses. On the completion of this ghastly task, the bodies were examined by an executioner and after he was satisfied that no spark of life remained in them, they were dug out of the trenches. Their loved ones requested permission to dispose of the bodies according to their customs but the hard-hearted Muslim officer refused to show any pity. In his eyes, the crime of killing the Chosen of God was so heinous that the punishment meted out was totally inadequate. What the living had been spared, the dead would suffer. He ordered the executioner to dig a deep pit on the outskirts of the town. The bodies were thrown into it, and the pit was covered. No customary rites or rituals were allowed.

This incident aroused great fear among the Hindus. But it was not the first atrocity that had been perpetuated by the sultan. When Alafkhan was on his way from Multan to Delhi, with the captured princes Arakalikhan and Kadarkhan, and the begum of the late padshah, Malekajahan, and many of their followers, he was met by Malek Nusratkhan, the kotwal. The kotwal carried with him orders from the emperor that the princes should be blinded. Preparations were made to carry out this pitiless deed at that very spot.

On that still, summer evening, the two princes were seated by one of the windows of the fort discussing their misfortunes. The burning heat of the day, which had seeped into all things, gave way gradually to a cool breeze which blew through the window and would have brought relief to the brothers, had it not been for the fever of worry and uncertainty. But the ill-fated princes were not concerned about their physical comfort. They were deeply suspicious of the motive behind their interrupted journey, and the dispatching of their mother and the womenfolk to Delhi. It was difficult for them to suspect Alafkhan of treachery so soon after being promised safe passage at Multan. They were filled with intimations of their impending doom as there seemed to be no reasonable explanation for their halt. On the other hand, they were well aware that promises could be easily broken, and were familiar with the sultan's cruel and selfish nature. While thus immersed in thought, wondering whether they would live to see another day, two men crept up quietly behind them, knocked them down, and bound and gagged them. The princes thrashed about desperately but were no match for their brawny assailants. The assassins threw them on their backs, and with sharp-bladed daggers gouged out their eyes. Overcome by terror and the agonizing pain of their wounds, the princes fell unconscious, blood streaming down their faces. Meanwhile, in an excess of zeal, Ulughkhan, the grandson of Gengizkhan, Ahmed Habibi and other minor courtiers were also blinded.

It is difficult to imagine the agony of the princes when they regained consciousness. When they realized that they had lost their eyesight they howled with anger and sorrow. 'Have we been kept alive for this?' they cried. 'It is a thousand times better to die than to live a life of blindness. **** Deprived of the ability to act, but endowed with the capacity to bear agonizing pain we must, like dumb cattle, helplessly follow where led. But even cattle can halt if they have the mind to, and kick and butt with their horns; but the blind remain forever at the mercy of their foes. O! How base is the greed to gain a kingdom! And how unfortunate it is to be descended from royal lineage. If we had been the sons of humble folk, this calamity would not have befallen us. We experienced happiness for a few years but setting our sights on greater glory we took our happiness for granted. What would we not give to go back to those former times. Now all is reduced to ashes. It was the greed of our foolish mother that has led to our dreadful plight. We had no desire for this kingdom, but she overruled us and crossed swords with Allauddin. And now we are reaping the bitter fruits of her actions. O Lord! Why have you been so cruel to us? We oppressed no one, harmed no one; on the contrary, we did all we could to help others. But what is the use of lamenting now? What has happened has happened. There is no remedy for it. We are only exposing our weakness to the enemy, so let fate do its worst. We are ready to bear whatever God has ordained and we will comply with His wishes.' From that moment onwards, the princes' lips were sealed.

Next day, Alafkhan's camp was dismantled and the soldiers marched to the town of Hansi. The two blind, half-dead princes were imprisoned in the fortress. Convinced that Allauddin would find no peace whilst the princes still lived, and that he would approve of whatever action they took against them, Alafkhan and Nusratkhan decided to have the princes killed. The task was simple. At midnight, two assassins with daggers drawn entered the princes' bedchamber. The princes were sound asleep, having not the slightest inkling that the fatal moment was at hand. Their innocent and sorrowful faces moved even the assassins to pity, but they knew that this was no time for compassion and disobeying orders would only lead to their own deaths. Hardening their hearts, one of the assassins plunged his dagger into Arakalikhan's stomach, while the other simultaneously attacked Kadarkhan. Kadarkhan died on the spot, but a single thrust was not enough to put an end to Arakalikhan. Thrashing in pain he cried, '*Shukar Allah!* You have brought a quick end to my agony!' The assassin quailed in fear at his botched attempt. The prince turned to him, 'You kafir,' he said angrily, 'you scoundrel, strike again immediately and snap the thread of my life. Can't you see the agony your clumsiness has caused? Finish your job and release me from this sinful world!' But the witless assassin stood immobilized; the dagger fell from his hand, and then, no longer in command of his senses, he fled from the room. Arakalikhan heard the dagger fall and realized that the assassin had taken to his heels. As the moments passed and his pain became unbearable, a superhuman strength possessed him. He sat up and groped for the dagger. With the cry of '*Bismillah ur Rehman ur Rahim*' on his lips he plunged the dagger into his stomach with such force that his soul was instantly freed to stand before its Maker.

A woman sat with head bowed in one of the rooms of the Delhi fort. The room reflected the condition of her mind. Darkness, darkness was everywhere. Not a ray of light penetrated the four walls. High above, through the barred skylight, a little air entered the chamber, enough to sustain the woman's life. But whatever dim light made its way through the aperture was lost in the thick darkness of the large room. If one could have got a glimpse of the seated woman one could very easily have fathomed the meaning of sorrow, and the effect that extreme sorrow can have on a person. She was the perfect subject for an artist or poet wanting to portray unbearable suffering. A living image of grief, a personification of sorrow, the woman sat with her head bent between her knees, oblivious of her surroundings. Grief had made her once beautiful face frightful. Her lips were swollen, her body emaciated. She was as pale as a corpse, and it was only because of the slight stirring of her body that one realized she was alive. Her red, staring eyes were devoid of brightness and intelligence. At times, she stared unblinking at some object, at others her gaze flitted ceaselessly about the room. The evidence of her eyes alone was enough to convince one of her insanity. But it was not merely the madness of her gaze; her speech, too, resembled that of a deranged person. She uttered meaningless broken words, wild and disjointed, like those of a person maddened by rage, and not only did she scream and wail uncontrollably, she pulled out her hair, tore her clothes, and beat her breast and head so relentlessly that it was a miracle that they survived such blows. She did not stop at that. From time to time, she ran across the room and slammed her head against the wall, biting her lips till they bled. Her face and clothes were covered with blood. Her body trembled as if a djinn had possessed it. Caught up in the turmoil of her emotions, she had no control over her mind, and life to her was meaningless. From this description the reader can clearly imagine the great despair of Malekajahan, the chief begum of the late emperor Jalaluddin Firoz, and the mother of Arakalikhan and Kadarkhan.

After her husband's death Malekajahan, strong-willed, ambitious and greedy for political power, had placed her youngest son Kadarkhan on the throne without any thought for the outcome of her action, without informing her older son or considering the enemy's strength. The plan misfired and she, her son and their supporters had to flee from Delhi to Multan; and like a bubble, her dreams of ruling the kingdom burst. This was not the end of her woes. She and her sons had been handed over to Alafkhan after he solemnly promised to spare their lives. Yet, while her sons were alive, a glimmer of hope remained, she still dreamt of regaining the kingdom, and this gave her the strength to live. It was when she was separated from the princes that hope began to diminish, and she was tormented night and day by terrifying thoughts. In her dreams she would see the shrouded corpses of her sons. Ultimately, her worst fears came to pass. She was informed by a spy of the blinding of her sons and, hearing this, she fell to the ground in a dead faint. When she regained consciousness her mind was permanently deranged.

When Emperor Allauddin heard of her plight he had her removed from her dark chamber and placed in a bright and airy room. But this change brought her no relief. On the contrary, being surrounded by people only increased the intensity of her grief and madness. She would sometimes stand at the window and gaze unblinking at passers-by. She was greatly pitied by most people who sympathized with her loss. Only the dervishes hated her, and even though she was incapable of understanding what was being said, they frequently reviled and taunted her. Once, when the begum was standing at her window, a dervish looked up and cried, 'Begum Sahib, have you forgotten the Sufi darvesh Sidi Maula? He was like an angel on earth. His charity knew no bounds. Thousands gathered at his doorstep where he distributed 1000 maunds of wheat flour, 500 maunds of meat, 200 maunds of sugar as well as rice, oil, ghee and other items every day. But your wicked husband, prompted by the dastardly infidels, had him put to death. Do you not see the fruits of this action? Do you not recall his dying words? The Creator Himself was filled with wrath at the death of Maulana Sidi. A storm raged for half an hour and darkness descended, making day into night. People crashed into each other and could not find their way home. The rains failed that year and drought spread across the land. Thousands of Hindus, wracked by hunger, fell lifeless by the roadside, and entire families, maddened by hunger and sorrow, drowned themselves in the Jamuna river. Dissensions rent the court. A grievous personal calamity befell the emperor, your husband. His eldest son Khankhana fell ill and died. The emperor died soon after. His nephew, the present king, had him put to death and usurped the throne from the rightful heirs. His remaining two sons, too, have lost their lives and you have been reduced to this hapless state. The curse of Sidi Maula has come to fruition, and you are reaping the fruits of your husband's sin.'

The dervish, whose sole aim was to tease out the queen's real opinion of the Sufis by needling her, failed miserably. Instead of reacting to his taunts, the begum remained as still as a statue and burst into mad laughter. The dervish's words evaporated into thin air and he went despondently on his way.

6

It was the month of Magh, and a festive atmosphere pervaded the town of Delhi. The day was a special one for Hindus and Muslims alike. At the temple of Kalikamata just outside the town, the Patotsav was in progress; while in Delhi, celebrations had been organized to mark the birthday of the heir apparent, Prince Khizrkhan. Many of the Hindus on their way to the temple were bundled in shawls and blankets, for the day was cold, but the poor could be seen walking with their arms tightly folded, bodies shivering and teeth chattering. The procession came to a halt near the Qutbminar. Begun by the first Muslim ruler of Delhi, Qutbuddin Aibak, and completed during the reign of Iltutmish, the Qutbminar is a beautiful structure. It resembles a minaret and has intricate carving on its balconies. It is 121 *sutari gaj* high. Part of the original structure collapsed as a result of an earthquake, but it still remains the tallest minaret in the world. Next to it stands a mosque. Even though it is unfinished, the architecture and decoration are not inferior to those of other monuments in India. An inscription tells us that it was built during the reign of Shahabuddin Ghori.

The Kalikamata temple stands next to the mosque. It is a small structure of no great artistic merit, but it was so renowned that Hindus not only from Delhi but from towns and villages forty to fifty kos away had flocked to it for the Patotsav. The variety of clothing and the colourful turbans of the visitors presented an attractive scene, but there was a lot more to see besides the picturesque crowd that day.

Kalikamata has a fierce and terrifying form, and in olden times blood sacrifices were offered to her. The goddess takes pleasure in bloody spectacles, and many cruel feats are performed during certain festivals. On that morning, a number of her devotees could be seen outside the temple—some had impaled their tongues with knives; others had built a bed of nails, the sharp points facing upwards, and leapt onto this from a scaffolding erected above. Several had inserted iron rings in their bellies, and suspending themselves with ropes from a wooden beam, spun round and round. Other worshippers stood about decked in flower garlands, their bodies smeared with red hinglok paste; yet others played musical instruments.

Amongst the crowd, which appeared to be enjoying the dreadful spectacle, was a man whose clothing and behaviour marked him as an outsider. He was lost in thought and did not seem to share the enthusiasm of the others. The task which had brought him to Delhi had not yet been accomplished; indeed its success seemed a long way off. For days and nights he had thought of nothing else but the execution of his plan and now, as he stood in the crowd, deep sighs escaped him.

The reader has no doubt guessed that this stranger was no other than Raja Karan's former prime minister, Madhav. He was amazed by the goings-on around him and could not help exclaiming, 'If causing harm to one's body is a way of realizing God, then these people will surely go to heaven!' A sannyasi who overheard him replied, 'O sir, if God is pleased by the mortification of the flesh, then he should be particularly pleased with us. The acts of these people pale in comparison to the torments that we

88

sannyasis subject ourselves to. They mortify their bodies for a day or two, we do so all our lives. Listen to what the *Manusmriti* has to say on the subject:

When the head of a family gets old and decrepit, when his hair turns white and he has seen his children's children, then it is time for him to renounce the world. He must abjure good food and material possessions, give up his family and go into the solitude of the forest, taking his wife with him if she so desires. He should carry with him the fire and the various items required for sacrifice, and keep a tight control over his thoughts and actions. Like the rishis, he must live on roots, tubers and fruits, and wear black deerskin or clothes of bark. He should leave the hair on his head and his beard uncut, and let his nails grow long. He should share whatever food he gets, and welcome any visitor to the ashram with food and drink. He should study the Vedas constantly. Regardless of the difficulties that come his way, he must have patience, help others and keep his mind firmly fixed on the Eternal Brahman. Unceasing in his giving but taking nothing, he must be compassionate at all times. He must slither and slide on the ground, do sit-ups, bathe at sunrise, midday and sunset, and perform the five-fire ritual in summer—that is to say, he must light four fires, with the blazing sun constituting the fifth. In the monsoons he must stand in the pouring rain without any clothing; in winter he must wear old, worn-out clothes. He must gradually increase the intensity of his austerities. Then, as is written in the shastras, he must not light a new fire; and must take a vow of silence. He can go into town to beg for food, carrying a bowl made of leaves, or a gourd, or simply use his cupped hands, but of what he receives he must eat only eight morsels. After observing all the prescribed rules of dharma for this, the third vanaprastha stage of life, he must then enter the fourth stage, and take sannyas. Now he must renounce worldy pleasures totally, and with full faith in the Universal Being, must neither seek death nor the extension of life. Just as a servant waits till the end of the month to be paid, he must wait for the appointed time of his death with patience.

'Now, the ritual for taking sannyas is as follows. Firstly, an auspicious day must be selected. On that day, the aspirant should have a bath, cut up a bolt of cloth into ten lengths, dye them ochre, and take them with him to a designated place. Of the ten lengths, he must keep four for his own use and distribute the remaining six to the brahmins who perform the ritual. Apart from this, the aspirant should keep certain items ready. First, a bamboo staff with seven joints; second, a gourd bowl; third, a deerskin; fourth, silver and copper coins; also flowers, rice daubed with red kunku and sandalwood. As a sign of his renunciation of the world, he must prepare and drink a foul-tasting brew. After a secret mantra is whispered in his ear, and the rules of sannyas explained, he must don the ochre clothing, snap his *janoi* to symbolize the break with caste and community, and cut off his top-knot. Once the ritual is over, the aspirant must take up the staff, the gourd bowl and deerskin, and sip three spoonfuls of water to the accompaniment of mantras. He is now a sannyasi, and will have no further contact with the world. From now onwards, he must smear his body with ashes after his morning bath, eat just one meal a day, give up chewing betel nut, not even so much as glance at a woman, shave off his beard, moustache and the hair on his head every month, wear wooden sandals and, whenever he steps out of his dwelling, he must carry his bamboo staff in one hand, the gourd-bowl in the other, and the deerskin under his armpit. The gourd is for water and the deerskin serves as a seat. The sannyasi has the right to beg for his food, and if he accumulates alms, he must give them away in charity, or use the money for the building of a rest house, temple, well or tank. His ashram should be situated near a river or pond as it is easy to bathe there.'

'This is all very well,' retorted a yogi who had overheard the conversation. 'But as the saying goes, there is no real substitute for experience. Compared to the way we wandering ascetics mortify our bodies, your lives are a bed of roses. Some of us keep our fists tightly clenched for so long, the nails curve over and penetrate the skin. Some stand for years in the same posture. Others hold their arms upright for such long periods that they wither and waste away from disuse. Still others carry heavy weights around with them, or attach a chain to some delicate part of their body, dragging it behind them wherever they go. Some yogis move around creeping on their stomachs like insects, often touring the entire country in this manner. And some make the pilgrimage to Jagannath Puri by a series of prostrations, or roll barrel-like all the way from the banks of the Indus to the banks of the Ganges, using any alms they collect on the way to build a shrine or a well, or in expiation of some secret sin. There are practitioners who swing above a blazing fire in the middle of summer, or hang themselves upside down for hours on end. They bury themselves in the earth, leaving only a small aperture for air; flail themselves with whips; sleep on beds of nails; tie themselves to tree trunks. If you want proof of this, all you need to do is to read Kalidas's *Shakuntala*.

'In it is written, "When King Dushyanta asked Maatali about the whereabouts of Rishi Maarichi's ashram, he replied:

Where stands the hermit, horridly austere
Whom clinging vines are choking, tough and sere;
Half-buried in ant-hill that has grown
About him, standing post-like and alone;
Sun-staring with dim eyes that know no rest,

91

The dead skin of a serpent on his breast:
So long he stood unmoved, insensate there
That birds build nests within his mat of hair."[3]

———

As Madhav watched the antics of Kalimata's devotees, listened carefully to the rules enjoined for sannyasis, and heard what the yogis did in the present and in the past, he wondered how the human body could withstand such punishment. How could the skin, which is so sensitive that even the tiniest prick causes pain, endure so much torment? When an insignificant cause—a stumble or a yawn, for instance—can cause death, is it not amazing that men who torture themselves for years remain alive? The human body adapts to the way it is treated. What causes death in one man may make another stronger. But be that as it may, what possible benefit could there be in mortifying the flesh? God has given man the wonderful and extraordinary gift of vision through which he can experience the world and discover its secrets and, beholding the unlimited power, the boundless wisdom and great compassion of the Creator, discovering the many signs of His divine presence, worship Him with greater love and sincerity. Should we then not make use of this wondrous gift? Should we shut the ears through which we hear the varied sounds of nature, the songs of birds, and the melodious strains of the human voice? Should we stop using the nose which allows us to discriminate between different scents, and ignore what each indicates? And why should we not utilize the tongue to experience different tastes? Should we wilfully ignore the fact that different foods taste different and that sweet and sour are not the same? Experience tells us that certain things which the Creator has provided in abundance taste good and have a beneficial effect, while others that taste bad have not been created for the purpose of nourishing human beings—should we now consider this experience invalid? Should we purposely damage the human skin, with its countless pores and nerves through which we experience the external world, until it can no longer perform its function adequately? All around us we have evidence that the world has been created to bring joy and delight to the senses; should we not then make use of our senses, rather than quit this world as we entered it, without leaving behind a trace of our existence? A study of man's natural instincts and inclinations shows that he is a social creature, one intended to live in the company of his fellows. If, in spite of this, he decides to live in isolation, what would be the point of qualities like compassion and forgiveness?

From all this we can infer that man is meant to live in this world, endure whatever sorrows that befall him and, as the bee sucks nectar from the flower, take pleasure in his surroundings. He has been given the capacity to discriminate and make rational decisions. So there must be a reason why some people believe in mortifying the flesh. Granted that the world has been created to delight the senses, that it is through them that we experience the bounty of nature, the scent of the chameli, champa and mogra, the difference between sweet and sour—the fact remains, they argue, that our senses are not always under our control. If we do not exercise dominance over them, they will control us. If they are a source of pleasure, they are in equal measure a source of pain. By becoming the slaves of our appetites, we become like beasts, incapable of distinguishing between right and wrong or aspiring to higher spiritual goals—faculties with which only human beings are endowed. The same eyes that strengthen the love of God in some, lead others to error—lost in admiration of the wonders of creation, they forget to notice the power and wisdom of the Creator; or pointing to a perceived deficiency, argue that He does not exist, and if He does then there is something lacking in his justice, compassion, wisdom, skill and goodness. To avoid falling into this terrible pit, many believers gouge out their eyes with their own hands. In short, our senses are both our friends and our enemies. They are like the current in a river: when it flows gently, it benefits everyone, but when it rages, it drags everything along with it. They are like caged tigers, safe enough when behind bars, but able to escape their confines quite easily. Keeping one's passions within bounds is a difficult task, and few manage it; hence it is wise not to indulge them in the first place. This is why sannyasis and yogis keep a tight check on their senses.

We are travellers on the perilous ocean of life. We set sail from port, each in his own boat, together with a few companions. But under the waters lie hidden dangers, big and small. Some boats run aground almost as soon as they leave the shore, drowning their passengers; others sail for a while before they, too, sink. As ship after ship comes to grief, new vessels embark on the journey of life, and throughout the voyage, until they reach the harbour of deliverance, they are tossed about by the great hurling waves of the ocean, and the fear of drowning is constantly with the passengers. Apart from the hidden reefs, there are many islands rising sheer-faced from the waters, idyllic with wooded hills. Alluring sirens sit on rocks, tempting passengers with sweet songs and seductive gestures. Among the passengers on the boats, some are true friends of the captain, but others are really agents of those women, constantly urging the captain to sail towards the islands. As long as Rationality is in control of the rudder, the vessel can be steered along a narrow but virtuous course, even against a headwind. But a few passengers—in reality the captain's ill-wishers—convince him that the narrow route is a boring one, and if they are not allowed to enjoy the pleasures of the journey, then the entire trip is pointless. Wresting control of the rudder from Rationality, they hand it over to Thoughtlessness. The sails of lust, anger, greed, delusion, intoxication and envy are raised, and the moment the rear winds of desire blow strongly, the ship is driven out of the passage of virtue into the open sea. It then makes its way to the nearest enticing island. Passengers on other vessels warn the captain of the dangers, and point out the hulks of vessels that have ventured too close, only to be smashed against the rocky reefs. But the foolish captain pays no heed. The spies and spokesmen of the sirens assure him that those who have not tasted the pleasures of the ocean of life cannot appreciate its delights; that those vessels that have run aground must have incompetent helmsmen or have taken the wrong route. Such a fate is not going to befall their own ship, they argue, and if there is the slightest possibility of danger, they will down sails at once and navigate back into the channel of virtue. What is the sense of remaining in a narrow passage because of uncalled-for fears without venturing out into the open sea and checking out the myriad delights of the islands? Convinced by these arguments, the captain pilots the ship towards the island, and regardless of the shipwrecks, continues onwards until his ship, too, is dashed against a reef. He may weep now, mourn and repent his foolishness, but it is too late. Before he knows it, the damaged vessel begins to sink, and either no one takes notice of his cries, or the efforts by neighbouring ships to throw ropes and send small craft to rescue the drowning passengers are in vain. One can only be thankful that there are people who, having resisted temptation themselves, are willing to put their lives in danger, endure the curses and taunts of those they are trying to save, and navigate others to their spiritual destination. The endeavours of these benevolent people are not entirely unsuccessful. Even if their efforts are too late and they are unable to save many ships from sinking, they do manage to steer a few away from danger and guide them to the right direction.

Yet the temptations of the islands, the alluring women with their honeyed voices, continue to seduce the passengers on deck. So long as Rationality is at the helm, a ship that strays into dangerous waters can be steered into the safety of the channel again. But those on deck remain at constant risk, for if the ship deviates even slightly from its proper course, it will be refused entry into the Port of Liberation. Because of this danger, some passengers voluntarily leave the deck and confine themselves in the cargo hold until the ship reaches the port. But the few who remain continue to take the ship off-course, thereby damaging it and ensuring that it never reaches its destination.

Such is the way of the world, reasoned Madhav, as he made his way back to his lodgings. It is to avoid getting trapped in the web of desire, and to stop the mind from chasing temptation, that people practise austerities. Besides, the mind and body are closely linked, and physical pain results in mental pain too, which perhaps prevents people from getting entangled in the web of maya.

———

Meanwhile, in front of the sultan's palace, grand celebrations were in progress to mark the birthday of Khizrkhan. A holiday had been declared, and all the leading nobles were present to offer greetings to the heir apparent and the sultan. Major changes had been made in the ranks of the higher nobility ever since Allauddin had ascended the throne. During the struggle for succession, several amirs had supported the claims of the dowager queen and her two sons, Arakalikhan and Kadarkhan, and had in return received enormous sums of money. Allauddin had not only confiscated this, he had also blinded all those who had sided against him and deprived them of all their lands. The money had swelled the sultan's coffers but it had not assuaged his fears, and he in turn had bought the loyalty of several other nobles with lavish gifts. Once his position was secure, Allauddin not only demanded that the money be returned, he accused many of the amirs of accepting bribes and stealing from the government's coffers. Allauddin's prime minister, Khajakhatir, had refused to support him and had even had the courage to speak out against the sultan's injustice and tyranny; and it was only Khajakhatir's reputation for integrity that saved him from being beheaded on the spot. As it was, his life was spared, but he was deprived of his position and Nusratkhan was appointed vazir. The new prime minister took it upon himself to execute the sultan's orders and began to extract the money from the amirs by force. Alarmed by the sultan's dictatorial actions, the nobles decided that they had no option but to take a stand against him. A revolt was organized but it ended in failure. As a result, not only did the amirs lose all their money, they were also thrown into prison. Repenting their foolhardiness, they repeatedly begged for forgiveness, but the implacable and heartless sultan would not relent.

Allauddin had now succeeded in isolating his various enemies and no longer feared for the safety of his kingdom. He, therefore, decided that he would free the rebellious amirs on his son's birthday: the gesture would add to the brilliance of the celebrations and earn him the approbation of the populace. The amirs were summoned to the palace and publicly pardoned. Brought back to life from the threshold of death, they could not stop praising God for their good fortune. There were a number of leading maulvis and qazis learned in Sharia law present at court that day, including the chief qazi, Modhisuddin. Allauddin now addressed him, saying that as it was a holiday that day and they were celebrating a joyous event, he would like to take the opportunity of asking the qazi a few questions regarding Sharia law. Hitherto, the sultan had never consulted religious leaders on any issue, in fact he considered them a lying, scheming lot, so his request stunned the audience and the qazi waited in dread for what lay in store for him. 'Your Majesty!' he said, 'From your request it seems clear that my days are numbered and death is at hand. If this is the case, and if it is your lordship's will, then I am prepared to die. But your slave urges you to consider that if you hang me for speaking the truth, and conveying the commandments of God without fear, then the burden of guilt will be on you. It is this that saddens me—there is no other reason.'

'But what makes you so fearful?' Allauddin asked.

'If I speak the truth and displease the king, then my life is at stake; if I lie and the king hears the truth from some other source, then, too, I will deserve to die.'

The sultan reassured the qazi and told him to answer his questions without fear on the basis of what the Prophet had revealed in the Sharia. Then he began to put forward his questions one by one.

The sultan started by asking, 'Is it correct to regard government servants who have accepted bribes or embezzled money as common thieves and to punish them accordingly?'

To this, the qazi answered, 'If a government servant who is paid according to the scope and responsibilities of his job accepts bribes or extracts money from those who need his services, then the government has the right to recover such sums by whatever means are deemed suitable. But it has no right to impose the death penalty, or chop off the hands or feet of the accused as would be appropriate for a common criminal.'

The sultan said that in this matter he had always acted in conformity with Sharia law, using all necessary means, including torture, to recover the sums acquired by government servants through fraud and deceit.

His next question was, 'Before ascending the throne, I had attacked the kingdom of Devgadh and returned with considerable loot, which I regarded as my personal wealth. Should this be handed over to the government treasury? Does the army have a right to any portion of it?'

The qazi answered, 'Your Majesty has a right to the same amount to which every soldier who accompanied you on the expedition is entitled.'

Displeased by this answer, Allauddin said in an annoyed tone, 'I am unable to understand how the state or individual soldiers have any right over the wealth I acquired when I was the commander, through my own efforts.'

To this the qazi replied that the sultan had a claim over that portion of the loot that he himself had collected, but that the spoils gathered by the soldiers must be shared between them and the sultan.

The sultan continued, 'What claim do I and my children have over this wealth?'

The qazi was now certain that his time was up—if his earlier answers had annoyed the sultan, what he was about to say now would surely enrage him.

'Speak,' the sultan ordered. 'I will not harm a hair on your head.'

'Your Majesty,' the qazi said, 'I can answer your question in three different ways. If you act according to the strict laws of justice and the edicts of the Caliphs, then you are entitled to an equal share of the spoils along with every other soldier who accompanied you. If Your Majesty wishes to follow the second course, then you could lay claim to an amount equal to that of the largest share claimed by an individual officer. But if you would like to follow the advice of those who, when consulted about the legality of some action, bend the Sharia law to curry favour with the king, you can claim an even greater amount than the largest share claimed by an individual officer. But there is no justification for this.'

Truly furious now, the sultan said, 'All the household expenditure I have to incur, all the gifts and rewards I must bestow, are these against Sharia law then?'

'When Your Majesty asks me to expound Sharia law, then I am duty-bound to speak as a Koranic scholar,' the qazi replied quietly. 'But if you authorize me to speak with an eye to the interests of the kingdom, then all Your Majesty's servant can say is that what you do is appropriate and right, since statecraft dictates that the more wealth you accumulate, the greater the splendour of your kingdom.'

'From soldiers who do not report for service, I deduct a month's wages for the next three years. Those who rebel are destroyed root and branch, and all their moveable and immoveable properties—no matter where they are located—are confiscated. Is it your opinion that immoral, thieving, drunken officials should go unpunished?'

The sultan's words, the tone in which they were spoken, and the expression on his face threw the qazi into paroxysms of fear and he started to make a hasty exit. But before leaving the hall, he bowed low to the sultan and said, 'Your Majesty, your actions are in complete violation of Sharia law.' And with those words, he left the assembly.

Returning home, the qazi drafted his will and tried to compose himself by focusing on God as he waited for the executioner. But his fears were unfounded. Allauddin was undoubtedly amazed and angered by the qazi's words and his abrupt exit, but the fact that he had spoken from the heart, with nothing but God as his guide, aroused a merciful response. Yet when he sent a messenger to summon the qazi, a wave of fear spread through the assembly.

The qazi was brought trembling into the hall, but to his and everyone's surprise the sultan showed no signs of displeasure, but rather, welcomed him with respect. Presenting the qazi with a brocade coat and 1000 tankas, Allauddin said, 'Qazi sahib, I have not studied the Holy Book, but I can never forget that I was born a Muslim. Hence, I cannot but agree to all that you have spoken. However, if I rule according to your advice, I will not be able to hold Hindustan for a single day. Unless I punish criminals harshly, crime will continue to flourish. If I act harshly, and according to my own judgement, I do so with complete faith in God, and pray to the merciful and pure One that he will show mercy on this great sinner.'

Astounded by this speech, the audience extolled the remarkable courage of the qazi and the fair-mindedness and wisdom of the sultan. The freed amirs bowed to the sultan and faithfully promised never to rise against him again. Allauddin now rose from his throne and the heir apparent Khizrkhan joined the nobles. The day's festivities began in earnest. Nautch girls gave performances and liquor flowed freely.

That afternoon, when the nobles gathered again at the palace, the shahzada showered them with gold and silver nuggets. So eager were these wealthy gentlemen to show their gratitude, they scrabbled like beggars for alms, losing their turbans, rolling on the floor, shrieking and trampling each other, much to the amusement of the heir apparent. The 'weighing' ritual then followed. A large pair of scales was brought in, gold, diamonds, rubies and other precious gems were placed in one pan, weighed against the shahzada, and distributed among his personal staff. Thereafter, Khizrkhan was weighed against silver bars, which were apportioned among the palace guards. Costly garments and spices were weighed next and handed out to the other servants; and finally ghee, grain and other food items were weighed and distributed among the poor.

An elephant-and-tiger fight had been organized in the enclosed courtyard outside the palace, and arrangements made for the populace to view it from atop the high wall. A huge crowd had gathered that afternoon. The sultan, the vazir, the princes and other notables watched from the palace windows. Ladies from the zenana sat behind curtained windows on the top floor. Amirs and courtiers reclined in comfort in the balconies below.

The elephant was strongly built and quick-witted, the tiger agile and fierce. The animals were set free and the courtyard resounded with the howls of the spectators. The tiger sprang first on the elephant and tried to grab hold of its trunk, but the elephant raised it high and thwarted his opponent. Now the elephant attempted to crush the tiger underfoot, but the tiger proved far too agile. Whenever either of the contestants seemed on the verge of death, the spectators went pale with anxiety, and each time a beast escaped its fate, they could hardly contain their joy. The contest went on for an hour without result. Desperate for the struggle to end, the two animals attacked each other with renewed ferocity. Finally the tiger succumbed: wrapping his trunk around the predator, the elephant dashed him to the ground and trampled him to death. This ghastly spectacle, rather than arousing compassion in the hearts of the audience, gave them a great deal of pleasure, and roars of delight went up from the crowd as though they had won a glorious victory over some powerful enemy. The elephant's trainer was given a generous reward, the spectators returned home and the celebrations moved back to the palace. The courtyard was empty and silent once again.

That evening, Khizrkhan was to visit the dargah of Sidi Maula and offer flowers at his tomb. Allauddin owed his throne to the death of the dervish, a man who in his lifetime had been regarded as an extraordinary individual, and who after death was honoured as a pir, his dargah visited by those seeking fulfilment of their desires. The entire town had been brightly lit and the route through which the shahzada's entourage was to pass seemed as if illumined by a blazing fire. The mansions of the nobility were also brilliantly lit, both inside and out; and the reflection of lamps and garlands sparkled in the waters of the fountains. Shops were decorated with lamps and flowers, and firework 'fountains' brought from China were planted at intervals along the way. Thousands of people, dressed in their finery, crowded the route. Fearful Hindus kept to the sides of the streets. Muslim fakirs pushed their way aggressively through the crowd. Haughty Pathans who held the reins of power in Delhi, swaggered past. People ran helter-skelter as Muslim horsemen, unconcerned for the safety of pedestrians, pranced and cavorted through the crowd. Careless soldiers pushed their way forward. Mongols, whose star had yet not risen in the political firmament, gathered inconspicuously in groups, talking quietly among themselves. Nobles and wealthy Muslims riding horses and elephants or in palanquins and carriages swelled the crowd, which had grown so dense that a plate could be passed over the heads of people without danger of its falling through a gap.

The shahzada's entourage started as it grew dark. Musicians and standard-bearers riding horses, camels and elephants led the procession, followed by a haphazard band of soldiers and cavalry. Finally came the royal elephant bearing a golden howdah, bedecked with rubies and diamonds. The heir apparent himself was a splendid sight. To say that he wore jewellery would be an understatement—he was laden with it like a beast of burden, visible proof that Allauddin had succeeded in extracting more loot from the country than even Mahmud of Ghazni and Shahabuddin Ghori had managed to do. Diamonds, pearls and rubies had been used as carelessly as if they were grains of sand; gold as if it were brass; and silver, mere plated metal. Behind the elephant came cart after cart piled with Chinese firecrackers. Lit by street lamps and the intermittent flare of the firecrackers, the shahzada's bejewelled body shone like the orb of the sun, blinding the eyes of those who dared to look at him.

The procession reached the marketplace. At least half the spectators had crowded there and there was no shortage of carts, horses and elephants in the narrow street. Firework 'fountains' had been placed at close intervals in the congested area; a panic ensued the moment the first one was lit, and there was a real danger of a stampede. The second 'fountain' exploded when ignited, sending sparks and debris flying on to the revellers, the horsemen, and the carts carrying the firecrackers. As firecrackers burst and turbans and clothing caught fire, terrified people tried to escape, but in vain. In the crush and the scramble, the flames spread from person to person. People tried to force their way into the open maidan, and those that happened to have swords or daggers did not hesitate to use them, but the wall of humanity made escape impossible. Howls from the burnt and wounded filled the air. The old, the frail and the young were crushed screaming underfoot. And as rockets, fountains and sparklers hissed and blazed, the marketplace resembled a battleground. Frenzied horses and elephants maddened by the chaos ran amok. They threw off their riders, and as if sensing that such an opportunity would never come their way again, stampeded mindlessly in all directions, crushing people indiscriminately. Rich and poor, young and old, noble and pauper—none were spared. All were equal as they writhed in the dust. Those accustomed to sleeping on the softest mattresses, those who employed servants to massage their bodies and fan them with cool air, in short, those who had never had to endure the hot winds of summer, now lay in the dust, their bruised and broken bodies not likely to need the services of a masseur again.

All this while, the shahzada's mahout and other servants had kept a tight hold on the royal elephant, preventing it from breaking loose as clouds of smoke enveloped it. Sparks had singed the shahzada's costly raiment in many places, but the timely assistance of those nearby had prevented him from being burnt to a cinder. But now a large ball of fire struck the elephant, and it started forward with such force that the mahout could no longer restrain it. Picking up the mahout in its trunk, the elephant hurled him down, and free at last, it began rampaging through the crowd. The howdah slipped and it looked as if Khizrkhan would fall off his mount. His clothes were on fire and with no help at hand, the shahzada's untimely death seemed inevitable. But what harm can come to those whom God protects? That the shahzada was terrified was certain. He knew that if he remained seated he was sure to burn to death, but if he jumped, it was equally certain that his life would be crushed out of him. When faced with death, princes and paupers think alike. No one is likely to come to my aid, thought the shahzada as he sent up a prayer to God. His clothes caught fire again, but just as the flames engulfed his body, a young man shoved his way through the mêlée, and clambering on the shoulders of some of the crowd hurled himself at the royal elephant and grabbed hold of the shahzada. By the grace of God, the amazed onlookers had moved away from the elephant, and the two men fell on the ground unhurt. Khizrkhan's saviour picked him up and with the same determination with which he had penetrated the crowd, bore the shahzada out of it and into an open maidan where both men collapsed.

Overcome by his close shave with death, the anxiety and the excitement, the shahzada fell into a dead faint. His saviour, equally overcome by the exertion, the mental strain, the relief that he had achieved his purpose without harm, and the hope that his deed would have its intended result, also fainted. In a short while, a cool breeze revived both of them simultaneously. His heart filled with gratitude, the shahzada embraced his saviour, and offered to grant him whatever he should desire. With tears of joy in his eyes—and with the intention of fulfilling the task that had brought him to Delhi and of assuaging the goddess of revenge who lodged in his heart—Madhav (for that's who the saviour was)

105

asked only for a face-to-face meeting with the sultan. Khizrkhan readily agreed, and having ascertained Madhav's name and other details, promised to send horses, elephants and grooms to his lodgings the following day and have Madhav brought before the king, and handsomely rewarded.

The shahzada's servants now arrived on the scene and he was escorted back to the palace. The spectators went home. The procession turned back. Madhav returned to his lodgings. And all night long, torches lit up the darkness as people went in search of the dead and wounded.

Madhav did not sleep that night. The hours passed swiftly as thoughts of what had led to his sudden decision to help the shahzada—how he had managed to approach the elephant through that mass of people, how he had borne the shahzada to safety, how he should conduct the meeting with the sultan, what he should ask for, whether the sultan would accede to his request—passed through his mind. The next morning he had a bath and put on his finest clothes. Then the sultan's elephants and men arrived, and a very satisfied Madhav made a grand entry into the palace. After a short wait, he was ushered into the sultan's presence. The sultan had been apprised of the facts and Madhav did not need to repeat them. Allauddin offered Madhav a seat and asked him his name, caste and occupation. After Madhav had described the background leading to the previous day's events, he said, 'Your Majesty, Gujarat is the wealthiest and most fertile kingdom in all of Hindustan. It is the granary of the land. All varieties of crops grow there. All the land is under cultivation. Rivers and canals abound. There are beautiful forests and tall mountains. In short, the country is like paradise. But the king, Karan Vaghela, is an evil, treacherous and stubborn man, and an unpopular ruler. His kingdom was once prosperous, but for some time now it has become enfeebled. Feudatories no longer pay regular tribute. Vassals are dissatisfied. The pay of the soldiers is in arrears and they, too, are discontented. The population in general is demoralized. People are disgusted by the way I have been treated, and I still have a large following in the country. The conquest of Gujarat will not be difficult: the other Rajput rulers have been cowed by your depredations and will not go to Gujarat's assistance; besides, many units will desert to your side out of loyalty to me. To one like you, conquering Gujarat will be like child's play. My request thus is that you flatten Gujarat, appoint whom you choose as governor, but place me in charge of the administration.'

Allauddin had given himself the title of 'Alexander II' and had it inscribed on his coins. Like the original Alexander, he too, dreamt of conquering the world. This opportunity was far too good to pass. He agreed to all of Madhav's requests, gave him a generous reward, promised to attack Gujarat soon, and bid him farewell.

7

From Patan our tale has travelled to Siddhapur and from there through Ambabhavani, Abu, Mewar, Marwar on to Delhi, where we have come to know a little about the splendour of the city, its emperor, his court and his regime. Now let us retrace our footsteps back to Karan Raja, the king of Anhilpur-Patan, narrate the incidents that have occurred since we left him, and describe the events that are to follow.

The people of Patan were greatly disturbed by the recent events—the abduction of Madhav's wife Roopsundari, the death of his brother Keshav, the decision of Keshav's wife Gunsundari to become a sati and the flight of Madhav from the kingdom—that had followed close on each other's heels. Wherever one went, one heard these topics being discussed endlessly. There were anxious discussions about the outcome of the king's act; and, to some extent, the fear proved to be justified. The third day after the events described above, a great fire swept across the town. Attempts to douse it only fanned the flames further, and house after house was devoured by the blaze. The terrified populace interpreted this as the wrath of God. A rumour spread that spirits had been seen flying across the skies torching the streets. The fire was finally extinguished but the townspeople were convinced it was supernatural retribution. That night, the windows of some homes were shattered by rocks, cooked food turned to excrement, the water in wells became blood, blood-curdling cries rent the darkness, and no one dared step out after the lamps were lit. Women keened as if possessed, new fires broke out through the night and confusion reigned.

The palace, too, was in turmoil. Karan Raja's favourite queen, Phoolrani of Janjmeer Talaja, began acting so wildly that few dared even to approach her. People were certain that a powerful demon had taken possession of their town. Now the *bhuva*s, astrologers and *tantrik*s came into their own. They went from place to place summoning the phantom to show itself. They hammered nails into all the gates, made offerings at all the crossroads, strewed sindur-smeared lemon slices on the streets, and scattered grains of sanctified arhad daal in every home. Many people lit lamps of mustard oil to drive away the spirit. But in vain! It refused to depart, and the harassment continued. All those the spirit possessed identified themselves as Babro,[4] thus proving without a shadow of doubt that Babrobhoot alone was causing all the mischief. The agitated populace could think and talk of nothing except the vexatious *bhoot*. One morning, while drawing water from a well near the town, some women heard a loud splash. As they ran for their lives, one of the women fell, or was more likely pushed into the well. A crowd gathered but no one had the courage to plunge into the well to rescue her, fearing that this was the handiwork of Babrobhoot. Just at that moment a Rajput on horseback arrived on the scene. In a trice he had divested himself of his heavy spear, undressed and jumped into the well. Soon he reappeared bearing the terrified woman, now all smiles. The crowd was amazed by the daring of the Rajput and delighted to see him emerge unscathed. The woman's husband and family arrived and thanking the Rajput profusely, invited him as an honoured guest to their home. The Rajput, in need of shelter for the night, readily accompanied them. While the hospitable couple prepared a meal specially for him, the Rajput sat in deep thought. He had come to Patan to meet Karan Raja and wondered how he would be able to manage this. As they ate, his hosts acquainted the Rajput, in great detail, of all the strange happenings that had occurred during the last few days—the havoc caused in the town by Babrobhoot, and the way he had taken possession of the queen. This gave the Rajput an idea: he would gain the notice of the king through an act of exceptional courage. He would vanquish Babrobhoot and rescue Phoolrani from the demon's clutches. But how was this to be accomplished? In his childhood, the Rajput had learnt a mantra to ward off evil spirits and he had often proved its efficacy in the past. He had not invoked the mantra for many years and was unsure of the outcome, but kali chaudas was just a few days away and he was determined to try out the mantra at the stroke of twelve on that moonless night. The Rajput spent the next few days gathering the materials he would require and waited for kali chaudas.

The cremation ground of Anhilpur was terrifying on that dark night of vad chaudas. It was pitch dark. Black clouds had gathered overhead and there was a steady drizzle. Intermittent flashes of lightning illumined the dark waters of the Saraswati, the trees that stood on its banks, the clusters of shrines, and the large Shiva temples. The sky thundered, the wind blew as if possessed, and the branches of trees crashed against each other and hit the ground in fury. Phosphorus released from the decomposed bones of cattle caught fire as it came in contact with the air. Inflammable gases from the boggy ground burst spontaneously into flames that leapt and crackled as the drizzling rain fell on them. Not a soul was around. In the distance, on both sides of the river, fishermen

110

could be seen warming themselves around huge braziers, their boats securely tied. The shrill cries of crickets and the discordant croaking of frogs could be heard. At this horrifying hour and place, a flash of lightning silhouetted a man walking along the river bank. One could not help admiring his courage. Another flash showed him to be the same Rajput rider who had rescued the woman from the well, and it should not be difficult to guess why he was in the cremation ground at such an unearthly hour. He walked with a confident step as if strolling on the streets of Patan on a sunny day. He appeared to be searching for something. After walking for a while he stopped and started digging with his crowbar. He dug vigorously for about half-an-hour then paused and, placing the crowbar on the ground, wiped the sweat off his face with his dhoti. As he prepared to descend into the pit he had dug, he heard a howl followed by a loud splash. Trembling, the man leapt back ten feet. Though momentarily overcome by fear, he did not succumb to it completely. Rushing to the river bank he saw that it was only a dog being swept away in the current. It thrashed about desperately but the stars were against the poor wretch who was soon swallowed up by the raging waters. This renewed the Rajput's confidence and he went back into the pit.

He emerged a while later, carrying a corpse. Most of the flesh had been devoured and it was crawling with worms; two deep sockets remained where the eyes had once been, the nose was half eaten and the skull protruded; a foul stench emanated from the pulpy flesh. Lightning flashed again, and now the Rajput saw that worms were creeping over his own body. He let go of the corpse in horror, struggled out of his clothes, shook them clear of the crawling creatures and put his clothes back on. Kicking the corpse with his feet he propelled it towards the shore. It was his intention to wash it clean in the river, but just as he pushed it into the water something bit into his leg. The Rajput leapt up in pain and saw the corpse being dragged away. At that instant, flames burst from the bog and fearing for his life, he took to his heels. He did not have the courage to follow the receding corpse. 'Alas! This is surely the work of some spirit,' he thought as he stood there. 'All my efforts have been in vain. What shall I do now?' He steeled himself and disregarding his fear, resolved not to leave the spot till he succeeded in his task. Ashamed of his faintheartedness, he hurried to take possession of the corpse once again. A flash of lightning revealed that it was being dragged by a jackal. As his fear subsided, the Rajput picked up a stone and hurled it in the direction of the receding corpse. There was a loud yelp and the patter of fleeing feet. The Rajput approached the body, rolled it back into the water, and stood guard over it to prevent the current from sweeping it away. Now and then he could hear the sound of splashing. Translucent fins shimmered in the dark, and snakes hissed near the water. He stood there for a while until he felt sure that the corpse had been cleared of the worms and muck. The night was short and the perils many. Seized by a nervous restlessness, riddled with doubts about the success of his endeavours, he was impatient to complete his task as soon as possible. But at the touch of the icy corpse, his limbs turned to jelly, every joint ached as if with rheumatic pain, and he was unable to take a single step. Courage, my heart, courage, he said to himself as he fled from the spot and ran for dear life till he reached a small shrine where he collapsed flat on the ground. Then composing himself once again he went back to the body and carried it into the shrine.

Everything was ready for the ritual. The Rajput's mind was now at peace, free of doubts and worries. He went to the river for the ritual bath. Reciting the prescribed mantras he bathed and still in his wet clothes re-entered the shrine. He created a spark with flint and lighted the wick he had kept ready in a lamp filled with mustard oil. Lemons, sliced and filled with sindur, were placed in all four directions. The Rajput hammered nails in the four corners and chanting mantras scattered arhad daal on the floor. He performed arti, applied vermilion on his forehead, smeared the water with which he had bathed the image on his body, tied amulets on his arm and an auspicious medallion round his neck. Protected by these weapons against the onslaught of ghosts, spirits, goblins, *shankhani*s and *yakshini*s, the Rajput straddled the corpse. So engrossed was he in the performance of the rite that he was oblivious to his surroundings—not that anything untoward happened. The wind blew harder, the flashes of lightning became more brilliant and the thunder more deafening. There was a sudden burst of rain and the darkness became more black. But the Rajput was impervious to nature's fury and continued chanting. Before long, however, the corpse on which he was riding began to move and jolt, tossing him up and down with it. He gripped the body hard with his feet to prevent it from escaping under him. As the corpse tried to unseat him, the shrine resounded with bloodcurdling shrieks and cries. He was encircled by wildly dancing demons; they laughed fiendishly, closed in menacingly, intent, it appeared, to kill him; some threatened him from a distance, their grotesque faces terrifying. *Chudel*s and *vantari*s balancing burning-hot braziers on their heads howled and screamed. Terrifying buffalo-headed rakshasas tried to devour him. It was clear that the Rajput was shaken: his hair stood on end, a deathly chill spread across his body, he was drenched in a sticky sweat and his heart beat furiously. At times he would start screaming. He had no strength to move even a fraction of an inch, let alone take to his heels. But even in this crisis he managed to remain in control of the situation. He did not allow his chanting to be disrupted. The corpse began to bounce up and down more vigorously. The spirits began to scream even louder, doubling their effort to destroy his meditation. But the Rajput remained blind and deaf to their ghoulish efforts. He had protected himself so well against danger from every direction that the disgusting creatures could not penetrate his defences. He continued his chanting for three hours and recited the mantra 108 times.

The recitation of the mantra came to an end, and the sway of the night receded. The sun rose, the light of the lamp grew dim, the silhouettes of objects could be dimly seen and all nature was transformed. The rain had stopped a little while ago, the clouds had dispersed and a gentle breeze blew; and now the fiends were suddenly desperate to leave. Both thunder and lightning had ceased. The trees clustered in verdant groves and the air was filled with the scent of flowers as the Rajput came out of the shrine. He had slung his bundle of ritual materials across his shoulder and had his stick in hand. His exhausted appearance was testimony to his terrible ordeal. His face was pale and dull, and lined with worry. Though inwardly pleased at the successful completion of his task, he had not yet had the time to shake off his fear. He strode hurriedly on, lost in thought, oblivious to his surroundings.

But this state of mind did not last long. When the Rajput neared the walls of the town, he saw a woman filling water from a well. The Rajput was thirsty and decided to approach her for a drink. He stood near her for a long time but she ignored him. Furious at the insult, the Rajput loudly demanded some water. But the woman was as deaf as the well to his command. Supposing her to be hard of hearing he was about to shake her by the arm when she suddenly became as tall as a palm tree. The Rajput was dumbstruck and froze in fear. After a while the woman spoke. 'Hey you Rajput, you want water, do you?'

Thoroughly ashamed at being frightened by a mere woman, the Rajput regained his composure and covered up his cowardice with bluster. 'You whore!' he shouted. 'Whatever you are, you cannot frighten me. I am a kshatriya. My ancestors have fought in countless great wars and have feared no one. I would be an unworthy descendant of my race if I were to be scared by a pathetic little creature like you. Even if you had touched the heavens and your feet dug into the netherworld, you will always remain a helpless woman, while I will always remain an intrepid Rajput. Therefore, whatever form you adopt, whatever height or width you attain, however fearsome you look, I will remain unafraid. I will extract water from you—whether by persuasion or by force. Then let what is to happen, happen!'

Impressed by his bold words, but determined to test him further the woman called out, 'Why, you midget! You can't even reach my hand. And you think you can wrest the water from me?'

The Rajput, who had witnessed far more frightening sights through the night and had held his own against far more terrifying fiends and ghouls, was not about to succumb to fear. He hit the woman on her legs with such force with his sword that she fell sprawling, transforming herself into a heavenly apsara the moment she hit the ground. She was as exquisite as a nymph and large tears fell from her eyes, but she kept her hand raised to steady the pot on her head, and would not let the Rajput seize it. The Rajput was about to hit her once more but how could he strike the delicate, flower-like hands of this lovely maiden? He stood undecided, aware that striking a woman was against kshatriya dharma. The woman divined his thoughts—she knew that she had never set eyes on a man like him, and was convinced that he was worthy of his Rajput lineage. Transforming herself once again into an ogress, she sprang on to the Rajput, grabbed him by the neck and threw him down. Now that she was no longer a lovely, helpless maiden but a terrifying demon, there was no need for restraint or pity. The Rajput tried to free himself from her grasp but he was being slowly strangled and he felt that the cord of his life would snap at any moment. Yama's emissaries were upon him, determined to hasten his departure from this world. He lost all hope, but the spark of life within refused to be extinguished without a struggle. With a superhuman effort he managed to extricate himself from the woman's hold and leapt onto her back. Again she changed into an apsara, but her water pot had disappeared. For once the Rajput was impervious to her beauty, for once he felt no pity, and for once he dispensed with his kshatriya dharma. He grabbed the woman's neck and squeezed it so violently that the blood rushed to her face. Her tongue lolled out, she frothed at the mouth, her eyes bulged and her body jerked wildly, but just when the Rajput was certain that he had dispatched her to the netherworld, the whore slithered serpent-like out of his grasp and stood before him in her true form. The Rajput was furious but concluded that she must be a nymph from heaven. After a while she said, 'Hey Rajput! Worthy of praise! You are indeed a true kshatriya. For years I have been in search of a valiant Rajput but I have searched in vain. I am convinced now that you are the very one I was seeking. But you still don't know who I am though you must have guessed that I am not of this world. I am Shakti, an emanation, a yogini of the great Goddess Ambabhavani. I have come down to this realm and wandered far and near to discover and taste the pleasures of the world. I desire to marry, and look upon you as a worthy mate. I will be pleased to live with you as your wedded wife. So hear my plea and marry me right now. I will do all in my power to make you happy and you will lack for nothing.'

The Rajput was delighted, and realizing how foolish it would be to lock the door when fortune came knocking, fell at the woman's feet and clasped her by the hand. 'My luck has finally turned,' he thought joyously. 'God's grace is upon me, my mission is sure to succeed and nothing will come in my way.'

The Rajput then went to the town to look for a suitable place for them to stay.

＿＿＿

Shakti had so far refrained from probing into her husband's past. From his looks, his speech, his courage and the qualities worthy of a Rajput, she was sure he was no ordinary mortal but of royal descent. She was eager to know all about his parents, whether they were still living, why he had left his country and what he intended to do in Patan. Her opportunity came at night when they were seated together after dinner.

She began, 'You know who I am and why I wanted to marry you but I do not know anything about you. I have married you without enquiring about your past, and you should now satisfy my curiosity. I am sure what you tell me will only confirm my impressions of you, so tell me your tale from beginning to end; then I will know that I have not been mistaken.'

The Rajput replied, 'Although you have married me in ignorance of my past, you must have inferred by my behaviour, nature and appearance that I am no ordinary person. Still, I will tell you my story in detail, so that you can be reassured and will never regret your decision. My name is Harpal.[5] My father was Kesar, the king of Kirantigadh in Kutch. And my mother was Karan Raja's aunt. From this you can gather that I do not come from a lowly family. I am the son of a king and the cousin of Karan Raja. But this alone cannot be considered a matter of pride. A king's son may turn out to be a fool, and Karan's cousin could prove an unworthy coward. I will recount the exploits of my father and grandfather, as yet I am young and have not had the opportunity to prove my valour. But, as it is said, a lion's offspring cannot but be lions, and a peacock's eggs need no embellishment to produce peacocks. When the time is ripe I, too, will bring glory to my forefathers. And if I do not surpass the valour of my father, I will consider myself unworthy of his name.

'My grandfather, Vahiyas, ruled Kirantigadh in Kutch. His Makwana ancestors had ruled the kingdom before him. When my grandfather was at death's door, his spirit refused to leave his body. His children and other family members undertook fasts and made numerous vows, but to no avail. Finally his son,

117

Kesar, asked him, "Why does your soul not depart from your body, Father? Tell me what troubles you and I, your dutiful son, will move heaven and earth to fulfil your dying wishes." Then Vahiyas answered, "The city of Samaiyu is ruled by my sworn enemy, Hamir Sumro. If you promise to capture and bring 125 of his horses here and give them away as gifts to the bards on the thirteenth day of my funeral rites, my soul will be released." Though Vahiyas was surrounded by his brothers and nephews, not one of them uttered a word of reassurance. At that time my father, Kesar, was a callow youth, but he took up the challenge. He approached his father, and pouring holy water into his hands, pledged to obey his commands. The moment he said this, Vahiyas's soul found release. When the thirteenth day drew near, Kesar turned his back on sorrow, readied himself and summoned his relatives to join him in the fight against the city of Samaiyu, but no one responded to his call. "Who would deliberately risk their lives accompanying an untried youth like you?" they retorted.

'Although no one came to his aid, Kesar did not lose heart. He decided to rely on his own resources. Just as a rain cloud is the best source of water, so a man's own courage is his greatest strength. Kesar's arms were unusually long and reached well below his knees. He could lift a spear weighing one-and-a-quarter maunds in one hand alone, his bow and arrow were constantly at his side and his horse was as swift as Vishnu's Garuda. Kesar attacked Samaiyu and brought back 125 horses and, on the thirteenth day of his father's death, fulfilled his promise by presenting them to the bards.

'When he had completed this task, Kesar summoned the royal astrologer to predict his life span. Examining the prince's horoscope, the astrologer regretfully predicted an early death for him. When Kesar heard this, he decided that it would be better to die a hero in battle, than to live unremembered at home. He attacked Samaiyu once again, this time capturing 700 of Hamir's camels that were grazing near the river, and distributed them among the bards of Kirantigadh. In spite of these unprovoked raids, Hamir neither expressed anger nor did he dispatch his army against Kesar. Since he bore the insults patiently, Kesar waited till the dust had settled and then set out to confront Hamir for the third time. He reached Samaiyu on the day of Dussera when Hamir's wife and daughter were taking a drive around the royal gardens. Kesar took them by surprise, and not only abducted the royal ladies but also carried away 125 Sumri maidens. Finally roused to action, Hamir sent his minister to Kirantigadh. The emissary informed Kesar that the women were the wives and sisters of Hamir, and should be sent back with gifts of gold and fine clothes, like daughters returning to their husbands' homes after a visit to their parents. Kesar burst out laughing. The captured women were now his property and his wives, he said, and would never be returned to Hamir. The minister carried this answer back to Samaiyu, and Kesar summoned all his kinsmen and bestowed a Sumri woman on each of them. He kept four for himself thus swelling his already large harem.

'Kesar continued his raids on Samaiyu for the next ten or twelve years. Meanwhile, he and his cousins fathered eighteen sons by their Sumri captives. Then, once again raring for war, Kesar challenged Hamir to battle. So far Hamir had shown no inclination to fight Kesar, but now he took up the challenge and sent word that though he was ready for a confrontation, he was worried about how he would feed his large army in the inhospitable terrain of Kirantigadh. Kesar replied that he would plant wheat in a hundred bighas of land for Hamir and his army. Then Hamir assembled with a mighty force and a bloody battle ensued. Many Rajputs lost their lives and the land was laid waste. In the end, a great confrontation took place in which Kesar and all his sons, except myself, perished. My uncles and cousins too fell in the battlefield. Hamir set fire to Kirantigadh and reduced it to ashes; and the Sumri women committed *jauhar* on the funeral pyres of their slain husbands. This was how it all ended—my family was destroyed, our lineage annihilated and our kingdom reduced to dust.

'I was the sole survivor of the carnage, and wandered hither and thither knowing not what to do. No king befriended me. I finally decided to seek out adventure in some distant land and perform valorous deeds to impress its king. Karan Raja of Gujarat is my cousin, so I set out to meet him and came here a few days ago. On my arrival, I heard about Babrobhoot and it occurred to me that if I could rid the town of this menace, the king would be very pleased and my fame would spread, not just in the town but throughout Gujarat. Then I would make known my kinship to the king and happily settle down here. In my youth I had learnt a mantra to exorcise spirits and since then I have often made use of it. But knowing how strong Babro is, I went to the cremation grounds last night to test its efficacy. Seated on a corpse I chanted the mantra. Countless ghosts, fiends, ghouls and other unclean creatures tried to frighten me but I persevered and completed my task. It was while I was returning from the burning grounds that I met you, and our present companionship is the result. Now, the next time the bhoot takes control of Phoolrani, I will disguise myself as an exorcist and go to the palace. And there, with your help, God willing, I will put an end to the spirit's mischief.'

Shakti replied saying, 'Your tale has made me very happy, and I am convinced that you are indeed the person I took you for. I will never regret marrying you. Your desires will be fulfilled. You will vanquish Babrabhoot. Courage alone is required for this task. But remember well the advice I give you, it will help you greatly. For if you do not heed my words, even your mantra will not be able protect you. You must remember to take hold of

Babro's top-knot the minute he emerges to fight with you. He will become powerless and bend to your will.'

The next day, as the couple sat together after breakfast, the news that Babrobhoot had again possessed Phoolrani and was creating havoc spread through the town. Harpal immediately put on the clothes of a northerner and prepared to go to the palace. Shakti gave him her blessings and reminded him once again to take hold of the bhoot by his hair.

No exorcist was prevented from entering Karan's palace at the time and Harpal soon found himself in the presence of the king. As soon as Karan Raja enquired about his mission he said 'I am an exorcist from Lakhnor, an adept in all the black arts. I am skilled in levitation, hallucination and control. I have travelled the length and breadth of Bharat, from Badrikedarnath to Setubandh Rameshwar, and from Dwarka to Jagannathpuri. I forged links with all the great sorcerers and bhuvas and learnt their mantras. But this was not enough for me. After wandering far and near, I reached the matriarchal kingdom of Kamarupa and was made welcome by its queen. For three years I remained with her, a man by night, and parakeet by day, gaining knowledge of the most potent science of mantras. Using the arts of deception, I escaped from there and was wandering in your kingdom when I heard about Babrobhoot. I was surprised to find that in the vast land of Gujarat not a single necromancer could be found who could exorcise this spirit, and was moved to pity for you, your queen Phoolrani and the populace of the town. I, therefore, present myself before you, and if you permit me to practise my art I shall rid you of this evil spirit.'

Karan was greatly astonished, for so far no exorcist had given him such convincing assurance of getting rid of Babrobhoot. He welcomed the sorcerer and ordered his attendants to lead him to Phoolrani's chambers. About a hundred brahmins sat in the antechamber reciting the *Chandipath*. In an adjoining room, many Hindu and Jain bhuvas and *jatis* muttered mantras. But not one of them, it seemed, could muster enough courage to enter Phoolrani's room. When Harpal came in, all of them dropped what they were doing and clustered around him to see what this great practitioner of the black arts from the north would do. Harpal bravely ordered the doors of the queen's chamber to be thrown open. The queen was seated on her bed. She was delicately built and appeared around twenty-years old. Her cinnabar-red eyes stared unblinkingly. Her face was pale and fierce, and she looked like an embodiment of the wrathful Shakti. Harpal took a few grains of arhad daal and sprinkled them on Phoolrani to the accompaniment of mantras. The instant the seeds fell on her, the dormant bhoot was startled awake and with one mighty leap the queen landed on the floor making it shake with the impact. This was accompanied by a blood-curdling scream that reverberated throughout the palace and was even heard in many parts of the town. Now the critical moment was at hand. Babrobhoot (as we shall now call Phoolrani) stood before Harpal and tried to grab him, but Harpal threw some more of the sanctified grain at the demon. This made Babro retreat a little, but he now revealed himself in his true, monstrous form.

The onlookers fled, but Harpal stood his ground and said in a loud voice, 'State your name and explain why you are tormenting the king, queen and the people of Anhilpur.'

Babro burst out laughing. 'Listen to me, you earthling!' he roared. 'I have not yet revealed my identity to anyone and I had no intention of doing so, but you appear to be a powerful sorcerer, so I shall disclose it to you. You look like a stranger to these parts so I shall tell you my tale from beginning to end, and then you may judge whether what I am doing is right or wrong. In my previous life I was a Nagar brahmin and my brother Madhav was the prime minister of this evil, despicable, ungrateful king. I lost my life trying to save the honour of my sister-in-law who was forcibly abducted by the king. As my wife committed sati, no bad karma can accrue to us, but to take revenge against the king's heinous deed I begged Yama, the god of death, to permit me to take the form of this spirit and take up residence in the queen's body. To harass the people is to harass the king, therefore, I trouble them too. When my desire for revenge is satiated I shall discard this body and dwell in the heavenly abode of Kailash.'

Harpal, though secretly sympathizing with Babro, was determined to exorcise the intruder for his own selfish ends, so, dismissing all questions of right and wrong from his mind, he said, 'You rascal! Enough is enough. Leave the queen and the city and go back to where you belong. If you don't agree to leave willingly I will use force; therefore, leave with dignity.' But Babro took no notice and continued his mad screaming and dancing. For the third time, Harpal threw the sanctified arhad daal on him. Angered, Babro rushed forward to strangle him. Both crashed on the floor and amidst the noise and shrieks, they rolled on the ground wrestling ferociously, now one on top, now the other. Until now, Babro had been merely playing with his opponent. He had not employed his full strength against the enemy. But when Harpal refused to give up the fight, Babro rose to his feet, lifted Harpal off the floor with one hand, and threatened to fling him to the ground and kill him. Harpal showed no fear. Before he hit the ground, he adroitly grabbed Babro's hand and enveloped him in a deadly embrace. Babro squeezed Harpal's neck and the Rajput's life would have soon ended had he not at that moment recalled Shakti's advice and with a superhuman effort seized Babro's top-knot. In an instant, Babro became as soft as rice gruel, a tiger turned lamb, and stood there like a docile cow. 'Let go of my pigtail,' was all that he could mutter.

Realizing that Babro had been finally vanquished, Harpal addressed the bhoot. 'It's time to come out, boy. Now you are well and truly caught. You might as well surrender.' Babro, now helpless, agreed to leave the town; but not before Harpal made him promise that he would come to Harpal's aid whenever required. Babro consented but set forward a counter-condition: that if he were left without a task to accomplish, he would devour Harpal. Harpal agreed to this and ordered a phial to be brought and commanded Babro to enter it. Defeated and defenceless, resigned to his fate, Babro entered the bottle. The phial was sealed with lac and mantras, and Harpal took it to the king. Karan bent low to touch Harpal's feet in gratitude, and promised to reward him with as much money as he desired.

Now it was Harpal's turn to speak and with folded hands he recounted his tale from start to finish. Karan could hardly believe his amazing story. When Harpal swore to its veracity the delighted Karan, his eyes filled with tears, embraced his cousin. The word spread from the palace to the town and there was a celebration in every home. People rejoiced to learn that Karan's cousin had rid the town of Babrobhoot. The phial was taken in procession through the town and escorted out of the kingdom. Then Karan rewarded Harpal with a ceremonial dress and the rank of Samant and urged him to remain at the palace, but Harpal wanted to live with his newly wed bride in a separate home, so the king gifted Harpal a magnificent mansion and with due honours sent him to his new home.

8

Free at last from the persecution and mischief of Babrobhoot, Karan Raja and Phoolrani, the residents of the palace and the inhabitants of the town celebrated New Year's Day with easy minds. It seemed as if it was Diwali as, in home after home, people got dressed in their finery early in the morning, and set out in the best of spirits to visit each other, offer gifts and exchange greetings. Meanwhile, in their own mansion, Harpal and Shaktidevi chatted cheerfully as they prepared to go to the king's durbar, and planned what they would ask for if Karan Raja offered Harpal a gift.

The durbar assembled at mid-morning. In addition to those who had gathered here the previous year for the Dussera celebrations, many prominent traders and financiers were also present that morning. As a richly attired Harpal entered, the raja offered him a seat to the right of the throne. After the usual salutations and the conclusion of the day's official business, Karan Raja congratulated Harpal and thanked him for the extraordinarily difficult task he had performed, and while acknowledging that he could never fully repay the debt he owed, offered to give Harpal whatever he should desire. Prostrating himself before the king, his hands folded, Harpal said that all he wanted was a gift of as many villages whose entrance gates could be garlanded in a single night?

The raja had not expected to be let off so lightly; he had feared that Harpal would be far more demanding. The Rajput's request thus came as a pleasant surprise, and calculating that it would not be possible to hang garlands at too many villages in just one night, the king readily agreed to the request. After the durbar dispersed, Harpal returned home and reported the news to his wife. Left to herself, Shaktidevi would have been quite capable of placing garlands on a large number of village gates. But Harpal doubted her capacity to accomplish the task to his satisfaction. As he thought about the matter, he suddenly remembered Babrobhoot. Babro had promised to come to Harpal's aid whenever he was summoned. Moreover, he had threatened to devour Harpal if he was not given a task to perform, so Harpal decided to summon the bhoot and ask him to accompany Shakti on her errand. Babrobhoot appeared the moment Harpal thought of him. He was delighted at the prospect of helping Harpal, not only because he was bound to do so, but because the more assistance he rendered, the greater would be Karan's loss, and he, Babrobhoot, would slake some of his thirst for revenge. Babro promised to come as soon as it got dark and bring his assistants with him. He arrived at the appointed time with a 100,000 goblin helpers, and together they set off with Shaktidevi to hang garlands on village gates.

The following morning, Karan sent his prime minister on a camel to determine the number of garlanded villages. The minister found that the first garland had been placed at Patadi at nine at night. Garlands had then been hung on all the 600 villages under its jurisdiction, and by four in the morning a total of 2000 villages had been garlanded. Amazed and alarmed by this unbelievable feat, the prime minister prepared a list of the villages and handed it to the raja. Karan's astonishment and rage can only be imagined. Two thousand villages! Must he give 2000 villages as a reward for expelling Babrobhoot? Why, Keshav's death had not cost him even two cowries, and now must he pay such an exorbitant price to get rid of his ghost? No king of Gujarat had ever granted so much land to an individual. He could not think of a single ruler who had paid such a price even to save his own life. Yet, thought Karan, I am bound by my promise; I have given my word, and the word of a king can never be broken. Besides, I can take some consolation from the fact that Harpal is, after all, my cousin. I must accept the situation, come what may. And to tell the truth, my days are out of joint; my stars are ill-favoured and evil times are at hand. Enough; there is nothing to be gained by thinking such thoughts; I must seal the reward deed.

When Karan went to Phoolrani's palace that evening, the queen was disturbed to find the king in low spirits. No longer in the clutches of Babrobhoot, she was in a cheerful mood and was looking forward to spending an enjoyable time with her husband, but Karan's expression was like cold water poured over her mood. Phoolrani attempted to discover the cause of her husband's unhappiness, but for the longest time he refused to confide in her. However, men are often helpless against the obstinacy of women, and so it proved with Karan. Despite himself, he felt obliged to confess to his wife the real cause of his sorrow. Phoolrani was shocked when she heard the story; but Rajput women are well known for their intelligence and quick-wittedness, and a possible way out of the situation immediately occurred to her. 'My lord,' she said, 'don't worry. I happen to be a distant relative of Harpal's, and he regards me as his sister. When the Raksha Bandhan festival comes around, I will tie a rakhi around his wrist, and in return ask him for several of the villages as a gift.' Karan's mood brightened when he heard of this plan, but then he remembered that Harpal was due to leave for Patadi the very next day and did not plan to return to Patan. Phoolrani told him not to worry about that either. Summoning a servant, she ordered her carriage to be made ready, and left forthwith to meet Harpal.

Harpal was still awake when Phoolrani reached his house and she was able to meet him right away. After the usual preliminaries, she thanked him profusely for ridding her of Babrobhoot and ending the torment he had caused her. A short while later, when the conversation came around to Harpal's departure for Patadi the next morning, Phoolrani said, 'Brother, you will leave, but who will have a care for me when you are gone? You know well that both my father and my mother are dead. You are the sole paternal relative I have left in the world, and if you desert me, who is there to take on the familial responsibilities you owe me? Who will look after my interests? So brother, make some provision for me before you go, and leave something behind for my needs.' Harpal felt trapped when he heard this request, but he knew that there was no escape. What option did he have? He had always regarded Phoolrani as his sister and there was no way he could disavow the relationship now. How could he deny her just request? Steeling himself, he fetched paper and writing materials and made over 500 villages in the district of Bhal to Phoolrani. She accepted the deed, and soon returned home.

The recovery of 500 of the 2000 villages was certainly a cause for celebration; even so, the loss of 1500 was no trifling matter. However, since nothing further could be done about this, Karan resigned himself to the loss and spent a pleasant night with his queen.

Meanwhile, Harpal and Shakti were busy discussing what to do with Babrobhoot. Babro had threatened to destroy them if he was left idle, and they tried to think of some unending task they could give him before they left for Patadi. Finally, Shakti had an idea. She asked Harpal to summon Babro, and when the bhoot appeared, she ordered him to fetch a long bamboo cane. The cane was planted in the earth and Babro was told to climb up the pole and then down again, up and down, over and over, and only when he had finished this job was he to ask for something else to do. The problem of Babrobhoot was thus resolved.

———

A month passed. Karan Raja had nothing special with which to occupy himself and his days were spent in idleness. His mind was in a heightened state of excitement and his thoughts began to affect his mood. As he recalled his actions during the brief period of his rule, regret wormed its way into his heart and began to slowly eat away at it. Food, drink, his usual pastimes—nothing gave him any joy; he could no longer sleep at night, and if by chance he fell into a broken, uneasy slumber, terrifying dreams would shatter both rest and peace of mind. The spirits of the dead women he had accosted that fateful Dussera night, the promise he had made to them, the advice they had given him, the sight of Gunsundari as she went to her death, the curse she had called down at the gateway of the town in front of all the townspeople, the screams from the funeral pyre he had heard in his imagination, the possession of Phoolrani by Keshav's ghost, Babrobhoot, the chaos the bhoot had wreaked on the town— all day and night these thoughts replayed endlessly in his mind. In the dead of the night, unable to sleep, his mind in turmoil, half awake, Karan would see Keshav and Gunsundari standing before him, their accusing voices striking like hammers on his brain, and he would break into a sweat and his body would turn deathly cold. The unbearable weight of regret and sorrow that he bore in his waking hours can hardly be described, but it soon took a toll on both his body and mind. His once strong body began to waste away. His once ruddy complexion became pale. His cheeks turned hollow and his eyes sank deep into their sockets. An anxious expression replaced his formerly open, smiling countenance, and he seemed to be continually lost in thought. His queens tried to arouse him from his melancholy, but lovemaking, womanly wiles and other distractions proved in vain. And as for Roopsundari, for whom Karan had brought such sorrow on himself, for whom he had borne the burden of disgrace and endangered both himself and his kingdom; the Roopsundari for whom he had consigned his soul into a pit of endless misery and, for a moment of ephemeral pleasure in this transient world, had surrendered the chance of gaining the highest, everlasting, limitless bliss in the world beyond—even she lay neglected, and far from savouring the pleasures of this ethereal nymph, now the very sight of her beautiful face, nay, the merest thought of her, was a cause of bitter remorse. Woe is you, Roopsundari! The happy vistas that Karan spread before you, the promises to make you his chief queen, have burst like a bubble. You have been abandoned by the king, and you count for nothing in the palace.

How fickle and wavering is the mind of a man! Until something he wants is within his grasp, he cannot stop hankering after it. He is ready to sell body and soul to acquire it; he plans what he will do with the object of desire once it is his; he wonders how he can possibly live another day without it and is amazed that he managed to do without it for so long. But the moment the object is his, it seems worthless, its value dwindling like a thin trickle of water, and what looked like a diamond from afar seems like a piece of glass, no better than a bauble. Like a child crying for a toy, only to put it down and pick up something else, a man's craving mind moves from the object attained to something new. His entire life is thus spent in futile pursuit, and the precious opportunity for seeking true happiness with which only humans are blessed recedes like a phantom flame.

Thus it was with Karan Raja. He was not yet aware of the storms and darkness that were heading his way, but his present misery was so intense that he lost all interest in life, and as he no longer had the will to confront his problems, he wondered if he should do what many rulers before him had done—renounce the world and go to some secluded holy spot where he could forget his cares and live out his days in devotion to God. But Karan was not yet free from the attractions of life or totally weary of the world. The desire to rule his kingdom and the longing for sensual pleasure was still strong. He persuaded himself that his present sorrows would soon pass, that happiness lay ahead, that the dark thoughts that clouded his mind would disperse, and brighter days would follow. His hopes were encouraged by soothsayers. Astrologers thronged to the palace, where they made so much money that many brahmins and ascetics put aside other subjects of study and concentrated on acquiring at least a smattering of astrology. Karan's horoscope was examined so often and had passed through so many hands that it was in tatters, and although no scholar would have set the slightest store by it, astrologers examining it with selfish spectacles discovered in the scraps wealth equal to that of Kuber's hoards, generosity like Karna's, the benevolence of Vikram, the integrity of Yudhishthir, the strength of Bheem and the heroism of Arjun. When someone is told the same tale again and again, it is not surprising that he believes it to be true. We know from experience that many reports become 'true' by virtue of constant repetition, and for someone who has implicit faith in the predictions of astrology, such reports are easy to accept. Besides, it is so much easier to accept opinions that one would like to hear than those that are inconvenient or unpalatable. Karan Raja accepted the words of the soothsayers and putting his trust in their predictions comforted himself with false hope. Like an exhausted and thirsty traveller who pursues a mirage, he was determined to walk calmly along the path of life.

But the worm of regret continued to eat away at Karan's heart, and the fire of his evil deeds raged through his body. The soothsayers had no remedy for this. They dealt in the future— they were not concerned with the present—and to deal with his current difficulties Karan had to turn to others. Now Puranic scholars came daily to the palace to console the king with tales of ancient monarchs who had overcome great misfortune and lived to see happier days. Brahmins learned in the Vedas recited verses, assuring Karan that the very sound of the sacred mantras would burn away his most heinous sins as easily as dry bamboo and restore his soul to purity. In exchange for large fees, pundits versed in the shastras explained the penances necessary to expiate different sins, including that of brahmanicide, and persuaded the king to undertake them. The king distributed cows, land and other gifts to all the brahmins. But when their measures failed to have the desired effect, his faith in religious remedies gradually diminished. Sensing that the good times were over, perhaps never to return, the brahmins became anxious. Finally, a group of their elders approached the king and enumerating the various holy sites and pilgrimage spots mentioned in the shastras, described the importance of each at length. They then said, 'Sites such as Kashi, Gaya and Prayag are located too far away for you to undertake a pilgrimage to them, O King. But close by, in our own kingdom, along the Saraswati river, is the auspicious site of Shristhala (Siddhapur). If you go there and bathe in the waters of the Saraswati, perform the prescribed penances, and visit the shrine of Rudra Mahakala, not only will your body be purified, not only will you obtain the wherewithal for liberation, even the poisonous thoughts that are causing such turmoil in your mind will be subdued and weakened. No harm can come to the kingdom if you go away for a short while. So take our advice and go on a pilgrimage to Shristhala. The rewards of being in the presence of the sacred are immense, but even apart from that, a change of scene will have a beneficial effect on your mind. Pilgrims who have heard of the power of holy sites and visit them with the conviction that their sins will be washed away, are never disappointed.

'Imagination can play tricks on the mind and body. A vivid imagination can make one see what does not exist, and hear what is not there. One's senses are dulled, and all kinds of superstitions and false ideas float in the mind. Imagination can lead to madness; it can make one live in a dream world that is removed from reality. So go to Shristhala with full faith in its sacred power—your very faith will bring you peace. Besides, visiting a new place has its own benefits. If those who are physically ill improve from a change of scene, why should the sorrows of the mind not be similarly removed? Those who are weighed down by remorse are bound to benefit by visiting a new place.

'Our experiences of the external world are imprinted as images in the storehouse of memory. But each image is wrapped up in a particular context, either happy or painful. When we retrieve an image from our memory, the associations surrounding it also come rushing out. When one thinks of one's own country when far from home, thoughts of one's parents, relations, acquaintances and friends, one's childhood and its joys, youth and its pleasures also come tumbling out, and some of these thoughts cause joy and others are painful. If a person who has committed murder remains close to the scene of the crime, terrible thoughts are bound to occupy his mind and he will never be at peace. If, on the contrary, he goes to some other place, his mind will be filled with new impressions and experiences, making it difficult for the suppressed thoughts to rise to the surface, and only rarely will he be tormented by them. As more and more new impressions fill his mind, their weight will push down the troublesome thoughts deeper still, and as a result he will become calm and tranquil.

'Besides, the pilgrimage sites chosen by the rishis of yore are places of breathtaking beauty. Many important ancient sites are situated along the course of great rivers. Rivers are truly a wonder of nature. It is amazing how rainwater that collects in some hollow on a mountain overflows and gradually becomes a

133

river that supports the lives of thousands of human beings and beasts. A river not only provides water to the towns lying along its banks and to the surrounding fields, it also serves as a place where Hindus, especially brahmins, can perform religious rites. Rivers wide enough for large ships allow trade to flourish, and prosperity increases as the specialties and surplus produce of one area are sent to another. Standing at a river bank, watching people bathing, women filling water or washing clothes, brahmins engaged in their daily rituals, the wind raising little ripples on the placid, glass-like surface of the water, the trees on the farther bank, boats and sailing ships bobbing effortlessly—a man is enveloped in tranquillity and memories of the past flow through his mind.

'A man's childhood is like a river which emerges as a trickle from the mountainside, making its playful way over pebbles and flower-filled meadows. And as the river flows onwards, to be joined by other streams, so a man's life becomes intertwined with many relationships as he grows older. When in full flow, the river's usefulness increases and it supplies the things that men both need and desire. In the same way, a man in the prime of life is a support to others and shoulders heavy burdens. And just as the river finally empties itself into the boundless ocean, so when this life ends, a man becomes one with the Infinite. This is why when standing near this wondrous creation of God, the man's thoughts turn to the meaning of life and he becomes aware of his own insignificance.

'Many pilgrimage spots are also to be found in the midst of thick forests empty of human habitation, surrounded by majestic mountains. Who could fail to be awed by their beauty? Face-to-face with the open-handed generosity of God, in a place where his own puny and ephemeral achievements seem laughable before the prodigious works of the Creator, in a place so hallowed and filled with His sacredness that the very idea of a sinful act seems impossible, a place which serves as a model on which primitive folk have created their vision of heaven—it is not surprising that in such a place a man realizes his insignificance and paltriness, and understands that there exists a Power far greater than his own; and with this realization, surrenders himself to that Power in all humility, and sings its praises, fully trusting that whatever happens is in accordance with the will of the divine.'

These words made such an impression on Karan Raja that he ordered arrangements for a pilgrimage to Siddhapur to be made immediately. A couple of days later, accompanied by a few retainers, and with minimum fuss, the king started out. There were a large number of Shaivite as well as Jain shrines at Siddhapur. Pennants stood atop the Shaivite shrines; but some years previously, the Jains had been forbidden to raise flags on theirs.[6] However, after Madhav's companion, the Jain merchant Motisha, had returned from Delhi, his support of the Jain cause and his quiet manoeuverings meant that flags had once more appeared on Jain shrines. The brahmins had complained to the king, but thanks to Motisha's cunning, their efforts had failed. Now the king himself had come to Siddhapur, and the brahmins grasped the opportunity that opened before them—unless Karan Raja ordered the flags on the Jain shrines to be removed, they would refuse to perform any rituals for him, even if he offered them 125 gold mohurs. The next morning, after the king had bathed in the Saraswati, he summoned the leading brahmins of the town so that the purificatory rituals could begin. But the brahmins told him in no uncertain terms that in a land ruled over by a Shaivite monarch, not only had the Jains ignored orders prohibiting the use of flags on their shrines, but the brahmins' complaint had been dismissed by the king on the advice of his Jain minister. Hence, unless the king granted their request, not a single brahmin would perform any rituals for him.

The enraged king dismissed the brahmins and informed Motisha of what had transpired. Motisha felt that this was the right moment to put pressure on the brahmins and to curtail their rights over temple affairs. He also tried to recruit Karan into the Jain fold and invited learned Jain munis from all over the kingdom to come to Siddhapur, where they put forward arguments, compared the two faiths and tried their hardest to persuade the king to join the path of Adinatha. But the king had little interest in religion, and the one-sided discussion had no effect on him. Fed up with the importuning of the munis, Karan suggested that a debate be held between the proponents of the two religions. Invitations were sent out to the brahmins in the town, and a large number of brahmins and Jain munis gathered together on the appointed day. The king sat on a raised throne, Motisha and other senior officials sat in a row facing him, and Karan's own men and invitees from Siddhapur stood behind them. The debate was begun by one of the Jain munis. 'Do any of you recall what happened in the reign of Kumarapala?' he asked. 'If you don't, I can recount the events to you.' Getting no reply from the brahmins, the muni continued.

'One day, when Raja Kumarapala was passing through the marketplace in his palanquin, he came across a pupil of the great Jain teacher Hemacharya and asked him if he knew what *tithi* it was that day. It was actually *amavasya* but the student mistakenly said that it was *poonam*, the night of the full moon. Overhearing this, some brahmins standing nearby burst out laughing. "What can you expect from a baldy?" they mocked. "It is amavasya, there will be no moon tonight." When Kumarapala returned to the palace, he sent his servants to fetch Hemacharya from his monastery. Before leaving, Hemacharya asked his shamefaced student what had happened and when he had heard the whole story, he told the boy not to worry. Then Hemacharya went to the king's palace where the brahmins were waiting. Once again the king asked, "What tithi is it today?" "It is amavasya," chorused the brahmins. "It is poonam," said Hemacharya. "Well," said the brahmins, "the matter will be settled at night. If it is poonam we will see the full moon, in which case we brahmins will leave the kingdom, but if the moon does not rise, then the Jains must be banished." Hemacharya agreed to this proposal and returned to the monastery. There was a particular goddess that he worshipped, and he now sought her aid. The devi created an illusion so that it seemed as if the full moon was indeed in the sky that night. The brahmins lost the wager and were ordered to leave the kingdom.'

To this account a brahmin retorted, 'You have told us how this episode began, why not tell us how it ended? However, if you are not comfortable doing so, I will recount the facts to this gathering.

'Faced with the threat of expulsion, the brahmins requested the renowned teacher Devbodhiacharya to come to Patan that very night. The following morning, when the king gave the formal order of expulsion, Devbodhi stepped forward and said, "What need is there to expel anyone from the kingdom? At nine o'clock, the great ocean will breach its bounds and engulf the entire land." Summoning Hemacharya, the king asked him whether the brahmin's prediction was correct. Hemacharya replied that there would be no such deluge: the world could not come to an end, because it had no beginning. "Let us set up a clock," Devbodhi said, "and see what happens." So a clock was set up and the three men sat around it. As the hour approached, they went up to the first floor of the palace, and when they looked out towards the west, they saw that the waves of the ocean were gathering speed. On they came, faster and faster, swallowing up houses as they advanced. The king and his two companions went up to the next floor, but the higher they climbed, so did the water; and when they finally reached the topmost, that is the seventh floor, they found that the entire town, the tallest trees, and the spires of the biggest temples had all been submerged, and there was nothing to be seen but a vast expanse of water. The terrified king turned to Devbodhi and asked whether there was any way of escape.

137

Devbodhi told him that a ship would come from the west and pass by the window where they stood. Whoever managed to jump into it would be saved. As the three men made ready to leap, they saw a boat coming their way. Devbodhi grabbed hold of the king's hand and said that he would help the king jump to safety. But as the boat approached and the king was about to jump, Devbodhi pulled him back sharply. Hemacharya leapt out of the window—only to fall to his death seven floors below, for the flood and the boat were nothing but a mirage. After this, Kumarapala ordered all Hemacharya's followers to be killed, and the king became a follower of Devbodhi.'

Once he had heard the arguments of both sects, Karan Raja said, 'Both sides are well matched. But Devbodhi's feats and superior wizardry surpass those of Hemacharya.' Then one of the brahmins said, 'Originally, one true religion prevailed in the world. The Vedas are eternal; whatever is written in them cannot be faulted by humans. Because their hidden truths are hard to grasp, great rishis wrote treatises and critical commentaries on them. Based on their teachings, the six shastras codified the rules governing man's duty and conduct. The first *Mimansa*, that is the *Purvamimansa*, was written by Jaimini, in which it is stated that the performance of Vedic rituals such as sacrifice are the path to salvation. The *Uttarmimansa* of Vyasa is a philosophical treatise. Gautama wrote the *Nyayashastra* on law. Kanad's *Tarkashastra* describes how the world was willed and created from atoms by God. The two final shastras, Kapilmuni's *Nirishvari* and Patanjali's *Ishvari* are known as *Sankhyashastras*. Of these six shastras, Gautama's and Kanad's adopt a materialistic standpoint. Kapila denies the existence of God, and according to Patanjali the universe is uncreated. Buddha wanted to reform the Hindu faith, but in order to leave his mark on the world, he propagated a new religion. Having studied the theory of an uncreated universe and the materialistic teachings of the Sankhya school, he went on to propagate the idea that there is no God. His teachings attracted so many followers throughout the length and breadth of Hindustan that for a while it was feared that Vedic dharma would be wiped out. At this time of crisis, God sent Kumaril Bhattacharya, Udayanacharya and Shankaracharya to the earth. They travelled across the whole country, debated with leading Buddhist scholars and completely destroyed their claims. Udayanacharya's arguments were recorded in a book that is available even today. He revived the Hindu faith. The Jain faith was established some years after Buddhism. The two faiths differ in certain respects, but there is no point in going into details at this time. However, I will try and describe, to the best of my abilities, the differences between Jainism and Hinduism.

'The Jains believe that God does not exist, or if he does, he is not capable of guiding the world. They believe that the universe is eternal. They regard their monks as worthy of worship. They go to great lengths to avoid harming any living creature. The lineage of their munis is not hereditary. The Jains do not believe in the revealed truths of the Vedas; they do not offer sacrifices or acknowledge the sanctity of fire. Instead they believe that to practise meditation with a mind that is still and focused is the highest bliss. Like Hindus, the Jains too, have caste distinctions. Although they deny that the Vedas are the foundation of their faith, they respect many Vedic teachings that are not contrary to their own beliefs. Their main quarrel with the Vedas is that they demand animal sacrifice; and they say that even other kinds of sacrifices cannot be performed without the unintentional taking of life. The Jains accept all Hindu gods and even worship some of them, but they consider the gods inferior to their own munis, whom they greatly revere. They believe that the munis have reached a higher spiritual plane than the gods. The munis are called tirthankars. Twenty-four belong to this yuga, twenty-four to the age gone before, and twenty-four to the age to come. The first tirthankar, Rishabh, is greatly revered, but it is Parshvanath and Mahavir, the last two, who are accorded the highest status. In the Jain texts many facts about the Hindu pantheon and the status of various gods have been altered. Certain gods are not recognized, and changes have been made to the number of divinities, for example by speaking of sixty-four Indras and twenty-two Devis.'

To this speech, a Jain monk replied, 'This is all very well, but the main difference between our two faiths is that you believe that the world was created by God at a particular moment in time, while we believe that it was never created and that matter is without beginning or end. Which of these views is correct remains to be decided. It is assumed generally that whatever exists must have an efficient cause. On seeing a stone statue one is certain that it was made by someone at some time. If one comes across a ruined dwelling in some desolate place, one infers that it was built by someone, and that the place was inhabited in the past. People are willing to grant that the chance coming together of different elements results in the creation of new substances, that when water is added to clay and other materials a variety of new and useful minerals are formed; but when they see complex objects whose composition they cannot understand, they find it difficult to believe that such objects emerged out of nowhere, without being created. When people see things that have clearly been made for a specific purpose—a building with many different types of rooms or a boat capable of sailing the ocean—they infer that not only were such objects designed by someone, but that their designer must be endowed with intelligence. In the same way, the complex human body, the structure of birds, and other objects in the world seem to hint that they, too, are the products of an intelligent Creator—but such inferences are based on the incomplete knowledge we have of the world. In truth, man cannot create matter. He can only modify or amalgamate it. We cannot assert that the atoms out of which complex substances are composed are the work of a Creator. Nor can we state that substances are the result of a spontaneous mixture of atoms. We have only partial knowledge of the nature of substances, so it is foolish to assert that a particular substance does not have this or that quality. For example, consider the quality of intelligence. It is assumed that intelligence is required for the formation of complex substances—which appears to indicate the hand of a Creator. We would have to admit this possibility if we were certain that intelligence does not inhere in matter. But there are three major objections against such reasoning.

'Firstly, nothing can be created from nothing. Those who believe that the world was created at some point in time must necessarily admit that prior to this moment there was only the void. Then how did the material world arise? How was it created out of nothing? This is impossible. Secondly, God is eternal, so what was He doing before He created the world? Was He sitting idle? Why did He feel the need to embark on creation at some particular moment? Why did this task not occur to Him earlier? No one has ever explained why the Creator finally found it necessary to begin the work of creation. Thirdly, matter cannot be destroyed. To say that a substance is destructible is incorrect. When we say that something is destroyed, it is really only in a state of transformation. When coal is burnt, some part turns to ashes, some rises in the form of smoke, some becomes vapour and the rest escapes into the atmosphere in a gaseous state. If we weigh all these substances together, we will find that they equal the weight of the original coal. Thus when coal is burnt, it is not destroyed; it merely changes form, and many of the particles simply occupy another place in a different form. Similarly, all matter is indestructible; and the world will never end. Its form may change, objects may break up into smaller parts—but the total matter in the world is not diminished. Thus if there is good reason to believe that the material world cannot have an end, then similarly, it cannot have a beginning. For these three reasons one must accept that matter is permanent. You cannot accept both: that the world has been created, and that the Creator is eternal; and if one accepts that the Creator is eternal, what difficulty is there in accepting that matter, too, is eternal? The only difficulty is that we have been conditioned from an early age into thinking that God has created the world, and that He is uncreated. But if we accept that the world is uncreated there is no room for confusion, and life becomes more meaningful.'

The brahmin found these arguments incredible, and wondered how anyone with a capacity for rational thought could use them to propagate the evil and unnatural view that God is absent from the world. He said, 'The three arguments that you put forward are so flimsy as to be worthless. It is true that the world cannot be created out of nothing. But God's power is infinite and we, with our limited intelligence, cannot grasp it; we cannot even imagine it. God can will phenomenal existence out of the void, even though our understanding is too limited and petty to grasp this. Secondly, what the Creator was doing in the endless time before creation is not only impossible to determine, it is also irrelevant. No doubt He created the world when He thought the time was right. But just because one is ignorant about these matters it would be foolish to conclude that there is no Creator. Thirdly, even if matter is indestructible, it does not follow that it is uncreated. No other religion apart from yours denies the existence of God, and all believe that He is the Creator of the world. His existence is proclaimed loud and clear throughout the world, and is engraved in the hearts of all men. The soft winds that blow across the land and the cyclones and storms that uproot houses and trees and wreak devastation, both proclaim the existence of God so surely that even the deaf cannot fail to hear. The birds that sing the praises of the Creator, the torrents of the rivers and the crashing of the waves drive home His presence. The miraculous heat of the sun that sustains life on earth, the cool light of the moon and the soft glimmer of countless stars that ornament the night—they too reveal the existence of God. The high and terrifying mountains whose peaks graze the clouds and attract the moisture that keeps the earth verdant and fertile, point the way to His existence—in short, every single thing in the world is testimony to the One that created it. And to think that, despite this, there are evil-intentioned and thankless people who close their eyes and ears, wilfully misuse their capacity to think and reason, and proudly assert that there is no God, and that the world was created of itself. O shame! To what evil purpose has the mind been put!'

The Jain muni was vastly amused by this forceful speech and the attacks on the Jain faith, which were based on complete ignorance of its tenets. 'Sir!' he said, 'your rhetoric seems to have surpassed your understanding. I never opined on whether God exists or not. Right from the start what I argued was that matter is eternal, and that therefore, the phenomenal world is uncreated. I did not state that God does not exist. What I went on to say was that complex substances themselves hint at an intelligent cause, and what is called "God" is nothing but a personification of these qualities combined with self-consciousness or I-ness.

'According to our beliefs, this God is immanent and quiescent, and does not exert His will in any way on substances. Our God is not like your God, a busybody, poking his nose in everyone's business. You earn your living by misleading people in your God's name, and like parents who frighten their children by invoking the threat of their teacher, you extract money from people by invoking in them a fear of God. This is the only difference between our two faiths. So now you must take back your words.'

The brahmin was unfazed by this reasoning. Instead he replied calmly, 'Whether one believes in your God or not makes no difference. Of what use is a teacher who neither punishes nor instructs? What good is your kind of God in the world we live in?

143

The world is constituted in such a way that its orderly progress is possible only when everyone follows God's law. But to follow the religious path is difficult and the temptation to deviate from it is great, since breaking the moral law often leads to immediate gain; and so with a God like yours, what inducement is there to lead a moral life at the expense of present pleasure? In this world of ours, good deeds are not necessarily rewarded and evil deeds often go unpunished, so unless there is the prospect that God will reward the good and the fear that He will punish the wicked, virtuous actions will be infrequent, evil will strengthen its hold, and the world will quickly come to destruction. Hence the fear of God is necessary. Moreover, when difficulties arise, when a person's body is wracked by disease, or his fondest hopes are shattered, when a loved one passes on, what brings him consolation? How is he comforted? Only by faith in God. Faith in God is a shield. It protects against the mortal blows of misfortune. It is a rock in the middle of a vast ocean, unmoved even when buffeted by rough and stormy waves. Without faith in a power superior to himself, man's sorrow would have no bounds. There is much to be gained by having a God who, as you put it, is a busybody, poking His nose into everyone's affairs; but to expound on this would take the entire day, so I will stop now.

'But I will take up one more point about your religion. That the taking of life is a great sin is something in which we too believe. But you carry this belief too far. You sweep the floor before you sit down, you cover your mouths before you speak—these, and the other ridiculous steps you take to avoid harming life, are mere pretence. You think nothing of killing people in the name of your religion, while taking a hundred precautions to save irrelevant insects. You surely know that the world teems with life. The air we breathe is filled with countless living things, and countless creatures live in the soil, and no matter what kind of cloth we use to cover our mouths, no matter how thoroughly we sweep the floor, thousands of living things enter our bodies through our breath, and thousands if not hundreds of thousands of tiny insects are squashed when we sit on the ground. This is not something we can control. We have not been given eyes sharp enough to see these minute creatures; so what is the point of all this show?'

As the debate continued and showed no signs of ending, Karan Raja interrupted, 'That's enough. Listening to all this bickering has given me a headache, and I do not wish to hear more. God has chosen to have me born a Shaivite, and I will observe that faith. I have no need for the Jain religion. There is truth in all religions. It is enough if one sincerely follows the faith that one is born into. Many different roads may lead to a town—some are long, some short; some difficult, some easy—but eventually, they all lead you to the same place. A woman once cast a spell on her husband and turned him into a bullock. The bullock grazed on some plants nearby and was transformed into a man once again. The bullock had no idea about the properties of the plant when he ate it, but he enjoyed its benefits nevertheless. We may not understand the deeper meanings of our religion but, like the bullock, we can also benefit by following it. The discussion is now closed. All of you may return to your homes.'

Unhappy and disappointed because their efforts had failed and their persuasive arguments had had no effect, the Jain munis left the palace grumbling about the dull-witted king. Motisha's bravado deserted him, and lamenting the foolishness of the munis, he too went home. The brahmins were overjoyed. The king ordered the flags on the Jain shrines to be removed and thus succeeded in restoring the goodwill of the majority of his subjects at this critical juncture. He gave generous gifts to the brahmins and persuaded them to perform the purificatory rituals. He then started on foot to visit the Rudra Mahakaleshwar shrine.

Along the way, the king encountered a large crowd gathered outside a house, and on enquiring what the matter was, he was told that the house belonged to a bania who, in order to meet the expenses for his son's wedding, had borrowed 2000 rupees from the banker Jethasha. Aware that the bania had a taste for the good things of life and was already heavily in debt, Jethasha had been reluctant to lend the money. But the bania's son's wedding was at hand, and expenses had to be incurred in keeping with the family's status, so he had looked around for someone reliable to stand guarantor for the loan. As nobody was willing to come to the bankrupt's aid, he finally approached a bard.[7] Now, when it comes to matters of money, bards are known for their reliability; besides, they have a way of recovering debts by one way or another, so when the bard agreed to stand surety for the bania, Jethasha lent him the money.

The marriage of the bania's son was celebrated with much pomp and fanfare, a lavish banquet was provided for the entire clan, gifts were distributed—and the 2000 rupees evaporated. The interest on the loan kept growing, but the bania was unconcerned, as he had no intention of repaying it. After a few years, the 2000 became 4000. Jethasha knew he would never be able to recover a sum larger than this so he filed a complaint, and since the bania was unable to pay, Jethasha recovered the entire amount from the bard.

It now remained for the bard to recover the sum from the bania. He pressed the bania for his dues day in and day out, but to what purpose? The bania did not have the money, and finally he flatly refused to pay. Bards generally do not lodge complaints about debt in the courts, and this bard too, did not do so. But even if he had, what could he have recovered from the bania? Instead, the bard sat down in front of the bania's house, and for three days refused to eat or drink and forced the bania to fast as well. The residents of the mohalla, apprehensive lest the bard die and give the neighbourhood a bad name, organized a collection in the area, put together 3000 rupees, and told the bania to give the sum to the bard. But the bania refused to budge. Neither would he give the money nor allow anyone else to do so. The helpless neighbours conveyed this message to the bard. The bard then brought his eighty-year-old mother to the spot and cut off her head with one blow of his sword. Still the bania remained adamant. Then the bard asked for his own son, a twelve-year-old boy and his only child, to be brought to him, and thrusting a dagger into his stomach, killed him. Collecting the flowing blood in cupped palms, he splashed it over the bania crying, 'Arre chandal! Here, take this offering! And as my lineage has ended, so may yours; may your married son die in the same manner; may destiny deal you blow after crushing blow; and may you die a slow lingering death.' The onlookers were terrified, but the stony heart of the bania was untouched.

It was just as the bard was about to kill himself that Karan Raja arrived on the scene. When the bard saw the king, he begged him to intervene, but Karan paid no heed. Maddened with rage, the bard hurled himself into the bania's house and within seconds dragged out the bleeding bodies of the bania and his blameless young son, flung them on the ground, and thrust the dagger into his own body. It all happened so fast that no one had time to intervene. Everyone just stood stupefied. The bania and his son died instantly, but the bard did not. As he thrashed about in the throes of mental and physical agony, his body flailing, his restlessly roving eyes fell on the king, and maddened him even further. Focusing all his remaining rage on Karan he said, 'O wicked king! The sin of killing a bard is even greater than that of killing a brahmin. You stood by and watched one of your own subjects die! Fie on your kshatriya honour! May your kingdom burn! You, a Rajput, could not save the life of an innocent bard! May the blood of all those who have died today be upon you!

The purpose for which you have come here will not be fulfilled. You are doomed to wander this earth homeless. Your people will desert you, and you will die alone, unremembered and unsung.' With these words, the bard fell down dead, and his soul was left to petition the final court against the bania and his unpaid debt.

Hearing the bard's curses, the king fell to the ground in a dead faint. His attendants carried him back to the palace. After he regained consciousness, the brahmins by his bedside dug up some rituals from the scriptures which would nullify the bard's curses and promised to perform them. This calmed Karan's agitation somewhat, but just then a messenger from Patan burst into the room and without pausing to take a breath said, 'Rajadhiraj! Word has come in from all over that a huge Turkish army is at the border, preparing to conquer all of Gujarat. With them is our former prime minister, Madhav. They have already attacked several villages and people are fleeing in panic.' The very thought that a Turkish force was planning to conquer Gujarat and that a major confrontation was inevitable made Karan's kshatriya blood boil, and with immense courage he spoke. 'Those mlechhas must be destined to be buried in the soil of Gujarat, which is why fate has lured them here. I have not yet donned a woman's bodice; the Rajputs have not yet forsaken their valour; and there are as yet brave men in our land. The king of Gujarat does not lack an army and we have many impregnable forts—so let the invaders come. I am not afraid, my hands are itching to kill the enemy, my sword is maddened with thirst and eager to draw blood. The time has come. I will show my mettle on the battlefield. Had things not transpired in this manner, I would have been forgotten. It is for the best. Make ready to march tomorrow. We will return to Patan and prepare for war.'

9

Allauddin's army lay encamped on the outskirts of Gujarat. The size of the army and the eminence of its commander reflected the importance of the task ahead. A hundred thousand horses, 1500 elephants, 20,000 infantrymen, and forty-five of the finest officers had gathered here. It had been decided that Alafkhan, the general commanding the forces and brother of Allauddin, would become the governor of Gujarat. Madhav would take over the reins of the administration; while Nusratkhan, the king's vazir, at present accompanying the army, would return to Delhi. The camp resembled a large city. Apart from the soldiers, it was populated with wives, children, shopkeepers, servants and other hangers-on. There were, in addition, lakhs of elephants, horses and camels meant for battle as well as for carrying provisions. Instead of houses there were tents of all sizes and shapes which could be rolled up and transported easily. The tents of the generals and nobles were made of expensive material covered with gold and silver embroidery. Markets had been set up at various places at which shopkeepers sold their wares. There was ceaseless activity in the camp and at night it was ablaze with naked torches. As the night progressed, most of the lights were extinguished; only the braziers on the outskirts of the camp around which soldiers kept watch remained burning.

In one of the splendid *zari*-embellished tents clustered in the centre of the camp, three men sat in deep thought. They were studying the geography of the terrain leading to Patan, and marking the route to the capital and the various villages and rivers along the way. Madhav had sent spies to the leading feudatories of Gujarat and the other chieftains in an attempt to turn them against Karan with promises of future rewards. He sent assurances that the Muslim armies would return home once Karan had been deposed or killed, and that as prime minister under the new ruler, he would reward all those who had sided with him. These attempts had not proved entirely successful. Only 360 cavalrymen had gone over to Madhav. However, neither Madhav nor Alafkhan were disheartened. Despite Madhav's best efforts, they had not depended on local support and had assembled a large well-equipped army. Everyone had his own reasons to wish for victory. Alafkhan wanted to increase the size of his brother's kingdom and hoped that some day he might rule it. Nusratkhan hoped that if the vast and fertile kingdom of Gujarat could be won through his courage and skilful diplomacy, he would secure Allauddin's favour and increase his power and prestige so that at some future time of political turmoil he might even be able to snatch the throne for himself. Madhav's main aim was to take revenge against Karan, and end his sway over Gujarat: Karan must either be deposed or killed in battle. He cared little about who would finally ascend the throne just so long as this goal was achieved. He was in good spirits that night as he anticipated a rosy future with himself as prime minister.

As the camp was to be dismantled the next day, Alafkhan, Nusratkhan and Madhav sat in consultation far into the night.

Alafkhan spoke, 'Madhavji, what do you think is the strength of Karan Raja's army? Will we face obstacles on the way to Patan? Will the king come forward to do battle or will he remain behind the closed gates of his city and keep us waiting? You are familiar with the king's tactics, the strength of the fort, the valour of the people and the effectiveness of his army, and are best suited to advise us regarding such matters.'

Madhav replied, 'Though Karan Raja is my sworn enemy and has utterly ruined me, I cannot accuse him of cowardice. Rajputs are reputed for their valour and Karan is no exception. Fear does not enter his vocabulary; he does not recognize it. He delights in battle and even though he has yet to prove his mettle and translate his boasts into deeds, yet when the time is ripe he will rise to the occasion and we, too, will be obliged to acknowledge his bravery. But praise be to God! He is more daring than is good for him. When our armies reach the outskirts of Patan, he will be so eager to plunge into war that he will abandon the impregnable fortress of Patan and face us on the open battlefield, saving us the task of besieging the fort. We will, therefore, not be held up outside the fort and will not suffer from shortages of food or drink; the outcome will be decided on the battlefield alone. If, by God's grace, we are victorious in battle, then the whole of Gujarat will be ours. In matters of warfare, Karan will not take anyone's advice. He will plunge headlong into the thick of battle and either die fighting or continue till he is mortally wounded. However, there are many wise and brave feudatories in Patan; and his bania minister is astute and level-headed. If the king listens to their advice he will wall himself up inside the fort. It is a formidable one and we do not have adequate equipment to capture it. It will be our misfortune if we are obliged to lay siege to every single fort in Gujarat; for then we will face an acute shortage of food and water. We will not be able to feed our vast army and many of our soldiers will die of starvation. The majority will become so disheartened that it will be practically impossible to persuade them to stay; and even if they remain, their hearts will not be in the fight. The local inhabitants as well as Karan's army will continue to harass our men and ultimately, we will be forced to make an ignominious retreat from Gujarat.

'Bear in mind the result of such an action. There is no knowing what Allauddin could do in a fit of impatient rage and frustration when faced with the failure of his plans, the colossal waste of men and money, the shame of losing for the first time, and the loss of face and prestige in the eyes of his feudatories, which in turn may lead to rebellions all across the kingdom, inspire unscrupulous nobles to aspire to the throne, and in the process jeopardize his life—and think what the consequences of this will be for us. But my intuition and limited experience tells me that this will not happen. Karan Raja is very stubborn and once he has made up his mind to prove his valour in battle, nothing on earth will change it. And the likelihood of victory is greater if we engage his forces in the battlefield. If Karan Raja can curb his impatience, he can muster a large and strong army of feudatory kings and their men. But we will not give him the time for this. We will quickly march to the gates of Patan and prevent the feudatories from mustering their forces. Karan is not going to wait for them. His confidence in himself is as great as his contempt for us and he will plunge into battle without waiting for their help. He already has the support of several chieftains who will bring their troops and together with his standing army the king will sally forth to war.

'As for the Rajput soldiers, there is no need for me to extol their bravery. Our soldiers have often fought against them. They are acquainted with their courage and their military tactics. On the other hand, Karan Raja is unlikely to garner the support of neighbouring kings. The raja of Devgadh, having been repeatedly harassed by our armies and tasted defeat, will not dare to raise his head against us. Moreover, he is a vassal of Emperor Allauddin and is duty bound to be on our side. The kings and princes of Udaipur, Jodhpur, Ajmer and other Rajpur rulers will not lift a finger to help their brethren. Unlike Prithviraj Chauhan, who was aided by Rajput princes when Mohammad Ghori laid siege to Delhi, Karan is not likely to be helped by the rajas of Mewar and Marwar with either men or money. These same rajas, in recent years, have been roundly defeated by the padshah; and the bitter taste of humiliation still lingers. They have experienced the strength of our forces and fear them greatly. They will not want to risk the padshah's displeasure by supporting Karan. Puffed with pride and supreme self-confidence, Karan will not deign to ask them for help; and even if he does, time is against him. If, for argument's sake, Karan was to win with their help, he would have to share the kudos for the victory. This would definitely displease him. He would rather fight alone than share fame and prestige with anyone else.

'The rest is up to God! The road to Patan is clear of obstacles. There are no strong forts or mountain ranges along the way. The land is flat for miles around. The towns on the route are large and prosperous; there is no dearth of food and water, so we will experience no hardship.'

Madhav's reassuring assessment of the situation put Alafkhan's mind at rest and as the night had far advanced, he gave Madhav permission to retire. The camp was shrouded in silence. Anticipating the long march and impending battle on the following day, most of the men had retired earlier than usual to get as much rest as possible. But here and there, across the camp, soldiers in small groups sat chatting amongst themselves around the lighted braziers. All the talk was centred around Gujarat, and the tone was boastful, for the men had won every encounter on the way. They harboured no doubts about the victorious outcome of the coming battle. The orthodox and fanatical fringe of the army prayed fervently for Gujarat to fall into the hands of the believers so that the infidel population could be turned towards the true path, the darkness removed from their minds by the bright rays of Islam, and the abominable idols and other diabolical handiworks of Satan be utterly destroyed. They had no doubt that to fulfil this holy purpose, Allah would weaken the infidels and make their own forces invincible. Yet, not all subscribed to this view. A vast majority had joined the army and left their families behind owing to abject poverty. They had one aim—to defeat and loot the enemy. All their thoughts revolved around money alone. Their dreams were filled with visions of the fabulous wealth of the king and the rich merchants of Gujarat. Even in their sleep they imagined plunging their hands into mounds of gold, silver and pearls, carrying back fistfuls to their lands, building mansions, buying slaves, swelling their harems and flaunting their wealth in every way.

Madhav made his way back to his tent in a dejected frame of mind. No matter how hard he tried, sleep evaded him. He thrashed about in his bed as scenes from his life unscrolled before his mind's eye. He remembered his parents, his childhood playmates, the dreams of his youth, and the castles he had built in the air. How innocent he was when he had first set foot in Patan! And now his mind was in turmoil, crowded by a stream of turbulent thoughts. The hope-filled days of his youth would never return. It seemed like only yesterday that he had come to Patan and accomplished his goal. He climbed the ladder of success, placed Karan on the throne and became his prime minister. Then the troubles had begun. His wife, Roopsundari, a true Padmini, was abducted by Karan, and in the skirmish that ensued, his younger brother Keshav lost his life trying to protect her. His sister-in-law Gunsundari committed sati, while he himself had slunk out of Patan like a common criminal and after many trials and tribulations, had finally reached Delhi. Madhav felt overwhelmed as he recalled the incident that had occurred in Delhi, his audience with the padshah, and the emperor's agreeing to conquer Gujarat.

Disturbed beyond endurance by his painful and conflicting thoughts, Madhav sobbed like a child. His success in persuading the Turks to invade his native land had slaked his thirst for vengeance, but in his heart of hearts he was deeply ashamed of this deed and repented it bitterly. A study of world history shows that Madhav was not alone in acting this way. In ancient times, Vortigern invited the Saxons from Germany to invade Britain, and Count Julian of Spain had welcomed the Muslim General Musa of Africa for the same reason as Madhav's. There are many more such examples of treachery prompted by the abduction of women, aimed at destroying the king under whose rule the wrong had been perpetrated, and delivering his land and people into the hands of outsiders. A man lays great store by his wife's chastity; great is his rage towards the one who violates her, and equally strong is his desire for vengeance. Yet revenge is invariably followed by repentance, and it is little wonder that Madhav, too, was overcome by remorse. Man's mind is so constituted that while in the grip of strong passion, his other faculties are weakened. They cannot assert themselves. But when passion loses its intensity, the suppressed feelings resurface and remorse sets in. This is what Madhav had experienced when he paced the steps of the Rudramal at Siddhapur on that dark night, his mind gripped by thoughts of revenge; but now that the time had come to put his cherished plan into action, more sober thoughts prevailed. Though pride in his country and religion had been pushed aside, it had not been completely destroyed. And now he was devastated by the thought that he had deliberately engineered the conquest of Gujarat, the suppression of its people, the supplanting of its lawful king by strangers, the enshacklement of his countrymen, the permanent enslavement of the land of his birth, of his youthful hopes and the fruition of his dreams; the land of his forefathers, his kith and kin, caste and clan, his friends and acquaintances; the land that he had once administered, whose people he had called his own and who in turn looked upon him as a father, and whose welfare and well-being he had considered his sacred dharma. The question of religion also caused him misgiving. Even though the Jains and the Shaivites were always at loggerheads, and in spite of the constant cat-and-mouse games they played, with the stronger side ever ready to plague the weaker opponent; even though the kings of Gujarat had often oppressed people whose opinions differed from their own and crushed dissent ruthlessly, ultimately they were all branches of the same tree. But now the Turks, staunch Muslims and sworn enemies of the Hindus, totally antagonistic towards Hindu beliefs and customs, were knocking at the doors of Gujarat. All idols—the Shivling, images of the Goddess, statues of Hindu deities, figures of Adinatha and Parshvanath—were equally anathema in their eyes. For them it was either the Koran or the sword, and compassion was limited to a choice between conversion or the jeziya tax. Hinduism would undoubtedly be attacked and perhaps some day would cease to exist. Temples would be turned into mosques; the sound of the bell and conch would be replaced by the call of the muezzin; the authority of the brahmins would pass to the mullahs and sayyeds; 'Ram' and 'Shiva' would be silenced and 'Allah' and the Prophet's name would be on the lips of men.

The religion in which a man is born and raised, the precepts which have been ingrained in him since childhood, his concept of the world, in short, the religion in which he has unshaken faith, is as precious to him as life itself. Any harm done to it is as wounding as a blow to the body. Often, a person is prepared not only to suffer great hardships for his faith, but thinks nothing of sacrificing his life for it. It is no surprise then that Madhav should have suffered the anguish of remorse. The thought that he was the cause of a devastating war, the rape of this beautiful and fertile land, the slaughter of its population, and the plunder of the hard-earned and carefully husbanded wealth of its people, tormented him, and guilt made sleep impossible.

At the break of day, the Turkish camp was a flurry of activity. The soldiers began their march towards Patan the moment the sun rose in the sky. The vast army of the Turks descended upon Gujarat like a cloud of locusts, and like these deadly pests, ravaged and destroyed everything in its path. It was the season of Holi. Winter and summer were competing with each other to retain their sway over the land. It was as if, exhausted by their fight, they had ultimately agreed to a compromise. Summer ruled during the day and winter by night. The winter crop had been harvested, and nothing but stubble remained in the fields. The threshed grain had been apportioned and the farmers were enjoying a well-earned respite. The mango was in bloom and from its bough the koel welcomed the spring. The village youth were doing their best to please the goddess of Holi with their lewd remarks and obscene gestures; and even the elderly joined in the bawdy revels. Water, mixed with the crimson dye of the kesuda flower, and red gulal and abeel powders were kept ready to play Holi. But this year, thanks to the deeds of the sons of Gujarat, Holi of a very different sort would be played. Holimata's insatiable appetite would demand the sacrifice of thousands. What need was there for red gulal when rivers of blood were soon to flow? This year men and women would not playfully spray each other with the colours of gulal and abeel; instead, Hindus and Muslims in their thousands would be locked in deadly embrace. Hatred, not love, vengeance, not enjoyment would rule the day. This year, the long-awaited festival which should have been an occasion for joy would only be lit by the fires of fear and death.

Panic spread as news of the advancing enemy and the preparations for war being made by Karan Raja began to circulate. Towns and villages kept their gates closed even during the day, cattle were grazed within their walls; men, their faces concealed by scarves, moved about the towns ready to fight or flee; and sadness and anxiety enveloped the land. Villagers buried their grain and whatever little money they had saved, blocked up wells, and deliberately laying waste the land, fled from their homes.

As the forces of Allauddin advanced, the ranks of fleeing people grew and swelled. Young and old, men, women and children looked back in horror and wept at the sight of their abandoned homes going up in flames. Overcome by hunger and thirst, bereft of money, many collapsed by the roadside. They were left to die as people made a desperate bid to reach Patan before the enemy caught up with them. Families feared for the safety of those who had joined Karan Raja's army. An old woman, whose only son had gone to battle wept incessantly, overcome by the possibility of never seeing him alive again. What would become of her? How would she survive? Troubled and sorrowful, the elderly feared to lose the staff of their declining years, the light of their fading eyes. Young women wept for their brothers and nephews. Newly married girls who had just begun to experience the joys of this world, who were not yet bound by the cares of parenthood, whose happiness, like the rising sun, was a promise on the horizon, whose hopes and aspirations were still but a dream, found themselves staring into a dark curtain of uncertainty, their hopes stillborn, the sun of their happiness overshadowed by a black cloud. Others, newly engaged, were inconsolable as, instead of tying the knot, their intended bridegrooms departed to take up arms against the cruel mlecchas. Their hopes of a happy future vanished as if in a dream and the buds of newfound love withered and shrivelled under the icy winds of war. The reader can well imagine what the future held for them. A menacing cloud had appeared in the clear skies of their happiness. Accompanied by terrifying flashes of lightning and thunder, a great storm was about to lash the land.

Meanwhile, in Patan, parents, children, wives, relatives and friends of those who had set out for the front were plunged in sorrow. Wealthy merchants who had piled up wealth, scoop by scoop for the generations to come, wept at the thought of the uncertain future. They buried their treasure in underground pits and waited anxiously for the outcome of the war. The more humble merchants followed their example. Shopkeepers turned to their gods. They prayed for the destruction of the barbarians, the victory of their king, the protection of their faith, and the safety of their country. No ritual was neglected, no stone left unturned to avert an evil outcome. But not all were overcome by fear. Those who possessed nothing had no fear of being robbed; while those hopeful of fishing in troubled waters, those who looked upon the country's wealth as theirs by right and saw no difference between another's property and their own, those who lived off the toil of others like drones in a honeycomb feeding on the honey extracted by their hard-working comrades, were delighted by the opportunities the situation offered, and planned to take advantage of them. The city was overflowing with villagers from the surrounding areas and soldiers who had already assembled there, and not an inch of empty space was available. Many people were camped in the open. Some had put together makeshift shelters, while others had paid through their nose to obtain lodgings. The army was housed in tents. The price of food and other essential commodities soared. The poor suffered tremendously and people began to die of starvation. Weighed down by problems, people prayed that the hostilities would end soon.

The fort, too, was in turmoil. Feudatory lords had arrived with their armies. Envoys had been dispatched to enlist the aid of vassal kings, but Karan Raja did not pin his hopes on speedy assistance. Ambassadors of friendly kingdoms offered to prevail upon their rulers to come to Karan Raja's help, but he felt that the support of a handful of kings would make little difference, while diminishing his own glory. He wanted the laurels of victory for himself alone and he courteously declined their offer. Karan was in high spirits, eager to prove his mettle. His strengths and abilities, dormant for long, awoke with full force. He was no longer indifferent and uninterested in matters of state. Just as fish need water, birds the sky and animals land to thrive, so too, faced with the prospect of a mighty war, Karan was in his element. He worked tirelessly, night and day, preparing for battle, not leaving anything to chance.

When news came that the Musalman army was approaching Patan, Karan decided to march out of the city and engage in combat. Before taking this decision, the king had convened a meeting of the leading feudatories and generals and discussed with them the various strategies for the defence of the kingdom. The older, more experienced generals strongly advised Karan to remain within the walls of Patan till contingents from all the vassal kings reached the city. Meanwhile the army of the Musalmans would reach Patan and lay siege to the fort, and in so doing would certainly be defeated. 'As our allies attack them from the rear, we will simultaneously strike from the front,' the generals said. 'They will be trapped, escape will be impossible, and defeat certain. Even if, God forbid, the army of Patan is defeated, the fort will protect the troops and enable them to hold out against the enemy. Though Allauddin's army is large it does not have the necessary equipment to breach the fort and in the event of a long siege, the soldiers will soon succumb to hunger, many will lose heart and desert him.'

This advice fell on unwilling ears. 'Though your advice is sensible and practical, it is hardly fit for Rajputs,' thundered the king. 'Should we hide in our homes like helpless women? Do we lack the valour to fight our battles? If by some chance we were to lose one battle, would this so enfeeble us as to make it impossible to fight another? Have the Rajputs lost their mettle? Has their heroism abandoned them? Are they totally spineless? Have they become namby-pamby merchants and traders? Are the heroic deeds of our Rajput ancestors in vain? If we kshatriya warriors remain holed up in a corner like aged widows, we will be mocked as eunuchs. Rajputs, afraid of the enemy? This can never be! O brave commanders! You must have succumbed to the advice of your womenfolk and are not in your right mind, otherwise you could never have spoken like this. Those chandal Turks, carried away by the promptings of that brahmin, have aroused a sleeping lion, shoved their fist into a cobra's mouth, tempted fate and invited death on themselves. They have come to be buried at our doorstep, not finding burial space in their own lands! Now the kites and the vultures will feast on their flesh, their remains will turn to manure, and our farmers will rejoice at next year's bumper harvests and thank the Lord for sending the enemy to be slain on our soil. So, onward soldiers! Fight to the finish! Do not hide behind the walls of the fort but, placing your trust in your swords and your just cause, face the enemy on the battlefield like men—and leave the rest to God. To die fighting in battle is a hundred times better than to win ignominiously.'

The feudatory chiefs, themselves Rajputs, were stirred by this impassioned speech and Harpal spoke on their behalf with vehemence. 'O King of Kings! We have not the slightest hesitation to join you in battle; in fact, the prospect delights us. But consider well this action, lest future generations judge it ill-advised and foolish. To engage an enemy one needs wisdom as well as courage. We have no objections against fighting but, God forbid, if we lose this battle and do not have the strength to face the enemy again, the kingdom will be lost forever, and then the people of Gujarat will never cease to criticize and revile us. Our advice is prompted by these considerations but if it does not please you, and you are determined to wage an open battle, we are ready to follow you. The astrologers should then be consulted and an auspicious time fixed to begin our march from here. May the Goddess Amba and the thirty-three crore gods come to our aid!' The Rajput braves twirled their moustaches in approval.

On the morning of the auspicious day, Karan Raja donned his armour and helmet and, weapons in hand, stood ready for battle. His generals, similarly clad, stood at attention. The palace priest placed a tilak on the raja's forehead and blessed him. Bards recalled the valiant heroes of the past. Pearl-studded rangoli patterns decorated the doorway. The army stood assembled in the maidan. It consisted of 10,000 cavalry, 500 elephants, 20,000 foot soldiers and 500 chariots. As Karan Raja mounted his armoured elephant, the assembled crowds roared a rousing call for victory, conch shells were blown, drums and other military instruments thundered. The crowds swelled, eager to get a glimpse of their king and his forces. Anxiety over the outcome of the war was writ large on their faces. They were dismayed by the inadequate strength of the army, which seemed doomed to perish like a vulnerable tiger cub surrounded by a herd of elephants. But the sight of their king lifted their spirits. Dressed in the austere garb of war, the glint of battle in his eyes, Karan Raja seemed like another Arjun or Indrajeet. His procession was greeted by a rain of flowers and fruits. Flowers were strewn in front of his elephant and the king left the city gates with the blessings of his people ringing in his ears. With a single stroke, the anger against his past deeds was wiped out. Valour is a potent force that excuses a multitude of sins. Physical strength and courage arouse admiration and awe, blinding men to all other shortcomings. Even those whose valour and daring result in death and destruction are immortalized rather than reviled, and the great scourges of the past are worshipped like gods and become shining examples for the whole world.

Karan's army encamped on a spot that was flanked on two sides by mountains, with the river flowing behind, and awaited the commencement of hostilities. The next day, the Muslim army led by Alafkhan arrived. He had received advance information of Karan's strategy and prepared his moves accordingly. The afternoon saw both armies facing each other. Dismayed by the size of the Turkish army, which outnumbered them ten to one, the Rajput soldiers seemed to lose heart. Realizing the grave consequences of this, Karan rode forward and addressed his men. 'The war between men and demons is now at hand,' he said. 'The demon army is large and appears invincible, but do not think for a moment that God will come to its aid. God is truth. And truth ultimately triumphs. The days of these barbarous Turks must surely be numbered for them to want to march unprovoked upon a foreign land and lay it waste. But by God's grace, not one of them will return to their country to bear tidings of their companions. Never forget that truth is on our side and therefore, God will never forsake us. Rajputs need no instruction on how to conduct themselves in battle. We are all kshatriyas. Our ancestors have fought mighty wars. For eighteen days they waged war at Kurukshetra. Their valour is legendary throughout the world. No Rajput is ever likely to sully the name of his ancestors. Soldiers! We fight for our beloved country. We fight for ourselves, our homes, our children; we fight to protect the chastity of our womenfolk, to safeguard our ancient religion, and for all that we hold most dear. Never forget this even in the midst of battle. We die but once, so why fear death on the battlefield? When I look at the sky, I see heavenly apsaras holding garlands in their hands, ready to receive the fallen brave. Lord Shiva waits in readiness to string a necklace of enemy skulls, and with him are countless *ganas*, *pishachas* and bhoots, impatient to join in the festivities. The *yoginis* stand by to drink the blood of the vanquished. And the gods eagerly await the outcome of the war. We fight before these celestial beings, their eyes are on us; therefore, O valiant Rajputs remain true to your kshatriya dharma. A dog may defeat a tiger; but such an occurrence is an exception and rarely happens. Therefore, take heart, be steadfast and slay the barbarians without mercy so that, once and for all, Bharatkhand is freed from the oppression of these Turks.'

Raja Karan's rousing speech stirred the hearts of his soldiers and they filled the battlefield with a mighty roar. The Turks trembled in fear and to instil them with courage, Alafkhan addressed his men, 'O soldiers of the pure faith! You have journeyed far, leaving your home and loved ones behind. There are two main reasons for this. The first and most important reason is to turn the kafirs towards the true faith, to destroy their temples and replace them with mosques, to smash their idols and to spread the message that *Laailaaha Ilulullad Mohammadur Rasul Allah*—there is only one God and Muhammad is His Prophet—throughout the land.

'The second reason is to expand the boundaries and the fame of our kingdom and thereby increase both the glory of our emperor as well as our own wealth. If it is God's will that we fail in our endeavours, remember well there is no place to flee. We must win or die on this very spot. There is no chance of escape and, in any case, why should we flee? Have our soldiers ever tasted defeat? Have not our braves vanquished the kafirs in innumerable battles? Then whence this fear? Does the bark of a dog unnerve a tiger? Never! Therefore, my brave warriors, scatter these puny opponents like rice-chaff in the wind. Conquer their land and make its fabulous riches your own. Rest assured, my men, Allah and our Prophet Muhammad are watching this battle from above. All the angels have gathered to help us. So, if you bring shame on them, you will have to answer for your conduct on the Day of Judgement.'

Resounding cries of *'Allah O Akbar'* rent the air. And now Karan Raja rode on to the battlefield and addressed Alafkhan. 'When elephant battles elephant, small trees and shrubs are needlessly trampled underfoot. Your emperor wants to grab Gujarat and I have sworn to keep it. Whatever be the outcome of this conflict, it will not benefit the soldiers. So why should they lose their lives? Send the most valiant of your warriors for single combat with me. If I win you must depart from this land, but if I die my army will likewise retreat and the whole of Gujarat will be yours.' There was no response from the Muslim side, prompting the Rajputs to shout in glee. Then Alafkhan said, 'Unlike kafirs we do not hold life to be without meaning. Allah has sent us down for a noble purpose. We should not throw away our lives without completing our appointed tasks. Besides, what guarantee is there that the armies of the dead king will give up the fight? We will fight as planned, come what may.' Having spoken thus he ordered his men to attack.

With the cry of '*Allah O Akbar*' on their lips, the Musalman soldiers rushed forward to dislodge the enemy, but the Rajputs stood their ground. The struggle was a prolonged one. The two armies collided like wind-driven monsoon clouds. The battlefield resounded with the deafening clash of swords. Lightning-like flashes of metal dazzled the eye. Not a bird could penetrate the mesh of arrows that crisscrossed the sky and rained to the ground. The battlefield streamed with blood and the cries of the wounded and dying rent the air. Thousands died on both sides, but the Rajput soldiers, true to their code and their dharma, did not retreat. Karan Raja, his eyes blood-red, fought like one possessed. His sword sliced right and left, cutting down all who crossed its path. When his elephant was slain, he fought on horseback. When even his horse was killed, he fought on foot like a common soldier, with no thought for his own safety. Only when he was wounded and some soldiers recognized him and realized that their king would surely die if he continued fighting on foot, was he persuaded to get back on a horse and fight with the cavalry. The feudatory chiefs, buoyed by Karan's courage, fought with renewed determination, and even the common soldiers discarded all fear and fell on the Turks. The enemy began to tire; many soldiers were killed, many wounded and, unable to make a dent in the Rajput ranks, retreated to their camp. After a brief lull they once again attacked the Rajputs only to find them well prepared for the encounter. Like the unsuspecting Keechaka, who fell into the arms of Bhima disguised as Sairandhri, the Turks were given a fitting welcome. The battle continued until the sun god, weary at the sight of the carnage and pained by the suffering of his devotees, turned his face away and disappeared into the west in a blaze of red.

Darkness spread across the land, birds flew home to their nests, one by one the stars began to smile, lotus blooms furled shut, travellers took shelter in the town for the night, and soldiers could no longer tell friend from foe. Then the moon rose and spread a faint light on the field, but the enemies had no strength left to fight and retired to their respective camps. Alafkhan sent word to Karan to cease hostilities for the night and renew the fight at dawn. The Rajput king readily agreed.

It was a moonlit night and a glow like beaten silver illumined the sky. But what a ghastly sight it revealed on the ground below. The vast battlefield was strewn with corpses, their faces hideously distorted in death, their dead-white countenances ghastly in the gentle moonlight. The wounded were carried away screaming and whatever medical aid could be given to them on the spot was administered. Crimson rivulets changed to black as they flowed across the land. Vultures, kites and crows had not yet arrived for the feast that was spread out for them, but bats circled overhead from nearby trees, owls hooted their inauspicious cries, and prowling jackals, attracted by the stench, disturbed the slumber of the dead. In the camps, all was quiet. Men who had gathered in the daytime, bent on slaying each other, were now reduced to fearful silence, afraid to disturb the spirits of the night and the spectre of death that hovered around them. Only the incessant call of crickets and the frenzied barking of excited jackals could be heard.

The Muslims spent three-quarters of the night in prayer, while in the Rajput camp, the Mahabharata was recited and the mighty exploits of Bhima and the other great heroes of the Kurukshetra war stirred the spirits of the soldiers. Bards sang tales of the valourous deeds of former Rajput kings. Now, only one watch of the night remained. The moon began to set, and the darkness increased. All was still in the Rajput camp when suddenly, without warning, the Turks attacked. The Rajputs were caught unprepared. Renowned for keeping their word and trusting their foes to do likewise, they fell prey to the enemy's perfidy. Taken by surprise, the Rajput soldiers panicked, their forces were in disarray, and in the darkness and ensuing chaos it was difficult to distinguish friend from foe. Only the cry of 'Allah O Akbar' announced the death of a Rajput soldier, and the frequency of this cry increased by the minute. Karan Raja tried in vain to regroup his forces. His men fell like sheaves of corn mowed down by the reaper's sickle. The king's horse was slain, and he once again fought on foot, but all hope of victory vanished. An enemy sword slashed his ribs and as the strength ebbed out of him Karan fell to the ground unconscious. He would no doubt have been cut to pieces but by God's grace, the dim light of dawn began to spread across the horizon and the valiant Harpal recognized the king. Convinced that if the king was saved he would eventually win back his lost kingdom, Harpal lifted the unconscious Karan and, seating him on a camel, hastened to the safety of the fort.

The morning revealed the extent of the devastation. Some soldiers had fled in the darkness of the night, many had been slain, but the remaining troops, though staring defeat in the face, continued to fight valiantly. At the commencement of hostilities, a few detachments under the command of feudatory chiefs had been stationed in a town nearby, ready to join the battle if required. But when the chieftains realized that Karan Raja's forces had been practically wiped out and that the king himself could not be spotted anywhere, they surmised that he must have been killed and felt that to enter the field now would be to plunge like moths into the flames of a lamp. To be alive is to hope, to fight again another day, and perhaps to achieve one's dreams. So why risk death unnecessarily? Some time in the future, at an opportune moment they would definitely vanquish the Turks. But till then it would be better to quit Gujarat, while continuing to harass the devils night and day, allowing them not a moment of peace. The chieftains mounted their horses and taking one last look at the hapless, bereaved city of Patan, they cried, 'O Gujarat! O motherland! What calamities have befallen you! Your children have been slain by barbarians and your lord has met the same fate. You, who have nurtured us and taught us to be brave, why are you dry-eyed when your sons are being hacked to death in their prime, when your indulgent lord is no more, and cruel widowhood is upon you? Is your heart as unfeeling as stone? Do tears not come to your eyes? Is it that you wish to marry once again? Is it your intention to wed the evil, blood-stained Turkish emperor on whose orders you have been condemned to barren widowhood? O you wicked chandal! You are no longer our mother. We will never accept a stepfather under the same roof, neither will we give you a moment's peace. Your new lord too will know no respite. Why don't you speak? If your intentions are otherwise, why don't you swallow the enemy hosts? Alas for Hindu dharma and for the fate of the kingdom! Today, both dharma and kingdom have ceased to exist. The gods are slumbering, unable to protect themselves let alone save us! O! where have the brave Vanraj, Mulraj, Siddharaj and Kumarapala vanished? Why don't they come to the aid of their children? They have washed their hands off Gujarat. They have allowed their motherland to fall into the hands of strangers. Perhaps God has ordained this and there is nothing we can do. All we can do is to leave and bid our farewells to this land.' So saying, the riders galloped away and the foot soldiers marched, stopping neither for rest nor for food until they had crossed the borders of Gujarat.

10

The news that Karan Raja had been defeated, his army totally destroyed, and that Turkish forces were on their way to Patan, set the city in an uproar. The rich became anxious for the safety of their wealth; those in power worried about losing it. The grief of those who had lost friends and loved ones was boundless. The old found themselves bereft of sons and means of support, children were left fatherless and unprotected, young women were widowed, affianced girls lost their fiancés to the apsaras in paradise, and the fleeting bonds of friendship were broken. The entire town was in mourning: in large mansion and humble hut, weeping and lamentation were everywhere.

In the royal palace, all of Karan Raja's queens had gathered together. The countenances of Roopsundari and Kaularani shone like the moon and the sun. Roopsundari was still as exquisite as before, but the many days she had spent in a forgotten corner of the palace, her mind and body starved of affection, neglected by the king, and with nothing to alleviate the memory of the horrors inflicted on her husband and family, had left her looking pale and careworn. But the radiant beauty of the chief queen Kaularani is difficult to describe. She was as beautiful as the women imagined by portrait painters, as ethereal as the figure of Mary, the mother of Jesus, created by the great Italian artists, as bewitching as the images of women dreamed up in the imagination of the world's finest poets. Her beauty was unequalled in all of India. And it shone even more brightly as she sat that day, her head bowed in sorrow. How wondrous is the work of God! So perfect was his creation, one could gaze at Kaularani all day long, without a thought for food or drink, and yet want more. With her were her two young daughters: like chicks clustering under the wings of the mother-hen in fearful anticipation of the falcon's eager swoop, they huddled by her side. Kanakdevi, the eldest, was eight years old, Devaldevi was four, but both looked older than their age. The children had taken after their mother, but their faces shone with the innocence of childhood and their golden hair had not yet turned dark.

While the grief-stricken queens waited for Kaularani to suggest what should be done next, Roopsundari's thoughts had taken a different direction. No strong ties of affection bound her to Karan Raja, and she did not share the pain of the others. On the contrary, she was filled with happiness at the prospect of Madhav's return. His victory over the king would soon bring him to Patan; he would be prime minister once again, and once she had undertaken the purificatory rituals, she would be reunited with him. But the other queens had enjoyed the king's love, and besides they had very high notions about kshatriya honour and the code of conduct expected of Rajput women who had lost their husbands.

Kaularani thought for a while and addressed them. 'My sisters! Today the sun has set on our happiness; today our lord, our shield and protector, has fallen on the battlefield, and the victorious mlecchas will soon be in Patan. Today, both we and our motherland have become widows. Widows. O Lord Surya, how is it that this word does not make you hide your face? Will you not cover the world in darkness to mourn the death of Karan Raja? O Lord Indra! Why does not the sound of this word make you rain blood? A man who was your equal in looks and strength has fallen; why then do you not grieve? O Sheshnag, why does this word not make you tremble and the earth quake? Will you not proclaim that you cannot bear the weight of the Rajput braves who have fallen on the battlefield? Hearing that word, O you mountains of Gujarat, why do you not weep? And what makes you, O birds and beasts, continue with your indifferent lives? Have you not heard that your lord, Karan Raja, has been killed? Or is it that your hearts are too stony to care? Though even stones, I think, should weep.

'But I forget myself. Why should you, my sisters, falsely mourn? We are Rajput women. Kshatriya blood flows strongly in our veins; and we, who have borne brave Rajput men in our wombs and suckled them at our breasts, shall we now sit around and weep? Is not our honour precious to us? Do we not want to protect our womanhood? Do we wish to cast a stain on the character of Rajput women by submitting tamely to our fate? Have we forgotten the example of the Rajput queens of yore who were in this very situation? Therefore, wipe your tears, my sisters; harden your hearts; forget the sorrows that have come upon you, and think only of what must be done. The Musalman troops are almost at the city gates; they will invade our private chambers; they will cast lustful glances at us—they may not be so vile as to take us by force, but we must take that possibility into account; their commander's desirous eyes may fall upon us and he may make us his wives. Then the vows of lifelong fidelity we have sworn to our husbands will be broken; we will have to give up our religion and accept the ways and habits of the mlecchas. Each of you must give your views on how all this can be prevented.'

None of the queens said a word. They told Kaularani they would do whatever she advised. Then summoning up all her kshatriya pride and Rajput courage, the chief queen spoke with great emotion. 'Death, death, death. That is our only option. We all have to die some time, so why be anxious about dying now? In the situation we are in, why should death be feared? We are filled with misgivings about our future. It is more than likely that it will be unbearable, and hence death is a thousand times more preferable than living. Into this world we are born, and in this world we must die. In the brief span that is available to us we must accomplish our allotted tasks and then wind up camp. Millions of souls have come and gone: what remains of them? Are there any signs that they once lived on this earth? The majority are swept away in the great flood of time, and it is as if they were never here; but a few stand firm like rocks in the sea, and will remain standing till the end of time. But what exactly is it that remains? It is their names, their reputations. A good reputation is invaluable; its worth far exceeds that of all the gold, silver and diamonds in the world. Gold and silver are perishable, but a good name lasts forever. Material wealth can diminish, and the man who has been responsible for amassing it is forgotten after a generation or two, but a good name remains as unchanging as the pole star.

'Most people hope to be remembered by their descendants, but they are remembered by one or, at the most, two generations, and after this they are nothing but ciphers. It makes little difference had they lived or not. But a good name is like an inheritance passed down to the entire world. Efforts are not needed to perpetuate the memory of a man who has left behind a good name: his reputation continues to shine like the rays of the sun. So a good name is like the philosopher's stone and all are eager to possess it, though few succeed. The names of those who, through their own efforts or the strength of their moral convictions, have accomplished great deeds are never forgotten. And the names of those who sacrifice their lives in the defence of truth and honour are etched in letters of gold. Who would not be prepared to die for such lasting fame? One who is prepared to sacrifice his name and reputation for the sake of a few more years embroiled in the cares of this world is truly to be despised. When he dies he is as little noticed as a useless garden weed that is trampled on, or an insect making its laborious way that is squashed underfoot, or some wild beast whose carcass is left to rot in some jungle. That such a person lived is a matter of indifference, and his death is as inconsequential as a grain of sand blown away at the seashore. No one respects him, no one sheds a tear, no poet sings a verse in his honour. Of course, not everyone is satisfied with only a few years on this earth, and most desire a long life. But when they find that this is not possible, they settle for a brief span on earth and a longer one in the memory of others. Even the humblest of men share this desire. It is for all these reasons, my sisters, that we must die untimely deaths, and be remembered as brave women who covered themselves in glory by their sacrifice. Now let a great fire be built in the palace, and together let us all perish in its flames.'

None of the queens showed the slightest uneasiness at the prospect of such a horrible death. They gave their consent and prepared to sacrifice their lives. Kaularani's thoughts now turned to her daughters. She did not think it right that the two girls, who had barely tasted the joys of life, should die in this manner. She summoned a servant, and handing over the girls to his care, asked him to take them to her father. So far, the chief queen had stood resolute for she was not afraid of dying, but now that the moment had come when she must part with her daughters, dearer to her than life itself, tears poured unrestrained from her eyes.

That this proud Rajput woman should break down in this manner did not reflect an abandonment of courage, nor did the queen's conduct deserve censure. All of us are caught up in the snares of love, and the love of a mother for her children is beyond compare. A mother's love for her offspring is an instinct

173

that the Creator has instilled in all human beings, whether high or low. Even hard-hearted women who lack empathy and are unmoved by the suffering of others are compassionate when it comes to their own children; they are troubled when they see their children unhappy and will go to any lengths to protect them. One need not be surprised then that Kaularani, while personally unafraid of facing death, should weep at the pain of parting from her daughters and fear for the safety of her innocent girls. Kaularani's tears were proof of a tender heart and enhanced her womanly nature. Bidding her daughters farewell, she said, 'O my dearly beloved girls, the light of my life, I have carried you for nine difficult months in my womb; I have raised you through difficult times and have not been parted from you for a single hour. To watch you grow was a great joy. To hear your childish babbling filled me with satisfaction. Your happiness was my happiness; your pain, my pain. Who will take care of you now? Who will pander to your every whim? And who will look out for you when you are older? Who will guide you along the right path and counsel you from falling into the many snares of life? But I must say no more. If I get caught up in my anxieties, I will not be able to carry out my resolve, so you must leave now. May all the gods protect you; may Jagadamba and the yoginis take care of you, and supported by a mother's love, may you spread the glory of our family. This is my prayer.' Kaularani stopped, and freeing herself from the clinging embrace of her children, ordered the servant to take them away. With eyes closed and ears shut, she left the room.

A great burning log was placed in a part of the palace that was built of wood. The room soon caught fire, wooden beams collapsed into the flames, the blaze spread to a section of the roof, tiles came crashing to the ground, billows of smoke filled the air and sparks chased each other playfully through the rooms. A huge crowd gathered outside. They were armed with pots of water, axes and everything needed to douse the flames and break down crumbling structures, but the conflagration continued to grow in intensity. Thus the palace which had been built by Vanraj when Patan was founded, where Mulraj, Siddharaj, Kumarapala, Bhimdev and others had been born and where they had died; the palace in which the cries of victory and the lamentations of defeat had so often reverberated; the palace which had witnessed so many changes and which for nearly 150 years had withstood the onslaught of wind, rain and time, embraced Agni, lord of fire. Like the physical body after death, the palace had become an empty shell with the departure of Karan Raja and was consigned to the flames.

But the glorious death sought by Karan's queens was not to be. The time had not yet come for them to leave this earth; they still had unfinished work, and had yet to taste life's joys and sorrows. So just as the flames were rising strongly and the women preparing to leap, the Muslim army arrived at the gates of the palace.

The wealth of Gujarat had been one of the main reasons for the invasion and, alarmed that the palace and all its treasures would be lost in the conflagration, Alafkhan ordered his men to extinguish the blaze immediately. Thousands of his soldiers descended on the palace and set to work with a will, the happy prospect of loot on their minds. Within a short while, the burning portions had been torn down and the fire put out. A way into the interior was opened up and a few bold soldiers, unmindful of death, made their way inside and returned with the queens and their attendants and whatever stray valuables that came to hand. Kaularani had managed to lock herself in a room and, terrified that she would fall into the hands of the enemy, had exchanged her clothing for that of a man's, disguised her beautiful face with cosmetics, and tied a spear and sword to her waist. Then leaning out of the window, she cried out for help. Moved by pity, one of the soldiers put up a ladder; assuming her to be a servant, and preoccupied with thoughts of plunder, he took no further notice of her.

Kaularani mingled with the chaotic crowd until she came across a Rajput whom she recognized. She got him to procure a horse for her, replaced her Rajput clothing for that of a Musalman's, and rode out of the city.

The Turkish troops soon had the entire palace under their control. Alafkhan took charge of the treasury and began to rule as the deputy of Allauddin Khilji.

Roopsundari was reunited with Madhav. The two embraced, laughing and weeping with joy. The tie between a man and wife is a strong one, and when it is severed by death the pain felt by the surviving partner can only be understood by one who has experienced a similar fate. Madhav and his wife had not been parted by death but the pain of separation was no less severe. He was fully aware that Roopsundari had had no role to play in her abduction. Separation had not lessened his love for her; on the contrary, his desire to rescue her and take revenge on her captor had only increased its intensity. He had not anticipated that he would get her back so soon, and so easily. When Roopsundari embraced him as passionately as before, his joy knew no bounds. Whether Roopsundari would have felt the same way towards her husband had Karan Raja wooed her with the passion he had felt when he had first seen her, is a question difficult to answer. But he had discarded her, and without another claimant for her love, it continued to flow, as before, towards Madhav, and distance only made it stronger. It was thus that Madhav and Roopsundari met again, their love as strong as it had always been. Madhav summoned an assembly of learned scholars and asked them to suggest the appropriate rituals for a brahmin woman who had been forcibly taken by a Rajput. The rituals were duly performed, the brahmins were paid their fees, and with no further impediments remaining, Madhav and Roopsundari resumed their lives as man and wife. In gratitude, Madhav had a stepwell built at Vardhamannagar (Vadhvaan) which is known as Madhav's *vaav* to this day.

The news of the victory over Gujarat had to be conveyed to the padshah. Alafkhan knew that a mere message would not be appreciated; it would have to be sent along with some special novelties and a token from the treasury. Aware of Allauddin's weakness for women, Alafkhan was sure that nothing would please the padshah more than the gift of a truly beautiful maiden. Karan Raja's chief queen was famed for her beauty; reports of her matchless looks and keen intelligence had spread as far as Delhi. Deciding that Kaularani would make the most fitting gift for the padshah, Alafkhan ordered a citywide search for the queen. But Kaularani could not be traced, and it was learnt from the other queens that she had left the town. How the queen had managed to escape from a burning palace and a city swarming with soldiers, where she was headed and which route she had taken, remained a mystery. Undeterred, Alafkhan sent his men in all directions with orders to bring back the queen unharmed.

—

While Alafkhan waited for news of Kaularani, the queen was making her way to her father's kingdom, Jhalavaad. She rode hard and fast, terrified of the dangers that could befall a beautiful young woman and constantly worried that her disguise would be revealed. Afraid to look anyone in the eye, she avoided the main road and took a circuitous route through woods and across mountains. She did not halt in any village, but stopped to rest in some quiet spot in the forest, where she ate what she could find and spent the nights. She, who had lived in the midst of flower-filled gardens, her body fanned by servants and cooled with fragrant sandalwood paste, had now to endure the intense heat of the summer sun. She, who was used to being carried in a palanquin was now forced to travel arduous hours on horseback. Accustomed to the softest of mattresses, coaxed to sleep with a hundred ploys, she now slept the exhausted sleep of a child on a bed of dried leaves, and even on the branch of a tree. Instead of her usual rich repasts, she lived on fruits and berries. She cooked her own meagre meals, and had no one but herself to attend to her needs. Travelling thus for several days, Kaularani came to a large forest. Surrounded by hills, crisscrossed by streams, it was a dark and frightening place, so thick with trees that even the midday sun could not penetrate its darkness. The wind soughed constantly and the howl of foxes, the roar of lions and the cries of other wild animals made the nights terrifying. Kaularani trembled with fear as she approached the place. It was not only the thought of wild beasts that terrified her, the possibility that her disguise would be uncovered and she would be handed over to the mleccha Turkish general was never far from her mind. Besides, there was the lurking fear of thieves. She had concealed many valuable jewels in her clothing, and she feared for her life lest she be accosted by bandits. Kaularani was after all a woman, albeit in men's clothing; the thought that her disguise might be exposed and she be molested filled her with dread. Luckily, she had disguised herself as a Muslim, and the local population had been so petrified by the the recent Muslim incursions that so far no one had dared challenge her. In fact, she had been treated with deference and readily supplied with whatever provisions she required.

But these untroubled times were not to last long. On one heat-drenched day, as Kaularani reached the edge of the forest, her doubts and fears momentarily at rest, she was stopped by a band of ten men. 'Remove your clothing,' they ordered. The blood drained out of Kaularani's face and she was on the point of falling off her horse. But she lived up to her Rajput name and said in a confident voice, 'I am a Muslim cavalryman. Our forces have defeated and killed your king Karan in battle. The whole of Gujarat is under our control and we are now its rulers. Our general has ordered me to convey news of our victory to Padshah Allauddin Khilji in Delhi. I am on an official mission, and if you try to stop me, rob me or obstruct me in any way, be assured that your days are numbered. Have you not heard of our padshah? He is the master of the world. And if you dare to obstruct one of his men, he will hunt you down whether you hide in heaven or hell, burn your homes, slay your wives and children, and torture you slowly to death. So move aside and let me pass without delay. Do what you will with others who come this way, but if you care for the safety of yourselves and those you love, get out of my way forthwith.'

Kaularani's threats had no effect on the dacoits. Her brave words dispersed in the air, and instead of causing alarm only produced mocking laughter from the men. 'Hindu or Musalman, emperor's servant or village bully—such distinctions do not concern us,' one of them said. 'We are not interested in who a person is, but what he has on him. We do not know who your padshah is, nor do we wish to know. What's it to us if he is Allauddin Khichdi or Allauddin Ghee? We are not in the least afraid of him. We live in close proximity with death, it is our constant companion, and we have come to terms with it. What more can your padshah or anyone else do besides send us to our deaths? So strip, or we will tear your clothes off.' As Kaularani hesitated, the bandits pulled her off her horse and yanked off her coat. They were amazed by the sight of the strings of pearls and diamonds around her neck, but when they discovered that she was a woman, they were paralysed with shock. Almost fainting with fear, Kaularani cried out agitatedly, 'Shiva, Shiva, Shiva! O my God! To what depths have I sunk! Me, a queen in the hands of these uncouth tribals! Not long ago they would not have dared even to glance at me; today they feel free to dishonour me. O husband mine! O Karan Raja! Wherever you are, why do you not come to the aid of your beloved queen? O Yama, if my husband is in your realm of death, send him back swiftly, so he can rescue his queen from the clutches of these thieves.'

Taken by surprise, the Bhil dacoits realized that their victim was in fact Karan Raja's queen. It was evident by her bearing, and the very expensive jewels she had on her. If they robbed her without first informing their leader, they would surely incur his wrath and be severely punished for breaking the rules of the clan. But one of the group, more avaricious than the others, was reluctant to let the lion's share of the loot fall into the leader's hands. 'What's in it for us?' he asked. 'Let's cut off her head, strip off her clothes and jewels and dump her body somewhere. Forget taking her to the chief.' The other Bhils disagreed. They were reluctant to kill a woman, that too a queen, for no good reason. Moreover, her jewels were no ordinary ornaments and disposing of them would not be easy as news of the transaction would surely spread. So they helped Kaularani back on her horse and led her to their chief with the consideration she deserved.

They found their chief reclining on a charpoy in his hut. He was around thirty to forty years old, but his energetic lifestyle made him look about twenty-five. His men greeted him and relating their tale from start to finish handed over the prize to him. The chief offered his congratulations and, promising to reward them soon, dismissed them.

Left alone with Kaularani, the dacoit chief surveyed her from head to toe, and the longer he looked, the more his desire was aroused. He ordered his wife's clothing to be brought and made Kaularani discard her male garb and change into it. Even with her face still disguised as a man's, Kaularani's beauty was evident, and had her captor seen her in all her splendour, there is no saying what he would have done to her.

The chief approached her cautiously. 'Just as Karan Raja was the ruler of Gujarat, so am I the master of this entire village,' he said, trying to assuage her fears. 'And just as he possessed a certain proportion of the country's wealth, so do I possess the same proportion of the wealth of this village, maybe a trifle more. You enjoyed a happy life in his palace, as you will here with me, and be treated with even greater respect. Your husband, the king, is dead, and will you now live out your life as a widow? Am I that objectionable? Fallen kings must perforce be content with jobs as schoolteachers; and I, after all, do rule over a realm, however small. You might think my occupation despicable, but look at it this way. Kings collect taxes from the peasantry in return, they claim, for protecting them; but in fact they squeeze out far more than they require and spend it on grand living. Is this not a form of theft? And when government officials, who are paid for their jobs, deceive and extort bribes from the poor, is that not also a form of theft? When carpenters, masons and labourers charge by the day and while away much of their time in idleness, what else can one call it but theft? Even professionals such as tailors and goldsmiths and others who routinely cheat their customers are nothing but thieves. In fact, it would not be too far from the truth to say that most people are thieves. The only difference between us and them is that they steal furtively while we do so openly. Actually, we may be better than them. They cheat, deceive and lie to their intended victims; we declare our intentions openly and at times secure our spoils after a fair contest. Thus it is us dacoits who are the most honourable among thieves; and yet the contrary opinion holds sway, with the result that the devious escape punishment and are held in high regard, while we are reviled, called wicked and sinful, and hunted down mercilessly. But we do not take this to heart.

We have as much pride in ourselves as the next man—and this is how you too, should think of us. So why are you so reluctant to live here? Why do you remain silent? Let me make this clear—whether you like it or not, you are a captive in my hands and I do not intend to let you go. I am going to keep you here, so you might as well submit with grace.'

Kaularani realized that there was no point resisting her captor, so after a moment's hesitation she agreed to his request. That night, the chief had a hearty meal and rather more than his usual quota of opium. As he got ready for bed, Kaularani opened up her heart to Jagadamba, the compassionate Mother of the World. 'O Arasuri! O Ambabhavani! O Protector of the Universe!' she cried. 'To what depths have I sunk! Like a diamond among stones, a mogra among thorns, a banana tree in a thorny thicket, a cow amidst lions, here am I, a queen, trapped in the hut of a bandit! This lowdown scum is about to rape me. If I resist, he will kill me. If I submit, I will be violated. O Mother, what should I do? No one but you can help me now. But wait! I have a dagger, and if I hide it in the folds of my sari, I can plunge it into this chandal when he attacks me. There can be no sin in killing such a man. On ten different occasions, when evil demons held sway over the earth and oppressed both men and gods, Lord Vishnu reincarnated himself and destroyed them. The Great Goddess too killed Shumbha, Nishumbha and other demons. Thus there can be no shame in killing this demon of a man who is intent on raping me.'

Kaularani concealed the dagger in her sari and steeled herself to perform the dreadful task. And when the dacoit, high on opium, approached her, she grabbed him by the neck with one hand and with the other, plunged the sword in his belly. The deed had been performed so rapidly and with such skill, that the dacoit did not have the time to cry out, and no one in the house was aware of what had happened. Kaularani rolled the corpse behind a chest and putting on the dacoit's clothes escaped into the compound. She selected a spirited horse from a number that were tethered there and rode out into the night. Supposing her to be the chief, no one stopped her, and by the time the dacoit's body was discovered and his men went in pursuit of Kaularani, she was far away.

Aware that the dacoits were bound to come in pursuit of her and that they would catch up with her if she kept riding, Kaularani decided to stop and seek refuge as soon as she came to a fairly large town. Her tale so moved the ruler of the place that he offered to give her shelter, despite the risks involved. How could he refuse to help someone in difficulty? And that too, a woman?

Meanwhile, as the Bhil dacoits rode in pursuit of their chief's murderer they came across Alafkhan's men who were seeking the same quarry. It soon became apparent to the Muslim contingent that the murderer sought by the Bhils was none other than the queen they were after. The two parties made their way together towards the town, but before long a dispute broke out between them. The Bhils intended to capture Kaularani and take her back to the village where she could be tortured and killed in front of the chief's family, but the Muslim soldiers had been ordered to take her back to Alafkhan unharmed. Arguments soon gave way to curses and curses to blows. Men from both sides lost their lives in the fracas; and had it not been for the intervention of two older men, that spot would have become the eternal abode of the men from both groups, Kaularani would have reached her father's home in safety, and Alafkhan's plans would have been shattered. But this was not what providence intended. The two elders decided that Kaularani should become the property of whichever group found her first. Both sides agreed to the proposal, but the Muslim contingent, afraid that the opportunity to win Alafkhan's favour—not to mention

183

a big reward—was unlikely to come their way again, secretly decided to kill the dacoits. Accordingly, in the dead of night, they murdered the unsuspecting Bhils. Then making their way into the town, they started their search for the queen. By a stroke of luck, one of the men they spoke to happened to be the king's barber. Now, barbers are universally known to have long tongues and small stomachs, and unable to retain the smallest morsel of news, the barber spewed out the information that just a day or two previously, a stranger had been seen entering the king's palace and was being treated there with utmost courtesy. Certain that the stranger was Kaularani, Alafkhan's men sent word to the ruler demanding that she be handed over to them immediately. At first the raja was reluctant to surrender someone who had sought his protection—it would be a dereliction of kingly dharma, and besides, Kaularani's desperate pleas had aroused his compassion. But when the soldiers threatened that a refusal would invite an attack by the entire Turkish army and that his kingdom would be annihilated, the ruler had second thoughts. He explained the situation to Kaularani and it was decided that she should try and escape from the town. However, the king secretly ordered the gatekeeper to apprehend any stranger attempting to leave the town and hand him over to the soldiers.

It did not take the soldiers long to confirm that their prisoner was a woman in men's clothing and that she was none other than Raja Karan's queen. Their mission accomplished, they hastened back to Patan. Alafkhan had been waiting for this moment and was looking forward to the padshah's response when he was presented with the beauteous Kaularani, but when the general saw the queen he was disappointed. Kaularani's complexion had darkened after many days of riding in the sun, traces of the heavy dyes she had used to disguise herself had not yet disappeared, and reports of her beauty seemed exaggerated. But the other queens persuaded Alafkhan to let her remain in the palace for a month,

and during that time—Kaularani's own wishes to the contrary—
the full bloom of her looks was restored.

A month later, the sight of her extraordinary beauty stunned
Alafkhan. She stood there, an apsara in human form, a marble statue
turned to life. Straightaway, Alafkhan told her that he was under
orders to send her to the padshah and that she must prepare herself
for her new life as the chief queen of Allauddin's zenana. Kaularani
had been prepared for the worst and she accepted the news of her
fate calmly. Without another word, she returned to her room.

It was only when a few days later, a small procession was
seen leaving the city with great fanfare that the citizens of Patan
realized that the beautiful Kaularani, former queen of Gujarat,
was leaving to grace the palace of the Turkish monarch. Sorrow
shrouded the town and not a single citizen came out to witness
the shameful departure. Kaularani wept bitterly as she left her
homeland, never to return.

Karan Raja! O husband mine,
Why have you left me?
Where do you hide?
Fate has turned her face from me.
Woe is me! O husband mine,
Unhappy wretch am I.

Without you I cannot eat
I cannot sleep.
Drowned in agony,
Your pain I cannot bear.
Woe is me! O husband mine,
Unhappy wretch am I.

To whom shall I tell
My ill-fated tale?

A boundless ocean,
This sorrow of mine.
Woe is me! O husband mine,
Unhappy wretch am I.

Wandering, desolate
Kanak my child,
Where can you be?
Unbearable the pain in my heart.
Woe is me! O husband mine,
Unhappy wretch am I.

O Rajputs! Justice personified,
My brothers, parents, those I hold most dear,
How will I bear
From you to part?
Woe is me! O husband mine,
Unhappy wretch am I.

Best of fathers, father mine,
In your care I knew no lack.
Your voice ceases not
To echo in my heart.
Woe is me! O husband mine,
Unhappy wretch am I.

Land of my birth, O Gujarat!
Forgive me.
To unclean shores
I must depart.
Woe is me! O husband mine,
Unhappy wretch am I.

Lost is my faith,
Gone my traditions.
How will I live
In the arms of that Turk?
Woe is me! O husband mine,
Unhappy wretch am I.

My lord is dead, my daughters fled,
Sunk low in shame, my land I leave.
Who will pardon me this sin?
I cry in vain.
Woe is me! O husband mine,
Unhappy wretch am I.

Lord of the Universe,
Who can fathom your ways?
Your compassion alone
Can give me peace.
Woe is me! O husband mine,
Unhappy wretch am I.

11

In a valley idyllic enough for apsaras to dwell lay the town of Baglan. It was spread across undulating hills and protected by a girdle of tall, impregnable mountains. This natural barrier was reinforced by massive stone fortifications and a smaller fort that stood atop a steep hill. Baglan was ruled by Ramdev, king of Devgadh. At sunrise and sunset, the majestic mountains that surrounded the town appeared so breathtakingly beautiful, it would have been well worth the money and effort to visit them. The hills were mantled in lush vegetation; teak and mango trees rose in ascending rows like the seats of an amphitheatre. Tigers, bears and other wild animals roamed freely in the forests and rarely did man intrude into their realm. Birds, large and small, filled the woods with their melodious calls. Their bright, many-coloured feathers danced in the sunlight and one could not but be awed by the Creator's wondrous display. Rivulets flowed down the hills, and as they splashed against rocks, crushed the little shrubs and flowers that came in their way and danced playfully over the black pebbles, they brought to mind days of carefree childhood. Large rivers cascaded down the mountain slopes. Their spray, lit by the rays of the sun, formed shimmering rainbows. Often the waters would flow on, but sometimes they would collect, forming crystal-clear pools. In many places, the swiftly flowing rivers had carved out deep gorges through which they moved at lightning speed. In the month of Ashadh, when rain clouds darkened the skies, and lightning flashed and clouds thundered, the scene was one of terrifying majesty. The clouds would appear like billowing smoke under one's feet and it was difficult to imagine them evaporating and returning to earth as drops of rain. The sound of splitting rocks and crashing trees rent the air as lightning streaked across the trees and hills. Thunder reverberated across the mountains. Torrential rains, unlike anything experienced by the people of the plains, swelled the rivers and filled the streams to overflowing. The devouring summer landscape with its scorched trees, burning rocks and bare hills was now unrecognizable. The land blossomed with renewed life, and cool winds carried with them the scent of countless flowers. The adage—things appear more beautiful seen from a distance—was proved wrong, as the hills appeared even lovelier when viewed from close by.

On one such monsoon day, in an inner chamber of the fort, two people, a man and a woman, sat engrossed in earnest conversation. The man was about forty, but time had taken a toll on his appearance and he looked older than his years. Seldom does good health desert a man of just forty. Indeed in some countries, a man of forty is considered to be in the prime of life. But this man had aged rapidly and seemed to have been considerably affected by the cares of life. His appearance was that of a man of fifty or fifty-five. His cheeks were hollow and his hair had turned totally white, yet it would seem that his spirit was not yet dimmed for his sunken eyes still glowed with the fire of courage. His visage still revealed an impatient and arrogant nature. He appeared to be a person worthy of respect, one who had seen better days.

By now the reader must have guessed the identity of this man, though nine years have passed since we last met him.

He was none other than Karan Vaghela, the last Rajput king of Gujarat. It has already been described how, on the day the Rajput army was massacred outside Patan, the day the mlecchas conquered the kingdom of Gujarat, the day Madhav's desire for revenge was fulfilled, the day when the brave feudatories bid their final farewell to Anhilpur and rode out of the country, Karan lay grievously wounded on the battlefield, was recognized by Harpal and carried away on the back of a camel to the borders of Gujarat. By the time they reached Baglan, Karan was in such an exhausted and enfeebled state that Harpal decided not to go farther. He sent word of Karan's condition to Ramdev, the king of Devgadh, in whose territory Baglan lay. Offering a helping hand to the weak was one of the noblest traits of the Rajput kings of those days. As a vassal of Allauddin Khilji, Ramdev was fully aware of the dangers of sheltering the emperor's enemy and arousing the wrath of Alafkhan. Even so, he agreed to grant Karan—a man superior to him in status who had been reduced to this pitiable state through his own sinful conduct—a safe haven in Baglan where he could live out his remaining days. Karan was brought to the fort and treated by the local physicians. They saved his life, but were unable to alleviate the pain caused by his injuries, and for many days Karan lay in agony, his mind in ceaseless turmoil, and his sleep shattered by memories of the dreadful events. It was only when Karan Raja cried out ceaselessly to God, entreating him to put an end to his life, that God had finally taken pity on him. A rivulet of joy had coursed through the wilderness of his despair. A ray of peace had pierced the darkness. And the scorched landscape of his misfortune was cooled by the dew of mercy as God sent two angels to drive away the demons of hopelessness.

Before setting fire to the palace of Patan, Queen Kaularani had entrusted her two young daughters, the princesses Kanakdevi and Devaldevi, to the care of a trusted servant, commanding him to take them to her father in Jhalavaad. On the way, the servant had learnt that Karan Raja was still alive and had been given asylum in Baglan. Convinced that Karan not only had a greater claim on his daughters than their maternal grandfather but that they would be a great source of comfort to him in his time of misfortune, he changed direction and made his way to Baglan. Facing many hardships and overcoming many dangers, the small party finally reached the fort of Baglan unharmed, and the innocent young girls found refuge in the arms of their father. It is impossible to describe the boundless joy of that unfortunate king at the sight of his daughters. Kanakdevi was eight years old. Skilled in the household arts she took up the responsibility of running the raja's home; and as a result of her tender care, Karan Raja's wounds gradually began to heal.

How essential women are for man's happiness and creature comforts become clear only in their absence. Women are not valued as they deserve to be and their worth generally goes unrecognized. God has endowed men and women with different qualities, and though we do find some instances of men possessed of feminine qualities and women of masculine ones, in general the two sexes are poles apart. As a rule men are more virile and tough while women are more gentle and possess a greater capacity for endurance. Compassion, tenderness, patience and the ability to bring happiness to others are qualities more prominent amongst women; and they are thus better suited to run the home and take care of their husbands' well-being. When a man is beset by difficulties, no one besides his wife can calm and comfort him. But it is when illness strikes a man and he becomes childish in his demands, when his irritability becomes so unbearable that no one can take it any more—it is then that a wife is desperately needed and her true worth recognized, and then it seems that God must have sent her with the express purpose of alleviating her husband's suffering. Her tender care banishes half his pain.

Her loving words act as a magic charm and her gentle touch cools his fevered body.

On every step of life's journey, a woman is a source of joy to a man. In infancy, the need for a mother is very great; in fact, a child's very existence depends on her or another like her. As an adult, a man's journey across the ocean of life is made more smooth and enjoyable with his wife by his side; and if, unfortunately, his wife dies before him, his daughter shoulders many of her domestic responsibilities. This is exactly what happened in the case of Karan Raja. All Kanakdevi's efforts were directed towards ministering to her father's needs, to looking to his comfort and lessening his pain. Towards this task she exerted herself as much as she was able to and, by the grace of God, she succeeded in her endeavours. Devaldevi, the younger princess, was only four years old at the time and though she could not do as much as her sister, her childish pranks, her winsome ways and innocent prattle went a long way to comfort Karan Raja. His two daughters were his most precious jewels, and while he had lost all, he yet had the good fortune to be left with such treasures. They were like soothing balm on his wounds, like food to the starving, water to the thirsty, medicine to the suffering. The more he was abandoned by the world, the more tightly enmeshed did he become in the net of his daughters' love. When men glanced askance at him, his daughters' eyes were brimful with love. When his fair-weather friends abandoned him like a flock of parrots, God united him with his girls. And when he was deserted by his retainers and soldiers, instead of having to buy loyalty, he had the unconditional love of his daughters.

Karan's happiness was destined to last only five years. The ways of the Lord are unfathomable. If one believes that God does not crush the already fallen and that the happiness granted to Karan Raja at the end of his terrible ordeal would last a lifetime, one might very likely be proved wrong. When calamities come, they come not singly but in hordes. Only one who does not lose his equanimity at such times, nor his firm belief in God, can be considered a man of true faith. Only a few pass this test. Now it was Karan's turn. Just as his pain had abated and just as he had begun to savour the taste of happiness, fate struck him a deadly blow. Death's messenger arrived at the secluded fort and without warning snatched away his beloved Kanakdevi, the joy of his life and support in his adversity, who had just turned thirteen. It is futile to try and describe the effect of this sudden and unexpected blow of fate. Therefore, let us draw a curtain across these events and resume our narrative in 1306, in the month of Ashadh, in a chamber where Karan sat with his younger daughter Devaldevi by his side.

Four years had passed. Devaldevi had blossomed into a maiden whose beauty eclipsed even that of an apsara. Her flawless, translucent skin, suffused with the glow of youth, rivalled the blush of a rose. She looked older than her age. Her slender, well-proportioned figure seemed to have been fashioned by the Creator himself. She moved with the grace of a swan and her voice had the sweetness of honey. When she sang to banish her father's sorrow her voice bewitched her listeners and left them spellbound. Just as the birds and beasts of the forest, unmindful of their innate enmities, were drawn to the music of Orpheus's lyre, so was the wind hushed by Devaldevi's voice, and her pet deer and other forest creatures gathered around to hear her sing. They followed her, mesmerized by her beauty. It wasn't difficult to surmise that she would grow up to be another Kaularani or even surpass her mother in beauty.

And what is more, she was but thirteen! This age has a charm of its own, and in tropical countries like ours it marks the passage from childhood to youth. Significant bodily changes take place at this age in girls who are brought up in health and comfort. The face fills out and glows with youth. The insouciance of childhood is replaced by a sweet thoughtfulness. The shoulders broaden and the breasts swell. The mind, too, does not remain unaffected. Thirteen! When a young girl, standing on the threshold of womanhood, looks back on her past, is it surprising that she sighs for the innocent days gone by? Those carefree days of childhood, like a flowing stream, will never return. Vanished forever are the freedoms which she enjoyed, the happy passing of her days, the indifference towards the future, the joys of the present, the frank and open interaction with young and old alike, the unresentful acceptance of criticism by family members or outsiders, the resilience that allowed her to shake off sorrow and bounce back to joy, the capacity to forgive and forget, the inability to perceive evil in others, the innocence that shielded her from the knowledge of sin itself, and the peace and happiness that resides in a sinless heart. Memories of such a childhood are enough to plunge a young girl into despair; and now, to add to that, she must confront an uncertain future. What does she see when she turns her gaze towards it? So far, she has spent her days in the freedom of the garden of innocence, but now on her thirteenth birthday she must cross the threshold into an unknown world. A veil of uncertainty obscures her vision and relying on her imagination she conjures a favourable tomorrow for herself. But it is not long before the harsh light of reality dispels her happy dreams. She becomes anxious at the very thought of crossing the ocean of life, and the unchartered joys and sorrows that lie ahead. And then an unfamiliar longing invades her heart and drowns all anxieties. It is the magical awakening of love. An inexhaustible stream of love wells up in the heart, and it craves an object towards which to flow. But bereft of such an object the heart is desolate. Longing for companionship, it flounders restlessly in all directions.

This fire of passion has been ignited by a wise, omniscient Lord for a profound purpose, and the more it is purified and divested of base tendencies, the more it resembles the highest love for the divine. When love is pure and unsullied it burns away all dross and cleanses the heart. It uproots and destroys negative tendencies of the mind. At such moments, men and women are so filled with love that it overflows and spreads over all those who cross its path, man or bird, beast or insect, tree or blossom. A heart full of love does not despair. Adverse circumstances are unable to crush it. It basks in eternal sunshine and love-filled eyes can see no shadows. The longed-for beloved, the companion on life's journey, monopolizes the lover's gaze. How beautiful was Laila in the eyes of Majnu! It mattered not if others thought her plain.

A study of other cultures makes it clear that in societies where child marriages are not prevalent, girls do not allow themselves to be meekly led like dumb cattle into matrimony. In societies where marriage is not looked upon as a form of barter; where the indissoluble bonds of marriage are not forged without taking into consideration the nature, inclinations and habits of the couple; where men and women have the time to get to know each other; where marriages take place with the willing consent of both the partners and their families—it sometimes happens that a youth from a humble background falls in love with a wealthy maiden or one whose station in life is above his. He may be deeply loved in return, but so long as he is poor, he does not entertain any thought of marriage. The girl's parents, out of pride or concern, would never permit such a marriage; neither does the young man desire to drag his beloved into a life of deprivation. Instead, he sets aside his own happiness and selfish needs and consoles his beloved with the promise that he will raise himself out of poverty by his own efforts, and will honourably ask for her hand once he has found employment, earned sufficient money and made a name for himself. It matters not if years pass before this goal is achieved. When, burning the midnight oil, immersed in his studies, the lover sees his beloved's form in front of his mind's eye; or when exhaustion and lack of money lead to despair and he is on the verge of abandoning his resolve, his beloved seems to chide him for his faint-heartedness and in her sweet voice urges him to be patient. And his burdens, however heavy and unbearable they appear to others, are made light by the goddess enshrined in his heart and the powerful mantra of love. She never gives up on him, encouraging him to persevere till his goal is reached. And, in the end, if his beloved remains true to him, their union will take place; but if she is fickle and forsakes him, he can console himself with the thought that he is fortunate to have escaped an unhappy future, and be content with the high position and status that his love has made possible.

Those who have not experienced such love find it difficult to comprehend. Yet it does exist and has united many a heart. But in a country where child marriages are the rule, duty triumphs over love. Where the relationship is that of worshipper and worshipped, where the woman's role is limited to the propagation of the family, the shouldering of domestic burdens and the raising of children; where a deceased wife is only mourned for the loss of her domestic services and a home bereft of comforts; where the widower's thoughts race towards remarriage, the concept of sublime, all-embracing love is rarely understood. Child marriages take place before the blossoming of such feelings, and therefore, there is neither room for them nor a sense of lack. It appears to be a law of nature that the true value of an object is recognized only when it is lost. For the child bride and groom, their untimely union only produces a forced bond, and they cannot experience or understand the natural flowering of mature love.

The gains that would accrue from a deep and lasting relationship are nipped in the bud. The desire to study diligently during one's youth and make a name for oneself, to obtain an adequate means of livelihood and, if need be, to better one's position to be worthy of one's beloved—such aspirations are strangers to those who have married young. Where a relationship is based on sexual attraction alone, it remains on the physical plane. Appearance is its driving force; other virtues play no role. Only when soul meets soul, when values and temperaments are in complete accord, when love rises above the sway of passions and is free of material considerations, when it is selfless, can it be defined as true.

When marriage is not based solely on lust there is a greater desire to protect the beloved and satisfy her every need. The more impoverished and unfortunate she is, the greater the desire to release her from her wretched condition and make her a companion in happiness. Love such as this grows stronger with the passage of time; death cannot destroy it and lovers can take comfort in the thought that they will be reunited in paradise. If only such pure love could be experienced by all, the world would be transformed. Love is the one constant that creates joy amidst unhappiness; it is a beacon of light in an ocean of sorrow, a rope for the drowning. Pure love is a gift from God, but it must be used well. Does not a mother shower unconditional love on her children even if they are weak, blind, dumb or wayward? The more dependent the child, the stronger grows her love. There is no taint of selfishness in it. The love of aged couples which is free of lust, and the friendship between men of the same age and class, untainted by selfish motives, is also of this nature. Just as lustrous diamonds emerge from insignificant pebbles when rubbed with abrasives, the dross of selfishness should be removed from feelings of love to render it pure and all-embracing. It is love such as this, vast and expansive, that man should feel towards his Maker.

Devaldevi had just turned thirteen, and tender shoots of love had sprouted in her heart. She, too, experienced the changes that have been described above. Living such a secluded life, the only men she came in contact with were her father, the servants and some villagers. It appeared doubtful whether her father's circumstances would ever allow her to place the wedding garland around the neck of her chosen one in the svayamvara ceremony, or if any suitable groom would approach her father to ask for her hand. Such thoughts made Devaldevi gloomy and depressed. And if God in His mercy had not cast a ray of hope on her unhappy life she would have slowly faded away. Just like a tree in full bloom, eaten away by woodworms, crashes to the ground without warning, the gnawing ache of unrequited love would have led to Devaldevi's untimely and incomprehensible death. But that was not to be. Devaldevi was to experience many upheavals in her lifetime. God had not intended for her to sit crouched in a corner, a silent spectator of life.

———

It so happened that ten kos from Baglan a tiger and his mate were creating havoc in the neighbourhood. Cattle had been killed and the villagers lived in constant fear. Many attempts were made to destroy the beasts, but they proved to be fierce and elusive, and not a few lost their lives in the process. When word of this problem reached the king of Devgadh, he immediately sent his two sons, Bhimdev and Shankaldev, to hunt down the tigers and come to the aid of the beleaguered villagers. Bhimdev was a mere youth of twenty-five, but in bravery he was second to none. Shankaldev was as handsome and intrepid as Indra, and endowed with those qualities that would make a Rajput proud. He was yet unmarried, not having met a girl who had won his heart.

Armed with bows, spears and other weapons, and accompanied by a retinue of men, the princes set up camp on the outskirts of Baglan. Aware of Karan Raja's fondness for hunting, the princes invited him to join the hunt, hoping that it would provide a temporary respite from his sorrow. Karan, eager for action and a chance to exhibit his skill, readily agreed to participate in his favourite sport. But he was reluctant to leave Devaldevi behind, as she had until then never been separated from him. So father and daughter both joined the princes in the forest. A *machaan* was built, and leaving Devaldevi with a few attendants on the platform, Karan Raja and the two princes of Devgadh set off in pursuit of the tigers. Villagers fanned out through the densely wooded ravines and with loud shouts tried to frighten the beasts into the open. Suddenly, out of the dense foliage, a tiger leapt out with a roar, and with a single deadly blow felled one of the men. As the villagers fled in panic, the enraged beast attacked again. Karan let loose an arrow, but it missed its mark and only grazed the tiger's tail. Soon only Karan and the two princes remained. The maddened tiger charged at Bhimdev's elephant, and if Shankaldev's arrow had not arrested that assault, Bhimdev's fate would have been sealed. But Shankaldev's arrow pierced the tiger's heart, and as the beast crashed to the ground, Bhimdev dismounted from his elephant and thrust his spear into the animal's mouth. With an earth-shattering cry, the mighty beast, the king of the jungle, deadliest of predators, the perpetrator of many a bloody attack, fell to the ground, lifeless.

His roar reverberated throughout the forest and was heard by his mate. She streaked out of the thicket like a flash of lightning to avenge the death of her mate. Before she could be shot dead she had charged into the machaan with such force that the entire structure crashed to the ground. Some of the hunters took to their heels, others lay on the ground numb with shock, and still others fainted with fear, unconscious of what was happening around them. The tigress mauled two of the men, and was about to pounce upon the unconscious Devaldevi. But just as this apsara, this innocent maiden, the apple of Karan Raja's eye, hovered between life and death, a man burst out of the thicket and slashed the tigress with his sword. And just as the beast turned around to attack him he plunged the sword into her open jaw with such force that it smashed her teeth and stuck deep in her throat. The wound proved fatal. With one ear-splitting roar, the tigress staggered to the ground and was hacked to pieces.

Though the danger had receded, the clouds of death dispersed, and the shipwreck averted in the stormy sea, everyone was still in a state of shock. Devaldevi lay in a dead faint and every remedy to revive her failed. Karan Raja stood by helplessly, crazed with grief. It was due to Shankaldev's single-minded efforts that Devaldevi finally regained consciousness. And as she came to, her eyes fell on the prince. That one glance, so full of gratitude and love, was enough. Shankaldev was undone. Even the potions of the most renowned physicians could not have worked faster to transform his life. Assailed by wave upon wave of feelings that overwhelmed him, he fled from the scene, and took refuge under a tree, lost in a world of dreams.

With the tiger and its mate dead and Devaldevi restored to consciousness, the little group prepared to leave the forest. Devaldevi and Shankaldev met only once or twice during the journey, and though their brief encounters convinced them that their hearts were in each other's keeping, they knew that the magical moment in the forest would never return.

———

Women are generally more sensitive than men and feel the pangs of love more keenly. Confined alone in the house for long periods of time, brooding endlessly over the beloved, the roots of love spread deep and firm in their hearts. A man, on the contrary, is more robust. He has other preoccupations. The desire to achieve success, to make a name for himself, to make his way in the world, weakens Kama's hold over him. It is to prove their love that women are ready to commit sati, it is for this reason that women of the higher castes are debarred from marrying a second time; and it is for this reason and no other, that a woman feels the agony of lost love more keenly than a man and often pines away till death releases her. A man seldom feels such despair; one rarely hears of a man sacrificing his life for his woman in any country or culture; nor has one heard of restrictions placed on a widower desirous of remarrying, or of one who has died of grief out of love for his deceased wife.

Devaldevi's heart overflowed with the intensity of first love, and she was fortunate to have it reciprocated by one who was worthy of it. It was made even stronger by the deep sense of gratitude she felt towards Shankaldev. It is not unusual for love to be born out of gratitude alone, and many get married under its sway without a backward glance at disparities in age or social standing. It is but natural that Devaldevi was overwhelmed with love for a man as young and handsome as Shankaldev who had saved her life.

It was the month of Shravan. New shoots had sprung up with the first rains. Grass carpeted the earth. Gardens were newly planted and the scent of flowers filled the air. The first sprouts dappled the furrowed fields. Farmers were hard at work; and in the evenings, the rhythmic tinkling of bells could be heard as well-fed cattle lumbered homewards from the meadows. Buffaloes spent their days lazing placidly in muddy ponds. The rivers were full, carts got stuck in the squelchy mud and travellers were obliged to ride on horses or bullocks. The roads of the towns were equally muddy and foul-smelling, and people walked barefoot on them, wrapped in blankets and shawls.

On one cloudy evening in the month of Shravan, Devaldevi sat pensively in the garden under a bower of sweet-scented flowers. A gentle rain was falling. She was oblivious to the world around her. Her body in turmoil with desire, the blood in her veins coursed with longing, and her eyes misted over with passion—all her thoughts were focused on her all-consuming emotion. The gentle breeze that blew across the garden only fanned the flames of her love rather than cooling it. The scent of flowers that it carried only inflamed her passion. Every pore of her body craved for union with her beloved. Devaldevi gazed at the swiftly moving clouds. Were they bringing her a message from her beloved Shankaldev or were they only hastening to join their companions in the sky? O, if only she could move like a cloud or fly like a bird to her lover! Everything appears yellow to a jaundiced eye and everything is rose-tinted to one in love.

Bees buzzed incessantly round the ketaki flowers, sipping nectar, but alas, there was no lover to taste the sweetness of Devaldevi's overflowing love. How tightly the vines entwined themselves around the mango tree! But there was no one to envelope Devaldevi in a passionate embrace. A creeper and a woman, both need support. Without that they wither away. Creepers find this support easily and clinging to it grow and thrive. A woman, too, may find support but often it proves inadequate or unpalatable. Not far from Devaldevi, peacocks welcomed the rains with a resplendent display of colour. Peahens, plain in appearance, surrounded them, participating in their joy. Poor, beautiful, unfortunate Devaldevi! Even an ugly peahen was not without a mate in this joyous season, while she languished alone. Birds flitted from tree to tree and birdsong filled the air. Envious of the birds, pining for her beloved, Devaldevi wished she too had wings. Her pet doe came to her side, expecting to be petted and fondled by her mistress as usual. In vain did the little animal wait—not a single, loving glance was cast before it. How could the poor creature know that all her mistress's love was now wholly fixed upon another? But when at last Devaldevi noticed the forlorn doe, she stroked it and said, 'You, too, are as unfortunate as I am. You, too, have no mate and you will not find one as long as you are with me. Therefore, I shall soon release you so that you can wander free in the forest and find a mate to love. Yet you are better off than me. You are happy to be with me and are content in my love and delight in my company. But there is no one to love and indulge me.'

As Devaldevi spoke, the sky became overcast. The rain fell in a steady drizzle. Flowers unfurled their petals to the sky, their thirsty mouths open to savour the life-giving rain. Birds stopped their playful flight to shelter under the branches of trees. Peacocks danced and strutted with renewed vigour. The doe bounded away from Devaldevi and she was left alone. But the rain could not quench the fire in her heart. Just as fire burns more brightly when a few drops of water fall upon it, the flames of love in her heart leapt higher as the rain fell around her. From a nearby thicket the koel's sweet notes bid the birds a final farewell. The papeeha's call sharpened Devaldevi's longing for Shankaldev. Frogs croaked ceaselessly from shallow puddles. The earth rejoiced. But nothing could assuage the longing in Devaldevi's heart.

O poets! You are mistaken to imagine the arrows of Kama to be fashioned from flowers. Even if made from flowers, they conceal sharp thorns that pierce the heart, and the wounds they inflict take long to heal. Devaldevi had no friends in whom she could confide. She had no mother to fathom the secret of her heart and find a solution for her predicament. Her older sister Kanakdevi was dead. If she had been alive, Devaldevi could have unburdened herself to her, and even if she could have done nothing to remedy the situation, Devaldevi would have found solace in her company. She could have confided in her maidservant, but she was an old woman who would not have been able to understand the longings of her heart. Both would have viewed the situation differently and would never have been able to reconcile their differences. And how could they? Can burning coals unite with ice? It is nature's law that opposing forces repel each other, and the old nurse could be of no help to Devaldevi. That left her father. But he was of no use in such a situation. How could he understand her plight? It wasn't possible to confide in him, and even if she did he would most probably be unable to appreciate her predicament and, perhaps, even worsen the situation.

These were not the only thoughts that troubled Devaldevi. She was wracked by other doubts. 'Is Shankaldev too suffering the pangs of love as intensely as I am? Is my love reciprocated or is it one-sided? My thoughts are focused on him as towards God, but who knows, he may be too busy to even remember me. Perhaps some other girl has stolen his heart, perhaps he is immune to love, perhaps he doesn't like my looks. If such is the case (O Lord! Let it not be so), then my agony is in vain. But I am doing him a grave injustice by thinking such thoughts. My heart and my mind are convinced that it is not so. Our love is mutual. He too longs for me, he too suffers as I do. Like me, for him too food has lost its taste. My image is enshrined in his heart. O, if only God brings us together once more, I shall never again leave him. I long to unburden myself to him and be sure of his love.'

As Devaldevi sat lost in thought, the sound of a flute wafted across the fields, its melodious notes sounding even sweeter on that rainy, monsoon day. Like the gopis of Braja intoxicated by the sound of Shri Krishna's flute, Devaldevi became wild with excitement. And before she could compose herself, a man leapt across the garden wall, and in the twinkling of an eye Shankaldev himself stood before her. The sudden, totally unexpected encounter was too much for Devaldevi, and she fell to the ground in a swoon. But with Shankaldev's anxious ministrations, she soon revived. The lovers locked their gaze. Who can describe their joy? Fakirs, sannyasis and sadhus who have turned their back on the world, and those who see only the darkest side of life, should realize that though the world seems full of evil, it is largely ruled by good. And though life is often beset by difficulties there are always moments of joy, as when a man and a woman come together in love. Devaldevi and Shankaldev, two separate beings, but one in mind and spirit, were unable to say a word to each other. But to say that they stood in silence would be misleading, for their eyes had begun to speak in a language of their own. Through a single glance, more effective than words, Devaldevi and Shankaldev assured each other of their mutual love and their readiness to go through life together for better or for worse. Yet the longing of their hearts called out for speech. Shankaldev was the first to break the silence, and then, mustering up all her courage, Devaldevi spoke. It is not necessary to convey what was said between the two. Love can give wings to speech, and what a person says under its influence may never be repeated again. So I leave it to the reader to imagine what was said between the two. Shankaldev looked on Devaldevi as one more divine than mortal. To him her virtue was priceless and it seemed that even the shadow of a base thought about her would be to plunge into the dark valley of hell. So anxious was Shankaldev that Devaldevi's modesty should not be violated, he resolved that it was far better for thousands such as he to be destroyed rather than her fair name be sullied in any way. For Shankaldev, to take advantage of a helpless maiden and deliberately trap her into temptation was not the conduct of a man, but rather that of a beast. It was the conduct of a coward, not worthy of a kshatriya. And so, when the time to part drew near, he stood beside Devaldevi. Clasping hands they looked towards the sky and with the sun god as witness, solemnly vowed:

'O Suryadev! You whose rays light up the whole world and can fathom not only the motives behind man's deeds but his innermost thoughts! O Vayudev! You are present in every breeze and witness every act of man. O Varundev! Guardian of every river and stream of this place. O countless ganas and godlings, the inhabitants of the air who are ever involved in the running of the world! O ye thirty-three crore gods! Wherever you are at this moment, you stand witness to our union. O omnipresent and omniscient God! We pledge this solemn oath in the vastness of your realm. Not a blade of grass can move unless you will it, no task can be accomplished without your knowledge. In the midst of this divine host, we, Shankaldev and Devaldevi, do solemnly vow to strengthen further our already strong love, to enjoy the happiness that flows from our affection, to beget children through holy matrimony, to use wisely the store of love the divine hand has placed in our hearts, and to be united in mind and body for the rest of our lives. This is our sincere promise. From today know us to be one, eager to share the joys and sorrows of this world. From now on, we will be true to the duties enjoined on men and women by dharma, and endeavour not only to be happy ourselves but to make others happy too. O Lord of the World! Seal this vow of ours. And O thirty-three crore gods! If we should break these sacred vows, know us to have sinned against our ancestors, ourselves, and the duties enjoined on all beings, and fully deserving of the severest punishments meted out in hell. Therefore, O Protector of the Helpless, Compassionate Lord of the World, look favourably upon us and sanctify our union. Bless it and let it attain a joyful fruition. Fulfil our hopes. O loving and compassionate Father, we entreat you to hear and grant this prayer of ours.'

Shankaldev and Devaldevi felt a great weight lift from their hearts. But all too soon it was time to part. It was time for lunch, and if Devaldevi was not seen at home an attendant would surely be sent to look for her, and their secret would be out. It was necessary for the lovers to part. But that was easier said than done. When lovers meet, a day seems but a moment, so how could an hour of togetherness satisfy either Devaldevi or Shankaldev? Can thirst be quenched by just a sip of nectar? Given the uncertainty of life, the ever-present possibility of death, and the fear of unforeseen obstacles, even a brief parting could mean permanent separation. The fear that this might be their last meeting made the lovers loathe to part. But they were helpless. Placing their faith in God and their destiny, they went their separate ways. Whether they will ever meet again or not will become clear as the story unfolds.

Happy and carefree days pass only too soon. Devaldevi felt that it was but yesterday when she had been with Shankaldev. Then one day, a bard accompanied by a royal priest arrived at the fort of Baglan. The bard, after the customary words of flattery went on to extol the wealth and splendour of the ruler of Devgadh and the vastness of that kingdom. He compared Shankaldev to Yudhishthir, Arjun, Vikram, Bhoj and other famous, virtuous and valourous kings, recounted all the events that had occurred from the day of the tiger hunt to the meeting of Shankaldev and Devaldevi in the garden, enumerated at great length the benefits that would accrue from a union with the House of Devgadh; and finally, on behalf of Shankaldev, asked Karan Raja for Devaldevi's hand in marriage.

Karan Raja turned red with anger. With a voice filled with displeasure he replied, 'Bard, listen well. Though I have lost my kingdom, though my dearly beloved wife has been forcibly dragged to Delhi by the Turkish emperor, though I am penniless and weak, and have been obliged to take shelter under Ramdev, still I have not sunk as low as you think. The blood of the Rajput still flows in my veins. My kshatriya dharma is unshakable, therefore I will never agree to such a union. What! A Vaghela princess to marry a Maratha! A swan to be a part of a family of crows!

A cow live amongst donkeys? This can never be. However great your king may be, however strong, rich and vast his kingdom, even if Shankaldev should possess the virtues of all the gods put together, a Maratha will never be fit to wed a Rajput maiden. During these hapless years I have been repeatedly humiliated and now it seems to be Ramdev's turn. But this insult is past bearing. I am still alive; I can still vigorously defend my name, my family and myself. And so long as I live, I shall not allow my reputation to be besmirched. A maiden of such high caste to be married to one so low! Even if dire calamities befall me, even if I am cut to pieces, I shall never allow such a thing to happen. For us Rajputs to lament the birth of a daughter is justified. It is not considered wrong to take the life of an infant girl in order to protect kshatriya honour. A Maratha to wed a princess! Let the heavens fall, the earth be destroyed, I will never permit it. So inform your king how greatly he has insulted me. Tell him that his hopes will never be fulfilled. Even if Shankaldev and Devaldevi have secretly pledged marriage, it is null and void. Devaldevi has not the right to make promises without my consent. She is still a child and my answer is no. The most you can do is throw me out of this place. But I do not fear this. The world is vast and I will find a corner in it to live out the rest of my days. After my death you can do what you will.' Saying this, Karan Raja bade the bard and the priest to take their leave.

12

'O Lord! You, who can turn an ant into an elephant, and create a mountain from a blade of grass! How can one even begin to understand the extent of your power!' Thus exclaimed a Hindu named Biharilal as he brought his horse to a stop in front of a large mansion on an avenue in Delhi. He was trapped in a difficult situation and had come here in a desperate attempt to try and resolve it. Under the new Sharia law, Hindus in Delhi who refused to convert to Islam were obliged to pay the jeziya tax. Those who protested against the tax, or tried to avoid paying what was demanded, were liable to the extreme penalty of death. Biharilal was accused of concealing the name of one of the members of his family, thus paying less than his due. Although the accusation was baseless and Biharilal innocent, although the whole business was due to nothing but the enmity of the jeziya tax collector, even so, given the climate of intolerance against Hindus, an atmosphere in which money decided which way the scales of justice would tilt, and judges who ensured that their judgements never harmed the treasury, it was not surprising that Biharilal was extremely worried. Not just worried—he felt certain that without immediate action, his days were numbered. But, God be thanked, in an oppressive, unjust state there does exist a remedy which, if one is in the position to employ it, can keep one safe. That remedy is money. 'With money anything is possible' is a saying that is very often true. A wealthy man can escape from an allegation whether true or false; he can even shift the blame on to another; but a man without money can be destroyed. The poor invariably suffer punishment, whether the accusations against them are true or not, and they often bear the consequences of rich people's culpability. God is their only protector—they must count themselves lucky just to be alive.

Biharilal was a successful merchant. He had amassed considerable wealth in just a few years but, thanks to harsh government policies, he had been unable to enjoy it. To avoid the hawk-eyed gaze of government officials, Biharilal lived in a small house in an obscure part of the city. He kept most of his wealth buried underground and wore such shabby clothing that it was difficult to believe that he was a rich man. But a despotic government has a keen nose for money. And just as hunting dogs sniff the presence of rabbits hiding terrified in their holes, vultures and kites scent a corpse from a long way off, and ants smell sugar from anywhere, so a whiff of Biharilal's wealth reached the government. No man is without enemies, but one who is rich must also contend with the envy of friends. Out of feelings of envy and dissatisfaction with their own lot, they spread rumours about his wealth to the authorities. Their information may or may not be correct, but it is certain that the very next day officials will appear at the rich man's doorstep, his property will be confiscated, he will be dragged to court on some pretext or another, accused of a crime and, after a needlessly prolonged trial, it will become clear that his only crime is his great wealth. By the time the matter is resolved, he will end up losing half or even more of his fortune. And as if such close 'friends' are not enough, there are government spies who scour the town for information. They have the lowdown on every section, locality and house in

Delhi, and the moment they spot a likely prey they pounce on it, claws extended. If at this moment, the victim hesitates to grease the right palms, his doom is certain. To escape from the frying pan he falls into the fire. He ends up being accused of much graver crimes and ultimately, has to gratify both the government and the spies.

The scent of Biharilal's wealth had reached the highest authorities, and the informant was no other than the jeziya tax collector, whom Biharilal—relying on his own innocence and wanting to discourage this kind of blackmail—had not bribed. Within a few days his home had been raided, his wife and children confined to a single room and he himself bound and taken to the police *chowky* like a common criminal. He had managed to get himself released that day on bail, but was sick with anxiety about the future. It was not just for himself that he was worried; what filled him with dread was also the possibility that the wealth he had put together with such effort, difficulty and risk could vanish in a moment, that the women of his household be left unprovided for, and his family punished for his actions. Just as in the Christian faith, the punishment that God rained down on the first man, Adam, for his sins is still visited on all of us; just as certain diseases are passed down from parent to child; so also, in an autocratic state, children are often made to bear the punishment for the crimes of their fathers, and close relatives too are often drawn into the conflict.

It may be possible to free oneself from the grasp of a tiger, but to escape safe and sound from the clutches of a tyrannical government is nothing short of a miracle. A fly trapped in a spider's web must consider itself lucky if by thrashing around a while, it manages to escape with only a broken wing or leg, for the spider is waiting and watching for its struggles to subside before it darts stealthily and ends the fly's life. Like a fly, Biharilal was trapped in a web of bureaucracy, and was flailing around trying to escape. He had made the mistake of not gauging the atmosphere of the times and the nature of the government that was in power. He had relied on the values of truth and integrity and assumed these to be as immovable as rocks. But in evil times, such values are often not enough to save a man from destruction; they get dislodged in the stormy sea of life, and those that cling to them for protection are swept away in the turbulent waters.

If one is to embrace the values of truth and integrity wholeheartedly, then one must be prepared to face life without fear. One must accept that reliance on these principles—invaluable as they are—may result in many difficulties, lead to financial ruin and even put one's life in peril; yet one must hold on to the belief that they are worthwhile in themselves, and rest assured that the virtuous will be rewarded with boundless joy by the omniscient Creator in the world to come. Of course, truth and integrity are often rewarded in this world, but it would be foolish to embrace them for this reason alone, for it is inadvisable to follow the right path in the hope of possible gain.

If, when faced with the difficulties and inevitable problems of life, virtuous people think that their honesty and integrity will please God and keep them safe from harm, they are bound to become unhappy and dissatisfied, and they will come to one of two conclusions: either that there is no God, or that he is blind and makes no distinction between the good and the evil, and hence to put one's faith in Him and expect Him to reward one for one's good conduct is pointless. Alternatively, they will conclude that there is no difference between good and evil, and that the notion that good will be rewarded and evil punished in this world is nothing but a false promise made by the wise in ancient times in order to prevent people from committing evil acts. But those who come to such conclusions have only themselves to blame, not God. In short, while good qualities may indeed be rewarded in this world, this is not the reason why one should adopt them. They are valuable in themselves, and will be rewarded by God in the world to come.

A man who lives in a country where integrity results in financial ruin should either leave it, or be prepared to lose his material possessions and everything that he holds most dear, including his life. The innocence of a goat does not prevent it from being killed by a tiger, and a sparrow cannot rely on its vulnerability to save it from a falcon. Biharilal did not seem to be aware of this truth, or perhaps he had forgotten it. When he had found himself in trouble, some of his more worldly wise friends, who knew how to blow with the wind, said to him, 'Forget this nonsense about integrity. Age seems not to have brought you any wisdom. Brother, you must adapt yourself to circumstances. If you had listened to us at the start and offered a little something to the tax collector, you would not be in such straits. But you were determined to rely on your truthfulness. How come your truthfulness does not help you now? Had you taken our advice, the matter would have been settled for a small sum. Now you will have to spend far more, without any guarantee of success. Truthfulness, indeed! If you want to follow such a moral path, why do you continue to live in this world? Become a mendicant or a wandering ascetic and then be as moral as you like!' The impressionable Biharilal had taken this advice, and regretting his earlier obstinacy, had come to the mansion bearing a bag of gold.

—

Soon after he had conquered Patan, Alafkhan learnt that the town of Khambat was home to many wealthy traders. In anticipation of great plunder, the general had captured the town and sacked it. His loot included a handsome slave who had been castrated and employed as a harem guard by a trader. The slave, who was known as Kafur, possessed many other qualities in addition to his good looks. In fact, he was blessed with all those qualities— both good and bad—which are essential for self-advancement and a high station in life. In matters where his self-interest was not involved, Kafur took care to display only his good qualities, and it was difficult to believe that he had another side to him. But when it came to furthering his own career, he did not hesitate from the vilest acts. As a slave, he had not had the opportunity to display his true talents, but his fortune was about to change: he was captured by the Turkish forces, Alafkhan had noticed his striking looks and, hoping to please the emperor, had sent the slave to Delhi along with Queen Kaularani.

Allauddin had been delighted with his handsome gift, and in a short while Kafur had risen to the highest rank. He was a master of the manoeuverings and intrigues that are an integral part of the royal court, and thanks to his efforts and intelligence he had secured such a hold on Allauddin that the emperor was practically his puppet. Kafur became in effect the ruler of Delhi; but the nobles and amirs who were obliged to kowtow to the upstart eunuch were bitterly resentful and envious of him. They referred to Kafur as Hazaar Dinari— Thousand Dinars—the sum for which he had originally been bought. Kafur wielded so much power that he often acted on his own authority, without bothering to consult the emperor, and he soon began to dream of becoming emperor after Allauddin's death. Blinded by ambition and unmindful of the many favours he owed the emperor, the eunuch had begun to plot against the man who had raised him up from the dust and installed him in a palace—the very palace in front of which Biharilal now found himself.

Dismounting from his horse, Biharilal made his way to the palace entrance but was stopped by the gatekeeper who pushed him aside roughly. However, the glimpse of a bit of gold lessened his opposition to Biharilal's entry. A further distribution of gold to other guards and functionaries secured Biharilal a seat in the durbar hall and a servant went into an inner chamber, where Kafur was in deep discussion with a dervish, to inform him of the visitor's presence. Kafur had by now developed a keen sense for the odour of money, and the scent of Biharilal's gold came strongly to him. Asking the dervish to wait awhile, Kafur went to the durbar hall. Biharilal had been well tutored by his friends. He threw off his turban, fell at Kafur's feet and implored the minister to help him. But tales of woe were not the way to Kafur's heart. What was required was the clinking of gold to reach his ears. It was only when this sound fell on Kafur's ears and his senses processed the information would his heart soften. When Biharilal saw that his actions only served to make the minister more angry, he emptied a bag of 100 gold *ashrafi*s and said simply, 'Forgive me my wrongdoing.' Kafur took one look at the small heap, kicked it aside contemptuously and said, 'Kafir! Infidel! You have cheated the government of crores and now you come to me with these miserable coins and your sobbing? You think this is some kind of child's play? I can do nothing for you. The matter has been put before the padshah. If you are found guilty, there will be no option but the death penalty.' Biharilal begged and pleaded his innocence, but finding that this was going nowhere, produced a second bag of gold. This too had no effect. True to his name, Kafur was too *kafar*—cunning—to relent so soon. It was hard to believe that such a handsome face concealed such a stony heart, and it was only after five bags had been emptied that Kafur relented and told Biharilal not to worry: he would see to it that not a hair on his head would be harmed.

This entire transaction had been watched secretly by the dervish. It made him furious that his love for money had prompted Kafur to act with leniency against an infidel, that greed had made the minister break a sacred law and waive the jeziya tax. As soon as Kafur returned to the room, the dervish broke out violently, *'Ya Allah! Ya Karim!* What is this world coming to! Greed has usurped faith from the throne of God. Have you quite forgotten your past? Did God in his mercy pick you up out of the dust and raise you to a high rank for this? So you could pardon an infidel? Is it not written in the Koran that idolators who worship false gods should be forced to embrace the truth that was revealed to the Prophet by the angel Gabriel? Yet you pardoned such a man! Why, unbelievers like him deserve nothing but the sword. Bismillah! Of what use are these people except to fill up the pits of hell? But alas, the day of reckoning is still a long way off.'

Kafur shrank from these words. He was an unlettered, superstitious man and, afraid that the dervish's curses would destroy him, he tried to defend himself. 'Dervish sahib! Forgive me, but I was only following the padshah's example. When it comes to matters of money, he makes no distinction between Hindu and Muslim.'

It was as if ghee had been poured on the flames of the dervish's anger. 'You ingrate of little faith! Just because the padshah behaves in a certain way, does that make it right? When Muslims these days think like this, it is surprising that the skies do not fall down, surprising that we are not all wiped out by the plague and drowned by flood. Can one compare the religion of these infidels with our faith? Is there no difference between the two? Why, it is the difference between earth and heaven. Yes! Between darkness and light. Yes! Between Satan and God. Allah! Our misguided people no longer recognize God. They no longer see the difference between true and false faith. Alas, alas. Of all the religions in this world, those who worship idols are surely the most impure. Let me explain. There are three religions that believe in one God and do not worship man-made idols: Jewish, Christian and Muslim. Of these three, only one is true. Arabs and Jews are both descended from Abraham, the former from Ishmael and the latter from Isaac. The Prophet has accepted the Torah and the claims of Adam, Noah and Moses to be prophets. Thanks to Adam's sin, mankind was expelled from Paradise, forced to struggle, suffer disease, endure hardship and face death. Thus his claim is tainted. Very few follow the teachings of Noah, and as for Moses, his laws were meant only for the Jews of that time. The Torah prophesies the coming of a saviour who will save the world. The birth of the Prophet Muhammad fulfils this prophecy. But the Jews reject this on the grounds that the Arabs are descendants of Ishmael, who was the son of Abraham and a slave girl.

'The religion propagated by Jesus, the son of Mary is also worthy of respect, as Jesus too was a prophet, whom Mohammad Paigambar met when he visited the seventh heaven. But no one can deny that Muhammad (blessed be his name) was the last and greatest prophet, and that his faith is the true one. Among idol-worshippers, the Parsis are the best—as worshippers of fire, they are of course, guilty in the pure eyes of God, but they are far better than the Hindus. The worst are the idol-worshipping Hindus.

'Firstly, instead of believing in one God, they worship thirty-three crore deities! Is it not clear that this wondrous world of ours is the creation of a single God? The countless diamonds in the sky that we call stars, the cold moon that lights up the night and helps plants to grow, the powerful fireball that gives life and heat to the earth and supports all living things, the untimely comets that pass by from time to time and bring calamity to people and are, for the ignorant, precursors of doom; the laws that apply equally to both the extraordinary phenomena in the sky as well as to a grain of sand and a blade of grass—all are subject to one, universal law that governs the minutest atom to the spheres that revolve through vast distances in space; all are proof of the existence of a single God. Unlike material objects that are destructible, God is not—that too is amply clear. Only that which is composed of atoms can be destroyed. Destruction involves a change of form, the dissolution and reconfiguration of atoms. But God is indestructible, which proves that He is beyond matter and not subject to the laws of nature. He is formless and resides in man's heart.'

Kafur spoke. 'I will speak if you will forgive me. The Hindus have a holy book called the Vedas where it is said that God is one and without form.'

The dervish replied, 'Lies. I cannot believe that the infidels have seen the divine light that God sent to the Prophet through the angel Gabriel. And if what you say is true, why do they not follow their holy book? It is clear that the Vedas say no such thing. And even if they do, what is the point? When the truth is clearly spelt out in the Koran, what is the need for other holy books? The sooner they are destroyed, the better. At a time when the Arabs were worshipping stars and other objects, when the Jews had abandoned the commandments of Moses, the hymns of David and the psalms of Solomon; when the followers of Christ were making golden idols of Jesus and Mary and placing them in temples, and the shrines of saints and the bones of holy men were being worshipped, it was at this time that Hazrat Muhammad Sahib proclaimed "There is only one God and Muhammad is His Prophet."'

'Praise be to Allah! And to His Prophet!' Kafur interjected.

Stroking his beard, the dervish continued, 'Amen, amen, amen. Further, Hindus regard their own kind, both dead and living, as gods. Rama and Krishna were humans in previous births, but as they performed miraculous deeds, they were worshipped as gods after their death. What foolishness is this! We do not worship men like Khalid, the Sword of Islam, or Amru, the conqueror of Egypt, or our caliphs Abu Bakr, Umar and Ali; or Hatemtar or Haroun-al-Rashid, though they were as great as Vikram or Bhoj. Why, Hindus even regard cows, elephants, monkeys and other animals as gods! Serpents and mongooses are worshipped on certain days! Just as God rained fire and sulphur on the inhabitants of Sodom and Gomorrah, so will this sinful land be one day swept into the sea. To honour cattle like gods! Why, such people need to be offered the Koran or death.

'Kafur my son! That is not all. They also worship material objects—the sun, the moon, stars, rivers, mountains—in fact, whatever they see on earth. What then is the difference between the Creator and the created? May God open their eyes so that they see that mankind has been endowed with the highest intelligence and the finest faculties, given overlordship over the earth, and that all things in this bountiful world have been created for their protection and pleasure. Humans are the highest of God's creations. Yet the Hindus see themselves as the lowliest. May God dispel their blindness.'

'Amen, amen.'

The dervish went on, 'It is to dispel this ignorance that God sent down the Prophet Muhammad, and each year, in the month of Ramzan, the angel Gabriel visited him in the diamond cave and revealed the verses of the Koran. He vanquished the guards of the Kaaba and their followers, and before his death, had spread the faith in Mecca and Medina and throughout all Arabia. Thereafter, the fearless armies of the caliphs took the faith to Iran and Turkey, and this way the true faith spread gradually across almost the entire world. All this was due to God's grace. It is thus our bounden duty to tear the veil of ignorance from the minds of the heathens.

'There is another reason for their blindness: they do not understand that God is beyond qualities and is, therefore,

219

unmanifest. When they want to pray to God, worship Him or make offerings to Him, they don't know who to address. So in order to represent the unmanifest, they fashion images in the shape of human beings or other imaginary creatures, and assert that He, being immanent, is present in these mud, wood or metal objects. This is the natural propensity of men and no matter how often the truth is explained to them, they continue to worship idols rather than pray to an unseen God. When the Jews fled from Egypt on their way to their homeland, they often made idols and worshipped them, and it was a hard task for the prophet Moses to convince them that their conduct was sinful. Finally, on Mount Sinai, God gave Moses a stone tablet on which ten commandments were carved. One of these stated quite clearly that images should not be worshipped. The great danger of this practice is that the deity gets identified with the image, and instead of offering respect to the Lord, it is offered to the servant. Such confusion is understandable, and it was to forestall it that Prophet Muhammad not only forbade image worship and the installation of images in mosques, he also proscribed the making of any likeness whether of God or himself or other saintly men.'

To this Kafur replied, '*Subhanallah*! How wonderful is the wisdom of the Prophet! Had he not forbidden such things, we too would have been idol-worshippers! Dervish sahib, I know well that the Hindus are an impure, sinful lot. I know that they ought to be brought to the true path, and those that are misled by the devil deserve to be put to death. But, dervish sahib, it is not feasible for kings today to follow this line of action, and even the caliphs of yore did not do so. The Sharia says that kafirs should be taxed to the maximum extent possible, and that if they do not pay they should be destroyed. Many of our learned scholars tell us that they should be offered the choice between Islam and death. But as Imam Hanif said, it would be better to avoid unnecessary bloodshed, and instead extract jeziya tax from the infidels and *khiraj* from vassal kings with such severity that it would be like a living death. As a matter of fact, this particular Hindu has done nothing wrong. His only crime is that he is rich. The jeziya tax collector wanted a bribe, and when the Hindu did not pay it, he decided to accuse him. I knew full well that the accusation was baseless, but I also felt that it would be a pity to surrender such a rich and providential catch. Besides, who knows to what base purpose so much wealth in the hands of an infidel could be put? So I extracted 500 ashrafis from the man, and would be obliged if you would accept half the amount and put it to good use in some right and virtuous cause.'

The dervish spoke, his eyes bright with the prospect of gold. 'Congratulations, my son! You have acted wisely. Continue on this path and use some of the money for charity and spare some for dervishes like me who will use it for God's work. If you continue in this manner, God will be even more pleased and raise you to greater heights.'

'Amen! May all this come to pass with your blessings. But there is no higher rank than the one I hold, except . . .'

'Hush! Say no more. Your meaning is clear. May God make your wish come true. But now enough. Even walls have ears.'

With a meaningful glance, the dervish took 250 ashrafis, blessed Kafur profusely and went on his way.

———

Biharilal rode back to Delhi as if on air, the heavy burden lifted from his heart. But when he reached the main square, a dreadful spectacle met his eyes. For the past few years, Hindustan had been subject to frequent and destructive raids by Mongol armies. A Mongol leader named Aibak Khan had descended with a thousand cavalrymen and numerous foot soldiers, devastated the town of Multan and encamped near the Shivalik hills. Allauddin's forces had successfully repelled the Mongols. Thousands of them had been killed, and those that escaped into the jungles died of thirst and heat. The 3000 men who remained had been taken prisoner and brought to Delhi along with their leader, where preparations for their execution had been made in the square. The captured Mongol women and children had been dispatched to a neighbouring town to be auctioned off as slaves; the men had been ordered to be killed without mercy. They were divided into a hundred batches of thirty, a hundred carts were kept in readiness, and Aibak Khan was made to sit at a vantage point so he could witness the proceedings. A hundred elephants, maddened with alcohol, were led by a hundred executioners into the arena, each to trample thirty men to death. The trumpeting of the crazed elephants, the agonized screams of the men as they were crushed under the weight of the mighty beasts, the terrified, bloodless faces of those awaiting their turn, the wild agitated looks of some, the uncontrollable weeping of others as they thought of their wives, children and loved ones, created a scene that beggars the imagination.

But this was not enough for the merciless padshah. As Biharilal watched, shocked but also fascinated, butchers sitting nearby sliced off the heads of the dead and piled them on to the waiting carts. He waited till the carts were full and followed them with morbid curiosity to the Badayun gate where they were unloaded and a tower fashioned from the severed heads.

The Mongol chieftain was now brought to the place. Aibak Khan was seated on a horse, his hands tied and his legs shackled. A huge crowd followed behind. Biharilal joined the procession as it moved towards the Yamuna river. The crowd lined the bank and waited eagerly for the show to begin. Aibak Khan was put into a boat and a few of Allauddin's men got in. The Mongol was a strong and well-built man of about thirty-five, but now that all hope had fled—his army destroyed, his soldiers dead of thirst and hunger, he himself brought to Delhi to watch his men, many of whom had been faithful old companions, die horrible deaths—and he was face-to-face with death, he looked worn-out and defeated. He was not afraid to die, but the thought that he had been unable to avenge the deaths of his predecessors, the Tartars—Amir Beg and Khwaja Khan—filled him with regret. The boat reached the middle of the river. Three or four of the padshah's men picked up the Mongol and flung him into the water. No cry escaped him as he sank. With his hands tied and his legs weighed down, he had no chance to save himself. His strong body rose up once, he took one last look at the world and disappeared into the deep. A slight turbulence marked the spot and then all was still. The black waters of the river enveloped him and the Yamuna became his grave. The spectators on the bank were unaffected by the Mongol's death. True, they were not so unfeeling as to applaud the scene, but it mattered as little to them as watching a lamb being slaughtered. This callousness was understandable. When the same event is seen repeatedly, it ceases to have much effect on the viewer. Of late, brutal spectacles had become commonplace in Delhi, and familiarity had numbed all feelings of compassion.

One could argue that such harsh methods were good for the security of the country, but one would be wrong. Brutal policies do more harm than good. The Mongols had made several raids into Allauddin's kingdom; they had been defeated every single time; their forces taken prisoner more than once, tortured and brutally killed; their women sold into slavery. On this occasion, too, they had suffered the same fate. Yet, instead of serving as a deterrent, at the very time the events described above were taking place, another Tartar chieftain named Balmand had invaded the country and Allauddin had sent an army to repel him.

As Biharilal was making his way home, Kafur was making his way to the sultan's palace. Kafur was now the most important personage at the Delhi court. He was the apple of Allauddin's eye and wielded so much influence over the padshah that he could do more or less as he pleased. Even so, he was not a happy man. He lived in a constant state of anxiety lest he lose the padshah's goodwill and fall out of favour. Moreover, the other nobles hated having to show him—a low-born upstart—the same respect they showed to the king, and Kafur had to be constantly on guard against their envy, resentment and intrigues. These causes apart, there were two other reasons for Kafur's unhappiness. The first was his avarice. The fact that his desires had been realized and his hopes fulfilled so often had made him crave for more, not less. Consumed by the worm of greed he now dreamed of becoming emperor, and it was towards this end that all his attention was focused. Secondly, he knew that to achieve this goal he would first have to earn renown, make a name for himself and win the admiration of the people. And the only way to do this was by undertaking some daring task and demonstrating his valour. So far, Kafur had not proved himself a man of courage. He had risen to power through a combination of humility and intrigue. His antecedents were the lowest of the low. He had been a slave, had spent years serving in the zenana, and was a eunuch. Until the doubts surrounding his manliness were dispelled and people were convinced of his courage and bravery, his hopes of becoming king would remain unfulfilled. We have many examples of eunuchs who though deprived of their manhood are not cowardly or effeminate. Kafur was one such.

Kafur had decided that the time had come to convince the padshah to embark on a military campaign that would give him a chance to show the world what kind of man he really was. When he entered the palace, he was told that Allauddin was in the zenana. As Kafur was freely allowed to see and spend time with the begums, he went there directly. Allauddin was having his evening meal. The table was spread with an array of liquor bottles, and glasses were being continually refilled. His favourite queen, Kaularani, sat beside him, and the two were busy conversing and enjoying the sparkling, ruby-red wine. Since the reader last met her, Kaularani had exchanged her Rajput dress for the clothing of a Pathan woman. Covered in beautiful, costly jewels, the queen looked like an exquisite houri now more than ever. The sorrow she had felt while leaving Gujarat had gradually faded, and time and habit had enabled her to accept her new life. One should not conclude from this that her earlier sorrow had been false, her lamentation mere pretence. God in his mercy has given mankind the capacity to adapt and, assisted by hope, even intense grief passes with time. Had it been otherwise, people would spend their entire life in sorrow. There are indeed some in whom sorrow takes deep root and convinces them to end their lives, but luckily such people are the exception.

After some idle talk, Kafur brought the conversation around to the issue of vassal rulers, pointing out that the ruler of Devgadh, Ramdev, confident of his strength, had failed to pay his dues for the past three years. This, he said, was an insult to the padshah, and Ramdev needed to be taught a lesson. An army should be dispatched immediately against him, and if the padshah so desired he, Kafur, would be happy to head it and not only recover the outstanding dues but bring back much wealth besides. Such a move would yield two benefits. It would increase both the wealth and the power of the kingdom, news of the padshah's might would spread and his name would strike fear throughout Hindustan. It would be clear that Allauddin had a powerful army and the resources to wage war, to bring new territories under his control and to punish rebellious feudatories. 'The war would also prove beneficial to me,' Kafur went on. 'As Your Highness knows, the nobles in Delhi hold me in contempt;

225

they suppose that because I am a eunuch, I am fit for only a woman's work. I may be low-born and deprived of my manhood, but God has given me courage and bravery in great measure, and just as I manage affairs of state with intelligence, so am I capable of leading the army with courage. So, O king, grant my wish and appoint me commander of the forces against Devgadh.'

The padshah had never denied his favourite the smallest wish, and there was no way he could refuse a proposal that was not only daring but that pleased him. And even if the attack on Devgadh did not turn out as Kafur predicted, the very thought of war, even one fought without cause, thrilled Allauddin. It infused him with vigour, excitement coursed through his veins, and he wanted to plunge into action. He would have liked to have led the army himself, but in the face of Kafur's protestations, he gave up the idea.

When Kaularani heard the conversation, and the words 'Devgadh' and 'Ramdev' fell on her ears, memories of the past came flooding back and her eyes filled with tears. She had heard that her former husband Karan Vaghela had taken refuge in Devgadh, that her elder daughter Kanakdevi was dead and that Devaldevi was with her father. The queen was happy in her new home, yet she was often lonely, and she longed to have Devaldevi, now grown-up, by her side. Women believe that the mother feels more for her children than the father and has a greater right to them. Blinded by her love for her daughter, Kaularani forgot that Devaldevi had now lived with her father for several years, that the bond between them must have grown strong, and that to take her away from Karan would leave him lonely and bereft. She begged Allauddin to instruct Kafur that after he had vanquished Ramdev, he should go to Baglan to find her thirteen-year-old daughter Devaldevi and bring her back with him. Allauddin disapproved of the idea, but as he did not want to disappoint his favourite queen, he gave the order, and Kafur swore to bring back Devaldevi to Delhi.

The next day a grand durbar was held. Allauddin received Kafur with full honour, conferred the title of Nawab Malik on him and personally presented him with a robe. The other nobles were ordered to show him the same respect they showed the emperor. Within a few days a 100,000-strong force was assembled and Khwaja Haji was deputed as Malik Kafur's second-in-command. The army set out to conquer the south in 1305. A number of the leading nobles of Delhi were present with their forces. The governor of Malwa, Ain-ul-Mulk Multani, and Alafkhan, now governor of Gujarat, had been ordered to join them. Aware that this might be the last time he would see his favourite, Allauddin bid Malik Kafur farewell, reminding him once again that he must bring Devaldevi back to Delhi, or be prepared to face his wrath.

13

When the first flowering of love between a man and a woman is thwarted, the misery is unbearable. When lovers are heartbroken and distraught, the entire world seems like a graveyard. Unless the stream of depressing thought is diverted by a change of scene or in some other manner, the personality can disintegrate. If the obstacles faced are temporary, if even a single, dim ray of hope is able to pierce the darkness of despair, the lovers can wait out the bleak present with patience. But when the door shuts on hope, it irrevocably shuts on happiness. Most men can forget their hurt by travelling to distant places, immersing themselves in new experiences, taking up a different occupation; and perhaps meeting another attractive woman. But this is practically impossible for women. They are more tender-hearted, and the imprint of love is more firmly stamped on them and harder to eradicate. They hardly ever have the opportunity to travel to distant lands or the luxury to wipe out memories of old hurts by a change of circumstance. They worry, pine, and if they are of a delicate constitution, they often fall prey to illness. No doubt there are exceptions to this. But when hope withers, women are prone to suffer more than men.

The sun of Devaldevi's happiness set when Karan Raja refused to allow her to wed Shankaldev. Her joy faded away with the fading of hope. Sorrow cast a shadow on her life, she began to waste away, and a deathly fever consumed her body. Devaldevi's laughter was silenced, her song lost its melody and her voice its sweetness, and she no longer walked with a joyous carefree step. Observing this change, Karan became apprehensive. He tried hard to tempt Devaldevi out of her despondency with all that money and love could do; but of what use is a poultice applied to the stomach of someone suffering from a throbbing headache? How can external remedies heal a wounded heart? As long as the worm of despair eats at the heart, all other remedies are futile.

One day, as Devaldevi sat despondently with her father who was trying his best to amuse her, a Muslim nobleman accompanied by several men on horseback entered the fort of Baglan. The sudden appearance of the stranger startled the king. The newcomer seemed a harbinger of calamity and Karan's heart sank at the thought that his precious jewel could fall into the hands of the blackguards. For his own well-being he was unconcerned. He could not imagine a worse future than the calamities that had already befallen him. What fears can a man robbed of all his possessions have?

As Karan watched, the amir rode straight towards the palace, dismounted his horse, ordered his men to different parts of the fortress and, after seeing that all the horses were safely stabled, entered the palace itself, certain of receiving a civil welcome from the Rajput. Karan sent Devaldevi out of the room and invited the stranger in. Muslims, by and large, are persuasive speakers. Their speech is soft and refined and pleasing to the ear; and they speak with great tact and politeness. The amir spoke with such consummate skill that Karan, though increasingly short-tempered of late, gave him a patient hearing. 'I am a nobleman from the court of Allauddin, the Emperor of the World, enthroned in the city of Delhi,' the amir announced. 'The raja of Devgadh has not paid tribute for the last three years and the rulers of the other southern kingdoms pay the emperor homage only in name. The padshah has sent a large army to permanently subdue these recalcitrant kings. He intends to conquer the whole of the south. I need not elaborate upon the strength and prowess of our army as it will only increase your unease, but in numbers it is beyond count. It comprises one lakh cavalry, and is led by General Malik Kafur. Kafur is a skilled tactician and indefatigable in his zeal. He is surrounded by advisors who are wise, and nobles who are experienced in the art of warfare. At present, they have set up camp at Sultanpur in Khandesh. I have been sent by Malik Kafur on the orders of the emperor to convey this message to you. You must know that your chief queen, Kaularani, is at present in the emperor's harem and is held in the highest esteem by him. She is now the padshah's chief queen and wields tremendous influence over him; and the emperor can refuse her nothing. Kaularani had two daughters, of whom one is no more, and the other, Devaldevi, who is thirteen years old, is with you. Her mother can no longer live without her. The sultana is eager to be reunited with her daughter whom she has not seen for many years. She certainly has a greater right over her daughter than you have, and her love for her child is so intense that she will fall ill if separated from her any longer. Besides, the girl will be far happier living with the sultana in the emperor's magnificent palace than staying with you. The Begum Sahib has importuned the emperor repeatedly to have her daughter brought to Delhi. The emperor has bowed to her wishes and has ordered Malik Kafur, on pain of death, to bring Devaldevi alive to her mother. In view of this, you have no option but to hand over your daughter peacefully and without delay. She is at an age when she needs a mother's care and must surely feel the lack of a mother's love. It is fitting that she, who is obliged to live a life in the shadows, should be brought into the light and her beauty made known throughout the world. At present, Devaldevi is like a priceless jewel sunk at the dark bottom of the ocean, when she should be lending her lustre to a ring fit for a king. At present, she is a beautiful, fragrant bloom whose scent is wasted in the wilderness when she should be plucked and placed in the centre of a rich bouquet. What kind of life does Devaldevi have here? Will she be content to gaze upon you forever? Can a man of your age be a fitting companion for her? As long as Devaldevi is with you, she is like a doe separated from the herd, a fish out of water—and if you do not put her back into the pond, she will die gasping for air. You have kept the moth away from the light. How will it survive? You have uprooted a tender sapling from the garden and planted it in the sandy Marwar desert. How will it grow? You have trapped the parakeet from the forest and confined it in a room. How can it be happy hopping on the floor when it should be flying in the bright sunlight? Therefore do what I say. If you obey my command, you too will benefit greatly; you might even get back your kingdom, and though you will have to pay tribute like other kings, at least you will be addressed as "Raja" and your life will once again be worthwhile. The emperor will look upon you with great favour; and instead of living in this pitiable, helpless state, you will be reinstated to your former splendour. Such an opportunity will not come again. In exchange for a thirteen-year-old girl you will gain lakhs of rupees; in exchange for a minor loss, your rewards will be immense. So think well about what I have said before answering me. There is no need for haste. Do not look a gift-horse in the mouth. You are descended from royal lineage and have ruled over a vast kingdom for several years, so I need say no more. I do not expect you to refuse this offer. But just in case misfortune and defeat have addled your mind and you do not acquiesce, bear in mind that a vast army stands nearby, ready to take your daughter by force. You will be humiliated and your reputation ruined.'

It was with great difficulty that Karan Raja managed to control the anger that had threatened to boil over during this insulting speech. But now, when it was his turn to reply, he could not control his fury. 'Let the skies fall and the earth be destroyed, let the emperor himself, or even God Almighty, approach me for my child, I shall never willingly give her up. Having lost my all there is nothing more to lose. I have faced every kind of trouble and no new or greater calamities can befall me. Therefore, I fear neither your emperor, nor your Malik Kafur, nor your vast army. The Rajputs have not yet abandoned their honour, not yet lost all pride in their history and traditions, that they would be ready to exchange one of their own for the sake of security or financial gain. No. Such a day has not yet dawned and will take a long time to come. Give my daughter to a mlechha! Send her to her father's sworn enemy, the usurper of his kingdom and the cause of his ruin! This will never be. So long as there is breath in my body, so long as blood flows through my veins and there is strength in my arms to wield this sword, I will not give up my daughter. To protect her I am willing to sacrifice my life. What may happen to her after my death is beyond my control, but let it never be said that while he was alive, Karan bartered his daughter for personal gain. Never! I would sooner slay her, sooner pluck out this delicate flower than let it fall into impure and base hands; I would rather crush this precious pearl than let it adorn the person of some brutish man. We Rajputs see no dishonour in committing such an act for it is sanctioned by tradition. We would rather drown our daughters in milk the minute they are born than risk the chance that they might fall into low-born hands and sully the family name. It was a mistake on my part to let Devaldevi live and to nurture her to womanhood. But all is not lost. With one stroke of the sword I can put this matter to rest. By a single blow, my honour and that of my family, my caste and my land will be preserved. One stroke will ensure that your padshah's desires will never be fulfilled, and my daughter's chastity will remain inviolate forever. O you wicked, sinful Kaularani! Why should I now address you as queen? What did I leave undone to make you happy? I indulged your every whim and hung on your every word. I made you my chief queen. And now you choose to repay me in this manner! Is this what you consider just and proper? You who deserted your husband, your children, your parents, your family, your community, and your land; who defiled your religion to sport in the zenana of a barbarous king; you who have wed another man while your husband still lives, and now nestle in his arms and live a life of luxury—know that I do not hold all this against you. But you who have so much have not the slightest pity for one who is forced to live like a mendicant: you are indifferent to my plight, you turn your gaze away from my great sorrow and wish to snatch away my daughter, the last remaining ray of sunshine in my life. O wicked woman! Reunion with your daughter will add very little to your already overflowing happiness, but parted from her I shall surely die. Let this sin be upon your head. Your desire to torment one who is already wretched will bring you no joy. You, too, will one day be as miserable as I am. At present the sun of your happiness is at its zenith. But twilight will inevitably follow, the sun will set, and the blackness of night will descend upon you. But why should I grieve in vain? Why delay the departure of this messenger? Amir sahib, please inform your general that as long as I live, I will not part with Devaldevi.'

The emperor's emissary realized that further discussion was futile; Karan's anger and obduracy could not be affected by soft tactics. As he arose to leave, he said, 'There is yet time to reconsider. If you do not, Malik Kafur will forthwith attack you; he will be victorious and take Devaldevi by force, and you will lose all the advantages you could gain by willingly relinquishing her. You will, in hindsight, regret your decision. So consider well what you do.'

Karan Raja's silence was proof of his refusal. Seeing that the Rajput would not change his mind, the nobleman left the fort and conveyed Karan's reply to Malik Kafur in Sultanpur.

Greatly incensed by the news, Malik Kafur sent a second emissary to Karan after a couple of days. He too returned with the same answer. Kafur knew that he had no choice but to bring Devaldevi to Delhi. Allauddin had repeatedly made this clear, and he had solemnly promised to do so. An attack on Baglan was thus inevitable. But Kafur disliked the prospect of deploying his entire army against such an insignificant enemy. His grand design was to wage a successful war against the southern kingdoms, loot them of their fabulous wealth, distribute some of it amongst the soldiers, generals and noblemen who had accompanied him on the campaign, and keep the balance for a future bid for the crown. His sights were set towards this end and he had no desire to get embroiled in this side-show. The task could easily be entrusted to someone else.

Kafur accordingly sent a message to Alafkhan, the governor of Gujarat, ordering him to proceed to Baglan with a large army, and by fair means or foul, wrest Devaldevi from Karan, protect her honour, and bring her to him. Malik Kafur warned Alafkhan that if he failed in this mission, if Devaldevi managed to elude capture, or he allowed her to escape, he should be prepared to lose his life. Kafur then disbanded his camp at Sultanpur.

In Baglan, an anxious Karan Raja was in a quandary. He knew that if he did not surrender his daughter, Malik Kafur would be furious. The emperor Allauddin was known for his vindictiveness. He never rescinded a command, and if it was not carried out the guilty person, whether nobleman or beggar, would be swiftly dispatched to the other world. Therefore, none of his subordinates would dare disobey him. What would Karan do when Kafur's army descended upon the fort? How would he fight it? He was without men, money or equipment. O Lord! he prayed. Take pity on me. Will I be compelled to surrender Devaldevi after all? Just the thought of this makes my limbs tremble and my blood boil. But there is no time to waste. I must not sit idly accepting my fate. Only if I strive hard will the gods come to my aid. Only if I make a sincere effort to face this calamity will they protect my helpless child. Only when I do all in my power to avert this danger will someone come forward to help save this innocent lamb from the jaws of the tiger. Begone, sloth! Fate, do not draw near. Come to my aid, my trusty shield and sword. I shall need your assistance now. Free me from my troubles and let me safeguard my beloved daughter's happiness forever. Like the embers in a brazier smouldering under its ashes, many unknown braves must surely exist in Gujarat; there must still be countless Rajputs thirsting for the blood of the enemy. There are surely many in Gujarat eager to take revenge on the Musalman. Are they such ingrates that they will refuse to come to the aid of their unhappy king? Are they so lacking in shame and pride that they will refuse to protect their motherland? Have they lost all feeling for their country that, like cowards, they would rather accept the yoke of the oppressor than put up a fight? In this hour of need, will they not join forces with me? No, I am convinced that matters have not reached such a sorry state and that Rajput valour has not completely disappeared. I will spread the word and request them to come to my aid.

Having decided on this course of action, Karan Raja sent messengers to all his former vassals. In a few days, armed Rajput braves could be seen wending their way towards Baglan. Several chieftains arrived with their contingents. It is testimony to the courage and loyalty of these Rajput men that they responded to the call of their former king to fight a war that held out little hope of victory. Leaving behind their wives and children, with death staring them in the face, some 5000 Rajputs arrived in Baglan. Karan was no longer their king; they had nothing to fear or gain from him: he was not going to pay them for their services, nor could he penalize them in any way. What motivated them to come? It was nothing but love for their king, pride in their motherland and the passionate desire to protect their country.

Alas, such courage is no longer to be found in our land! And it is for this reason that our people are no longer free.

Karan Raja could not have imagined, even in his wildest dreams, that he would have an army of 5000 in such a short time. When he saw the men, eager to do battle for his sake, his spirits lifted and he began to prepare for the coming struggle with renewed vigour. Damaged portions of the fort were repaired, large quantities of wood for quivers were procured from the forest, ironsmiths' furnaces burned brightly as arrowheads were sharpened and hammered into shape. In anticipation of a long siege caravans laden with grain came from Khandesh to feed the residents of Baglan, as well as the army and its camp followers. Arrangements were made to replenish supplies as and when needed. For once, Karan tried to keep his obdurate nature in check and controlled his destructive habit of having his own way in everything. He consulted the chieftains at every step, and even the most humble soldier was allowed to express his opinion. If a suggestion was valid, Karan acted on it; if not, he would explain the reason for rejecting it. If only Karan had exhibited such reasonable behaviour in the past, he would not have lost his kingdom; and even if he had eventually lost it, it would have been only after a determined resistance and the infliction of heavy losses on the enemy. But wisdom usually comes after the event. Very few can think wisely and act accordingly from the beginning. Man learns through his mistakes. This time around, Karan's well-planned strategy did produce results. Yet circumstances beyond his control would prevent a favourable outcome.

Nine years had elapsed since Patan had fallen into the hands of the Musalmans. A lot had changed even in this short span of time. A succession of governors, far removed from Delhi and the authority of the emperor, ruthlessly oppressed the local population. The governors lived in a state of perpetual insecurity, not knowing when they would be sacked from their posts, and they did not think it prudent to rely solely on their official salaries. Since, in any case, the emperor was convinced that all his administrators were corrupt, there seemed little point in being honest. The outcome was both a heavy loss to the royal exchequer and an increase in official rapacity as extortionate taxes were extracted from the ryots only to be transferred to the governors' private coffers. Land taxes soared and peasants began to die of starvation. Trade was crippled by a four-fold tax increase. Merchants reeled under heavy losses and the prosperity of the town declined. At the slightest pretext, even men of integrity were arrested, threatened and tortured. People quietly paid up whatever was demanded to avoid falling into the hands of the police. The minute it came to be known that a certain person was wealthy or highly regarded, false charges would be made against him and his reputation destroyed. Only when the pockets of the governor were adequately filled would the man be released. A number of new, hitherto unheard-of taxes were clamped on the people, the worst of these being the jeziya, which was extracted with unfeeling severity. Life and property were precarious. Each day that passed was like a gift from God. A man could be sure of only that wealth which remained with him at the time of his death. And only when he awoke unharmed to greet another day, could he be sure that he was still alive. Women lost the freedom they had enjoyed under Rajput rule. A woman, even one from a cultured family, if seen walking unescorted on the street would be treated like a whore and subjected to insults. In the houses of the well-to-do, women disappeared within curtained rooms. Only the womenfolk of the very poor ventured into the open, having no alternative but to step out of their homes to earn a living. They walked in trepidation and the prettier ones cursed their good looks. The religion of the land was treated with contempt. Temples were strictly forbidden to sound the bell or blow the conch during the muezzin's morning call to prayer. Hindus were banned from playing musical instruments in front of mosques. A Hindu believed to have obstructed Muslim religious observances was in danger of losing his life. Muslims, on the other hand, it was tacitly understood, could hinder the religious practices of the Hindus without the slightest fear of reprisal. Every Muslim, from the governor down to the sweeper, was convinced that the Hindu religion was the creation of Satan—utterly false and hypocritical—and that it was his bounden duty to eradicate it. It was believed that merit could be gained by harassing and insulting Hindus and forcing them to convert to the true faith. Motivated by greed as well as the desire to protect their self-respect, more and more Hindus began converting to Islam. Conversion held out the possibility of becoming part of the ruling elite, and thereby transforming victim to oppressor. Some Hindus were forcibly converted and some bribed.

Hindu priests suffered the same fate as their gods and temples. Many of the rights enjoyed by religious institutions were abrogated, priests were denied their customary fees, brahmins lost many of their privileges and the yearly allowance given to them by previous Hindu kings. Gods were thrown out of the temples where they had resided for thousands of years. Many temples were destroyed or refashioned as mosques and where, previously, you could hear the sound of bells and the conch, now echoed the mullah's call to prayer. Even homes were destroyed and replaced by mosques. On the orders of Alafkhan, the great Shiva temple that stood in the centre of the town was razed to the ground to make way for the Juma Masjid. Built of white marble, this splendid many-pillared edifice where Alafkhan and his ministers used to pray still stands—now a neglected ruin.

The Jains and the Shaivites, abandoning their former enmity, came together to mourn the plight of their religions. But to whom could they take their grievances? Delhi lay far away. Having no other recourse, the populace would resort to rioting every time an oppressive measure was enacted. But the Musalman army stood prepared to quell such disturbances and protestors were ruthlessly mowed down. Nothing was gained by such protests: many lives were needlessly lost, and the oppression only increased. It was not long before the population was reduced to dumb, cattle-like submission. Cowed down and drained of energy, the people lost the will to resist. Lying, hypocrisy, cunning and vulgarity became second nature to them. Like subject peoples all over the world living under oppressive foreign rule, the Hindus of Gujarat became indolent and demoralized. The ill effects of this are evident even after 500 years.

―――

The moment Alafkhan received Malik Kafur's orders, he mustered an army of 10,000 and set out from Patan. It was a very different scene from the one witnessed nine years earlier when Karan Raja had marched from here to wage war against the Turks. The enthusiasm displayed by the people, their eagerness to see him return victorious—all such exhibitions of feeling were absent now. The roads were empty except for the marching soldiers. In their heart of hearts the citizens of Patan longed for the utter destruction of the army. The memory of Karan Raja was yet green in the hearts of his former subjects. They ardently prayed for the safety of his daughter and for the victory of the Rajputs who had gone to Karan's aid. But knowing well Allauddin's nature, his dogged determination, and the size and capability of the Turkish army, they had little hope of a successful outcome. If the present army failed in its mission, Allauddin was bound to send another; whereas, Karan's resources were limited, he had no reserves and no neighbouring ruler was likely to come to the rescue of a king without a throne. The people of Patan surrendered themselves to the will of God, and awaited the outcome.

Within a month, Alafkhan had reached the foot of the mountain passes which led up to Baglan. Four roads led to the town from four different directions. Winding through the mountains, these paths were extremely narrow and could only accommodate a few men, at the most five, marching abreast. To secure them against the Turks was thus easy. A handful of soldiers stationed at strategic points could block ten times the number of the enemy. Moreover, the advancing forces could easily be fired upon from the mountains. It was in this manner that a handful of Greeks at Thermopylae had obstructed the march of the Persian army. In the same way, 300 Rajput soldiers now prevented the army of Alafkhan from reaching Baglan.

Karan had stationed his men at various points to protect the passes and, accompanied by a few of his soldiers, observed the enemy's movements from a mountain summit. After setting up camp a short distance away, Alafkhan sent a message to Karan. 'If you hand over your daughter immediately, we will withdraw peacefully, thereby saving our time, money and men, for which we shall put in a good word on your behalf to our general, Malik Kafur. He will in turn inform the emperor, and you will be suitably rewarded for your cooperation. So, if you value your life and that of your men, if you do not want to squander your wealth on a hopeless cause, if you want to live in peace—do as we demand without further delay. You are needlessly courting death. Do you really believe you will win against our vast army with a handful of men? Can you dam a raging river with your bare hands? You are as foolish as the lapwing who tries to hold up the sky with legs upraised to prevent it from falling on her brood. This is a totally unnecessary war. So be sensible, think well, and set aside your earlier decision, made, I dare say, on the advice of a fool. Do not plunge unthinkingly into a raging fire. If you were a worthy foe we would not hesitate to cross swords with you, but it would be shameful and contemptible on our part to fight one who is in such a sorry condition. We feel nothing but pity for you. What honour is there in fighting a fallen enemy? If a lion were to slay a mouse he would gain no glory. By overpowering a child, what honour would accrue to a wrestler? Set aside this pretence of a confrontation, for we are not about to be frightened by your childish sabre-rattling! Hand over Devaldevi to us. What is the point in sowing grain that is already roasted? There is great wisdom in promptly executing the inevitable. Therefore, give us your answer without delay.'

'We Rajputs do not fear death,' Karan replied. 'We will not shrink from battle. We hold your emperor and your army in contempt. God is our shield. We fight in the name of truth. And if we lose, we will have the satisfaction of knowing we have done all that was in our power to do. So long as there is breath in our body, we shall never hand over Devaldevi to you. Never, never, never. If you want her, come and get her. This is my final answer. Convey it to the one who sent you here.'

Enraged by Karan's reply, Alafkhan ordered his men to march at once against the foolhardy Rajputs. His soldiers set out confidently, convinced that they could crush the enemy as they would some miserable insect. But when they tried to dislodge the Rajputs from their path, they realized that they had underestimated their foe. The minute they were within range of the enemy, the Rajputs let fly a stream of deadly arrows. The Turks faltered; they lost heart and dared not advance farther. Alafkhan tried hard to rally his men, but they seemed unnerved by this first encounter and the unexpected resistance of the Rajputs. They stood for a while, numb with shock, and then took to their heels. A furious Alafkhan found himself helpless. He halted operations for a day to restore the confidence of his troops. But the next morning he mounted another attack. That day too, the Rajputs rained arrows at the Muslim army, but Alafkhan's men continued to press forward. Karan had stationed his men at various vantage points along the mountain. As the Muslim army made its way along the narrow mountain pass they found themselves attacked from several directions. They had not anticipated this. If they tried to defend themselves against the arrows from above they were speared by the men below, and if they concentrated on the soldiers in front they were killed by those above. Unable to march more than five abreast, the Turks could not take advantage of their superior numbers. Their men began to fall, their ranks were in disarray and they began to run helter-skelter. Taking advantage of the disorder, the Rajputs inflicted heavy losses on the enemy before returning to their former positions.

For once, Karan Raja's notion of valour was tempered by reason. Had he been foolish enough to pursue the enemy, his men would have been forced into open battle and the larger Muslim army would have had the upper hand. If only he had exercised such caution nine years ago and had taken the advice of his experienced generals, he would not have been reduced to a state of pitiful dependency. This time, the result of his circumspection was that the Muslims found themselves outmanoeuvred. Each day they attacked and each day their attacks were repulsed. Frustration made them fearful and angry. Their furious general vowed not to give up till victory was won. He had sent for reinforcements to strengthen his dispirited army, but they had not yet arrived. He was ashamed of losing face and feared the fearful consequences that awaited him once Malik Kafur and the emperor learnt of his inability to dislodge a handful of Rajputs from his path. All his previous victories, all his valorous deeds, would be set at naught. He tried in vain to discover alternative routes by which he could circumvent the enemy, but whichever way he turned, he was confronted by the Rajputs. Karan Raja, like a disembodied spirit, seemed to be here, there and everywhere, ready to repulse him.

For two months, Karan fought wisely and well, blocking every attempt Alafkhan made to reach Baglan. Seeing that his soldiers were exhausted and his army depleted, Alafkhan halted hostilities till reinforcements arrived. The respite proved beneficial to Karan too. Exhausted by the continuous fighting, his body wounded, his mind distraught with anxiety, he was greatly in need of rest. His contingent of 5000 men—now reduced to a force of only 2000—also welcomed the lull. Karan knew that this number too would inevitably decrease, for he had no hope of reinforcements. The Muslim army on the other hand would be replenished with new recruits. His own men would not be able to fight it. It seemed certain that Baglan would fall and Devaldevi be abducted. Everyone, from the commanders to the foot soldiers, agreed that further fighting would only postpone the inevitable.

What was Karan to do? Should he allow his men to die in a hopeless battle? Should he take his own life? Should he put an end to the life of his daughter, she who was the root cause of this war, and thereby wipe out the very reason for it? All three alternatives were equally dreadful. To carry on fighting was to invite the slaughter of innocent lives. But to take one's own life, which he knew was a grave sin, was an equally ignominious proposition. It was a path that would lead to hell and tarnish his name. Moreover, when there is life there is always hope. The third option, to kill Devaldevi, was cruel, ghastly and unnatural. One could not imagine that it befitted a Rajput. And yet Rajputs seldom think twice before committing such acts. They hold very different views regarding family honour and are prepared to go to any lengths to uphold it. According to them, it is the bounden duty of their womenfolk to guard against any slur on their reputation. Examples of women sacrificing their lives at the altar of honour abound in Rajput ballads and folktales. Accordingly, Devaldevi ought to take her own life rather than allow herself to fall into the hands of the Muslims. But as she showed no inclination to do so, someone would have to do the deed for her.

243

It was thus that Karan sat one night lost in thought. The household was fast asleep. An oil lamp burned dimly, casting a sinister glow and as midnight approached, the room itself seemed ready to suffocate him. Karan sprang out of his bed in a fit of frenzy, and drawing his sword he advanced towards the room where Devaldevi lay in deep slumber. With her hair in disarray and her bright eyes half closed in sleep, she resembled a lotus with its petals folded against the night. Fragrant breath escaped her lips which were parted like the petals of a rose. Her face shone with innocent joy. Even the heart of a hardened criminal would have melted at the sight of such an apsara. How could anyone want to hurt this blameless girl, let alone murder her? Karan's sword fell from his hand. He stood transfixed, his eyes never leaving his sleeping daughter, more dear to him than life. 'What kind of a man am I! Am I a rakshasa or a wild beast that I was ready to commit this monstrous act? O merciful Lord! Had you not stayed my hand in time I would have plunged this sword into the heart of my beloved daughter. Shiva! Shiva! Shiva! What has come over me that I was about to destroy the very reason for my existence? Far better she should marry Shankaldev. She is languishing for love of him. Parted from him, she has become a shadow of herself. If I marry her to the prince of Devgadh this war will automatically come to an end. The king of Devgadh is capable of protecting her and has his own axe to grind against Allauddin. It is true that his caste is inferior to that of the Rajputs. He is only a Maratha. Still, he belongs to the Yadav clan, and in such dire circumstances nothing is to be gained by being too fastidious about the antecedents of the family. I will accept their secret betrothal.'

A few days after this incident, Karan's camp was abuzz with the news that an army was approaching from the direction of Devgadh. Convinced that they were reinforcements sent to assist the Muslim army, Karan's men became alarmed and braced themselves for a renewed offensive. Alafkhan, on the other hand, was sure that the army had been sent by an anxious Malik Kafur, and his troops waited eagerly to welcome the reinforcements. But when the army drew nearer, it was discovered that it was a small force headed by Bhimdev. The reason for Bhimdev's arrival was unclear, but since there was no doubt that the advancing forces would prove to be foes rather than friends, Alafkhan decided to stop them in their tracks and send them packing.

Karan was perplexed. Why had Bhimdev come here with an army? Was he intending to take Devaldevi by force? If this was his plan, Karan would himself make known his willingness to give Devaldevi in marriage to Shankaldev. Could it be that Bhimdev had come in person to ask for Devaldevi's hand on behalf of his brother? This then would be an ideal opportunity for Karan to show his magnanimity. In any case Bhimdev could never have come to assist Alafkhan, for Devgadh and Emperor Allauddin were sworn enemies. Well, the mystery would be solved soon enough.

When news of the approaching Muslim forces reached Bhimdev, he decided to avoid a confrontation and to try and reach Karan's camp as quickly as possible. He altered his route and led his men to Baglan by a little known path. The Muslim contingent that had been sent to intercept Bhimdev's army could find no trace of it. The local people deliberately misled the soldiers who were soon helplessly lost in the dense forest. Then, together with the hill tribes, the villagers fell on the Muslims. What could the handful of Turkish troops do? They were determined to fight to the bitter end but their resolve was no match for their enemy's cunning. Trapped between the dense forest and the mountains, with an unseen enemy relentlessly showering arrows upon them, they had little chance of success. In a couple of days, not a single Muslim soldier from the contingent was left alive.

Karan welcomed Bhimdev warmly and treated him like an honoured guest. As soon as he had recovered from his arduous journey, Bhimdev broached the subject of Devaldevi. 'There

245

exists an extraordinary bond between Shankaldev and Devaldevi,' he said. 'Separated from his beloved, Shankaldev has lost all interest in life and will die if not reunited with her. Devaldevi, too, must be pining for him. What objection can you have against their marriage? Only that of ancestry. But I don't think you are so foolish that you will destroy your daughter's happiness and let go the benefits that will accrue to you by such a union for such a paltry reason. Lineage is a relatively trivial matter. You are Rajputs; we are Yadavs. A union between our families will not tarnish your name. In fact, think of all the advantages it holds for you. This conflict is only on account of Devaldevi. When Alafkhan hears that the princess he has come to capture is already the wife of another, he will wind up camp. Then it will be a matter to be settled between him and Devgadh. Moreover, till we reach Devgadh you will be protected by my troops. So it would be wise to agree to my proposal.'

This was exactly what Karan had hoped Bhimdev would say, and he had his answer ready. But he feigned despondency and remained silent for some time. And only when Bhimdev repeatedly importuned him, did he say: 'All that you say is true. I know that I will gain much from Devaldevi's marriage to your brother, but I hesitate on account of the disparity between our families. To give a daughter to a family of inferior caste demeans the Rajputs. On the other hand, if I disallow this union with Shankaldev, there is a distinct possibility that she will fall into the hands of the Turks. Though we consider you inferior in status, you are a thousand, nay a million times better than the Muslims. So I will accept your proposal. But how do you plan to take Devaldevi to Devgadh? Alafkhan is awaiting reinforcements, which should be here in a day or two. You must leave immediately. I will accompany you to fight beside you and help you in every way. We can take a circuitous route to Devgadh.'

14

Alafkhan was worried. He had sent a force to prevent Bhimdev from joining Karan Raja, but Bhimdev had reached Karan's camp and there was no news of his own men. Several search parties had been dispatched, but four or five days had passed and the fate of his soldiers remained uncertain. The absence of the men and the losses suffered during two months of incessant warfare had greatly reduced the strength of his army. A murmur of discontent rose among his soldiers. They had anticipated a speedy victory, and were unhappy. In Karan Raja's camp on the other hand, the mood was optimistic and upbeat. The opportune arrival of Bhimdev seemed like a special sign of God's favour. Everyone was hopeful that Bhimdev would soon take Devaldevi back with him to Devgadh and bring the war to an end.

Even the humblest of Alafkhan's soldiers would have hesitated to be in his shoes at this time. His was an unenviable situation. It seemed to him that all the acclaim he had won so early in life would be washed away by this insignificant conflict. His sweeping victory over the kingdom of Gujarat would count for nothing. Alafkhan owed his high rank to his military successes and his kinship with the padshah, but he did not have the slightest doubt that if he did not hand over Devaldevi to her mother very soon, if he allowed Bhimdev to carry away the girl with him to Devgadh to be married to Shankaldev, Kaularani's fury would know no bounds and, notwithstanding Alafkhan's rank and family ties, his property, his life and indeed the lives of his family would be in grave danger.

Alafkhan's reputation and life hung by a slender thread. Only if the final throw of the dice was favourable and God took compassion on him would his mission succeed and his life be safe. He prayed fervently for the reinforcements which he so desperately needed. It is not for us to fathom the inscrutable will of God. But it was His desire that Alafkhan's prayer should be answered, the strength of the Muslim forces increased, and a crushing defeat inflicted on the Hindus. And He would fulfil His purpose by taking appropriate action. So, because it was ordained that Alafkhan's life and reputation were to be safeguarded, that Devaldevi was not to be married to Shankaldev, that she was to suffer much misfortune, that she too, like her mother, was to fall into the hands of the mlecchas, and finally die a lonely, painful death; that Karan's belief that his troubles were finally at an end was to be proved false, that his beloved daughter was to be snatched away from him and his cup of sorrow filled to overflowing—because it was all thus ordained, it came to pass that billowing clouds of dust appeared on the horizon one evening and 5000 fresh and energetic soldiers arrived in Alafkhan's camp shortly afterwards. Alafkhan's spirits soared once again and the cries of jubilation, the excitement and the joy of his men made it seem as if victory had already been won.

Alafkhan immediately decided to take swift, decisive action. He drew up battle plans and the next morning summoned his lieutenants. Sending small batches of soldiers to block all exit routes from Baglan, he gathered together the rest of the army and set out against Karan.

Meanwhile, Karan surveyed his camp with satisfaction. He believed that Alafkhan's army lacked the men and equipment to attack Baglan. Now that Bhimdev's forces had arrived, Devaldevi could be escorted to the safety of Devgadh and the war could come to an end. It was, of course, unfortunate that Devaldevi would be marrying a Maratha, but that was infinitely preferable to her falling into the hands of a mleccha. His men, too, were in a hopeful mood. They were weary of the war. It was only because they were Rajputs and determined to defend their reputation for bravery that they had not abandoned Karan so far, but now they looked forward to returning home, their honour intact. Orders were given to disband the camp, and the soldiers collected their belongings and prepared to march. Devaldevi donned her finery and mounted her horse. Karan and Bhimdev joined their men, but they had ridden only a short distance when a messenger came running up to them. Without pausing to take a breath he announced, 'Five thousand reinforcements have arrived in Alafkhan's army; all exit routes have been blocked; he is on his way to do battle with you.'

'You evil man! How dare you bring me such news!' shouted Karan. The entire army came to a dead halt. The countenances of the men paled. Karan and Bhimdev looked uncomprehendingly at each other, stunned by the news. A sepoy caught Devaldevi as she fainted and almost fell from her horse. It was as if the whole army had been struck by lightning, as if some magic spell had metamorphosed the men into statues. All was deathly silent.

It was not cowardice that was responsible for this reaction to the news. Rajputs are never afraid to fight: they glory in combat, warfare is their dharma, to die on the battlefield is to live with the apsaras in paradise. They have been taught since childhood that war is a sport, that to be afraid of fighting is a disgrace, to retreat from the battlefield a slur on their honour. The stunned reaction of the soldiers was because their hopes had been shattered like a ball of crystal, and they had lost what was so nearly in their grasp. It was the suddenness and unexpectedness of the news, absolutely contrary to what they were expecting, that overwhelmed them.

Ordering the troops to go no farther, Karan, Bhimdev and several senior and experienced feudatories gathered to discuss their future course of action. They felt that it would be risky to engage in battle, for the Rajput soldiers, though momentarily buoyed up by the arrival of Bhimdev's men, were exhausted and dispirited. If they lost the battle the casualties would be enormous, and Bhimdev feared that this would increase the chance of Devaldevi falling into enemy hands. He, therefore, opposed the idea of immediate battle. The other chiefs, too, felt that nothing would be gained by rushing into war. There seemed to be no option but to withdraw into Baglan fort. The army could hold out there until it was ready to take on the enemy, and if defeated could easily retreat into it for safety and prepare to fight again. True, such a move might seem unmanly and to fight from within the fort cowardly, but given the circumstances this seemed to be the best course of action. What was the point in sacrificing so many lives? It was better to run from the fray and live to fight another day.

On the other hand, to barricade themselves inside the fort had a major drawback. Baglan was a small town: it had few large traders; the surrounding areas were sparsely cultivated; most of the foodgrain came from elsewhere; the shops lacked adequate supplies and people had little to spare. Ordinarily, there were enough stocks to last the inhabitants for two or three months, but if the army were stationed there, these would run out in less than a month. Karan would have to either defeat Alafkhan or hold out long enough to exhaust the besieging forces, but either course of action would have to be completed within a month. If the Muslims succeeded in capturing the fort, or if the siege continued longer and supplies were blocked, the Hindus would be starved into submission and compelled to sue for peace. Escape might not be possible. Given the situation, however, Karan had little choice but to withdraw into the Baglan fort.

The dejected soldiers made their way back to Baglan as if marching to the realm of death, bidding silent farewells to family and friends, all hope of seeing them again gone. Alafkhan's army followed, his men brimming with confidence and certain of success. The Muslim army too was inadequately provisioned, but Alafkhan had made arrangements with traders and had secured the routes to ensure an uninterrupted flow of supplies. The advancing army looted the villages of grain, forcing the villagers out of their homes. By the time Karan's army reached Baglan, the town was already overflowing with desperate peasants fleeing for their lives. Preparations to strengthen the fort's defences began immediately. Metal-workers worked tirelessly to make spears, arrowheads and other weapons, and able-bodied youths from the town made ready to help defend the fort.

Four or five days later, Alafkhan's army arrived at the outskirts of Baglan. He set up camp and, in anticipation of a prolonged conflict, ordered the construction of strong, durable barricades. It was evident that the general was in no hurry and that he was determined to achieve the success of his mission, however long it took. He did not plan an early attack, but focused on taking defensive measures against the enemy. His strategy was to avoid a pitched battle that was bound to lead to a great loss of life. He knew that supplies within the Baglan fort were likely to run out in a few days, that riots would ensue and that Karan would be compelled to make an unconditional surrender. To this end, he cut off all communications and, making sure that not a single grain of food was allowed into the fort, sat back and waited to achieve his purpose.

Karan's worst fears about food shortages soon came true. Food prices had risen and stocks of grain were rapidly disappearing from the shops. The entire town was abuzz with this news. Karan would have to engage the enemy as soon as possible and get his men out of Baglan. One dark night, at about two o'clock, he led his army out of the fort. Only the sound of crickets could be heard; occasionally, some wild animal roared in the jungle and foxes howled from nearby streams. It was a moonless night and the faint light from the stars was dimmed by the trees and hills that encircled Baglan. The soldiers stumbled in the darkness and it was only because of skilled local guides that they could make their way forward. The enemy camp was discernible only by the light of great braziers that had been lit by the sentries. The unsuspecting Turkish soldiers were fast asleep and even the sentries had dozed off. Karan assembled his forces and reminded the commanders of his special instructions about how to engage in a surprise night attack. The men advanced silently, and the first dozing sentinel was cut down, but his dying screams alerted the other guards and the light of their braziers revealed the presence of the Rajput army. The news flew across the camp; all was confusion as men woke up hurriedly and grabbed their weapons, and Alafkhan came out to take charge.

Meanwhile, the Rajputs fell upon the unprepared enemy, slashed and slew without mercy. The Turks would have suffered even greater casualties had Alafkhan not quickly restored order and with great courage stood his ground. If the night had been brighter, Devaldevi and Karan might have managed to flee to safety, but the darkness and confusion prevented a quick escape and gave time to the enemy to put up a resistance. The loss of so many of their comrades only served to spur the anger of the Turks, and they swore to fight to the last man. As the rallying shout of 'Allah O Akbar' filled the air, cries of 'Har Har Mahadev' resounded from the Rajput army. It was a frightful moment as the roars reverberated across the mountains, drowning out the cries and lamentations of the dying and the screams of the wounded.

Swords sliced like streaks of lightning in the darkness. The very heavens seemed to be at war. Strong winds attacked from all four directions, trees swayed and snapped. Rocks and debris crashed and collided in mid-air. Dust, leaves and stones were picked up by the swirling winds. The cries of wild animals were lost in the din, the sounds of bugles silenced. Rational men, men bound together by the common bonds of humanity, endowed by the Creator with compassion and the ability to discriminate between right and wrong, were as if possessed, raring to kill each other, every human quality swamped by the worst and most destructive urges, no longer rational, no longer different from the beasts of the jungle.

Anyone who desires the good of the world opposes warfare. God has created human beings to help one another, given them the desire to live in cooperation; but all this good is negated by war. Only wars fought in self-defence are justifiable, though even these are to be regretted. The frequent wars in the world suggest that mankind is not as evolved as it is believed. This was not an honourable war. To abduct another man's daughter was anything but just. But, as the saying goes, might is always right. There is no further point in debating the rightness or otherwise of the war. What we need is to examine its consequences.

The two armies came together like giant waves in a turbulent ocean or thundering clouds in a stormy sky. This was no embrace of love; rather, it went against every norm of just behaviour. Arrows were useless in such a close struggle. The men fought with spears, swords and daggers, determined (perhaps mercifully) to dispatch their opponents as swiftly as possible. To kill or get killed, that was the only goal. Cries of 'Allah O Akbar' and 'Har Har Mahadev' competed with the clash of swords. The din of bugles and trumpets added to the frenzy. Hundreds were cut down like blades of grass. Many more were wounded, left to be crushed underfoot or flung aside, where they lay, their shrieks

253

and cries renting the air. The carnage continued for three hours, but neither side retreated. Dawn arrived: the night surrendered its hold, the rays of the rising sun turned the clouds rose-pink, the stars disappeared one by one, and birds and beasts emerged from their resting places to begin the new day. The growing light revealed a ghastly scene. The two armies were still attacking each other like packs of ravenous wolves. Blood was everywhere, flowing in streams, forming pools; corpses, Hindu and Muslim, lay sprawled, mouths agape, eyes open, faces hideous in the agony of death. Severed limbs lay scattered, headless bodies twitched convulsively. The wounded lay abandoned, screaming and weeping, with no one to tend to their wounds or say a consoling word. They thought of their loved ones and begged God to put a swift end to their suffering.

While the life-giving warmth of the morning sun spread across the tranquil land, the battlefield was a scene of death and lamentation. As the creatures of the forest went about the business of the day and birds sang with the sheer joy of being alive, rational men, men who had the capacity to know the difference between right and wrong, blessed with immortal souls, the highest of God's creations and masters of the world, had become like beasts, had broken one of nature's most sacred laws, and were busy massacring their own kind.

Daylight revealed the extent of the carnage on both sides. Although fewer of Karan's men had been killed, his numbers had been smaller to begin with and his losses were proportionately greater. Besides, Alafkhan had not deployed his entire army in the night, and now, as a number of fresh soldiers fell upon the exhausted and diminished Hindu forces, they panicked. They themselves could not expect any reinforcements and who could say how many more Turkish forces were waiting in reserve? The demoralized state of the army alarmed Bhimdev, and in his mounting concern for Devaldevi's safety, he threw off all notions of kshatriya honour and ordered his own men back to the fort. This was just what his troops had been hoping for, and the moment their commander gave the signal, they left the battlefield and made for Baglan. Discovering their desertion, other Rajput soldiers broke rank and joined them. Soon the stream became a flood as more and more Rajput soldiers, like unthinking cattle, joined the exodus. As they retreated they were pursued by the Musalmans, and many lost their lives. It was not until they reached the moat surrounding the fort that the Muslims turned back. And Karan's men, battered and exhausted, entered Baglan.

They were safe for the moment, for the attacks stopped. But now Alafkhan encircled the fort and effectively blocked the movement of both men and materials to the town. Karan's men were already demoralized by their defeat and had lost the will to fight. What would happen if the enemy were to assault the fort? Karan knew that the army must be strengthened and if possible, a second attack launched against Alafkhan. Keeping his men penned up in Baglan was to deplete already scarce supplies, invite famine and hasten a surrender. If only he could manage one more surprise night attack, there was a chance of inflicting casualties on the enemy, escaping from the fort and averting a calamity. Karan attempted to recruit some able-bodied townsmen into his army. But they were unused to war, and were unwilling to fight for him. Some made excuses, others went into hiding, and a few flatly refused to join. The people of Baglan were furious with Karan. They blamed him for all their troubles and cursed him silently. Food was getting more and more expensive and the poor were dying, all because of Karan and Devaldevi. In the end, only a few men joined Karan. They made very little difference to the strength of the army, and Karan gained little but the curses of their parents and wives. Finally, Bhimdev summoned all the leading citizens together and addressed them. 'Do not forget,' he said, 'that the Musalmans are fighting this war not against Karan but against Ramdev, ruler of Devgadh and your king. All of you know the reason for this—Devaldevi. The mlecchas want her for their own, but she is already promised to Shankaldev and is your future queen. If you allow her to be captured by the mlecchas, do you suppose they will hesitate to steal your wives and daughters? Rise up now, for the sake of your people and for your motherland, fight for the honour of your king! Are you such cowards that you will let your future queen fall into the hands of the enemy? I do not think that you are so unmanly. So consider your reputation, discard your womanly fears, and putting your honour above all else, make ready for battle. Why are you so indifferent? Have you no courage? Are you so afraid of death that you will not fight for your king? Shame on you!' Bhimdev stopped then, too angry to say more.

But his words were like hot air. They passed over those apathetic men without a trace. The people of Baglan were convinced that the war could not be won, and they were not prepared to barter their lives for it. But the lives they held so dear, and for which they were willing to sacrifice their honour, the lives they did not want to risk for the sake of their king—those lives were in any case going to be cut short. For the Musalmans were not the only enemy. Another foe was stalking the town. It moved silently and was difficult to evade, and there was no question of dying a noble death at its hands. The enemy was famine. Had the people of Baglan followed Bhimdev's urging, had they all joined together and attacked the Muslims, then perhaps they could have escaped the clutches of this new enemy and kept their pride intact; their king would have achieved his purpose and the war would have come to an end. But it is rightly said that in times of calamity, men cannot think straight. Like unthinking cattle, the men of Baglan went tamely to their deaths, their wives and children followed them, and all was lost.

As has been explained, the arrival of the garrison and peasants from the surrounding villages had led to rising food prices. At first, in anticipation of an early end to the conflict, the citizens of Baglan put up with the additional expense patiently, but as supplies disappeared and corpses began to litter the streets, looting began and riots broke out. One morning, a group of hooligans, the scum of Baglan, went on a rampage, armed with crowbars. Joined by a number of soldiers, they broke into the houses of the rich and ransacked them of grain and provisions. Bloody clashes ensued as the mob fought over the spoils. The rich tried to safeguard their possessions as best they could, and many lost their lives, but to no avail. Left with nothing, it was now their turn to look death in the face. However, the looted grain did not last very long, and rich and poor were soon back on the same level playing-field of death.

The demon Death now revealed his true colours and treated everyone impartially. It is impossible to give an accurate picture of the horrific suffering of the people. The description would be too harrowing. Starving men, their bloodless faces unnaturally pale, walked the streets. Their bodies reduced to skin and bone, their skin rough and shrivelled, they looked like living ghosts. Hatred, envy, anger, utter indifference to killing or being killed, every ugly emotion which rises in a person when death approaches was reflected in their frightful expressions. In short, they looked like death personified. So much for their physical condition. As for their mental agony, only a skilled physician or one who has personally experienced extreme hunger can understand their suffering. Some of the starving collapsed and died instantly; others lingered for two or three days. They lay side by side with the dead till they too died, for there was no place for compassion in the town, no one to take care of anyone else. Corpses lay rotting in lanes and by-lanes. Some people were too enfeebled to venture out of their homes. They lay quietly weeping in their beds, waiting for death. Mothers scrounged frantically for food, furtively feeding their skeleton-like children a piece of roti they had managed to hide, their darting eyes on the alert for thieves. Those that had nothing sat slack-mouthed and expressionless as their children died before their eyes. Infants sucked at dry breasts. Young and old, rich and poor, no one was spared.

With no grain available, people tried to live on wild fruit and berries. The fortunate, whose cows and buffaloes were still alive, survived on milk while others were reduced to eating leaves, chewing on pieces of leather or swallowing mud to calm their unbearable hunger. They filled up their stomachs with water. Soon, the eating of food unfit for human consumption and the noxious vapours from decomposing corpses led to an outbreak of cholera. The business of death flourished as those who had survived the famine were felled by the fearful epidemic. No one was prepared to remove the bodies that lay on the streets. Vultures, kites and crows fed on the corpses during the day, dogs and cats attacked them, and at night jackals and other jungle beasts came to the town to feast. They had cause to celebrate as cows, buffaloes and other farm animals, with no one to feed or take care of them, were also dying in large numbers, their corpses adding to the stench in the town.

The physical effects of famine and disease were matched by psychological changes. The basest tendencies came to the fore. All semblance of civilized behaviour ceased. Family ties were broken, links of friendship snapped, and people looked to nothing but their self-interest. The love that binds parent to child, husband to wife fled. It was each one for himself. Faith in religion too receded. God was forgotten, and people no longer feared death or felt grief for the dead. Instead of turning their thoughts towards God and focusing on serious issues, the imminence of death made the men and women of Baglan desperate in their frantic search for pleasure. Hunger had driven them crazy. Day and night, for no apparent reason—except perhaps to occupy their time or drown out thoughts of death—gangs of starving, wild-

258

looking people made loud music and sang in the streets. Some individuals delirious with hunger ran about, singing, shouting, talking nonsense and laughing hysterically.

Meanwhile, back in the fort, Karan, Bhimdev, Devaldevi and the principal chieftains had managed to survive by strictly rationing their food supplies, and they still had just enough to last a few more days. But the townsfolk were bitterly resentful. There they were, dying because of the war, while the people who were the cause of it were alive and well. It was only because they felt sorry for the unfortunate king of Gujarat, and were concerned for the reputation of Prince Bhimdev, that the people of Baglan did not rise up against those in the fort. Certain disaffected and rebellious men were often on the point of infiltrating the fort to loot it, but wiser counsel had prevailed. It was pointed out that the stolen grain would not go very far in the town, while without it their leaders, who were indispensable in this crisis, would certainly die. The mutineers had desisted from their scheme, but Baglan had continued to simmer with resentment. One other remedy was readily available to the townsfolk: they could get together and open the gates of their town to the Musalmans, and their misery would end immediately. If the people of Baglan did not carry out this plan, it was only because they would not stoop to treachery. It was only because of their unshakeable sense of honour that they had suffered so much for so long, allowed famine and cholera to invade their town, watched their loved ones die slow and agonizing deaths, and lost all care for death themselves. Their conduct was truly admirable. But now they could endure no more, and the less scrupulous among them resolved to open the gates and put an end to the suffering. What was the point of continuing like this? they thought to themselves. We no longer have the strength to fight. Karan and Bhimdev's forces have suffered grievous losses, and those that have managed to survive are too weak to offer serious resistance. By remaining besieged many more will die, and we will gain nothing except a little more time. And for such a small benefit it is not worth prolonging the siege. The townsfolk decided to send a large delegation to Karan and put matters frankly before him.

Karan listened patiently to the delegates, expressed his sincere gratitude for the immense suffering they had borne for his sake and for the sake of his daughter. He felt genuine sympathy for the people of Baglan, and in his heart of hearts knew that what they said was true: that there was no longer any hope of victory, far too many soldiers had lost their lives, and as for the men who remained, it was hard to know whether they occupied the land of the living or the dead. To prolong the fight was pointless. Karan requested the delegation to be patient for just one more night, and gave them his permission to throw open the gates the next day. Satisfied with this answer, the delegates returned home and waited for the morrow.

What should be done next? Up till now, Karan had taken for granted that once the supplies in the fort were exhausted, he and Devaldevi would starve to death, either together or one after another, after which the conflict would come to a natural end. But such an outcome was now ruled out. The people had lost patience, and there was just one course open to him before the night ended: either he or Devaldevi would have to die. Once before, he had raised his sword to kill Devaldevi but had been unable to commit the unnatural act. How could he kill an innocent child? It would be far better to die himself. His was, anyway, a meaningless existence. He was getting on in years and was unlikely to go back to the happier days of his past, so it was better to end his life now rather than spend the rest of it in misery. And so, in the dead of night, when all were asleep, Karan took his sharpest sword and came out of the fort. Anyone seeing him at that moment would have guessed that he was out on some fearful mission. He did not even wake up Devaldevi to

260

bid her farewell, but blessing her silently, and with a prayer to God to keep her and her honour safe, he left. Moonlight covered the maidan, the trees and the surrounding hills. Not a leaf stirred in the windless night. As he walked across the hilly terrain, his footsteps clearly audible in the silence, Karan's thoughts turned to God and to the world he would soon be leaving. After a while he reached a temple. It was a Shiva shrine of considerable size. It was well-known in that area, and kept open day and night, but that night there was no one around. Karan went inside and stood in front of the Shivling. His mind fixed on Shiva, he prayed and did puja, offering the deity the flowers he had brought with him. Then standing up straight and firm in his resolve, Karan brought out the sword from its scabbard and holding it to his neck said in a resolute voice, 'O Mahadev, O Bholanath! O Shankar! You know well the crisis I face. I know not how to extricate myself from it. So, Destroyer of the Universe, either show me a way out or let me die.' Karan was about to bring the sword down on his head when he felt something holding back his hand. His sword fell to the ground and a voice as if from heaven echoed from the *shikhara* of the temple. 'Karan Raja, your troubles are endless, but do not take your life. Let whatever is to happen, happen. Be patient. You will find a way out of your difficulties tomorrow.' Karan heard the words clearly. Convinced that it was indeed Shiva himself who had spoken and that what was prophesied would come true, he sheathed his sword, bowed to the Lord and returned to the fort, reassured.

The next morning, a group of Baglan citizens went to the ramparts and made an offer of surrender. When Alafkhan's emissaries arrived, the townsfolk put the facts clearly before them. They told the envoys of the great hardships they were suffering in a manner calculated to arouse their sympathy. The whole town was ready to admit the Turks, they said, but on the condition that they did not destroy any property or harm its citizens. It made no sense to deal a death blow to those who were already dying. Karan Raja and Devaldevi would soon be theirs, and Alafkhan would achieve his objective, so what was the point of killing innocent townsfolk and looting their property? The envoys were requested to convey this message to their leader and if he was willing to accept the terms, the town would be immediately surrendered. Moved by this report, and realizing that there was no harm in acceding to the proposal, Alafkhan gave his word. The gates of Baglan were opened that very night and the Turkish forces entered the town.

A hunt for Karan and Devaldevi was immediately launched. A number of spectators had come out onto the streets, and suspecting that Devaldevi might be among them, the soldiers dragged the women aside and began questioning them. Their husbands protested strongly, but when their words had little effect, they came to blows with the soldiers, and a full-scale riot was soon underway. The Muslim soldiers held the people of Baglan responsible for the long-drawn-out conflict and for the death of so many of their fellow soldiers. They welcomed the opportunity to vent their pent-up anger on the townsfolk. Many people who had escaped from the clutches of famine and cholera now died by the sword. The trouble spread to the main bazaar, where a shop was set alight by some Muslim miscreants. It was the signal that the soldiers had been waiting for. They resented Alafkhan's unconditional promise not to harm the people or plunder Baglan, for it had been the promise of loot that had kept them going all these months, only to be dashed by Alafkhan at the last moment. But now that a fire had broken out and was likely to spread, there was nothing to prevent them from looting gutted homes. The soldiers made no attempt to put out the blaze; instead, small fires were surreptitiously started in two or three other places. A strong wind came up later that night and the flames spread unobstructed. The soldiers did nothing to contain the conflagration, the people of the town were too debilitated to do much, and soon the whole town was enveloped in the fire. Baglan presented a dreadful spectacle that night. Houses burnt down like grass. There was a complete breakdown of discipline in the Muslim army as soldiers disregarding Alafkhan's orders, entered and ransacked homes.

A fire is always terrible, but a fire in a town already ravaged like Baglan was devastating. Weakened by cholera and starvation, and with no one to help them, many died in their homes. Some abandoned wives, children and property, and fled for their lives. A few women and children managed to escape, others were snuffed out by the flames. Those who ran out clutching their valuables were accosted on the streets and their belongings snatched. The empty-handed were beaten up and bullied into returning to their homes and made to surrender their jewels. Soldiers broke into houses and forced people to reveal where their wealth was hidden. Those that would not, or had nothing to hide, were beaten nevertheless. Demands of 'Hey kafir! Hand over your money!' echoed in the streets and anyone who failed to respond had his head sliced off.

Alafkhan was furious that his orders were being disregarded. The chaos was not merely a slap to his authority, it had far more serious consequences. Devaldevi was not yet in his hands. If he lost this opportunity to capture her, he would not get a second chance, the war would be in vain, the padshah would be furious, and his life worthless. If Devaldevi were to try and escape, there would be no one to stop her. There was not a moment to lose. He had to restore order immediately. Once she was in his hands, the men could continue looting to their hearts' content. He tried to reason with his soldiers, he threatened them and offered inducements, but they would not give up the looting.

When Karan got word of the situation in the town, he was delighted. With Alafkhan's men absorbed in looting, what better opportunity to escape? What the heavenly voice had prophesied seemed about to come true, as there was no one to obstruct or stop him from escaping now. He made plans to flee. And within a short time, he, Devaldevi and Bhimdev, accompanied by a small force, left the fort from the rear gate and, mounting the horses that had been kept ready, were soon on their way to Devgadh. They did not meet a single Turkish soldier as they escaped, and were able to make swift, uninterrupted progress.

Once Baglan had been emptied of all its wealth, the contrite soldiers went to Alafkhan and begged forgiveness for their conduct. It was now midnight and Alafkhan led his men straight to the fort. They wasted a lot of time in the darkness trying to find their way in, until they came across a man who led them to the back entrance. The gate was open and a dismayed Alafkhan realized that the birds had flown. But then he wondered if the entrance had been kept open on purpose, to mislead him into thinking that the occupants had fled, when they were still hiding inside; and having come this far, Alafkhan decided to enter the fort and make certain that his quarry was not hiding there. Large torches were lit and every corner of the fort searched thoroughly. When morning came, and there was still no sign of Devaldevi or Karan, Alafkhan was filled with apprehension. He cursed his soldiers for ruining his chances. He felt certain that the stars were against him and that to fight against Karan was to fight against fate. He was convinced that bad times had come, that the sun had set on his luck, and that whatever he did would yield the contrary result. Devaldevi was already well on her way to Devgadh, and once she reached there and married Shankaldev, all would be lost. Still, determined not to give up while even a glimmer of hope remained, he gave orders to his men to proceed swiftly towards Devgadh. They marched all day without pause and then, just as evening fell, they spotted a cloud of dust on the horizon. Alafkhan went in hot pursuit and soon Karan's small force was clearly visible.

Karan realized that the enemy was almost upon him. His men were too weary to outrun their pursuers, but he took satisfaction from the fact that night was falling and that the road ahead was thickly wooded and difficult to negotiate. The local village guides were bound to mislead the Musalmans and this would give him time to reach Devgadh. But then Karan saw that Alafkhan's men had lit torches to guide them in the darkness and were rapidly gaining ground. He acted swiftly. He split up his party, sending Devaldevi with Bhimdev and a few men by a less-known route, while leaving Alafkhan to follow the main portion of the army, led by himself. The ruse worked. Alafkhan did not realize that Karan and Devaldevi had separated and he concentrated on following Karan. It was a difficult night for both pursuer and pursued as they made their way through the dense forest, but when morning came the Muslims found themselves in an open field and were told that they were only a day's march away from Devgadh. The bad news was that there was no sign of Karan. It was clear that he had either reached Devgadh or would soon do so. A disheartened Alafkhan decided that there was no point in giving chase. He stopped to rest, and sent out teams to reconnoitre in all four directions. But the whole day passed and Karan could not be found. Karan had reached Devgadh safely, while Bhimdev who had taken a more circuitous route, had halted in a village on the way. There seemed to be little likelihood of the enemy finding him there, so Bhimdev stopped for the night and planned to leave for Devgadh the next morning.

15

The next day, as evening drew near, a small village bustled with unusual activity. The neighing of horses could be heard and the village square teemed with horsemen. Soldiers wandered about aimlessly. Some searched for fodder for their horses on the outskirts of the village. Cows and bullocks, having grazed in the meadows all day, ambled back contentedly, leaving a cloud of dust in their wake. Farmers, exhausted by the day's work, slowly wended their way home accompanied by the sound of bells swaying from the necks of their bullocks, as the animals tossed their horns from side to side, eager for a good night's rest. It was an idyllic time of day. The sun god was preparing to leave by the western gate, the sky was awash with different hues, and the scent of blossom-laden trees filled the air—though at times it was overladen by the stench of filth created by man's carelessness and indifference. In front of every house stood a rubbish dump, overflowing with garbage. This poisonous heap of animal droppings, rotting food and other waste emanated deadly vapours and was the cause of innumerable diseases and the short lifespans of the villagers. But these simple folk were totally unaware of this. They spent their days in happy ignorance, surrendering themselves to their fate, accepting all that befell them as the will of God; little realizing that the untimely deaths of parents, children, spouses and relatives was often due to their foul surroundings; and that it was in their own hands to keep death at bay.

In a humble hut, two people could be seen whispering softly as the evening drew to a close. One of them was a woman; the other a man of around forty who appeared to have aged prematurely. Of shrivelled face and dark skin, he sat, scratching himself incessantly. His eyes were bloodshot and sunken, and his bald pate shone like a polished mirror, the occasional patch of hair looking like an oasis in the African desert. He appeared to be greatly enfeebled by some debilitating addiction. In fact, he was an opium addict. Without four or five seers of *bhang* he was unable to function. But bhang alone did not satisfy his craving; he consumed *afeen*, *ganja*, and various other intoxicants. All day he lay in a stupor, unable to earn his livelihood as a village priest. He had to pay half his earnings to the brahmin who generally substituted for him. And with the other half he had to maintain his large family of a wife and five children. Had he been single, he would have lived a contented, if wretched, life. But his wife had other ideas. She nagged and threatened him by turns for money; and had he not been in a constant state of blissful unconcern, he would have succumbed to her incessant harangues. Her curses fell on deaf ears and her harsh words bounced off his elephant-thick hide. This made his wife seethe all the more with rage. Often she punished herself in frustration, starving both herself as well as her husband. Her anger spilled over in other ways too. But her husband countered her rage with stoic silence, a quality he possessed in ample measure. This angry female was thirty-five years old and of hefty build; one look at her was enough to strike fear in a person. It was truly a misfortune to be married to such a shrew. She was a slave to anger, jealousy and cruelty. But greed for money was her worst fault. Night and day she thirsted after money and it was impossible to tell what lengths she might go to obtain it. However, it was God's will that the more she hankered after wealth the poorer she became. She never had enough to satisfy her innumerable desires, and was unable to meet even the bare necessities of life. And so, her husband became the target of her frustration.

On that day the *bhattani* had to entertain important guests. Bhimdev and Devaldevi had taken shelter in her house. She did not know how she would be able to take care of guests of such exalted status. She hoped that by keeping the prince happy she would be richly rewarded and that her life would take a turn for the better. The bhattani did whatever she could for the guests, but doubted whether her arrangements would result in the longed-for outcome. She would have to contrive some other means by which to attain her ends. Perhaps she could secure the costly jewels that Devaldevi was decked in; then the remainder of her life could be spent in utmost comfort. She could creep to Devaldevi's side at night, suffocate her, and decamp with all her jewels. With the Muslim army so near, Bhimdev would not dare to pursue her. The more the chandal thought about her evil scheme, the more determined she became, and her greed triumphed over every other consideration.

But who should execute this deed? The bhattani summoned her husband to her side, put the facts forcefully before him and finally informed him that he would have to carry out her plan. He could hardly believe the extent of his wife's cupidity and that she could contemplate such a heinous deed. Angry and shocked, he cried: 'O you wicked chandal! O you heartless witch! How much sin have you accumulated in these terrible times! You murderess! How could you think of this? To make me kill a woman! And that too, a princess betrothed to the heir apparent of our land! Alas! Surely this is the full flowering of Kaliyug. It is bad enough that men have turned to wickedness in this cursed age, set aside truth, plunged into the well of deceit, entangled themselves in the net of maya not fearing the wrath of God. But women? Soft-hearted women, who fear to step out into the dark, who tremble to see a fly being swatted—when such women, who should be more compassionate than men, plan to kill an innocent being— that is truly beyond belief. O Lord! What kind of future is still in store for us! I pray I do not live to see it. Am I to commit murder? To kill a woman is considered the worst sin in our scriptures. Ah, Lakshmi, great goddess of wealth! You truly rule the world! All the other gods have been forgotten and men yearn to serve you, ever ready to commit crimes in your name. My wife wants to murder a woman, that too a princess, who has taken shelter under our roof; but not just that—she wants me to do the deed for her! Life has truly become meaningless now. It is better that I become a sannyasi and abandon this vile and deceitful world. I am but a poor brahmin, harassed by my wife, barely able to make both ends meet, but I manage to forget my sorrows with drugs and alcohol and sail serenely through the Ocean of Samsara. Let the heavens fall, but never shall I commit this sinful deed! I have no desire for money and I will not do it.'

Emboldened by alcohol, the *bhatt* stood up to his wife for the first time in his life and dared to defy her. The bhattani was astounded by his response. She knew full well that he was incapable of pulling off such an act on his own and had only wanted his help to accomplish her plan. But her husband's words awakened the demon in her. Anger coursed through her body, her face became livid, her eyes bloodshot and her hair stood on end. That she had remained silent throughout her husband's tirade was surprising, but anger had frozen her responses and rendered her speechless. The moment her husband subsided into silence, the pent-up fire smouldering inside her exploded in a volley of curses. 'You *bhaangi*! You opium junkie, *ganjakhor*! Rotter and coward! You are nothing but a woman in man's clothing. Lord Brahma surely erred in making you a man. What evil did I do in my past life to be dependent on you now? My parents must have been blind to choose you for my husband. They must have ferreted you out with the help of torches. Had every other suitor dropped dead that they had to yoke me to you? In the glare of the afternoon sun, with eyes wide open, they flung me into a well of darkness. What happiness have I gained by marrying you? You who lie all day in a drunken stupor, what do you know of my plight? Have you any idea how other women of our community live? Dressed in fine raiment, adorned with jewels, every desire of theirs fulfilled by their husbands who toil night and day to please their wives? They shower them with affection and wait upon their wishes. But unfortunate me! In all my life, I have never experienced such happiness. My birth has been in vain. My only pleasures are those in my dreams. My hopes have been crushed in the bud.

'O Fate! Why have you heaped such calamities and pain upon me? Forget the expensive clothes and ornaments, I have not even been blessed with a loving husband. You are a good-for-nothing wretch, incapable of earning a livelihood. But enough. One can't fill one's stomach by breast-beating. It is only because of me that you, and the hungry mouths of our little ones, get even a morsel of food. What more is there to say? If I sat around all day, indifferent to our plight, not struggling to procure food, we would starve. Have you forgotten all that, you ingrate? And today you dare to lecture me! Kaliyug and Satyayug; Brahma and Vishnu is all you can blabber. If you had been a rock you would at least have been of some use to people. What good have you done by being born a man? You cannot even take care of your family. Damn you and damn your existence. A curse on you for living off your wife! It matters little whether men like you are dead or alive. You spend all your days in a drunken stupor. A hundred times better to be a widow, neither witness nor victim of your slothful ways. You are barely alive anyway. What difference will it make when my bangles are smashed and my hair lopped off after you die? I am as good as a widow anyway. As it is, I do the work that you should be doing. If only you worked hard we would never have to stoop to such evil.

'This is not the flowering of Kaliyug or any other yug but is the result of a flaw in your character. I know that this terrible sin will close the doors of salvation for us. For murdering a woman we shall be scourged by Yama in hell, and will be reborn as vermin. But what alternative is there? How else can one survive? Are we to spend all our days in sorrow and penury? Are we to sit back and watch our children starve to death? Is that not murder, you moron? It's all right to murder our children, but to murder a woman is a sin? Who does not sin for the sake of money? From the king down to the beggar, they are all willing to cheat for wealth: merchants deceive their clients, government officials take bribes, and artisans certainly steal time not to mention materials. But a brahmin is not supposed to steal, so what is he to do? Money is needed; which is why one is forced into sin. I told you my plan only to test you; I know you don't have the courage to perform the deed. But your hypocrisy drives me crazy. It is said that a saintly garb is the refuge of the weak. Your holier-than-thou attitude is a cover for your cowardice. It is I who have shouldered a husband's responsibility. You are an insult to manhood. Give me your turban and wear my blouse instead. And if you cannot stomach such an act at least keep your mouth shut.' The tirade felled the poor brahmin, and he slunk into a corner muttering, *Shiva, Shiva, Shiva.*

Now the bhattani began her preparations in right earnest. First she had to ascertain the number of ornaments and jewels that bedecked Devaldevi's person. She put on a pleasant face and went and sat beside Devaldevi, chatting away in a friendly manner. After a while she touched on the topic of ornaments and while talking, observed Devaldevi closely. As night fell she began preparing dinner,

271

but her mind was not on the cooking. The daal was scorched, the rice burnt and the chappatis raw. It was not surprising that she was so preoccupied. Her heart was full of turmoil. At one moment thoughts of pity triumphed, only to be defeated by the prospect of wealth. Virtuous thoughts were immediately crushed by visions of her helpless state and her miserable starving children. Such was the storm raging in her heart that she was unable even to serve the food properly. The gentle voice of her conscience was no match for the clamour of the arguments ranged against it. The guests, unable to understand the reason for her distracted behaviour, remained silent. They assumed that she was embarrassed by the presence of a male guest. Now and then, the bhattani composed herself: she was greatly honoured to receive such royal company, she said, and upset at not being able to entertain them with all the pomp and splendour that was their due. This, she explained, was the reason why she was so flustered. Bhimdev and Devaldevi responded with words of comfort and encouragement. To help, protect and shelter them in their hour of need was indeed the greatest favour she could bestow upon them, and she would definitely be rewarded for it. But for the bhattani, their words were like a poultice applied to the forehead, when it was her stomach that was on fire! Ever since her childhood she had been told that a king's promise was not to be trusted; and that a favour once done is soon forgotten. And besides, a bird in hand was better than two in the bush. She foresaw no impediments to the completion of her deed and was convinced that she would not be caught. O, how foolish is man! Most crimes in this world are committed because of such false reasoning.

After the meal, everyone retired for the night as they had to begin their journey early the next morning. Bhimdev's men were soon fast asleep, and the brahmin lay down, sprawled in drugged slumber, oblivious to the world and the earlier conversation with his wife. The children too dropped off to sleep. Only three people remained awake. One was the bhattani who tossed and turned, a sword in readiness in her bed, eagerly awaiting the midnight hour, a single moment stretching out like an age. The second was Bhimdev who was too excited to sleep. Relieved to have escaped the clutches of the enemy, his thoughts raced to the following evening when he would reach his capital and hand over Devaldevi to his brother, Shankaldev. But a full day still lay ahead, a day that might be fraught with untold difficulties. Uncertainties and doubts kept Bhimdev awake for a long time, but finally he, too, fell asleep. Devaldevi fluctuated between happiness and despair. At times her heart would be filled with joy at the thought that though the path of love is uneven and strewn with obstacles and dangers, even though it often seems endless, in the end true love triumphs, and the joy of reunion more than makes up for the anxieties of the past. She was but a child with no experience of the world. She had only basked in the sun and knew nothing of the dark shadows of life. She was unaware of the many impediments that fate could place in her path. Restless with longing for the one whose image was engraved in her heart, the one who she thought of night and day, her first love, the keeper of her heart and soul—she was unable to sleep. Poor Devaldevi knew not what lay in store for her on the morrow. Her mood was affected by her surroundings and since Bhimdev and his men appeared outwardly composed, she was not worried. Before her swam the vision of her beloved Shankaldev, her reunion with him, their mutual outpouring of love, and the promise of future joys. Imagination created a pleasurable picture. But alas! A dark curtain had been drawn across her future and it was only because of the compassion of an all-merciful God that she could not see beyond it, and all appeared rosy and bright. She at last fell asleep in the arms of her imagined future.

It was two in the morning. The moon had set and all was enveloped in darkness. Only the harsh calls of the owls pierced the silence. It was the time when thieves were abroad and evil and unclean spirits roamed the night. Good rested and only Evil was awake to count the hours. The bhattani got out of bed and picking up her sword, crept towards the sleeping Devaldevi. She gazed at Devaldevi as the girl lay on the boundary of light and shadow in the intermittent glow of the lamp. Only a consummate artist could portray the strange and terrifying scene. Two women, one a youthful, lovely and innocent maiden, sunk in deep slumber; the other a middle-aged, heartless female, a deadly weapon in her hand, poised to strike. On one side Indra's beautiful celestial nymph, Rambha, on the other an evil witch; on one side a lotus-eyed maiden, her eyelids closed like petals in sleep, and on the other a bloody-eyed tigress staring at her prey. On one side the guileless girl, sleeping the sleep of virtue; on the other a woman, a dark blot on womankind, her mind roiling with emotion, ready to commit a dreadful crime. The woman raised the sword, but before it could fall on her victim it was arrested in mid-air. In truth, it appeared as if some goddess, protector of the innocent, had intercepted the weapon. The bhattani's hand became limp, the sword slipped from her grasp, and she started shaking uncontrollably. She was drenched in perspiration and her forehead was beaded with sweat. The blood fled from her face. These outward changes reflected an inner transformation. The reader will naturally wonder how such a change came about. It was wrought by the bhattani's heartfelt repentance. Had she immediately carried out her resolve her goal would have been accomplished, but she had hesitated and stood gazing at the sleeping girl, giving time for nobler thoughts to enter her mind. The bhattani's sleeping conscience awoke. The fever of hatred raging in her heart was cooled by the balm of Devaldevi's innocence; and pity, together with gentler feelings, rose to the surface and came to her rescue. A feeling of remorse welled up within her. How could she murder this blameless girl, pluck this delicate blossom, axe this exquisite tree? It comes as no surprise

274

then that the bhattani lowered the sword and lay down to sleep once more. Compassion and repentance are powerful emotions. Given time, they can work miracles. If an evil deed is delayed, it is likely that it will not be committed at all.

As dawn drew near, the contours of the world began to change shape. Birds and beasts awoke. Village dogs barked. Horses neighed impatiently and Bhimdev's men got ready to march. Bhimdev and Devaldevi mounted their horses. The bhatt appeared with folded hands, blessed Bhimdev with mantras and waited expectantly for his dakshina. His wife stood with head bowed respectfully in front of Devaldevi. She was too ashamed to look her in the face. She would have gladly sunk into the earth if that were possible. Devaldevi appeared cheerful that morning. She called the bhattani to her side and thanked her profusely for her hospitality and help in her hour of need. Placing all her jewels in a box she gave them to the bhattani, and promised to invite her to Devgadh once she was settled there. The brahmin, too, was given a hundred gold coins and promised a permanent place at court where he would be well looked after for the rest of his life. The reader can well imagine the joy of this wretched poverty-ridden couple at such good fortune dropping into their laps! If the brahmin had not been used to existing in a permanent state of inebriated euphoria, this sudden torrent of good luck might have unhinged him completely. Likewise, if the bhattani had not possessed a strong constitution, she would have dropped dead delirious with joy. Their hearts overflowed with gratitude, and to repay this generosity and assuage her guilt, the bhattani with her children in tow, joined Devaldevi's retinue. Her husband trailed behind her.

As the procession left the village, the villagers showered flower petals on their prince and their soon-to-be-queen. Young and old blessed them and prayed fervently for their safety, imploring God to protect them from the enemy and to lead them to Devgadh without harm. About a hundred youths, armed with whatever weapons they could muster, accompanied Bhimdev.

———

While Bhimdev and his retinue wend their way to Devgadh, let us turn our attention towards Alafkhan. The general had set up camp in the open field where he had halted, and it was soon transformed into a bustling township. Colourful tents ringed a large makeshift bazaar. Everything an army could possibly need was being sold here, to the great satisfaction of the local merchants and shopkeepers. But the general himself and his senior officers were despondent. Alafkhan was the most disheartened of the lot and the reasons are not hard to see. There was no solution in sight to his predicament and the future was bleak. He saw no point in advancing further. Devgadh was only a day's march away but to attack it with his depleted force would be futile. In fact, it would be courting disaster. His men would be slaughtered. To retreat was the only option left. But what a humiliating one! Alafkhan's men were equally unhappy at the thought of retreat. All their efforts would be nullified and their hardships crowned with ignominy. To be bested by the Hindu kafirs was like rubbing salt on their wounds. If they had lost against their co-religionists it would not have been half as bad. The solders twirled their moustaches in a show of defiance and pretended that they had not a care in the world. As night fell, they gathered in groups around huge, lighted braziers. In one of the groups two soldiers could be seen engrossed in conversation.

Sobhaankhan said, 'Mian Ibrahimkhan, Allah keep you safe! Of course, there's no doubt that Alafkhan's clout is weakening. He has fallen in the eyes of the emperor. That whore has undoubtedly given him the slip. But, believe me, Alafkhan is not to blame. He did all he could in his power to capture her. God must have willed otherwise.'

'What you say is true,' Ibrahimkhan replied. 'The whore has indeed escaped from his clutches, but Alafkhan is not at fault. Yet it would have been better for him if he had taken our advice. Relying only on his own counsel has landed him in this mess. How can he face the emperor now? This entire farce is the work of that eunuch. What more is there to say? He ordered this attack on a worthless kingdom to enhance his own reputation, and now we are trapped in this godforsaken place. Only God knows the outcome, but in the meanwhile Alafkhan's neck is going to be axed. May God protect us.'

'Now that you have broached this subject, let me tell you that the eunuch has no interest in the whore. He only wants to teach the raja of Devgadh a lesson. The problem is our emperor, who is completely bewitched by the Rajputani bitch in his harem. She is a celestial beauty, a houri from paradise. The padshah is totally besotted by her. It's nothing to be surprised about. That's the nature of women. It's on the insistence of the whore that Alafkhan was sent here. The escaped girl is her daughter whom she wants by her side in Delhi. Allah knows what the emperor will do with the child! Having married the mother, will he now wed the girl? Or will he keep her for the crown prince? Kafir women are undoubtedly beautiful, fashioned no doubt for our pleasure. But if the emperor appropriates them all, what hope is left for us ordinary soldiers? There is no justice in this world.'

Malik Jafar interrupted the conversation. 'How now, *mian sahibs*! Have you forgotten yourselves, sirs? Are you so afraid of life that you insist on inviting death to your doorstep? If the emperor gets to hear about this he will cut you to pieces. You have no idea what Allauddin Khilji is like. He has spies in every corner of his kingdom and nothing can be hidden from him. So weigh your words before you speak. Such talk will only harm you. Let us change the subject, there's no dearth of other topics.'

'*Istagufrulla*! You're right,' Sobhaan agreed. 'Let's talk of other things. Well, are there any places of interest in the vicinity? Let us at least amuse ourselves while we are forced to encamp here.'

'*Subhanallah!*' Malik Jafar changed the subject. 'I can show you a place that will amaze you. Not far from here there are temples of the kafirs the like of which cannot be found on this earth. Of course, they are not a patch on our mosques at Medina and Mecca. But in the nearby village of Verul are caves which cannot be praised enough. One cannot take one's eyes off the paintings and carvings. The Hindus certainly produce great craftsmen. They are an intelligent race except in the matter of their satanic religion. *Alahudilillah!* May God grant them the light!'

'Tell us a little more about these caves, mian sahib,' Sobhaan requested.

'It is impossible to describe them. You have to see them for yourselves; but bowing to your wishes, I will try to describe them as best I can. About half a kos from the village of Verul (Ellora) there is a semi-circular mountain with cave temples cut into it—Hindu, Buddhist and Jain—filled with a variety of carvings; the pillars are decorated with exquisite patterns of leaves and creepers, and there are splendid images of gods and goddesses, gigantic in size, that leave the viewer wonderstruck. Some of the caves are shunned in disgust by the brahmins who refer to them as the abode of untouchables. The caves with their exquisitely carved exteriors look charming during the monsoons. A small river runs past them and becomes a waterfall as it rushes down to the valley below, forming a fine, transparent curtain in front of the temples. Two low parapets stretch across from one end of the caves to the other, where students, scribes and shopkeepers used to sit. Between them a path leads to the image in the very last cave. I will say no more for fear of talking too much, but I am sure you can visualize the place. But how is one to visit them, however lovely they are? We will have to get Alafkhan's permission and who can dare approach him at this time? The very idea of our wanting to go on a ramble will make him explode and instead of giving us permission he will throw us out. So what do we do now?'

Sobhaankhan and Ibrahimkhan and several of the other soldiers indignantly protested their loyalty to the Muslim cause. Had they not fought willingly for the padshah? Just because they had enrolled in his army to serve the emperor did not mean they had sold themselves to him. There was really no need to beg Alafkhan for permission. And, anyway, what could he do if the whole group decided to visit the caves? He could hardly send them to the gallows and it mattered little if he dismissed them from the army. Their mission here was over. After facing so many hardships, they undoubtedly deserved a day's holiday. What would happen would happen. Trusting in Allah they would go ahead and enjoy themselves. It was not likely that they would ever have a second opportunity to visit this place. It was better to live life fully and risk death than live a long, unadventurous existence. It was decided that around 200 to 300 soldiers would set out to explore the caves. As they weren't going to ask for permission, they would gather together clandestinely.

Completing all their preparations for the trip that very night, around 300 soldiers, weapons in hand, left for Verul before dawn. They carried out their operation so skilfully that hardly anyone in the camp knew about their plan, and the few who did, remained silent. The soldiers passed through many picturesque spots as they walked across undulating ground and hills mantled in vegetation. Rivers flowed in the valleys, their waters crystal clear. How lovely was the morning! And what a contrast to those hardened soldiers, men to whom slicing off heads came as easily as cutting fruit, and whose only companions were their weapons. If there was even one amongst them who was drawn to the glorious works of God, he was soon rewarded. As the sun rose, a glow spread across the mountain peaks, and though the lower slopes were in darkness, its rays danced on the waters below. The trees revealed their drapery of green. The songs of myriad birds resonated through the land and now and then the roar of wild beasts could be heard.

⁓

Meanwhile Bhimdev and Devaldevi, along with their horsemen, soldiers, servants, attendants, the bhatt and his wife, and the rest of their retinue, were making their way to Devgadh. At first their journey proved uneventful. Full of hope and free from fear they rode light-heartedly on their way. Seated on a beautiful and spirited horse, deep in thought, Devaldevi allowed her steed to lead the way. This was the most important day of her life, the day her desires would be fulfilled. On this day she hoped to see the face of her beloved. On this day her life would begin anew. It would be the first day of her long-imagined bliss. So it was not surprising that on such a day her happiness was tinged by apprehension.

As the morning gradually progressed to noon, the sound of sobbing could be heard from far away. The frightful wail in the middle of the afternoon startled the travellers. Someone was obviously in great distress, and Devaldevi ordered her attendants to halt and investigate. Bhimdev was strongly opposed to the delay: dangers lurked ahead and it was best that they march without interruption till they reached the city. But as Devaldevi was unwilling to proceed, he too, halted by her side. The wailing could now be heard clearly, and going towards it, they came to a woman sitting under a tree, weeping bitterly. She was the epitome of misery and poverty. Her body was clearly visible through her rags and her rags were so filthy that it was impossible to guess the original colour of her dress. Her clothes crawled with lice and vermin. It appeared as if she were in the throes of some great misfortune. Her frightful demeanour aroused feelings of fear, even on that sunny day.

As Devaldevi's horse approached, the woman sprang up, grabbed the reins and dragged the animal back. The horse took fright and bolted with the woman clinging tight to the reins. The soldiers stood frozen with fear. Surely the woman was a spirit, a witch or a *shankhini* and there was not the slightest doubt that she would drown Devaldevi in the river or kill her in some other way. Human intervention was useless; there was no point giving chase. Everyone stood rooted to the spot. It was only after Devaldevi's horse had been spirited away a great distance that Bhimdev recovered his presence of mind and gave chase. He rode like the wind and it seemed certain that he would be able to overtake Devaldevi. A few horsemen followed him. When Bhimdev finally spotted Devaldevi's horse in the distance, he spurred his horse to go even faster, but it took another hour for him to catch up with her.

Enraged by the sight of the witch, Bhimdev raised his sword to smite her but he might as well have been slicing air. The woman transformed herself into a burning flame that leapt into the sky and she landed two *kadam*s away. Bhimdev was a brave warrior and yet his limbs turned to water. Terrified, but holding true to his kshatriya dharma, he regained his composure and cried, 'Who are you? What do you want of Devaldevi? Where were you taking her? What did you intend to do with her?' But now the woman transformed herself into an apsara. Her face glowed. She was attired in rich zari and decked in priceless ornaments. Her expression was sad and her eyes full of pity. Before answering

Bhimdev she turned and gazed lovingly at Devaldevi, and from her lotus-shaped eyes tears began to flow. But after a while she wiped away her tears with the edge of her rich garment, and with a voice like gently falling dew, she began to speak. 'I am Devaldevi's destiny. I have protected her so far. But now you must proceed no further. Halt here for the night and resume your journey in the morning. Heed my advice. If you defy fate and continue your journey tonight, I will not be able to protect you from the consequences. This is my final warning. Follow it if you will. I must leave you now. Farewell!' So saying the apparition vanished.

Bhimdev and Devaldevi looked at each other in disbelief, not knowing what to do. It was only when their companions joined them that their courage returned. They determined to settle the issue then and there. Bhimdev felt that if they retreated now, having come so far, it would demoralize the soldiers. Moreover, it was the dharma of the kshatriyas to fear nothing. So why be overcome with fear now? And that too, because of the words of a woman? This was rank cowardice; so, setting aside all fear they would march on. Besides, Devaldevi was so eager to be reunited with Shankaldev, she could not bear the idea of even a moment's delay. She was in the bloom of youth and fear had very little hold over her. Her eagerness to meet Shankaldev that very day made her doubt the apparition. Refusing to believe that it was the guardian of her fate, she persuaded herself that it was a witch or a filthy beggarwoman bent on luring her away. Bhimdev and Devaldevi turned back to join the rest of their party and pretended that the incident had never taken place.

The grassland narrowed to a path flanked by tall mountains on either side. As the convoy moved forward, smoke was visible in the distance. At first they thought it emanated from some village or a kiln, but as they went further they could see that it was a group of men cooking around a fire. They were Muslims—Alafkhan's soldiers resting on their way to the Verul caves. As soon as they saw the convoy approach, the soldiers dropped what they were doing and were instantly on their guard. They gathered up their weapons and discussed their next move. For some time there was complete confusion. Shouts of 'Rasulkhan!' 'Pirmahommad!' 'Jafar!' 'Behelim!' mingled with cries of 'Allah O Akbar'. Some of the men waited in silence, while others swaggered and bragged about their exploits. But this was no time for boasting. A decision needed to be made quickly. They had only 300 men while the advancing enemy seemed to have twice or thrice as many troops. To face them or flee was the question. Some advised caution, but the young Turkish *mirzas* felt nothing but contempt for the Hindus and were convinced that God was always on their side: therefore, to run away from battle, and that too, one against the effeminite kafir Hindus was out of the question—a deed only fit for cowards. The Muslims decided not to retreat even an inch. With 'God protects and the pir helps' on their lips they stood in orderly ranks to face the enemy.

Bhimdev on his part was greatly perturbed. He had not expected to come across the enemy and had made no preparations for combat. Moreover, he was escorting Devaldevi and it was imperative to get her safely to Devgadh. There was no knowing what would happen in a skirmish. If he lost the encounter, Devaldevi, who was finally under his protection, would be snatched away. He could not help recalling the words of the tattered apparition and bitterly regretted not having heeded her advice. Now he was convinced that her dire predictions would come true and his courage failed him. He lost heart and grew pale with fear. What was he to do? He could not turn back and there was no other way to reach Devgadh, so fight he must. Bhimdev tried to rally his men with words of encouragement, telling them how they greatly outnumbered the motley Turks and could oust them easily. But the expression on his face belied the enthusiasm of his words. His men had never seen Bhimdev so disheartened before; they felt that there was some ominous reason for his despondency. They lost all will to fight. They put up a brave front, but their hearts beat fast with dread and their legs turned to lead. It was thus that they marched forward to face the Muslims.

The enemy was ready for them. They were greeted with the blood-curdling cry of 'Allah O Akbar'. The kshatriyas had heard this battle cry innumerable times in the past, but this time it had a particularly chilling effect. Though outnumbered, the Muslims launched a fierce attack. The swords of Shirohi clashed with the scimitars of Arabastan. Men were mowed down like grass. With another cry of 'Allah O Akbar' the Muslims attacked with renewed vigour. The Hindus were unable to withstand the onslaught. Their ranks broke and the soldiers fled in all directions. Wounded by an arrow, Devaldevi's horse fell down dead and she was flung onto the ground, unconscious. Her maids gathered around but before they could take her away to safety, Muslim soldiers had surrounded her. To some she appeared to be a houri from paradise and they could not turn their eyes away from her. Others were so overcome by desire, they could hardly restrain themselves from carrying her away to their harems. Some older soldiers looked on her as a gift from God. They imagined her in their homes, cooking and ministering to their needs. Some thought greedily of the huge price such a woman would fetch in the slave markets of Delhi. Devaldevi lay helpless, encircled by a hundred lusting bulls. There was a general scuffle as each tried to drag her away. Swords that had been raised against the enemy now fell upon each other. One misdirected blow could have ended Devaldevi's life, and several times she managed to escape death only by a hair's breadth. Her maidservants, adhering to

Rajput norms, would sooner let her die than reveal her identity. But the bhattani could restrain herself no longer, and cried out, 'O you wretched Turks! Why are you killing each other? Here at your feet lies Devaldevi who is about to wed Shankaldev. Idiots, stop fighting and take the princess to your general.'

On hearing the name 'Devaldevi' the men immediately threw down their swords. Delighted at discovering the prize they had fought for so long, they despatched a messenger to Alafkhan and placing Devaldevi on a horse, hastened back to camp. Alafkhan's joy was indescribable. He thanked God with all his heart and rewarding his men, left with Devaldevi for Gujarat.

16

A man and a woman sat at the window of a large mansion in the village of Patadi in Jhinjuvada. Both were middle-aged, and the man looked anxious and careworn. Ever since Anhilpur had fallen into the hands of the Muslims, the governor of Gujarat had subjugated a number of Hindu kings, chieftains and landlords. Several smaller principalities had been swallowed up; others had agreed to pay tribute; but a few chieftains, relying on their own courage, their impregnable forts and the size of their armies, had held on to their independence. The thakur of Patadi, who sat at the window of his mansion, had so far courageously managed to safeguard his freedom, but he was worried that he would be unable to do so for much longer. His equally courageous wife did not allow her husband's confidence to falter. She pointed out that the manner in which they had obtained Patadi and other villages from Karan Vaghela had all the signs of divine favour. No mortal could have tied garlands on 2000 villages on his own. And the same divine grace that had bestowed so much territory on them would remain with her husband and his descendants forever.

As the two conversed, they heard a commotion outside, and on looking out they saw that a mad elephant had charged into the courtyard where the thakur's three sons, Shedo, Mangu and

Shekado, and his daughter Umadevi were playing. Trampling everything that came in his way, the rampaging elephant lifted up one of the boys in his trunk and was about to hurl him down and smash another underfoot, when their mother thrust her arm out of the window, extended it right up to her children and snatched them away from certain death. Harpal was surprised and delighted to be reminded of the supernatural powers of his wife, and to ensure that her exploit would never be forgotten, gave the title 'Jhala' (Seized) to his sons. Harpal's descendants are known as Jhala Rajputs to this day.

The mad elephant, discovering that nothing of interest remained in the courtyard, now moved onto the street, where he knocked down a passing cart with a blow of his trunk. The driver was thrown to one side, the two occupants to another, and as the startled bullocks reared forward, one of the cart wheels ran over the couple. The man's leg was crushed and his wife badly injured. They lay unmoving, and supposing them dead, the driver screamed so loudly that his cries could be heard within the mansion. Harpal sent his servants to investigate what had happened. They returned a short while later, carrying the injured couple on stretchers. As a Rajput, Harpal knew that it was his duty to offer shelter to the unfortunate strangers, make arrangements for their care, and let them stay in his home until they had recovered, so he had the two brought to a room in his house.

The doctor and apothecary were sent for, and thanks to their efforts, the couple regained consciousness after a while. When they realized that they were in the house of a total stranger, and that he had done so much for them, they were overcome with gratitude and were impatient to convey their boundless thanks to their benefactor. By the time Harpal visited them that night, the man had recovered sufficiently to talk to him. In his eagerness to tell Harpal who he was, recount his past exploits and explain why and how he had been reduced to his present condition, the man narrated the entire story of his life.

Harpal could not believe his ears. The discovery that fate had brought to his doorstep the very man who was the greatest enemy of Gujarat, the one responsible for the ruin of the king, who had delivered his countrymen into the hands of the mlechhas, and was the cause of Harpal's own troubles and anxieties, filled him with rage. Stamping his foot he said vehemently, 'O you evil man! You chandal! You traitor! You great sinner! So you've finally reaped the fruit of your wrongdoing? You no-good Nagar! You think it does you credit to brag shamelessly to me of your despicable conduct? A pox on your birth! Cursed be your name! You, who were born a Hindu, sold the land of your birth to worshippers of a false god. For shame! Why did you not perish in your mother's womb? Why were you not aborted? Why did you not die in childhood? You have destroyed the reputation of seven generations of your family. Brought dishonour on your caste. Heaped shame on all Hindus. Better to be a stone than a man like you!'

Harpal rained curses on the man and would have used even stronger language, perhaps raised his hand against his guest, but the injured man interrupted. 'Forgive me, sir! Forgive me. I am guilty of all that you have accused me of and of whatever you have left unsaid. I am truly an evil, sinful chandal. I am not fit to live much longer in this world, and am surely destined for a low status in the next, but what am I to do now? The past is past. What's done is done, and it's no good hoping that it can be undone. But you must consider the situation I was in at the time. Bear in mind the extraordinary pressures I was under. Revenge was what motivated me. Revenge goaded me. Revenge perverted my judgement and dictated my actions. Wouldn't most people in my situation do the same? I admit that what I did was unforgiveable. Had I personally taken revenge on Karan

Raja, I would not consider myself at fault. But I got another to take revenge on my behalf, and that was wrong and caused all the misfortune that followed. And how did it benefit me in the end? So long as Alafkhan was the governor of Gujarat, I had a high post, but even then I did not command the kind of authority I had wielded earlier. I was continually anxious. I was surrounded by envy and enmity and had to walk on a razor's edge. My life hung by a thread, and in the end my apprehensions proved correct. Alafkhan's successor deprived me of my position. My home and possessions, my wealth—everything was confiscated. My wife managed to salvage a little money and flee, but I was thrown into prison like a common criminal. Several times I tried to escape, and to send word to the emperor of my plight, but in the din of drums, can the sound of a small trumpet be heard? My pleas went unheeded, and it was only after there was a change of authority that I, through a combination of coaxing and cunning, managed to escape. I left Patan and joined my wife who was hiding in Siddhapur, and then we went for darshan to Somnath and were returning home when the accident happened. I am filled with remorse for the great evil that I have done and cannot rest night or day. All I want to do now is to go to Benaras, pray every day at the Vishveshvara temple, bathe in the Bhagirathi river and live out the rest of my days. I pray to God that my sins are washed away by my penance and remorse. I have got the punishment I deserve, and have no cause for complaint. Merciful God, forgive me! Goodbye, sir. I will leave tomorrow morning; I beg your forgiveness for the trouble I have caused.'

Madhav and Roopsundari left the next day. They made their way to Modhera and took shelter at a dharamshala attached to the temple. That evening, after dinner, as they stood at the ghats, they saw a man pacing slowly up and down, his head bent. It was the full moon night of Ashvin, and silver sheets of moonlight fell bright on the still waters of the *kund* and cast shadows of the shrines on the steps of the ghat. The Shiva temple was large, with two *rangmandap*s: one of the pavilions formed part of the temple, the other was detached. Victory towers stood on either side. The complex was 125 yards long and 25 yards wide and the kund covered four times this area.

Although it was still early, all was quiet. The wind had dropped and the leaves on the trees were still. In the dharamshala, an ascetic had built a large fire and he and a brahmin were making preparations to smoke ganja. The solitary man was clearly visible. His hair was snow-white, and his sunken eyes were like those of a corpse. Not a spark of life nor any sign of intelligence was visible in them. His hollow cheeks, bloodless complexion and skeletal body were enough to strike terror in the fainthearted. To the opium smokers, he did not appear human but seemed like a cadaver risen from some grave.

The reader must have guessed who the man was. In case he has not done so, I must reveal that he was Karan Ghelo. His mind was as broken as his body. He seemed incapable of lucid thought. But something in his face and manner of walking suggested that he had not always been in this wretched condition, and that some dreadful calamity or stroke of fate had changed his life. At the moment Karan was deep in thought, and the subject of his musing was someone close to his heart.

It is difficult to describe the despair Karan had felt in Devgadh when he had received the news that Bhimdev's forces had been wiped out and that Devaldevi had been captured by the Muslims. He refused to eat or drink anything for days on end. The eventuality which he had struggled to prevent, against which he had fought a difficult war, endured adversity, endangered his own life and watched the men he loved die—that eventuality had come to pass and was not to be easily borne. The jewel he had treasured for so long, which had been the source of so much joy and given meaning to his empty life, had slipped from his hands—and into what hands it had fallen! He had refused a matrimonial alliance with the king of Devgadh to avoid sullying his Rajput lineage, and it was only to prevent Devaldevi from being captured by the Muslims that he had finally, and with great reluctance, accepted Shankaldev as his son-in-law. But all that had become irrelevant with her capture. What was the point in living? For whom? For what? Karan had attempted to put an end to his life several times, but each time he was prevented. The king of Devgadh did his best to console Karan and keep up his spirits; he tried to persuade him to eat, and to divert his thoughts from his daughter, but Karan was no longer in his right mind: he sat grieving all day and had forgotten how to laugh. He had remained in this state for several days, but then Malik Kafur's forces had arrived and encircled Devgadh. Ramdev had left Shankaldev in the fort, and had gone out to meet Kafur with costly gifts and an offer of surrender. He accompanied Malik Kafur to Delhi, where the title of 'Raiarai' was conferred on Ramdev. The padshah not only gave him back his kingdom, he extended its boundaries. The district of Navsari was gifted to Ramdev together with one lakh tankas for his journey home.

The news of this surrender had enraged Karan. He found his situation unendurable and left Devgadh secretly. For the next five years, adopting different disguises, he wandered around homeless in Gujarat. He had finally arrived in Modhera and taken shelter in the dharamshala attached to the temple.

Madhav and his wife were discussing the recent events that had befallen them, and the many ups and downs of life. They spoke of Karan and how sorry they felt for the unfortunate king. 'If Karan had been alive now, it would surely break his heart to know that Devaldevi has forgotten him and is living in luxury with her mother, happily married to the heir apparent Khizrkhan. But the poor man is most probably dead. Wherever he is, may he be at peace.' Madhav's words were heard clearly by Karan. He fell to the ground in a dead faint. Hearing the loud sound, Madhav rushed to the stranger's assistance, but a closer look at his face made him jump back in horror. Dragging his wife behind him, Madhav hurried back to the dharamshala, packed his belongings and left the ashram that very night.

When Karan regained consciousness, he was red-eyed with rage and had a crazed expression on his face. The news that his daughter had completely disowned her debt to her father, and had put him out of her thoughts, was something he could not bear. That Devaldevi, for whose sake he had been reduced to such depths, should think that it was fine to live in a palace while he was obliged to wander homeless! That she should, like her mother, forsake her faith, forget him, erase Shankaldev's love from her heart, and marry the son of a king who had seized her father's kingdom, destroyed his happiness and brought him to such straits! Ungrateful child! Why, it was each for himself in this world. Love meant nothing, life was a fraud, affection a pretence—of that he was now convinced. Why should he continue to live this miserable existence when those for whom he had lived had betrayed him? He would end his life right now, Karan thought as he paced around the temple tank. But death is no easy business. No matter how weary one is of living, it is difficult to surrender to the messenger of death when he actually arrives. How hard then must it be to voluntarily seek out death, how hard to plan one's end! Karan walked about, his mind seething with doubt. Waves of anguish were succeeded by moments of composure. When his thoughts tormented him, he prepared to jump, but then his mind would become calm and he would start pacing again. This went on for a while, until finally, in a moment of frenzy, he plunged into the water. The sound of his falling body echoed loud in the lonely night.

The sound startled the *vairagi* and the brahmin as they sat smoking ganja in the dharamshala. The ascetic pushed aside his pipe in disgust as if it were poison. 'What unfortunate creature could have fallen into the tank in the night? Must be a dog or something. Hardly likely to be a person. Whatever it is, it has broken my rhythm and the ganja has been wasted. The ass has ruined my day. Some chandal must certainly have crossed my path this morning, to have my pleasure interrupted this way. Forget it. Let whatever it is, die; I'm not about to rush to the rescue.' The vairagi filled up his pipe again. But his companion, the brahmin, was less callous. He was no stranger to sorrow. His wife had been captured along with Devaldevi, and ever since then he had wandered restlessly from place to place before arriving at the dharamshala in Modhera. He felt sure that some human being had fallen into the water, and that if he sat and watched while the person died, he would have to bear the consequences of the sin; so he abandoned his pipe and went over to the tank.

A head was bobbing in the water. Karan had sunk to the bottom when he fell, but had swum back to the surface again. The innate instinct for self-preservation had taken over. He had forgotten all his problems in the desperation to save himself. But as he thrashed about in an attempt to stay afloat, his strength gradually weakened, he got cramps in his legs and his arms would barely move. He began to sink once more, and by the time the brahmin reached the tank, only his topknot was visible. The *bhatji* leapt into the water. He was not weighed down by much clothing. Flinging off his cap, he jumped in with the dhoti he was wearing. Luckily for Karan, it was a moonlit night and the brahmin was able to grab hold of the topknot. But rescuing a drowning man is no easy matter. To him it seems as though the whole world is drowning and his frantic efforts to save himself

293

succeed in putting the rescuer's life in danger. As soon as he surfaced, Karan gripped the brahmin so tightly that, had the latter not been a strong swimmer, two death rites would have had to be observed on that day. But the bhatji managed to swim despite his heavy burden, and when he could hold out no longer, he bit Karan's arm so hard that he let go his hold. Then in a single movement, the brahmin flung Karan out of the tank. He got out himself, picked up Karan and dumped him besides the vairagi.

The renunciate was now on to his second pipe and, looking at the body with complete indifference, said angrily, 'Hey *bhamman*, why have you brought this corpse here? The tank and the dharamshala are now both polluted. What was the need for this unnecessary gesture? Dump him in some corner somewhere. We will announce the news tomorrow morning and some loved one or acquaintance of his can take him away or the town's dignitaries can help remove him to the cremation ground. You can't keep a corpse here in Shiva's shrine. It will defile the whole place. You will have to spend a lot of money getting everything purified. People will criticize us. We will have to answer to the raja for our conduct. Who knows what will happen then? If he asks us why the man fell into the tank, what will we say? And if we are unable to give a satisfactory answer, the king will suspect us of foul play. The raja here is crazy; one can't depend on him. We may be sentenced to death like stray dogs or banished from the town, and then we won't be able to earn a living and will starve to death. So get rid of the corpse. Get out of your wet dhoti and warm yourself with a fresh pipe. Come on, son. Hurry, now.'

The speech made a strong impression on the bhatji. The vairagi's arguments seemed sound, and the brahmin started to regret his action. But it was too late; the past could not be undone. And meanwhile he was cold and the effects of the ganja had long since worn off. The bhatji had never spent a day without the assistance of opium, and the sight of the vairagi smoking his pipe and the aroma of ganja smoke made him frantic. His eyes clouded over and he could no longer think straight. Without another glance at Karan, he put on a fresh dhoti, and took a long drag at his pipe. This revived him somewhat, and picking up a lamp he examined the corpse closely. Its chest rose and fell and a sharp breath escaped from its nose. Relieved to find signs of life in the corpse, the bhatji decided to do something to resuscitate it. By placing weights on the man's stomach and sitting down on him, the brahmin managed to expel about four to five seers of water from the prostrate body. When no more water seemed forthcoming, he tied a rope around the man's legs and hung him upside down. A little more water escaped from the man's mouth. The bhatji kept him hanging for an hour or so, then took him down, wrapped him in a blanket, and let him sleep near the embers of the fire.

The warmth soon had an effect on Karan. He started moving slightly, opened his eyes and realized he could speak. The ascetic and the bhatji were overjoyed. Happy that his apprehensions had been belied, the vairagi said in a satisfied tone, 'Well, son! So who are you? What is your caste? What work do you do? What brought you to this place? Did you fall into the tank by accident or on purpose? If you jumped in on purpose, what was the reason? Are you suffering from some illness? Do your children make you unhappy? Has your wife run away with someone? Has she made an ass of you? Are you frightened of her bad temper? Has your business suffered losses? Has someone fleeced you?' The vairagi would have continued longer in this strain, had Karan not become nervous. How was he going to keep so many questions in mind and how was he going to answer them all? So he interrupted the torrent, and instead of answering each question, gave a summary of his life. So far, he had kept his name and the circumstances of his life secret, but he could hide the truth no longer.

Moved by Karan's story, the vairagi felt that it was his duty to try and counsel him. 'Son, listen carefully to what I have to say. It concerns your well-being. If you follow my advice, your suffering will be a thing of the past. This world of ours is but for a moment. It is a bubble in the water. A magician's trick. Everything in it is transient. Whatever can be named must die. Only God is ageless and deathless—all else is unreal. The world does not belong to us, nor will it ever be ours. We are linked with each other only like passengers in the same boat. They come together for a brief period, then go their own ways. Which is why one should not get entrapped in the net of attachment. It is this which leads to man's ruin. It prevents him from walking on the spiritual path, and he is left to wander the eighty-four lakh rounds of existence. He is wise who abandons the world and becomes an ascetic, with his thoughts focused on God alone.

'Like everything else, the body, too, is perishable. Today it blooms like a flower; then, in a moment, it is as stiff as wood. It is beset by a host of problems caused by entanglement in the worldly life. For an ascetic, such problems are rare, and even if they arise, he pays no heed to them. Happiness and sorrow are the price we pay for being born human, but to one who has snapped all ties with his body, happiness and sorrow are all the same. Such a man is not unhinged by happiness, nor is he overwhelmed by pain. He accepts what God sends him with equanimity. And what's more, son, wives and children are not what they seem. They are part of the net of illusion. They entrap us in this world. They divert our attention from God. They induce us to commit grave sins and condemn us to endless cycles of birth and death; so what is the point of it all? None whatsoever. No happiness comes from wives and children. And if it does, it is momentary. On the contrary, wives and children are the cause of much misery. The whole basis of our relationship with them is false. We are bound to them by ties of duty, and when these are broken, we leave one another and move on. They cannot free us from death, nor can we save them from its clutches. We bury or cremate our loved ones, grieve awhile, and then forget them. This is the nature of relationships, which are essentially false, which is why the wise stay clear of them, live alone and meditate on God, searching for a way to free themselves from these bonds.

'And likewise, wealth is also treacherous. It is the root of all evil. In this Kaliyug that we live in, wealth takes up residence in the homes of the evil and flees from the virtuous. Lakshmi lures men, but she is a mirage, and brings unhappiness, not joy. No wise or thoughtful person should mourn the loss of wealth. So son, put aside your grief—yes, you have lost your kingdom and are a king no more, but you must consider this a blessing. The shastras tell us that hell awaits the king at the end of his reign. Think of all the measures you had to take when you were king, recall all the wrong you were obliged to do, and then ask yourself, was the loss of your kingdom a good thing or bad? Understand that the loss of your kingdom was for the best, and now live according to my advice, for it will be your salvation. Utilize well what little time you have remaining. Detach yourself from the world. Come and live with me. You have seen how those you loved most behaved towards you. Your wife, whom you loved more than life itself, abandoned you. Your daughter, whom you raised, for whom you endured so much, and for whom you grieve even now, has married and is luxuriating in the home of your greatest foe. So much for the relationships of this world. And it is because of them that feelings of passion, anger, desire, lust, envy—which are the enemies of the self—arise. It is these feelings that lead us astray and embroil us in this world. The five senses do their bidding, and man finds himself isolated from God. It is difficult to overcome such foes. One who lives in the world cannot help but fall into their clutches. This is what has convinced the wise that the world is a lie, and that we must give it up and concentrate on what is real. As a man's desires weaken, he is brought closer to God, and when he is finally without desire, he becomes one with Him. This is the highest state, and one who reaches it attains a state of pure bliss. So come and live with me and strive for this state of desirelessness.'

The bhatji listened closely to the vairagi's sermon but it did not impress him, nor did it have the slightest effect on Karan. The brahmin had travelled widely and had often discussed religious issues with sadhus, sannyasis, devotees and babas, and was well versed in these matters. He held totally opposing views on the subject of happiness. Keen to show off his learning, he said, 'Bavaji! What you have said may be correct, but let me tell you what I have learnt from my guru. In my opinion, the world is not an illusion, nor are one's relationships based on deceit. To renounce the world is a sin. Man cannot free himself from desire. To claim this is sheer hypocrisy, and even supposing such a state were possible, there could be no happiness in it. The world in which the Creator has placed us is real; to argue that it is unreal just because it is impermanent, is not logical. Nor is it fair to characterize all mankind as evil just because a few men are scheming and deceitful. When we look closely at human attributes, it is clear that God has created man to be a social animal. To shun one's fellow men is to waste several of the qualities with which one has been endowed. Of what use are gentleness, politeness, compassion, forgiveness, or anger for one who lives in the forest? If man has been given these qualities, he must use them and hence he must live in the society of others. Besides, co-operation is the bedrock on which society is based—living in society allows man's innate altruism to come to the fore. From this it is clear that even God does not approve of the ascetic life. Moreover, if everyone took your advice and became sannyasis, that would spell doom for the world, and that is not God's intention. You might argue that only a few people are likely to give up the world and therefore, there is no need to fear its imminent end. But if you believe a principle is worthwhile, then it should be beneficial when *all* practise it. For example, although there is no possibility of everyone speaking the truth, even so, if everyone *did* speak the truth, this would be a great benefit for the world; but if the majority of people were to renounce human society, far from being a boon, this would destroy the world.

'Besides, even the most detached are not totally free from desire; if nothing else, then at least the desire to worship God or to attain moksha is present. Look at the two of us! At the accustomed time, don't we crave for a fix? Deprive us of opium at this moment, and we go out of our minds. Man cannot become desireless, and if he does then he is as one dead. It is not advisable to suppress one's senses and feelings. They have been given to us to use and they have been instrumental in man's progress. Of course they should be kept in check, but if they are used in the appropriate manner at the appropriate place, this will surely lead to happiness. Money cannot buy happiness; it is one's thoughts that determine whether we are happy or not. Even great power does not bring happiness because it leads to dissatisfaction and anxiety. The happiness of the senses is not true happiness either. Such happiness is momentary and soon leads to boredom. Real happiness comes from within and good qualities are at the root of this. The man who nurtures virtuous qualities, lives in the world and does good to others according to his abilities, is truly content. Living with equanimity, with complete faith in God, trusting that adversity is God's will and intended for his own good, his happiness can never be diminished. But he must not give up his desires and hopes, because aspiration is the wellspring of action: it is essential for progress, and it is through the fulfilment of aspiration that happiness is increased. Hope is the anchor on the voyage of life. So by living with love for

God and mankind, one will not only get success and fame in this world, but gain great bliss in the next. So my advice to the king is that he should not renounce the world but live a virtuous life.'

Karan listened attentively to the arguments of both the ascetic and the brahmin, but he was not convinced by either. He believed that man cannot achieve success by his own efforts. The inspiration comes from elsewhere. Man is merely a tool. He acts according to his abilities, but he is not the active agent. He is like a puppet that dances and jumps according to how the strings are pulled, and the one who pulls the strings of life is the omnipresent Creator. Accordingly, a man does not have to answer for his own deeds before God. These, both good and bad, are performed through God's will. Karan did not see the need to renounce the world and become an ascetic since whatever had been preordained for his future was bound to happen anyway. So also there was no great need to atone for his past by living a virtuous life, since whatever had happened thus far had been God's will and could not be changed. A certain number of good and bad deeds are part of a man's destiny and he has to perform them for a particular length of time. The world is a stage on which man takes on many roles. He plays one role for a while and when that is over, he is given another and so it goes on. The same person performs a number of different and contradictory roles. We cannot understand the reason for this. But in the greater scheme of things, all these contradictions come together and form a whole. The events of a man's life from the moment he is born are written down, and there is no point trying to go against them. You may be able to swim against the tide, but nothing can change what has been written by fate. God, demon and man—all are dependent on the Supreme One. A man says, 'I did this.' But more fool he. Not even a blade of grass moves at his will. Pride is my downfall, reasoned Karan. It is the result of ignorance. I must be calm. Those who are wise have renounced pride. This is the meaning of the teaching that Shri Krishna imparts to Arjun at the beginning of the Bhagvad Gita:

> Bound by attachment, puffed with pride
> The fool makes plans.
> Know that without Me you cannot take a step.
> What is destined will surely come to pass.

> Sheltering under a cart,
> The dog doubts not
> That his is the strength that holds it up.
> What is destined will surely come to pass.

> The board is set, the die is cast,
> Man is but a pawn in the game of life.
> Many are dragged by its raging currents.
> What is destined will surely come to pass.

> Proud to judge,
> He punishes the wicked, flays the sinner.
> But justice rests not with man.
> What is destined will surely come to pass.

> Men sin again and again,
> The burden of sin heavy on their heads.
> Yet who is man to condemn?
> What is destined will surely come to pass.

> Good and evil, truth and falsehood, high and low
> Are not for man to judge.
> Yet many sing their own praises.
> What is destined will surely come to pass.

Who is noble, who wicked?
It is not for man
To apportion praise or blame.
What is destined will surely come to pass.

Deeds of past lives
Bear fruit in the present.
You cannot swim against the tide.
What is destined will surely come to pass.

Give up the ego,
Be one with God.
What has to be will be.
What is destined will surely come to pass.

This is what Karan believed. Yet he had little choice but to remain in the ashram and listen to the vairagi's discourses, not that they had the slightest influence on him. Just as a tiger remains passive when caged, and only reveals its true nature when it has been set free, so also to an outsider it seemed that Karan was living a quiet life in the ashram. But his mind was not at peace. His kshatriya spirit could not be tamed, and he was waiting for an opportunity to pick up his sword and take revenge on his Muslim enemies. He could not sleep at night and woke up frequently screaming 'Bring me my sword!' and 'Cut these evil men to pieces!' Even in his dreams he would do battle with the Muslims. What is surprising is that he remained in the dharamshala for so long. But one morning, when the vairagi awoke and went in search of Karan as usual, he discovered that Karan had left.

The ruthless policies of Allauddin Khilji and his generals had spread terror across the land. The very mention of Allauddin's name was enough to make the independent rulers of Hindustan tremble. No one had the courage to stand up against him. The rulers of the south paid the exorbitant tribute that Malik Kafur had extorted from them without a murmur. As mentioned earlier, Ramdev, the king of Devgadh, had done the same during his lifetime. But things had changed after his death. His son Shankaldev and Shankaldev's brother Bhimdev were made of sterner stuff. Though Shankaldev had continued to pay tribute for a while, he was a true kshatriya and for him, death seemed preferable to a life lived in subjugation. Having made preparations for an inevitable war, he had stopped paying tribute. Year after year, the padshah's officials would be sent back with promises or insults. As if to add salt to Shankaldev's wounds, the person responsible for collecting tribute was none other than Khizrkhan, the heir apparent and commander of the south. Although Shankaldev had married another woman, he had not forgotten Devaldevi. She was his first love and, as generally happens, her memory was still fresh in Shankaldev's heart. He had been enraged when the Muslims had snatched her away from him, but he had been helpless then, and could do nothing about it. But when he had heard that Devaldevi had completely forgotten the past and had married Khizrkhan, he was devastated, and from that time onwards he had sought for a pretext to take revenge on her and her husband. Shankaldev felt sure that sooner or later, the padshah would despatch Khizrkhan to attack Devgadh. He would then fight Khizrkhan, defeat him, capture Devaldevi and get her back. But the success of this plan was not in his hands. Man may have many dreams, but the Almighty alone can make them come true.

———

The kind of influence that Malik Kafur commanded at Allauddin's court must be clear to the reader. Through cleverness, treachery and courage, he had brought the leading nobles under his control, and he had so much influence over the padshah that the sultan did not undertake a single project without first consulting him, and the eunuch could make his master do whatever he wanted. Kafur's influence had increased as the padshah grew older and feebler in both body and mind, and the sultan became a puppet in Kafur's hands. He danced to Kafur's tune. In truth, Malik Kafur became the uncrowned king. Yet all this power had not satisfied the eunuch. It is a law of life that the more a man has, the more he wants. He is never satisfied and there is no end to his needs. Was it not enough that Malik Kafur, who for several years had been a slave in Khambat, had become the virtual ruler of a large and prosperous kingdom? The eunuch had succeeded beyond his wildest dreams; even so, he longed to rise higher and to ascend the throne after Allauddin's death. It was a dream not impossible to realize, especially in those times. But one stumbling block still remained—so long as Allauddin's sons were alive, Kafur's hopes of securing the throne were faint. He waited day and night for them to die, and when they did not oblige him, he decided to do something about it. Kafur filled Allauddin's ears with talk of his eldest son's wickedness and disloyalty and his repeated insinuations had the desired effect. The feelings of the sultan turned against the heir apparent, and Malik Kafur was untiring in his efforts to remove any lingering traces of affection. He knew well that Allauddin put great store by bravery and admired anyone who was victorious in war. So Kafur had ensured that Khizrkhan never led an army in battle and that no talk of his valour reached the padshah. If the slightest whiff of praise was to reach the sultan, his former affection for his son might resurface. Kafur had seen to it that Khizrkhan was given no opportunity to prove his prowess in battle. Instead, Kafur had demonstrated his own courage in many ways, and this had not only strengthened the padshah's fondness for him, it had also endeared him to the populace. He was regarded as a hero and the stigma of castration had been wiped out. He was also very popular with the army, and there was a good chance that with its support he would one day be able to ascend the throne. Kafur's last campaign against Karnataka and Dwarasamudra had met with great success and he had returned with 312 elephants, 20,000 horses, 96,000 maunds of gold and jewels, and trunks full of pearls. But this had been a while ago, and the glory it had brought him had begun to fade, when a new opportunity for war luckily arose.

A gift, including 200 elephants, was sent to the padshah by the raja of Telangana, and with it came a letter stating that the raja was prepared to pay the tribute that had been agreed by the treaty he had signed with Malik Kafur. The letter gave Malik Kafur an excuse to persuade the padshah to send him to that region. He said that he would not only collect the tribute from the raja of Telangana, he would also recover all unpaid dues from the rulers of Devgadh and other kingdoms. He asked the padshah to send him south with a large army. Kafur knew that a war against the southern kingdoms was only a matter of time and that this region was considered to lie in Khizrkhan's sphere of influence, and he was afraid that the padshah would order the heir apparent to lead the attack. This was an opportune way to forestall such an eventuality. The padshah loved a good war, and was restless when not involved in conflict, so he was very pleased with Kafur's suggestion and agreed to send him south immediately. A large army was assembled at once and in the year 1312, Malik Kafur left Delhi.

One day as Shankaldev, Bhimdev and the leading officials of Devgadh sat together, a messenger rushed panting into the durbar hall and bowing his head before the king, said 'Maharaj! The king of Delhi has assembled a huge army and the eunuch Malik Kafur is on his way here. His orders are to collect tribute from the raja of Telangana, and to recover unpaid dues from

Your Majesty and other rulers. I have seen the army with my own eyes and have come in haste to give you the news. So you must be on the alert and prepare for war.'

The king's expression remained unchanged. He had expected such a move and seemed pleased rather than alarmed by the news. He felt that Devgadh's earlier humiliation was due to his father's faint-heartedness. Now that he was in complete control and there was no one to give him cowardly advice, he was bound to be victorious. He longed to prove his mettle in battle and was pleased that the opportunity to do so had arisen. He offered the messenger a reward but the man folded his hands and said 'Maharaj, I did not do this for money. I am your well-wisher. I want to see your fame spread and the mlecchas destroyed. But, O king, I have one request. I am used to bearing arms. I have fought against the enemy in the past and long to fight them even more today. Those chandals have destroyed my home. I want to take revenge on them. So if you will do me the honour of giving me command over a small contingent, I will show to you the kind of man I am and prove my valour on the battlefield. Do not hesitate, Maharaj! I may look old and my body seem weak and feeble. But this is the result of past misfortunes. Do not judge by outward appearances. My mind is strong, I am still brave. My inner resolve is as strong as ever. I will owe you a debt of eternal gratitude if you grant me my wish.'

Shankaldev was surprised by the request, but there was something about the man that convinced the king that he was a person of courage, and he appointed him commander of 1000 horses. Then the preparations for war began in earnest—soldiers were assembled, weapons were procured, the fort was repaired, supplies of grain were brought to the city, and continuous efforts were made to raise the morale and fighting spirit of the army. But Shankaldev's soldiers were fearful at the prospect of war. They had never tasted victory against the mlecchas and had suffered a great deal at their hands. To them it seemed that God was on the side of the enemy, and to fight against them was simply asking for death. Many did not want to fight at all. But since they could not disobey the king's summons, they arrived in Devgadh, determined to bring the conflict to a speedy end. How to achieve this was the question. If they refused to fight, they would be considered cowards, their reputation would be ruined, and they would incur the displeasure of the king. What other option did they have? They could not think of a way out of the dilemma. One of the soldiers suggested that the king should be murdered and thus the root cause of the war removed, and the new king made to pay the tribute to Malik Kafur. Most of the soldiers were shocked into silence by this suggestion. Some showed their approval but others were so enraged that they had to be prevented from beheading the soldier then and there. The meeting ended without a formal decision, but many were secretly convinced that the suggested course of action was the only possible one.

The next day the soldiers gathered in the palace courtyard as usual and busied themselves with preparations for the impending battle. Some led their horses through their paces, or made them canter up and down; others engaged in mock battle, brandishing swords and shooting arrows at a target. Raja Shankaldev arrived in their midst. He came on foot, and the newly appointed sardar followed behind. The soldiers were reminded of the talk of the previous evening, but when they saw the king approach, trusting so completely in their loyalty, many found that their resentment had fled and they decided that they would fight by his side, whether to win or die. Yet not all shared this sentiment. Some were indifferent, while those reluctant to go to war were pleased that the opportunity to carry out their design was at hand. The soldiers carried on with what they were doing but their minds seethed with turmoil. The archers missed their aim again and again. The men were unable to look their king in the face and when he gave a short address, their applause was half-hearted. Most remained silent. The king was surprised by this response, but he said nothing. As he prepared to leave, a sepoy came up to him. He requested to be excused from the war, pleading many reasons for returning home. And before the king could respond, the man thrust a dagger into Shankaldev's stomach. Fortunately, it was winter: the king had worn a padded coat and the dagger did not penetrate deeply, but he lost his balance and fell to the ground. There was consternation in the ranks, but the soldiers, either from shock or satisfaction, stood unmoving, thus giving the traitor time to strike again. The second blow was about to fall on Shankaldev and put an end to his life when a sword flashed and the traitor's head fell to the ground. 'Shabash! Shabash! Well done! Well done!' resounded across the courtyard. The king sat up, shocked to see the newly appointed sardar standing with sword in hand and the assassin's body still twitching on the ground. Everything had happened so fast that Shankaldev wondered if he was dreaming. His life had been saved, and who was the saviour? The very man who had once seemed so old and wizened! He was now totally transformed. It seemed to Shankaldev as if he was a divine being who had taken human form for the sole purpose of saving the king's life.

The incident unnerved the king. He lost courage and wondered whether it would be wiser to pay the tribute to Malik Kafur after all. But now he had a new counsellor by his side. Since he had saved the king's life, the sardar had risen in Shankaldev's esteem and had been given a position second to none. He was constantly by the king's side and held the chief place in his regard. The king depended completely on his advice, and the sardar constantly urged him not to give up the fight. He reminded him that it was preferable for a kshatriya to die than pay tribute to a mleccha. The king's earlier resolve thus remained firm: he gave up the idea of paying tribute and resumed preparations for war.

A fortnight passed. Then one morning, the entire town was in an uproar. People from neighbouring villages had fled into Devgadh in the night to announce that a large Muslim army was approaching. The advancing enemy had set fire to the villages and spread terror in the countryside. Standing crops were burnt, cut down and trampled. Malik Kafur had spared the lives of the villagers but had forced them into the fort in the hope that, in the event of a siege, the added population would put a strain on supplies, lead to starvation in the Devgadh army, and bring the war to a speedy close. As soon as Shankaldev got the news, he armed himself, bid farewell to his family and left the palace at the head of his troops. Bhimdev accompanied him as did the new sardar, now a close and honoured confidante of the king. Drums beating and trumpets blaring, the army set out. But only a few citizens lined the streets to cheer the troops. The doors and windows of most homes were shut and people remained inside. Intuition, or perhaps experience, had convinced them that their king's defeat was certain, and they were unhappy at his insistence on going to war. Devgadh was bound to suffer and its citizens were fearful and depressed. Some people offered garlands to the king and prayed to God to grant him victory and destroy the mlechhas. But it was only a few who prayed and even fewer believed that their prayers would be granted. The lukewarm support disheartened the king and he felt his courage desert him. Even so, he reassured himself that victory would bring him fame, and that the lack of enthusiasm displayed by his people would be matched by equal pride in his success. A lack of enthusiasm was evident in his soldiers as well. They looked as if they were marching to meet death. They had no hope of winning this war. They had said their farewells to their wives and children and had little confidence that they would return home. The stars, too, were unfavourable. Although the astrologers had made reassuring predictions to the king, in private they muttered about inauspicious omens and the imminent destruction of the kingdom. It was rumoured that the position of the moon was not propitious for the king. But Shankaldev's hour was at hand. Disregarding the omens, he led his army out of Devgadh and took up position in an open field.

The Muslim forces arrived soon after. At the sight of the enemy arrayed before them, ready for slaughter, they let out a bloodcurdling yell. The Rajputs responded but their cries lacked conviction. When Malik Kafur came face-to-face with the enemy, he ordered his soldiers to halt, and summoning one of his men, gave him a message to be delivered to Shankaldev. 'Oh king! Naib Malik Kafur, the commander-in-chief of the forces of Allauddin Khilji, Emperor of the World, reminds you that several years ago the padshah defeated your kingdom, but showing great favour to the king, offered to reinstate him on his throne on condition that he pay tribute. Your father Ramdev became the padshah's vassal, he was bestowed the title of Raiarai, and presented with *jagirs*. He returned to Devgadh and paid regular tribute as long as he lived. Since his death, you have stopped paying your dues. You are aware that the raja of Telangana has agreed to pay tribute and it is to collect this that we have come south. We have stopped en route only to ask how you are doing and to give you some advice. You cannot escape paying what you owe us. No matter where we go, we do not turn back without completing our mission. Our army has never been defeated. So be sensible and pay the tribute that was voluntarily agreed, together with the cost we have incurred coming here and the accumulated penalty, or be prepared to face the destruction of your army, the devastation of your kingdom and the slaughter of your people. Consider this well and act reasonably. Belligerence is pointless. Do not start something that you will later regret.'

The soldiers and commanders of Devgadh waited expectantly for their king's reply. When Shankaldev hesitated, the sardar went up and said something to him which seemed to assuage his doubts. Then Shankaldev spoke, 'That my father paid your padshah tribute was both wrong and cowardly. It is true that we were defeated, but this was the fruit of past sins. So long as we call ourselves kshatriyas, we will not live in subjugation. The blood of the warrior runs in our veins and we will not pay tribute without a fight. Whatever the outcome, we are prepared to accept the will of God. Inform your padshah accordingly.'

The Muslim assault began shortly afterwards. With cries of 'Allah O Akbar', the army of Islam fell upon the Devgadh forces with fury. But the Marathas and Rajputs were not yet so spineless as to be felled by the first attack. They resisted the advancing forces with great determination—war drums beating, horses neighing. The Muslims attacked with renewed fury. But the Rajput ranks were like a stone wall and the enemy could not penetrate it. Clouds of arrows choked the air. They were pierced by flashes of lightning as sword clashed with sword. Spears smote thick and fast, and every moment some unlucky soul fell to the dust. All was tumult and confusion with the clamour of battle, the shrieks of the dying and the howls of the wounded. Vultures, kites and crows circled happily overhead, anticipating a great feast. Blood flowed in streams. Cries of 'Allah O Akbar' and 'Har Har Mahadev' rent the air. The Rajputs, so dispirited a short while ago, now fought like lions, displaying the famed valour of their blood. Three men could be singled out for their bravery and daring. Shankaldev performed extraordinary feats of valour and many of the enemy lost their lives attempting to cut him down. Bhimdev gave it his all. He led from the front, fighting as if convinced of his immortality. Arrows rained down on him and how he survived is a mystery. But it was the bravery of the newly appointed sardar that was truly remarkable. He seemed to have taken on a new avatar specifically for this occasion. He fought as if some demon had taken possession of his once feeble body. He inflicted destruction on the enemy and remained constantly

311

by the raja's side, thwarting all attempts to kill Shankaldev. He was badly injured but in the frenzy of battle took no notice of his wounds. He would fight unto death. The heroic example set by the king and the sardar infected the soldiers and they fought with desperate courage.

The Turks had not expected the Hindus to put up such resistance. They had anticipated an easy victory, and the determination of the enemy struck a blow to both their confidence and courage. The more they lost their nerve, the more emboldened the Hindus became. They mounted a fierce attack. The Turkish forces were thrown into disarray and fled for dear life. It was not until they had retreated a full kos that Malik Kafur managed to stop them. He berated them for their faint-heartedness, but his men seemed to have lost the will to fight. Adopting a new tactic, Malik Kafur appealed to their religious sentiments. He attached verses of the Holy Koran to the Turkish pennants and assured his men that as they were under God's protection, they were invincible. This had the desired result. The soldiers plucked up courage and returned to the battlefield. As they approached, Malik Kafur bent down, picked up a handful of dust from the road and shouting, 'Death to the Rajputs!' flung it towards the enemy. The Muslim onslaught was so fierce that the Rajputs could not withstand it. Their ranks broke and so many of their men were killed that they were forced to retreat. Shankaldev urged his men to fight to the death. 'He who runs is a coward,' he shouted, 'and will sully the reputation of his clan for seven generations!' But the enemy assault was irresistible. Many Rajput commanders lost their lives. The slaughter continued unabated. Malik Kafur was determined not to let Shankaldev escape, but to either kill him or take him captive. But his indomitable gallantry, and that of the sardar, foiled all Malik Kafur's efforts. Several soldiers around Shankaldev began to flee and the contagion spread. Soon the Devgadh army was in complete disarray. Shankaldev was unable to restore order and his soldiers scattered in all directions. Two or three Pathans now surrounded Shankaldev but a sword appeared as though miraculously and the head of one of the men fell to the ground. But the second Pathan thrust a spear into the man who had killed his companion. The king was captured alive. Bhimdev lay wounded on the battlefield. The rest of the men fled for dear life. The valiant sardar who had been injured by the spear lay writhing on the ground.

His suffering did not last for long. His eternal soul soon left his wounded body to stand before the all-powerful Creator. And thus, the successor to the renowned kings of Gujarat, the descendant of Vanraj, Siddharaj and Kumarapala the last of the great Rajput rulers met his end. Rajput rule over Gujarat ended, never to be restored.

Readers! Pause to shed a tear over the corpse of Karan. His death widowed Gujarat. It fell into the oppressive hands of the mlecchas. Mohammad Begada and others wreaked destruction on the land. The Marathas invaded and looted it. The kingdom disintegrated into petty principalities. Gujarat lost its independence and, with it, its greatness. Today, only the broken remnants of its past glory remain. The Rudramala of Siddhapur, the Sahasralinga of Patan and a few other structures bear testimony to its past splendour and reflect the great architecture of the Rajputs, but all this was a long while ago.

Since Karan Vaghela's death, 550 years have elapsed. Much has changed since then. Those Rajputs, those Muslims, those Marathas—where are they now? What has become of them? Who would believe that the indolent, weak and decadent Rajputs of today are descended from the valiant race that once ruled the land? Who would believe that the weak, starving, illiterate Muslims of today have descended from the Muslims of yore? And as for the Marathas, no trace of their former glory survives. All have been subjugated by the white man. The bhats and *charans* who once graced the courts of kings, now wander the hills and jungles. The whole of Gujarat is under British control. But by God's grace, this province will once again flourish and achieve greatness in a different way, and knowledge, art and social reform will spread over this beautiful land. May it once again become a garden of paradise, the abode of Lakshmi, the storehouse of all virtue. *Astu! Astu!* So be it.

AFTERWORD

The story of Karan Vaghela, the last Rajput ruler of Gujarat (c.1296–1305), has occupied a permanent place in the collective memory of the Gujarati people for over 700 years. It is a classic tale of love and passion, revenge and remorse. Karan Raja, the brave but thoughtless and pleasure-loving Rajput king, abducts Roopsundari, the wife of his trusted prime minister, Madhav. Madhav's brother is killed as he tries to protect her. In revenge, Madhav goes to Delhi where he persuades Sultan Allauddin Khilji to attack Gujarat. The attack succeeds and Karan loses not only his kingdom but his wife Kaularani and, a few years later, his daughter Devaldevi as well, to the Turkish sultan. And gains the epithet, 'Ghelo' (foolish).[1]

The Turkish conquest was a turning point in the history of Gujarat, and it was not long before the story of Madhav's betrayal, the humiliating defeat of Karan Vaghela, and the fall of the great city of Anhilpur-Patan became a staple of bardic repertoire, to be told and retold by the bhats and charans of Gujarat over the centuries. Apart from oral tradition, Allauddin

---

1 'Ghelo' is the singular of 'ghela' (literally, 'mad') and is a play on Karan's dynastic name, 'Vaghela'.

Khilji's invasion was recorded in contemporary Jain chronicles such as the *Prabandhachintamani* of Merutunga (1305), in the *Dharmaranya* (written between 1300 and 1450), and in the *Tirthakalpataru* of Jinaprabha Suri.[2] Padmanabha's famous medieval epic, *Kanhadade Prabandha*, written in 1455, gave a graphic account of Allauddin's invasion and the response to it.

Karan Vaghela's story was not confined to Gujarati sources alone. The events that led to his fateful second encounter with Allauddin Khilji's forces and the capture of his daughter Devaldevi, were described in considerable detail by Amir Khusrau, Allauddin Khilji's famous and prolific court poet, in the masnavi *Deval Devi Khizr Khan*, popularly known as *Ishqia*. The episode, which forms the background to the tragic romance between Deval Devi and Allauddin's son Khizr Khan, after she is brought to Delhi, was later summarized in prose by the renowned sixteenth-century historian Ferishta.

It is perhaps not surprising, therefore, that when Nandshankar Mehta published his historical novel *Karan Ghelo* in 1866, it was an immediate success. As the first modern novel written in Gujarati, the book was a landmark in Gujarati literature. It remained immensely popular right into the twentieth century and, until a few decades ago, was used as a textbook in Gujarati-medium schools. The lyrics 'Karan Raja, O husband mine, why have you left me, where do you hide?' were put to music and became so popular that students learnt the Lalit metre to its words. The novel was translated into Marathi and serialized in a widely read magazine, *Vividha Jnana Vistara*.[3] What is remarkable is that *Karan Ghelo* has never been out of

---

2 K.M. Munshi, *Bhagnapaduka*, Ahmedabad, published on behalf of Bharatiya Vidya Bhavan by Gurjar Prakashan, 2003, 'Introduction', p vi.

3 Vishwanath Maganlal Bhatt, *Sahityasameeksha*, Ahmedabad, Ravindra Vishwanath Bhatt, 3rd edition, 1984, p 209.

print. It has gone through nine reprints, the last one in 2007.[4] Recently, the novel has caught the attention of academics seeking to probe the roots of Gujarati regional identity.

The story of the ill-fated Karan was a source of inspiration to others as well. As early as 1868, the Parsi Theatre in Bombay enacted *Gujaratno Chhello Raja Karanghelo* (Karanghelo, the Last King of Gujarat). Karan's misadventures were the subject of a film (Shree Nath Patankar's *Karan Ghelo*, 1924), and a play (Chandravadan Mehta's *Sandhyakal*). Two new interpretations of his life were written in the 1950s during the agitation for a separate state of Gujarat: K.M. Munshi's *Bhagnapaduka* (1955), and Dhumketu's *Rai Karanghelo* (1960).

A Short Biography of Nandshankar

Nandshankar was headmaster of an English-medium school in Surat when he began writing *Karan Ghelo* in 1863. 'I wrote in the mornings and late evenings, afternoons I spent at school,' Nandshankar says. 'Only occasionally did I have to score out what I had written.' His wife, Nandagauri, adds: 'There was a room in the attic of the house with plastered mud floors. He would keep his written work there. Seated on the floor, paper on his knee, he wrote with abandon. The room contained neither chair nor table; himself and the *chattai* on the floor were sufficient. So absorbed was he in the writing that the time to be at school would arrive, and I'd have to go upstairs and awaken him from his trance.'[5]

'When *Karan Ghelo* was published,' Narsimhrav Divetia (son of Nandshankar's close friend, Bholanath Sarabhai) would recall later, 'all his friends, including my father, were surprised

---

4 Published by Gurjar Grantharatra Karyalaya, Ahmedabad.

5 Vinayak N. Mehta, *Nandshankar Jeevanchitra*, Mumbai, 1916, p 167. Translation: Radhika Herzberger.

to discover that this man of few words had managed to write, in complete secrecy, such a fine novel. When my father chided him for his reticence, Nandashankar simply laughed in his usual way.'[6]

By this time, the East India Company had been ruling over Bombay Presidency for nearly fifty years. The appointment of Mountstuart Elphinstone as governor of the Presidency in 1819 had spearheaded significant changes in the educational system of Gujarat. The need to impart Western education to the local population was keenly felt and the lack of indigenous textbooks was seen as a major impediment to its spread. In response to this need, in 1825, Col. George Jarvis, head of the Board of Education, tried to encourage educated Indians to come forward as translators and writers of textbooks by promising handsome rewards for those willing to take up this challenge.[7]

In his preface to the first edition of *Karan Ghelo*, Nandshankar describes the impulse behind the writing of the book: 'Most people of this province are fond of reading stories set in poetic form, but only a very few examples of these stories are readily available in prose; and the available ones are not well known. In order to fulfil this lacuna and to recreate versions of English narratives and stories in Gujarati, the Educational Inspector of this province, Mr Russell Sahib, urged me to write a story along these lines. On that basis, in approximately three years, I wrote the book.'

Born in 1835 in a Nagar brahmin family, Nandshankar was sent to an English school at the age of ten. The young student soon became the protégé of Mr Green, the headmaster. Green's close friend, Captain Scott, opened up his well-stocked library to

---

6 Narsimhrav Bholanath Divetia, *Smaranmukur*, The Sahityaprakashak Co. Ltd., 1926, p 108. However, according to Vinayak Mehta, Nandshankar 'would read out the text to his friends as he wrote the novel'. (Ibid. p 167)

7 Tridip Suhrud, *Writing Life: Three Gujarati Thinkers*, New Delhi, Orient Blackswan, 2009, p 2.

the bright young student. 'I gazed at this storehouse of knowledge with thirsty eyes and like the chataka bird, eagerly lapped it up. I began to feel a kinship with the wider world,' Nandshankar confessed.[8] He soon became an avid reader of English novels, histories and essays, the works of Scott, Lytton, Gibbon and Macaulay becoming special favourites. Shakespeare, too, had a great impact on him.

After Nandshankar's marriage in 1855 to Nandagauri, he began work as an assistant master in the same school where he had studied and, in 1858, became its first Indian headmaster. Later he would become the principal of the Teachers' Training College in Surat. Fondly addressed as 'Mastersahib', Nandshankar was a frequent visitor at the home of Bholanath Sarabhai, the founder of the Prathana Samaj in Gujarat. He would sit 'along with five or ten of my father's other friends in our living room', Narsimhrav remembers. 'Leaning against a bolster, taking frequent pinches of snuff from his snuff box, he would speak little, but now and then his laughter, as nasal as his speech, would fill the room and his head would shake from side to side, his hair flying.'[9]

When Sir Theodore Hope, associated with the Government Textbooks' Committee, joined the Surat Municipality, he recognized Nandshankar's abilities and urged him to join the Civil Service instead of wasting his talents as 'a mere *pantuji*' (humble teacher). He was convinced that Nandshankar, whose standards of integrity and efficiency were very high, had the capacity to advance to great heights in the Civil Service. Nandshankar joined the Revenue Department as a mamlatdar of Ankleshwar. In 1880 he became the Diwan of Kutch, and in 1883, the Assistant Political Agent at Godhra.

Despite the success of *Karan Ghelo*, Nandshankar did not write another novel (though he translated R.G. Bhandarkar's

---

8 Vinayak N. Mehta, op. cit., p 38.

9 Divetia, op. cit., p 107.

Sanskrit *Margopadeshika* and an English textbook on trigonometry into Gujarati, and was a frequent contributor of articles to newspapers). Narsimhrav met him for the last time at his home in Dummas in 1903. 'As usual, he was entertaining himself with mathematical problems, erasing each from his slate as he solved it. He stopped what he was doing and we spent a pleasant time chatting with each other. Not long after that, in 1905 . . . I heard that he had fallen ill. My wife and I immediately rushed to his house but we were unable to see him. We learnt . . . that he had suffered a third stroke and was in unbearable pain. Exactly a month later, on the 16th of July, I stopped in Surat on my way to Ahmedabad and went to visit him. He was hovering in that twilight state between life and death. I paid him my respects at this solemn spiritual moment, and left. What would I have not given to know for sure that he could hear the call of the divine.'[10]

Sources

Nandshankar's 'love of history', writes his son and biographer Vinayak Mehta, 'knew no bounds'. This interest in history is clearly reflected in Nandshankar's meticulous use of historical material, whether indigenous histories, heroic tales of the bhats and charans, Jain chronicles or Persian sources, in his novel. Unlike some later nationalist Gujarati authors, he generally sticks closely to the story described in these sources and does not gloss over or reinvent inconvenient episodes.

Karan Raja's Story

According to Vinayak Mehta, Nandshankar decided to write a historical novel which would focus on a pivotal moment in the

---

10 Ibid., p 110–11.

history of Gujarat, a moment that signalled the end of one period of history and the dawn of another. He had considered writing about the destruction of Somnath or the fall of Champaner, but finally decided to write about the conquest of Gujarat in 1297–8 by Alladuddin Khilji. It seems incredible that Nandshankar chose to write, not about one of the great Rajput kings of Gujarat, like Mulraj or Siddharaj, but about a man who had failed his land and his people. Unlike traditional hagiographies, he would write, he decided, a historical novel in the Western sense, one in which historical fact would be enriched with psychological insights and a poetic vision.

The contemporary Persian historian Ziauddin Barni (who goes into great detail while describing the political and administrative conditions of Allauddin's reign) dismisses the Sultan's conquest of Gujarat in five sentences: 'At the beginning of the third year of the reign, Ulugh Khan and Nusrat Khan, with their amirs, and generals, and a large army marched against Gujarat. They took and plundered Nahrwala and all Gujarat. Karan, Rai of Gujarat, fled from Nahrwala and went to Raja Ram Deo of Deogir. The wives and daughters, the treasure and elephants of Rai Karan, fell into the hands of the Muhammadans. All Gujarat became prey to the invaders...'[11]

Whether iconoclastic zeal, political ambition or plain greed provided the main motive for Allauddin's invasion of Gujarat is still debated by historians. There is however little doubt about the effects of the unprovoked attack on the people of Gujarat. A century-and-a-half after the event, Padmanabha recalled the horror: 'After the flight of Karan, Patan fort was destroyed, its well-filled stores and treasures captured ... What

---

11 F.N. John Dowson, *The History of India as Told by Its Own Historians*, Vol III, edited from posthumous papers of H.M. Elliot, p 163. Barni's *Tarikh-i-Firuz-Shahi*, which covers the reigns of eight Delhi sultans from Balban to first seven years of Firuz Shah Tughluq's rule, was completed in 1357.

took place in Anhilpur had never happened earlier, nor would happen again . . . Everywhere in Gujarat terror spread . . .' 'Where Shaligram was worshipped and Hari's name recited, where yagnas were performed and charities given to the brahmins, where tulsi plant and pipal tree were worshipped and Vedas and Puranas were recited . . . in (sic) such a country Madhav brought the Mlecchas!'[12]

Allauddin's invasion and the displacement of Rajput rule by the Turks was a traumatic blow to Rajput pride and swept away many old certainties. Rajput chroniclers trying to make sense of Madhav's treachery and the subsequent attack came to terms with it in their own way—by suggesting that it was divine retribution for the decline of kshatriya dharma, with Madhav, Karan's prime minister, as the agent of Providence. In their version of the events, Karan had neglected his duties as a Rajput king, and had provoked Madhav beyond endurance.

Nandshankar too follows this line of reasoning. He describes how Karan's peasants are oppressed, how the Raja alienates an important and influential section of Gujarati society, the Jains, how he is absorbed in sensual pursuits and neglects his duties as a king. While Karan himself attributes his misfortunes to the working of fate, Nandshankar never lets us forget that the raja is in fact hostage to his own deeds. Wilfully disregarding the warnings of the female spirits and against all norms of kshatriya honour, he abducts the beautiful Roopsundari, wife of his prime minister, in a thoughtless moment of lust, thus setting in motion a chain of events that leads to his defeat, the loss of his kingdom and his chief queen Kaularani.

It is interesting that while Nandshankar makes no attempt to absolve Karan of his responsibility for the invasion of Gujarat,

12 Padmanabha, *Kanhadade Prabandha*, translated by V.S. Bhatnagar, Voice of India, New Delhi, 1991, p 2, 7.

and criticizes his notions of honour that held valour as preferable to strategic withdrawal and death to defeat, he does—against all evidence—credit Karan with heroic qualities. No source—Rajput, Jain or Persian—suggests that Karan put up any semblance of opposition to the invaders.[13] Yet Nandshankar depicts him fighting valiantly till he is grievously wounded and carried away from the battlefield.

The second half of *Karan Ghelo* is based in Baglan in southern Gujarat where Karan has managed to establish himself with the assistance of Ramdev, the Maratha ruler of Devgadh. Here he lives a solitary life, his only consolation being his daughter Devaldevi. In the historian Ferishta's account, Kaularani, now a favourite of Sultan Allauddin Khilji, asks the sultan to get her daughter back from Karan. The sultan orders his generals to secure Devaldevi, 'either willingly or by force'. When Karan refuses to give her up, he is attacked by the sultan's forces. In need of Maratha support, Karan reluctantly agrees to marry Devaldevi to Shankaldev, the prince of Devgadh, though he deems him inferior in status. But it is too late. Before she can reach her new home, she is captured and taken to Delhi.

Several Gujarati writers have cast doubts on the story of Devaldevi's capture and marriage to Prince Khizr Khan, regarding it as little more than poetic fiction. Describing Amir Khusrau's masnavi as an 'absurd story of a lecherous woman asking her paramour to snatch her daughter from her natural guardian into a life of infamy', A.K. Mujumdar says that the poet 'seems to have been suffering from a delusion that the Hindus had no sense of honour and their women no sense of chastity'.[14]

---

13 S.C. Misra, *The Rise of Muslim Power in Gujarat: A History of Gujarat from 1298 to 1442*, Asia Publishing House, 1963, p 60.

14 Ibid., p 76.

Nandshankar obviously did not share these sentiments, and follows Ferishta's account of the events that lead to her capture.[15] But he gives a completely different slant to the story by inventing a love affair between Devaldevi and Shankaldev. As described in Ferishta, Devaldevi is nothing but a trophy to be fought over by Allauddin and Karan. Her marriage to Shankaldev is a matter of political expediency—an option to which Karan agrees as the lesser of two evils: it is better she is married off to a Maratha than fall into the hands of a mleccha. However, in *Karan Ghelo*, Nandshankar makes us see the issue from Devaldevi's point of view. His moving account of her clandestine meeting with Shankaldev, her feverish longing, her dreams of love shattered because fate wills otherwise, make us see Devaldevi as more than just a prize to be fought over by Turks and Hindus, but as a young woman capable of independent thought and feelings.

Social Dimension

The blossoming of love between Devaldevi and Shankaldev gives Nandshankar an opportunity to make an impassioned plea against arranged marriage and child marriage in particular. It is one of the many digressions and asides which are interspersed in the tale of Karan Raja. They reflect the reformist agenda of the nineteenth century with which Nandshankar was so closely involved, and provide an added dimension to the novel.

Born into the Nagar brahmin caste, which was known to value education and which prohibited bigamous marriages, Nandshankar was part of the English-educated intelligentsia

---

15 In Dhumketu's novel, *Raikaranghelo*, Devaldevi never enters Allauddin's realm. She marries Shankaldev and begets two sons by him. She remains a true Arya wife to the end. Chandrakant Mehta, *Kathavishesh*, Mumbai/Ahmedabad: Ashok Prakashan, 1970, p 119.

of nineteenth-century Gujarat. He had joined hands with reformers like Durgaram Mehta, Dalpatram and two other colleagues to establish the Manav Dharma Sabha, and was an enthusiastic member of the Buddhivardhak Sabha which was set up in Bombay in 1851. Both organizations were strong champions of issues such as women's education, widow remarriage, and the removal of the caste ban on foreign travel. They were vocal in their condemnation of untouchability and challenged superstitions, the belief in magic spells, ghosts and spirits. By reflecting some of these issues in his novel, Nandshankar engaged his readers at two levels—grappling with a traumatic period of Gujarat's past and providing a new perspective on issues churned up by the social and religious reform movements of the nineteenth century.

At a time when even some renowned Gujarati social reformers believed in the innate superiority of men, and defended child marriage on the grounds of protecting women against their innate unbridled sensuality, Nandshankar advocated the desirability of marriage based on mutual respect and consent. In a lengthy aside in *Karan Ghelo* he makes a strong case in support of a relationship where the lover works hard to be worthy of his mate even if it means a wait of several years before they can marry. The lover's determination to stand on his own two feet before proposing marriage reflects some of the values the Victorian age glorified—self-discipline, hard work and self-control.

Perhaps even more daring is the manner in which Nandshankar portrays the relationship between Madhav and Roopsundari. As a woman who was abducted and had to become part of the king's harem, she is a fallen woman, a 'polluted commodity'. Yet Madhav does not reject or abandon her after Patan falls and she is rescued. On the contrary, the two embrace 'passionately . . . laughing and weeping with joy', their love as strong as before. The mandatory purificatory rites that custom demands the couple undergo are treated as a mere formality.[16]

Nandshankar appears to be clearly uncomfortable with customs such as sati and jauhar, which were common among the upper castes even in his time. While remaining true to the traditions of thirteenth-century Gujarat, and describing the immolation of Gunsundari, widow of Madhav's slain brother, in vivid detail, he puts persuasive arguments against the custom in the mouth of Gunsundari's mother. In contrast to writers like K.M. Munshi who censure Karan's chief queen Kaularani for not upholding Rajput traditions and for preventing her daughters committing jauhar, and who lament her misfortune for being captured alive,[17] Nandshankar is far more understanding of Kaularani's plight and presents her predicament in a more sympathetic light.

Recreating the Ambience

In 1858, about a decade before *Karan Ghelo* was published, a British administrator, Alexander Kinloch Forbes, with the help of the poet Dalpatram Dahyabhai, had compiled *Rasmala*, a rich repository of bardic tales, Jain chronicles, Persian texts and folklore relating to Gujarat. What Forbes had done for his English-speaking audience, Nandshankar wanted to do for his Gujarati readers. In the first edition of *Karan Ghelo* he wrote: 'My intention in writing the book was to draw as accurately as possible a picture of how things were at the time of the story— the manners of the men and women of the time and their way of thinking; the principles of government of the Rajput kings

---

16 This episode, as well as Madhav's remorse at the end of the novel—both of which redeem Madhav's treachery to a certain extent—are inventions of the author. According to tradition, Madhav was killed during the Turkish attack on Somnath which followed the fall of Patan.

17 K.M. Munshi, *Bhagnapaduka*, Ahmedabad, p iii.

326

of Gujarat and the Muslim emperors of Delhi; the heroism and the pride of caste of the men and women of Rajasthan, and the passion and the religious fanaticism of the Muslims.'

Nandshankar owes a debt to Forbes's *Rasmala* not only for the core story in *Karan Ghelo* but many other details. In several instances, (e.g. the description of the condition of peasants and the trading community in Gujarat in Chapter 1, or the description of the shami puja) it seems as if Nandshankar has simply translated the English *Rasmala* passages, without paraphrasing or changing the text. However, since Forbes himself quotes extensively from Rajput bardic sources and early texts, it is impossible to say whether Nandshankar also referred to the same sources, or simply relied on the *Rasmala*. What we do know from Nandshankar's biographer is that the author 'steeped himself in the poetic study of the annals of Gujarat and her oral story-telling traditions' since he wanted to give his readers 'a true vision of the past'.

Accordingly, we are given a flavour of medieval society through vivid description: Kalikamata's devotees suspended by ropes from iron rings inserted in their bellies, brahmins and Jains engaged in acrimonious debate, a bard who impales his son and himself in protest over non-payment of a debt, Harpal straddling a rotting corpse in performance of a tantrik ritual.[18] We get a picture of the fierce (and often self-destructive) Rajput pride in lineage and tradition, their chivalry, code of honour, and elaborate etiquette through the sentiments expressed by

18 It was Nandshankar's description of superstitious beliefs that brought him into open conflict with British authorities, and led to perhaps the first instance of official censorship of an Indian novel. The first edition of *Karan Ghelo* had been published at government expense and the copyright lay with the government. In 1882, Nandshankar was informed that the new edition would be reprinted for schools on condition that all mention of spirits and ghosts was removed. Nandshankar refused to have his book 'repaired by censors'. He suggested that the copyright revert to him and thereafter the book was published at his own expense. Vinayak N. Mehta, op. cit. pp. 168–9.

the characters, and accounts of customs, rituals and war scenes. Nandshankar is so concerned with familiarizing his readers with the history and culture of their land (he wrote at a time when very little prose literature, fiction or non-fiction was available in Gujarati), that he does not mind breaking his narrative flow by launching into long descriptions at the most improbable moments—for instance, he breaks off from Madhav's journey to Delhi in search of revenge by making him go on an extensive tour of the sites at Mount Abu. The inclusion of digressions and stories within stories within the narrative is a traditional storytelling device and one which would have been familiar to Nandshankar's readers.

For scenes set in Allauddin Khilji's Delhi, Nandshankar relies heavily on contemporary Persian sources. Amir Khusrau's description of how Allauddin Khilji had Mongol prisoners 'tied into bundles' to be 'pounded into meat for birds and beasts' by elephants; and Barni's account of Allauddin's murder of his uncle Jalauddin, serve as the basis for Nandshankar's portrait of the Turkish sultan. His description of the condition of Allauddin's Hindu subjects echoes that of Barni. 'To pre-empt any attempt at rebellion,' writes Barni, 'Allauddin decided to tax them to poverty.' Regulations were so harsh that the people were 'not able to ride on horseback, to find weapons, to get fine clothes or indulge in betel . . .and in their homes no sign of gold or silver . . . was to be seen.'[19]

Conclusion

One of the verses of the nineteenth-century poet Dalpatram Dahyabhai's poem *'Harak havé tu Hindustan'* (Now rejoice, O Hindustan) reads:

---

19 John Dowson, op. cit. pp182–83.

Look! Even the timid goat wanders at will without fear.

Thank the Lord for such blessings O India, and rejoice.

Dalpatram, like many other liberal, Western-educated Gujaratis, including Nandshankar, was convinced that whatever the drawbacks of British rule, Pax Britannica would restore Gujarat to its former glory. In the last paragraph of *Karan Ghelo* Nandshankar laments the passing away of a glorious past. 'Who would believe,' he asks 'that the indolent, weak and decadent Rajputs of today are descended from the valiant race that once ruled the land? Who would believe that the weak, starving, illiterate Muslims of today have descended from the Muslims of yore? And as for the Marathas, no trace of their former glory survives.' But Nandshankar does not end on a note of despair. He prays that under British rule Gujarat may rise from the ashes once more to 'become a garden of paradise, the abode of Lakshmi, the storehouse of all virtue'.

NOTE ON THE TRANSLATION

While translating this book, we have tried to be as faithful as possible to the style and spirit of the original. Nothing has been omitted from the text except in very rare instances, where a few sentences, mostly of a descriptive nature, have been removed to avoid repetition. These are indicated with asterisks.

Notes

1 After defeating Ravana in Lanka, Rama initially rejects his wife Sita, requiring her to undergo a test of fire to prove her chastity. Although Sita passes the test, Rama's ungrateful subjects in Ayodhya (over whom he has ruled with such benevolence) continue to question her chastity, causing him to banish her from his kingdom.

2 *Veercharya* or walking incognito through the streets of the town at night to gauge 'the very hearts of men' was one of the duties enjoined on medieval Rajput kings. The king would often go beyond the town walls to 'some spot frequented only by the filthy birds of night, the Yogeenee and the Dakin, female sprites whom he compels to reply to his questions and to inform him of future events'. Alexander Kinloch Forbes, *Ras Mala: Hindu Annals of Western India*, New Delhi, Heritage Publishing House, 1973, p 191.

3 Prof. Arthur W. Ryder, *Shakuntala and Other Poems of Kalidasa*, London/New York, Everyman's Library, J.M. Dent and Sons Ltd /E.P. Dutton, 1933, p 83.

4 The spirit of one who has died a violent death becomes a *bhoot* (ghost) and returns to plague the person who has caused him harm by possessing one of his family. The bhoot can be brought under control by cutting off a lock of hair or topknot and keeping it in one's custody. A subjugated bhoot should never be kept unemployed; otherwise it torments its master. R.E. Enthoven, *The Folklore of Bombay*, New Delhi, Asian Education Series, 1990, p 158.

5 Harpal Makwana, from whom the Jhala Rajputs claim descent, was a historical character. In ballads he is described as the grandson of King Vahiyas of Kirantigadh in Kutch and the cousin of Karan Vaghela. The Jhalas were a military-pastoral clan who were driven eastwards by the Sumris and took refuge with Karan, receiving land as reward. The legends relating to Harpal—his marriage to Shakti, how she helped him to vanquish Babrobhoot and acquire vast territory, how the clan got the name 'Jhala'—played an important role in the assimilation of the clan into the Rajput hierarchy, a major criterion for this being descent from a mythological or historical hero. Harpal played an important role in Karan's war against Allauddin Khilji.

6 The absence of a flag over a temple indicates that it is no longer in active use.

7 The *bhats* (bards) of medieval Gujarat, who recorded the genealogies and histories of their Rajput patrons, served another important—if little known—function. They provided surety for the performance of commercial transactions, acting as guarantors for loans, the safe passage of goods, etc. 'As the descendant . . . of the gods, his person was sacred in the eyes of men'. A bard extorted compliance using the rites of 'dhurna'—sitting outside the house of the offender along with other bards 'who fasted, and compelled the inhabitants of the house also to fast, until their demands were complied with'; and 'traga'—'shedding the blood of himself or of some member of his family, and calling down upon the offender . . . the vengeance of heaven'. This custom of 'bardic security' fell into disuse under the British. (A.K. Forbes, op. cit. p 558.)